Will Bryant was born in Arizona and spent his boyhood years on the move in the Western states of America. In all, he attended forty schools, including the universities of Utah and Arizona. He was a naval aviator in World War II. He has been an illustrator and designer, and in illustration he has followed the antique art of wood engraving. Most of his work has been concerned with the American frontier, including his previous novel *Escape from Sonora*, published in 1973. Will Bryant now lives with his wife Nancy and their four children near the village of Katonah, New York.

Also by Will Bryant

Great American Guns and Frontier Fighters
Kit Carson and the Mountain Men (for young people)
The Big Lonesome
Escape from Sonora

Will Bryant

Blue Russell

Design and Wood Engravings by Will Bryant

MAYFLOWER
GRANADA PUBLISHING
London Toronto Sydney New York

Published by Granada Publishing Limited
in Mayflower Books 1978

ISBN 0 583 12839 4

First published in Great Britain by
Martin Secker & Warburg Ltd 1976

Granada Publishing Limited
Frogmore, St Albans, Herts AL2 2NF
and
3 Upper James Street, London W1R 4BP
1221 Avenue of the Americas, New York, NY 10020 USA
117 York Street, Sydney, NSW 2000, Australia
100 Skyway Avenue, Toronto, Ontario, Canada M9W 3A6
Trio City, Coventry Street, Johannesburg 2001, South Africa
CML Centre, Queen & Wyndham, Auckland 1, New Zealand

Made and printed in Great Britain by
Richard Clay (The Chaucer Press) Ltd
Set in Linotype Plantin

For my mother

One misty August morning in 1899, a passenger-mail train of the Frisco line was stopped by a fallen black walnut tree between Neosho and Seneca, Missouri. As the locomotive slowed and nudged into the tree branches, a masked man sprang up the gangway and jammed a revolver into the engineer's backbone. When the startled fireman protested, the man slapped him across the jaw with the pistol barrel and dropped him to the steel floor of the cab.

The train was strung out along a curve, with a small bridge just ahead. The masked man leaned out of the cab and waved. A second man, waiting at the rear of the express car, broke the coupling linkage there.

'Plow that tree out of the way and run her across the crick,' the engineer was told. The locomotive's cowcatcher scooped the tree aside. Drive wheels grumbled, steel on steel, and the locomotive chuffed across, separating engine, tender and express car from the rest of the train. As the express car cleared the bridge, the second bandit dropped off and struck a match to a fuse taped to a steel girder. He fired two shots over the heads of curious passengers who had alighted from the coaches, and then ran after the express car. Thirty seconds later a dynamite charge exploded and dropped one end of the bridge into the stream.

A nine-year-old farmboy was turning some cows into a pasture nearby. Terrified by the explosion, he switched his mule to a gallop and headed for home, a quarter-mile away.

The two bandits, lately known in a Carthage, Missouri, boarding house as John Mullins and Russ Burrows, left the engineer and still-unconscious fireman bound with wire and pounded on the door of the express car with pistol butts.

'Roll the bastard back if you want to live!' Mullins shouted, and heard a muffled 'Go to hell!' in return. Mullins took a stick of dynamite from a satchel slung over one shoulder, lighted the fuse and placed it on the slotted doorsill, then ducked back to the shelter of the tender as the charge blew the door to splinters and ripped away the steel frame and part of the roof. The agent rose tottering to his feet in the wreckage, smoke curling from his hair and clothes. He was holding his sawed-off shotgun in one hand, though he was too stunned to lift it. Seeing the shotgun, Mullins fired. The agent fell. The two bandits vaulted into the car, but stopped where they stood when they glimpsed the massive black safe through the smoke and blown dust.

'Judas!' breathed Russ Burrows.

'Will you *look* at that son of a bitch!' Mullins growled.

The safe, centered squarely over the car's forward trucks, squatted within a framed crib of timbers like a sullen, brooding idol, its combination dial gleaming through the gloom like a single baleful eye. Above the dial, in an arc of gold leaf and vermilion, was lettered THE INVINCIBLE. On the doorframe above was the legend *Kruger Safe Co – Chicago.*

Mullins unslung the satchel from his shoulder. 'I'll blow the guts out of her, by god,' he said. Kneeling, he taped four sticks together in a single-fused charge, placed them under the safe and lighted the fuse. Turning to run, Russ Burrows tripped over the agent's body. On impulse he snatched the coat collar and dragged the body to the blasted doorway and dropped it onto the cinders. 'What the hell!' complained Mullins, but Burrows leapt down and pulled the body into the bushes off to one side. The two men dropped into a ditch and seconds later the charge exploded. The blast blew out the end of the express car, ruptured the tender's water tank and drove the engine forward several feet; but when the bandits staggered dizzily back through the smoke and wreckage, they found the safe fallen through the floor onto the axles of the trucks, where it now sat undamaged.

In the next seventeen minutes they exploded four more charges of dynamite. At the end of that time the safe lay intact on its side in a hole blasted in the cinder roadbed, flanked by bent rails amidst the mangled fragments of what had been the express car. The two bandits were crouched in the hole, shakily fumbling a last charge into place when police officers arrived aboard a switch engine from Seneca, summoned by the farm-boy's father, who had ridden his mare bareback to town for help.

The bandits had scorched faces and hair and their clothes hung in tatters. They were too dazed and deafened to hear the approaching switch engine or to resist capture.

Because of the fallen bridge the prisoners were taken to Neosho in a borrowed surrey and thrown into jail. They gave their names as John Mullins and Russ Burrows, but otherwise refused to answer questions. That night a mob gathered, threatening to lynch them for the brutal murder of the express agent. The prisoners were secretly put aboard a train and transported to St Louis and there lodged in the old Four Courts city prison to await trial.

Newspapers celebrated the event. BANDITS HUMBLED BY MIGHTY SAFE trumpeted one story and the district superintendent of the Pinkerton National Detective Agency was quoted as saying, 'Crime ceases when it cannot be made to pay. I foresee a twentieth century delivered from the clutches of criminals by the mailed fist of science.' An editorial headline put it more simply: *Iron Nerve and Dynamite No Match for Cold Steel.* Diagrams of the Invincible's construction showed that even had the bandits penetrated the outer doors, there were still not merely one more set of doors, but two, inside the first set; multiple layers of hardened steel with burglarproof bank locks on each pair of doors; and a time lock on the inner chest.

A reporter thought to interview the safe's manufacturer, Herr Kruger, who said in a marked accent, 'Quite simply, the Invincible cannot be broken by the hand of man. Every conceit of the criminal mind has been foreseen.'

THE APPRENTICE

St Louis
October, 1899

CHAPTER I

A wavering dark curtain of rain swept across St Louis. Driven by gusting icy wind, it thrummed noisily on roofs and cobbles and the afternoon traffic of the city streets.

A light one-horse farm wagon moved through the pelting rain on a street walled by red brick warehouses and industrial buildings. The wagon was driven by a young woman wearing a yellow slicker and a battered man's hat pulled down over her red hair. An electric trolley car clanged across the intersection ahead of the wagon. The horse shied and balked, skittish between the shafts,

'You, Joe!' the girl said and sawed on the reins. 'You want me to strip the hide off you?' She urged the shivering, blowing horse through the intersection. A few blocks further on, near the corner of Tenth and Spruce streets, she pulled into a narrow alley between two old buildings and parked the wagon next to a littered loading ramp. She pulled the corduroy-faced collar of the slicker up around her neck and waited.

In the next block, beyond Eleventh and Spruce, only a few score yards from where she sat, prisoners milled in an exercise areaway deep inside the Four Courts jail. In a few minutes they would file into the mess hall to sit down to a meal of stew, grits, corn bread and thin coffee.

Two barber chairs manned by trusties were set up in the narrow, smaller end of the L-shaped areaway, near the door to the cell-block wing. Two men lay back in the chairs, the barbers scraping their lathered jaws. They were John Mullins and Russ Burrows. Minutes earlier they had been escorted in from the cellblock under special guard – the guard, a glowering, beefy man, now stood close by, swinging his long riot stick by a leather thong. Several prisoners were lined up along a wall waiting their turns, loafing and smoking and covertly watching the two notorious prisoners in the chairs with that mixture of awe and admiration that some men reserve for fierce fighting cocks or coiled rattlesnakes.

At the far end of the areaway, near the barred door leading to the mess hall, the chief jailer rattled his stick on the bars. Guards armed with rifles stood on the alert behind him. 'Grub line, boys!' he barked.

Prisoners crowded into line, making up files, but close to the door a prisoner turned to the man next to him and hit him in the jaw, knocking him back against the others, who not only kept him from falling but promptly stood him on his feet and threw him back, swearing and swinging with both hands. Men shouted and crowded around, shoving and jostling. One man took a running dive into the fight. Others began swinging.

The chief jailer was blowing his whistle and other guards struggled toward the fight, jabbing with riot sticks. Back by the barber chairs the beefy guard snarled, 'You men freeze where you are!' and hurried toward the fight himself. He was not being negligent because he knew that the only place the men around the barber chairs could go was back into their own cellblock.

Instantly Mullins and Burrows threw off their towels, leaped from the chairs and ran through the doorway into the cellblock. On sudden impulse, another prisoner – a wife-poisoner named Eddie Lynch – saw what he took to be his chance and followed them. The three men ran through the cellblock to the stairway and sprinted up, the rasp of their shoes on iron treads lost in the sound of the fight.

The cells were built in three iron-decked tiers rising about a central airshaft, so that banks of cells in each tier faced each other across the open shaft. Above the third tier, the roof was supported by arching steel trusses. The ridge of the roof, some sixty feet above the concrete floor, was crowned by a glassed skylight cupola.

On the top tier the three prisoners ran out along the gallery past the open cell doors. Midway they stopped. Russ Burrows, a tall, limber man, climbed onto the guard rail next to an iron post, caught an arching girder with his fingertips and pulled himself up, then climbed upward through the webbed girders above the open airshaft. The other two quickly followed him.

The noise of the fight funneled up, ringing through the steel decks. Up under the skylight cupola, Burrows reached a cross-brace, a heavy rod drawn tight by a turnbuckle. He hung there for a moment, his legs dangling free, then swung his feet up and lashed out, kicking. Glass broke away, showering down. He kicked again and tore through the wire mesh in the glass, then skinned up onto the truss. He grinned down at the other two, his face glittering with glass flakes. Rain pelting through the hole in the skylight spattered his denim jacket.

Below him, John Mullins, whose half-shaved jaw showed blue stubble through patches of lather, said, 'Go on through, goddammit,' in a voice like splintering wood.

The third man, Eddie Lynch, had reached the center of the arch beneath them. He tried desperately to keep his eyes turned upward. Suddenly he had to look down – there was nearly sixty feet of open space to the concrete floor. He hugged the girder, his face pressed tight against it, his eyes clamped closed now. 'I caint go it!' he gasped.

Burrows was already through the hole and onto the roof. Mullins looked back and saw Lynch, frozen to the girder. 'Turn loose of that thing and climb up here.'

'Oh, Jesus, I'm tellin you I caint do it.' He was biting his lip as he clutched the girder, and a trickle of blood ran down his chin, drops beading there and falling.

'Go to hell then,' Mullins said. He climbed through the hole, glass tearing at his jacket. Stung by the cold rain, he rolled off the cupola onto the steep-sloping roof. Russ Burrows was crouched at the gutter, looking over.

'There aint nothing under us here,' Burrows said. 'We've got to get over to that other wing.' He pointed. The cellblock wings spread from a central domed structure like petals on a huge and ugly flower. The two men ran along the guttered edge of the roof to the central structure, then out onto the south wing. At the end, they looked down. The roof of the prison hospital was twenty feet below them. Below it, the paved prison yard was separated from the yard of the jailer's house by a tall iron fence. The jailer's house was built into the prison wall at the corner of Eleventh and Spruce streets.

They swung down, dropped and struck crashing on the roof below. Shaken, they scuttled down the steep pitch to the copper gutter. Another twenty-foot drop was below them. Mullins eased himself over the gutter, caught at a drainpipe and started down. Metal screeched as the pipe tore away. Mullins fell with it, hit heavily and lay twitching feebly, his face upturned to the rain. Burrows heard whistles blowing over the shouting in the mess hall. He caught the gutter and swung down to drop, but the brackets holding it ripped loose one after another, dropping him in a series of ripping jolts, along with a solid sheet of water from the broken gutter. He landed staggering, turned and hauled Mullins to his feet. Together they limped toward the iron-barred fence and began to climb.

An aged black porter in the morgue directly behind them looked out the glass window of the corridor door and saw the two men. Greatly amused, he continued to sweep, grinning and murmuring to himself as he watched.

Inside the prison the shouting had stopped. A single voice was now bawling orders. A team of guards ran into the cell-block, their footsteps ringing through the empty tiers. Uncertain, they stopped.

One started to turn when something fell past his line of vision. He looked down and saw spattered drops of blood; while he watched, another drop struck and burst into spray. He looked up and saw Eddie Lynch, still clinging to the steel girder more than sixty feet above. An instant later he saw the hole in the skylight. 'There's one of the bastards,' he shouted, pointing. The guards all ran for the stairs. Halfway up, one realized that some of the escaping prisoners would already have squirmed through the hole. He turned back to sound the alarm.

Mullins and Burrows topped the iron fence, jumped into the tidy rows of the jailer's garden and ran for the house. In the kitchen an elderly woman was peering into the oven of the nickel-trimmed coal range when the back door slammed. Startled, she stood straight as two men entered. Walking past her, Burrows bowed slightly and smiled agreeably. 'Tolerble nasty rain falling, aint it, ma'am?'

As they reached the front entry hall, the woman suddenly shrilled, 'You tracked mud on my clean floor!'

'I do beg your pardon, ma'am,' Burrows said; then they

were through the door and out onto the street. Walking rapidly but not running, they crossed the street in slanting rain, dodging between moving buggies and wagons. On down Spruce Street they turned into an alley. A wagon was parked there.

The horse snorted, tossed its head as the men approached. The girl rose from the seat, put a foot on the iron tire and let Burrows lift her down. He swung with her once, then stood holding her clear of the ground, his yet-stubbled chin passed close to her neck.

'Here now, behave yourself,' she said after a moment. 'You're lettin rain run down my neck. Put this on.' She pushed him away, took hats and slickers from the wagon seat and handed them to the two men. 'Seems like hours I been waitin,' she complained. 'Mighty cold, waitin in the rain.'

Mullins was already in the wagon, back of the seat. 'Let's get the hell out of here,' he said. He pulled a tarp up over him and settled down under it. Burrows and the girl seated themselves, then Burrows let off the brake and shook out the reins. The wagon rolled off down the narrow alley.

Entering the street at the far end of the alley, they heard a bell clanging and the clatter of iron-shod hoofs on cobbles. Two police wagons thundered by. The policemen saw a farm wagon pulled up obediently to let them pass, and the farmer on the seat waved. The police wagons rounded the next corner skidding on the cobbles. The farm wagon turned left toward the river and the horse moved into a trot.

CHAPTER II

Rain drummed on the shingled roof of the old carriage barn above Blue Russell's head. He looked down at his bed where his things were laid out on a frayed patchwork quilt and a square of old canvas. They didn't come to much, he was thinking. When it came down to what a man could carry, there was a whole lot he could shed and not miss.

Through the rain he heard the clop of horses' hoofs and the

growl of iron tires on cobbles, then the urgent *ding-ding* of police bells – from the direction of the river front, he thought, two streets away. Another wagon rumbled by in the street outside.

He went to the gabled window and looked out, but the wagon was already gone. Yellow lamplight glowed in the kitchen window of the big house across the stable yard. A shadow smudged the window, and then the door opened and yellow light spilled into the yard.

She carried a bundle in one hand and with the other held a sheet of oilcloth over her head, the oilcloth streaming flashing glints of light in the rain as she hurried toward the carriage barn. A horse nickered from one of the stalls below. Then Blue heard the whisper of shoe leather on the stairs, and a moment later her head rose above the stair opening in the floor at the end of the room, his loft room, built a century earlier as groom's quarters.

She let the oilcloth fall onto a pile of old harness and came toward him, eyes gleaming in her dark face. She looked at his things on the bed, then held out a paper-wrapped bundle for him to take. 'I spect you be gittin hungry, Blue, on the road somewheres.'

He took the bundle, then put an arm around her and squeezed her shoulders. 'I figured you come to cry and carry on and beg me to stay, Cassie.'

She laughed, a deep rich sound. 'Land, no. Time you went. I loved that little boy, used to run loose here, but he gone now – I spect the goblins eat him up, leave this big ugly one to spite Cassie.' She sniffed, fussed with the sleeve of his shirt. 'No, it time you went, Blue.'

'Today was near too late,' Blue said. 'Israel picked up a piece of red-hot bar stock and I thought he was going to feed it to me.'

'Cassie hear bout that. That man got to take out his troubles on somebody, like a man who chainwhip his hounds cause he losin at cards.'

'You mean I get it because I'm family?'

'That's it. He aint always so cussed mean. He love your ma, sure enough, his baby sister. Mighty cruel for him too, when she die.'

'He took us in, all right – but except for her, I would have skinned out long ago. I should have left the day she died. How about you, Cassie? Do you mean to stay?'

She took a deep breath. Down below, one of the horses was scratching against his stall. 'With you gone, you ma gone – I spect not. Nothin to keep me here. I'll go back to my own people, over round Jeff City.'

Blue pulled some bills from his pocket. 'Take this, Cassie. Israel, he held out on my wages or I'd have more —'

She pushed it away. 'Don't you worry none bout Cassie, Blue. She got a jar of arnin money laid by, ratholed. When you git where you goin, you write Cassie a letter. I git somebody read it for me. Tell me how you gittin rich. Now I got to go, fore he start hollerin.'

But Blue tucked the money in her apron pocket. This way, he thought, I'll leave clean, without a nickel of Israel's money. Her arms went around him, pulled him close. He smelled the dried lavender in her dress. It was one of the first things he remembered, from the dim memory end of time before he had words, when she stood vast and tall above him. She sniffed again. 'Leave Cassie bawl a little.' Then she pushed him back and turned away, laughing at her own foolishness. At the stairs she turned. 'You know, Blue, that little boy the goblins eat – when I used to wash him, I always wished he was black, like Cassie.'

He smiled. 'First time you ever told me that, Cassie – but then you named me too, didn't you?' Outside, another wagon was passing.

'Ha. You mama, she gawn call you some ol' family name, I cain remember what. Not Cassie. That baby name *Blue*.'

'What's it mean, Cassie? Why?' The wagon was not passing. It was turning through the gates in the high board fence and into the stable yard, halting there. The horse blew and stomped.

'Blue Russell.' Cassie cocked her head, savoring the delectable mystery the syllables held for her. 'So-o pretty. What it mean is —'

Voices sounded in the stable yard. Blue and Cassie stepped to the window and looked down. Israel – heavy-bodied, massive – was standing there by the wagon. His voice drifted up through the thrumming rain. 'I can't do it – you want to ruin me?'

'You'll do it,' a man answered. 'But get us in the house. We caint set out here in the rain, jawing.' And the figures were climbing down from the wagon then. One in long skirts. And two men. Blue could not see their faces. Grumbling, Israel led the three toward the door of the back stoop.

Blue shrugged and turned away from the window. 'It's just some people come to see Israel.' He began to roll his bundle of clothes in the canvas. He heard Cassie gasp and looked up. She was staring out the window, covering her mouth with her hand. 'What, Cassie – what is it?'

Her fingers fluttered down, smoothed the front of her dress. She shook her head. 'Nothin.' She touched his cheek. 'Got to run now, Blue. You stay warm and eat good, hear?'

'Cassie —' But she was already on the stairs. A moment later Blue saw her dart across the stable yard and run into the house. Blue shrugged into a slicker and caught his old hat off a wall peg. There was nothing to keep him now. He looked around the room one last time, the room he had grown up in, an apprentice in the smithing trade – GUNS LOCKS & FINE SMITHING read the sign out front over Israel's door. He saw on the walls his old lithographed posters from the gun companies – Winchester, Colt, Remington, Marlin – with their paintings of scouts and hunters, and grinned at his favorite. It showed a mounted man looking back over his shoulder at a band of Indians, his carbine at the ready, and below, the promise: *A resolute man armed with this weapon cannot be captured.* Blue bent to blow out the light in the oil lamp.

'*You, Blue!*' Israel's voice, shouting from the house. 'Answer me, Blue!'

Blue hesitated. He wanted to be gone now. In an hour he would be on a freight, bound west. But he remembered suddenly how Cassie had gasped, looking down at Israel's visitors. Israel barked again. '*Blue!*' On sudden impulse, Blue called down, 'Here I am, Israel – I'm comin.'

He left his bundle on the bed and ran down the stairs and out across the stable yard, the rain pelting on his slicker, but he stopped short of Israel, who stood back in the shelter of the doorway. Blue looked to see if the big man's hands were empty; then he advanced. Israel glared at him. In the street another wagon passed. *Ding-ding-ding!*

'By god, Blue – you *jump* when I holler, hear?' Teeth showed under his mustache as he snarled, 'Hitch two horses to that old butcher's van for me. I want em right away. Use the nag that come in with this wagon and one of ours. Make it Brownie. You hear me?'

Blue walked to the horse, put a hand on its nose while Israel spoke. The horse nuzzled him and stomped repeatedly with its near forefoot. Blue picked up the foot and examined the hoof, turning it to the light.

'Damn you, Blue, you aint listening to me,' Israel said.

'I'm listening. This horse has throwed a shoe.'

'Ketched it on the damn cobbles, I shouldn't wonder – then see you get a shoe on the bastard while I'm gone. I'll have to take Brownie with this wagon, instead of the van. When you're done shoeing, you git straight to your room and stay there till I git back and call you. I won't be long – but stay out of the house, understand? There aint a thing there to do with you.' Israel turned back into the house and closed the door. Through the streaming rain and the window curtains Blue saw shadows of figures move back toward the kitchen. A block or so distant, in the direction of the river, Blue heard again the sound of horses and the urgent *ding-ding* of police bells.

Blue unhitched the horse from the wagon, led it into the horseshoeing shed at the end of the house near the big gate, and tied it there. He went into the barn and harnessed Brownie, then led him out into the rain and hitched him to the wagon. Israel burst out the back door wearing a hat and slicker. He mounted the driver's seat, muttering to himself. 'See you mind what I told you, Blue,' he growled as he shook out the lines and set off at a brisk trot, through the gate and onto the cobbles.

Blue went back to the horse in the shed, where he clipped its halter ropes to iron rings set in posts to right and left. He dumped a quart can of oats into a nosebag and pulled the strap up over the horse's ears. At the forge, he raked carefully. Coals glowed dully deep in the fire bed. He shook some coke onto the fire, caught the slick ash bellows handle overhead and began to pump air to the fire. The windy roar of the bellows mingled with the thunder of rain on the iron roof.

Blue lighted a hanging oil lamp and put on his leather apron. He looked again at the horse's hoof and saw that it was split. He trimmed and filed it, then took a new shoe from a keg and fitted it, heating and reshaping it until it was just right. He put the shoe back in the coals, pumped the bellows and watched the swirling plume of sparks gush upward around it. Then he took the hoof on his leather-aproned thigh and with his tongs clapped the hot shoe on the hoof and held it there with the yellow-white smoke curling up and stinking, the horse placidly munching oats in the nosebag. He tubbed the shoe and it buzzed like a bucketful of bumblebees.

Through the thrumming of rain on the iron roof, he heard a girl's laugh. It came from inside the house – upstairs, he thought. Holding the cold gray shoe, he stepped back and looked out through the open side of the shed at the dark looming wall of the house. Light glowed softly behind an upstairs window. As he watched, the figure of a woman appeared, her face lost in shadow, the light behind her touching coppery glints in her hair. She unlatched the window, swung it partly open; then she was laughing again as a man's arms wrapped around her, the man lost to sight behind the curtain. She laughed and pushed at the hands, twisting her body. As she turned, the light fell on her and Blue saw that the buttoned front of her dress was open. In that instant a hand caught the top of her white undergarment and pulled down, and he saw the spill of white-round quivering flesh. Her laugh turned to a startled *'Oh!'*; then she was pulled away from the window and her voice went shrill and scolding, the words themselves blurred in the sound of the rain. The light in the window dimmed then as someone turned down the lamp.

Blue filled his mouth with horseshoe nails. His hand was shaking as he caught up the horse's foot, cradled it and nailed the shoe onto its scorched bed. He clipped the nail ends and clenched them over, his mind holding feverish memories of the quivering bare flesh.

He led the horse back into the carriage barn and tied him

there, still in harness. Don't think about it, Blue thought. Israel was apt to have visitors at night, but it was not a thing Blue asked questions about next day. He had long since learned better.

He went back to his room. Pushing his things aside, he stretched out on the narrow bed on his belly, his chin on his fists, where he could see the house through the gable window. The window where he had seen the girl still glowed dimly. Downstairs, light showed in the windows of the kitchen and back parlor where Israel liked to sit around of an evening, rocking and drinking and doing business with his night visitors. On a quiet night Blue could often hear the squeal of spindles in Israel's rocker as he rocked. Or sometimes voices, a sudden sharp cackle of laughter. Tonight the rain drumming on shingles slanting close overhead drowned any sound from the house.

I meant to be gone by now, Blue thought. Just as well I didn't, with all the rain. He saw himself trying to get to sleep in a boxcar, or trying to crawl into a strange woodshed someplace, with dogs barking at him. Yet a few hours ago, with fear and fury burning sharp in his throat after Israel in red-eyed rage swung at him with a pair of tongs, he had meant to go. Funny, he thought, how a couple of hours' time and a cold rain could take the fire out of him.

His eye fell on an old postcard tacked to the wall next to his bed. On it, an Indian maiden in gaudy chromolithograph knelt by a fanciful pool, a spotted fawn in her plump arms. And next to the picture his own name was scrawled in faded pencil: *Master Blue Russell.* The postmark read Silverton, Colo., and was dated 1893. He pulled the card loose and turned it over. *Dere Blue*, it read, *Im skining Mules here – packing ore for a Mine calld the Old Hundred – Could Show you some dandy Fishen – when you come to See me will get us a little horse ranch – As ever Yr. Bro. Clay ps Take good care of Mom*

It was the last he had ever heard from Clay, but now, with his mother gone and Blue himself about to leave Israel's place, he wanted to find Clay again. Once he got to Denver, he thought, he could start asking questions. It ought not to take long. Maybe they could still get that little horse ranch. Maybe

Clay was just stringing him along when he wrote that, but it was just the kind of promise, joking or not, that a lonely thirteen-year-old would read and never forget.

He was not even sure he would recognize Clay, it had been so long. Whenever he thought of Clay anymore, it was to see him the way he was that last night at the old Russell farm near Dixon: running past the kitchen door to saddle his horse under the black walnut tree by the barn, drawing the saddle girth snug as Blue approached, turning, with his black hat and round-skirted suit coat and saddlebags over his shoulder, to rough Blue's hair. *'Caint stop to jaw, Blue.'* But memory was a tricky thing. Blue, seeing all that in memory and hearing the voice clear, still could not bring back Clay's face. He would see the shaggy fair hair, the ice-blue eyes and the sharp, lean jaw, and hear that quick, reckless laugh, but just as he thought he almost saw him whole, it would all skid away and he would lose him, seeing his coattail fly and the chickens scatter as he galloped off.

The old misery that burdened his nine-year-old self heaved within him again, battered at his ribs. Blue swallowed and blinked. Memory rushed again and he saw himself jolting in the back of the spring wagon, bundled amongst the traps behind his mother and Cassie, with Cassie's brother Tom driving through most of a day. Then the long night hours in the coach car. And Uncle Israel, in the lofty Union Depot where the trains came in, looking down upon him, vast and black-bearded, saying, *'A likely boy, sister. A learner, is my judgment.'* And he took them in a shabby surrey along dawn-gray streets crowded with freight teams and dray wagons and overalled workmen, iron tires grumbling on damp and greasy cobbles, smoke-blackened buildings hulking huge over them.

They came to the house, Israel's house – two blocks back from the river, a big house it was, fronting right on the street: two stories of sooty red-black brick, a steep greenish roof with many gables beetling from it. Blue saw the carved wooden three-foot-long cap-and-ball Colt hanging over the street door, paint flaking from it, and he marveled, thinking at first that it was real, big as a cannon. Beneath it on the wall, patchy gilt letters winking through streaks of bird lime – GUNS LOCKS &

FINE SMITHING. Rolling through the gateway in a high board fence, Blue smelled for the first time the sharp, acrid iron-forge smell that would be in his nostrils from that day on. He saw the forge shed built off the end of the house, and on their right as they drove in, the scrap pile that marked the place a smithy as much as the sign out front – a fifteen-foot mound of old horseshoes, axles, nails, bolts, spikes, and scraps of rod, bar and strap stock of every description under the sun. Beyond the scrap pile to the right sat the carriage barn and more untidy sheds against the back fence, along with a clutter of battered or wrecked surreys, buggies and wagons.

Looking now at the dark and gloomy bulk of the house, Blue thought of his ancient friend Scipio, now gone, who once pushed a junk cart along these streets and claimed he had been stableboy in this very house back when it stood all alone in green fields sloping to the river. Scipio did not know his age for certain, but thought he was near a hundred.

Israel gave them rooms back by the kitchen, Ma and Cassie downstairs and Blue above, off the back stairs. The old house was a warren of rooms, halls and alcoves. Scipio remembered with glee a time – it was after he was grown and the house swallowed up among buildings of the spreading waterfront – when it had housed fancy ladies. It was a long time before Blue understood what the old man meant by fancy ladies. Most of the rooms had carved plaster around the ceilings and many had marble fireplaces, all now grimed and chipped, far gone in neglect, though Ma and Cassie had laboriously cleaned their rooms, every inch, and kept them spotless. Israel's shop took up the front parlor and what they called the Grand Room. Here there were workbenches, banks of machine tools, shelves and another forge built in against a huge marble fireplace.

Israel himself lived in a big corner apartment of the ground floor, the rooms filled with heavy, carved furniture. For a long time he shared these rooms with a grim-jawed woman Blue knew as Aunt Justine. Blue often awoke at night to the sound of their voices arguing, then one day Aunt Justine was gone. When Blue asked where, Israel glowered and both Ma and Cassie *shush*ed him.

Israel, for all his fearful temper, was a superb smith, known for his ingenious modifications of fine sporting arms and for the custom barrels and stocks he turned out. From the beginning Blue loved the forge, the shaping of metal with fire and anvil, file or cutting tool. He hung on in school for a time, but schooling was an unseemly luxury in hard times for a boy who could learn a trade instead. Blue's schoolmasters became a succession of smiths and machinists, most of them German or Swiss, drinking men often, with a craving for moving on, especially if they had occasion to lock horns with Israel Cawley.

Blue heard again the rumble of a wagon and the chink of trace chains.

'Blue!' He snapped alert. 'You get that horse shod?' It was Israel.

Blue cupped his hands and called down. 'It's done. He's inside.' He was putting on his hat and slicker.

'Get down here then,' Israel said. Blue snatched up his slicker and ran down. Israel pointed to the wagon. 'There is some sides of meat under the tarp. You load them into the butcher's van, hear? Then throw a couple of saddles in behind the seat, along with maybe half a sack of oats.'

'What do you want me to do with the horses?'

'They will be going out early, so leave em harnessed under the shed.'

'What is all the commotion?'

'What do you mean, "commotion"?'

'Police wagons,' Blue said. 'There must have been a bank robbery or a shooting someplace.'

Israel hesitated, then he said, 'There's been a jailbreak. Someone broke out of the Four Courts – I don't know nothing about it.' He sucked in his breath. 'What the hell are you askin me for?'

'No reason,' Blue said. He threw back the tarp covering the wagon's cargo, saw the hog sides stacked there. He wrestled one out, shouldered it and carried it toward the van.

'See you keep your mouth shut then,' Israel snarled. 'And when you're done with this, get back to your room and stay there.'

The back door opened suddenly. Light splashed into the

dark and Blue was awash in it. 'What the hell, Israel!' a voice said. Blue saw a dark figure, the glint of metal.

'Put that thing away,' Israel said. 'It's only the boy.'

'He's just damn lucky I didn't punch his ticket for him,' the voice said.

'By god, Blue,' Israel snapped, 'get on with it.'

Blue opened the back of the van and heaved the side of meat in. His heart was pounding and his mouth was dry.

CHAPTER III

Kathleen Brody, widow, aged sixty-four, born in Limerick, bent to her mop in the third-floor corridor of the Wainwright Building. Cables sang in the elevator shaft behind her. She glanced back as the grilled cage stopped and a tall man stepped out.

The man's hat was dented and sweat-stained, he wore no collar and the bosom of his shirt was spotted with filth. His dark suit was slick with grease and hung on his gaunt frame like sacking. She turned away, sniffing loudly; the man was trash and had no business in her building. She sent a swirl of water along the floor with an expert flirt of her mop.

The man's footsteps whispered close. Stopped. She saw the cracked shoes next to her mop bucket. She smelled him – swine, she thought. Then his hands touched her shoulders. She gasped and turned. His eyes were fierce and glittering in the dark bearded face.

'Kath, you darlin girl,' the man said softly, 'give us a kiss now.'

She collapsed against his chest. 'Bassett, you beast, you've stopped me heart. Clean your filthy face, so's a body would know ye.' She pulled back, wrinkled her nose. 'And how ye stink! If ye were me own man, I'd scrub ye down with lye soap and holystone.'

He pulled a paper bag from his side pocket and pressed it into her hands. She opened it, saw the flat bottle with rock candy lumped in the amber whiskey. Rock and rye. Her wrinkled lips twitched. She slipped the bag into her apron pocket and touched his cheek. 'Go long with ye, Bassett. And *scrub*, man.'

Bassett went to the end of the corridor and opened a door with a panel of frosted glass in it bearing the agency's name in an ornate cartouche of gold-leafed lettering. Within the cartouche was the black-line image of an eye over the italicized legend '*WE NEVER SLEEP*.' Inside, a young woman at a telephone switchboard expressed shock at his appearance, then recognition. She smiled, recoiling slightly as he passed. He walked on through the room and rapped at the oak-paneled door of a private office on which was lettered ASS'T. SUPERINTENDENT – G. HAVENHURST. Behind the door a man was talking. The voice broke off, then barked, 'Enter!'

Bassett entered. Havenhurst hung the telephone instrument on the wall box next to his great roll-top desk and glowered at Bassett. After a moment he rolled his chair on shrieking casters back to the window behind him. Lifting the sash, he exhaled noisily. He was a massive man with a heroic mustache and an enormous head covered with tight curls that made him look curiously like a buffalo. 'Christ, Bassett!' he protested.

'I crossed Indiana in a boxcar loaded with tubs of rancid hog lard,' Bassett said.

'Did you set eyes on the yeggmen?'

'No. I was about twenty-four hours behind them, according to the boys I talked to in the hobo jungles. Followed them to the yards here yesterday, but they went on through – they were gone and the place was crawling with coppers on account of the jailbreak. A man couldn't move without getting pinched.'

The super looked up at his wall map and shook his head. 'No telling which way the yeggs might have gone from here. Suppose we set that aside for the moment —' He slapped rumpled copies of the morning newspapers on his desk. Reading upside down, Bassett made out a headline: NEOSHO TRAIN ROBBERS IN DARING ESCAPE FROM FOUR COURTS. 'We *told* those people at the Four Courts to keep the men separated and locked in their cells, even for meals. Told em!'

'No leads at all?' Bassett said.

Havenhurst consulted a yellow pad that was covered with scrawled pencil notes. 'This just turned up. Those men were arrested and booked as Jack Mullins and Russ Burrows. Aliases, of course. But the one who called himself Mullins had a tattoo on his arm.' Havenhurst pushed a photograph toward Bassett. It showed a tattoo of a rearing horse. Arm hairs curled crisply over it. Beneath the horse was the word *Gitmo*. Bassett nodded. 'Turns out,' Havenhurst went on, 'that this stands for the regimental nickname of a U.S. cavalry regiment that saw service in Cuba. A volunteer regiment, something like the Rough Riders, see? These boys called themselves the Gitmo Studs, Gitmo being short for Guantanamo. Notice the pecker on that horse – not the sort of thing that would get attention in the papers, of course. All right, no sooner was the regiment disembarked in Florida and busy discharging soldiers than the regimental payroll was hit. Four masked men, but the paymaster was low on funds so the take was only a couple of thousand. I learned all this after we sent an operative to the War Department. The regiment had been disbanded, but our man talked to a sergeant in Fort Myers who identified two of the men from their photographs. Zachary Murdock and Clay Russell. Good soldiers, he said, when they stayed out of the guardhouse. And they were discharged the day before the payroll was tapped.'

'None of this was in the papers,' Bassett said.

'No, we just uncovered it. And there's more. The men enlisted in Denver, but army records show that the man Russell came from Dixon, which is near Rolla, over on the Gasconade. One of our men looked into that. The family had a farm there. The old man was killed in a shooting years ago. The boy Clay got into trouble and left home not long after that, around 1889. The widow took another youngster named Blue and left the place.' A trolley bell clanged in the street below.

'Is that where the story stops?' Bassett said.

'No. A neighbor of the Russells remembers that the widow's maiden name was Cawley, and that when she left, she was headed for St Louis. If we had known that yesterday, we might have had those two men back in irons by now. We would have had a squad of men watching Israel Cawley's place.'

'Are you certain of the connection?'

'Not dead certain. But Cawley has been suspected of being a receiver of stolen goods and of course he deals in firearms. So if it isn't a lead, it's a *suspicion.*' The super spread his big hands and shrugged. 'Look into it, Deacon, before you take a bath.'

Bassett left the building and walked east the few blocks to the river, then turned south along the cobbled levee, away from the splendid and graceful span of the Eads Bridge. He threaded between great stacks of cargo, savoring the sights and smells of the river, the steamboats taking on or discharging cargo, the freight wagons and teams of mighty dray horses. He stopped to admire a handsome cap-stacked 4-6-0 locomotive hogging a string of freight cars slowly along the Iron Mountain tracks that ran along the levee. In twenty minutes he passed Cherokee Street and was about to turn away from the river when he saw Zumbach's Saloon.

On impulse Bassett went into the saloon and ordered a five-cent beer at the bar, then made himself a corned-beef sandwich at the free lunch counter. Two minutes in a saloon, Bassett thought, was sometimes worth hours nosing around anyplace else. It was the noon hour and the place was doing a brisk trade. A waiter came with a tray of cold meats to replenish the counter's supply.

'Cawley's been around, I spect,' Bassett said.

The waiter was a small blond man with a great red mustache and soft white hands. '*Ach*, sure,' he said looking around, 'like always, but I caint see him now. Maybe for *bier* he vill send der kid.'

Bassett paused, his mouth full of corned beef. 'You mean the Russell kid?'

'Plew,' the man said, slapping down cuts of braunschweiger.

'Plew?' Bassett frowned uncertainly.

The man stabbed a finger aloft. 'Like der schky – plew!'

'Blue? You mean Blue?' Bassett tried quickly to cover himself. 'Little shaver, right?'

The waiter smiled frostily. 'Christ, mister, you aint here for a vhile.' He picked up the tray and moved away toward the kitchen.

Bassett finished his sandwich and beer and left Zumbach's, turning away from the levee along a narrow canyon of a street that was walled in between four- and five-story brick warehouses and commercial buildings. Shortly, he was standing at the street door of a splendid but decrepit old corner house. He looked up at a big carved Dragoon Colt that hung over the door, then tried the door. It opened. He went up several steps into a foyer – once elegant, the chipped plaster acanthus-leaf moldings were heavy with dirt. His reflection leered at him through a cracked mirror in a rococo frame. He went on through a double door and found himself in a vast room with great mirrors and carved marble fireplaces at both ends.

But there was a forge built against one of the fireplaces, and the room was filled now not with elegant furniture but with workbenches and with two banks of machinery. Bassett saw grinders, buffers, a drill press, lathes for wood and metal, and a long rifling machine. The machines drew power from a long overhead idler shaft by means of heavy leather belts, all driven by a great brute of a Monarch electric motor which was floor-mounted at the end of the room under a big knife switch on the wall. A streaked sign read BE WARE BELTS. The motor was silent, the room empty of people. Bassett looked at his pocket watch. Still lunchtime.

He heard a man's explosive grunt, then a crash. 'Hang it on him, Augie!' a voice cried. 'Git the ear holt!' another shouted. There was scuffling, thudding. Another crash. Bassett walked past silent machines to an open door and looked through it, and through a blacksmith's shed that opened into a stable yard. There was a forge and a big stump-mounted anvil in the shed, and a long metal horse trough alone the open side. Beyond in the stable yard Bassett saw four or five men sitting around on crates among dismantled parts of wagons and running gear.

The workmen were eating from lunch pails and watching a young man pick himself out of a splintered stack of packing crates. He was a big kid, well over six feet, Bassett judged, and must have weighed close to a hundred and ninety. He was shirtless and wore a smith's leather apron. There were red marks on his big shoulders and lean ridged belly and ribs.

A trickle of blood ran from his nose. He was staggering a little as he turned to face his opponent, but he was laughing.

Blue, thought Bassett. *Blue Russell.*

'Lay it on him again, Augie!' one of the men bellowed.

'Watch Augie's elbows, kid!' another man called.

Bassett stepped into the shed and leaned against a post. From there he saw Augie. Astonished, he craned for a better look. Augie shuffled forward, crouching low, his union suit pulled down over his belt to reveal heavy shoulders humped with muscle and long, knotty arms; yet the powerful body with its immense spread of arms was borne on stumpy bandy legs – Augie was at least a foot shorter than the kid.

Augie snorted through a nose that was a mushroom of pulped cartilage and offered his bullet-shaped skull for a target, a skull covered with a crinkly pelt of white fleece from which two funguslike growths protruded in place of ears.

'... 'm tellin ya, kid, save ya dukes fer playna pyanna, gemme?' – the scarred lips mauled the words – 'Man thinks he's Jim Corbett, gim a shotta yer headbone. Lem bust a duke on it, see? Take da fight outta im quick, gemme?'

And Augie stepped in close, the knobby shoulders twitching with deception, forearms spinning as he tied Blue's hands, slashed the kid's ribs with an elbow, then battered his jaws and head with quick blows of his own shoulders and skull. 'Lissena Augie, kid, and gim ya headbone.'

'Belt the kid, Augie!' a fat man shouted merrily through the foamy collar on the tin pail of beer he held to his lips.

'Right, Augie!' the kid said. Suddenly he sprang close, caught Augie by neck and crotch and lifted him over his head. Wheeling, he plunged him headfirst into the horse trough and held him there. 'You're next, Axel!' he shouted to the fat man. He let Augie collapse into the trough and plunged after Axel, who was scrambling to get away among wagon wheels and running gear. The kid caught him by the crossed straps of his overalls and dragged him toward a carriage barn a few yards away.

Bassett saw a rope pegged down to a cleat at the door of the barn. Above, a bale of hay had been hauled up to the level of the hayloft door, and the bale hung there now just below the pulley. The kid caught the rope, pulled it free of the cleat and took two quick hitches around Axel's ankles, then hurled him aloft. Axel rose shrieking and flailing his arms as the bale of hay dropped. The kid pulled it on down and sat on it. Axel's feet were jammed against the pulley. 'I dint mean nothing, Blue,' he wailed.

Augie surfaced in the trough and blew spray, his face crumpled in what Bassett intuitively took to be a laugh. He regarded Bassett calmly. 'Damn good thing fer Axel the kid aint mad,' he confided. 'The kid ever gets mad, ainta sumbitch inna country gonna takim, gemme?'

'Getcha,' Bassett said. Augie climbed out of the trough. Axel shrieked again. 'Goddammit! Lemmee down from here, Blue!'

Blue stood up and released the bale, which now shot upward as Axel plummeted down to land in a heap, his fall slowed by the bale acting as a counterweight and broken somewhat by his arms. He rolled over and began groggily trying to untie the rope from his feet.

A small man wearing a derby hat and neatly pressed overalls, who appeared to be the foreman, rose to his feet and snapped his watch open. 'Time to throw the switch, boys. Let's get to work.' To Bassett he said, 'Mr Cawley aint around, mister, but the young feller will see to you.'

He put the watch away and strode into the shop, followed by the other men. Moments later Bassett heard the deepening hum of the big Monarch motor, then the whir and slap of drive belts. Axel tottered past, roughing Blue's hair with a big meaty hand. 'Py gott, Blue, you damn near kill me.'

Blue bent over the trough and splashed water on his head and body. He caught a whiff of Bassett and winced. 'There's room for two here, mister.'

'Hog lard is my line, not flowers,' Bassett snapped testily. 'Wagenbach is the name.'

Blue dried himself off with a piece of sacking and pulled on a flannel shirt. 'I didn't mean nothing, Mr Wagenbach. How can I help you?'

How indeed, thought Bassett, He needed a lead, some way to get the kid talking. It was a gun shop – he could let the kid think he needed to buy a gun. 'I run a little slaughterhouse, south of here, and I been robbed two-three times already, so I figured I would just talk to Mr Cawley —' He hesitated. 'You sure he aint around?

'He went out early,' Blue said. 'A slaughterhouse, you say – would this have to do with —' He broke off uncertainly.

'With what?' Bassett prompted, seeking a hint, an opening to probe.

'With them sides of meat he brought here last night?'

'Well now, it might,' Bassett ventured cautiously. The kid was apparently mistaking him for a creditor.

The kid frowned. 'I don't know nothing about it, Mr Wagenbach, but you'll get your money. It was only last night.'

'A man hates to get robbed,' Bassett persisted. 'I wisht I had it all back.'

You can't hardly do that, Mr Wagenbach,' Blue said. He was very uneasy.

'Why not?'

'It aint here no more.'

If it was only last night —' Bassett said.

'I know, but he must've brought it for somebody else, because I loaded them sides into another wagon myself, and the stuff is gone now.'

'You mean to tell me he took it away with him this morning?'

'No, last night. But he didn't take it. It was —' The kid broke off suddenly. 'Look, I just don't know nothing about it. You'll have to talk to Mr Cawley.'

'What kind of wagon was it?'

'A two-horse van, like any butcher wagon. Spose I ask Mr Cawley to get in touch with you.'

'Never mind,' Bassett said quickly. 'I'll find him, don't worry.'

Obviously relieved, the kid turned away. 'Hold on,' Bassett said. 'What I said about bein robbed – I mean it, son. I do business along the waterfront, have to carry cash money. This is a gun shop, right? Spose you could show me something in the way of protection?'

'If that's what you want, you've come to the right place,' the kid said. He led Bassett back into the shop and through another door off the entry foyer into what must have been a library at one time but was now a gun room and office. There was a littered desk in back, shelves and racks of guns along the walls, and glass cases filled with more guns in the middle of the room. Pistols, rifles, shotguns, guns of every description, including curiosities and relics. Bassett saw one case filled with sword-guns, knife-pistols, knuckle-duster pistols, umbrella pistols and incredibly, a cigar-case pistol. He laughed. 'A man asks for a smoke – he would get a surprise, right?'

'He might,' the kid agreed. 'Is that the kind of thing you had in mind?'

'There is nothing sociable about a holdup,' Bassett said. 'I believe I would just want to come right straight out and shoot the bastards – last time it was three men set on me with lead pipes.'

'Ouch,' the kid said. 'That's worse than tangling with Augie.'

'Augie don't have no use for Queensberry rules, right?'

'There was a machinist here last year,' the kid said, grinning, 'trying to teach me Queensberry style. The manly art, he called it. Augie is tryin to break me of it – he says it aint manly and it won't defend nothing. Here is something that might do you some good.' He held up a huge hand gun with a big flat block of metal riding forward of the trigger guard. 'This is the latest thing, a Mauser self-loader magazine gun. You cock it once and it shoots ten shots. Just keep pulling the trigger. The holster is wood – it can be clipped onto the butt and that makes a carbine out of it.' Expertly, Blue fastened the wooden stock on and shouldered the weapon. The action clicked.

'I would be curious to see it work, all right, Bassett said. 'It don't even look like a gun, except an artillery piece maybe, and I aint talking about starting a war.'

'Here is another self-loader, a Browning,' the kid said, showing Bassett a flat, sleek, compact weapon. 'You could carry it in your hip pocket. You won't find this stocked many places, it's that new. It will cost eighteen fifty.'

'Hell of a lot of money,' Bassett said.

'How much did the robbers take you for?' The kid grinned. 'Plenty of guns around for two-three dollars, if you want trash, but not here – we don't deal in trash.'

'It don't look like much to me.' Bassett did not really want to buy a gun or spend any money. But the kid was taking a box of cartridges out of a drawer, shaking some into his hand. He began to fill a magazine he slipped from the butt of the pistol.

'Why not come along with me?' he said. Carrying the pistol, he led the way through the back door of the room into a hallway, then down a flight of steps into a cellar. He turned a wall switch and light flooded the room. 'Edison lights, see?' One side of the room was filled with shelves and bins and boxes of parts and stock. But on the other side there was a narrow counter against the wall below a circular, dark opening. Blue turned another switch and light glowed deep within the opening. Bassett found himself looking down a tunnel with corrugated iron walls, like a culvert. It was an underground firing range. A clothesline ran on pulleys to the far end where a paper target hung from clothespins on the line.

Blue loaded the magazine into the butt of the gun, worked the slide and handed it to Bassett. 'Try it.'

Bassett took it, purposely sighted awkwardly, let his hand tremble and jerked off a shot. The sound in the tunnel was a muffled *pop*. He shot twice more, slowly, jerkily. The paper twitched once. He put the gun down and shrugged. 'It *shoots*, I spose. A man could say that. I best be going.'

'Wait,' Blue said. He slipped more cartridges into the Browning's clip. 'Say the gents with the lead pipes were coming for you. You said you would —'

'Come right straight out and shoot the bastards,' Bassett finished for him.

'Right.' The kid whirled, thrust the Browning straight out ahead of him, letting the butt rest in the palm of his left hand. He fired, a ripping burst of sound, until the gun was empty. Spent cartridges flew. The paper twitched and jerked and a piece tore free of the black center of the target and fluttered down. Bassett swallowed. Even in his line of work he had never seen such a torrent of gunfire from a single weapon.

'Mr Cawley, my uncle, has me practice, so as to make it look easy,' Blue said apologetically.

'I'll take it,' Bassett said suddenly and with conviction. 'But

I'll want to keep it under my coat, understand. Out of sight in some kind of harness.'

'A shoulder rig. It will take us a few days to get one made up to fit the Browning, it being such a new model. What will you want me to tell Mr Cawley about the sides of meat?'

'Not a damned thing,' Bassett said.

Bassett kept a room in an old hotel a few blocks from the agency's offices. He walked there rather than take a trolley and endure the outrage his present odorous condition was certain to arouse in the other passengers. Once in his room, he shed the filthy suit; then in his robe he crept furtively down the hall to the bathroom, where he drew a bath in the great iron ball-and-claw-footed tub. He soaked for thirty minutes, from time to time splattering shots of bay rum into the water. Out of the bath, he decided he had better not shave until after he picked up the Browning.

He returned to the office in another old suit, but this one was clean. Finishing his brief report to Havenhurst, he said, 'Piecing it together, I would say that Russell and Murdock probably left Cawley's place and went through police lines at dawn with a wagonload of meat, posing as butchers, along with all the other workingmen, market people and farmers.'

Havenhurst sighed. 'A van was found south of Jefferson Barracks this morning. Horses gone, some hog sides in the van and some butcher's aprons. No doubt they saddled the horses and rode off. We are just a little late. Now, what are we going to do about Cawley and the kid?'

'We could try to nail Cawley on some kind of complicity charge, but without having the culprits in hand, I doubt if it would stick. Besides, my impression was that the kid was in ignorance of what took place.'

'Clay Russell's own brother? The kid is certain to be involved in it.'

'Bassett shrugged. 'I thought so too, at first – he was reluctant to tell me anything about the sides of meat. But look, he thought I was a creditor. When I pushed him, he told me what he knew, which wasn't much. The kid wasn't trying to hide anything, I'm sure of it.'

'I can't believe it, Bassett.'

'All right, but either way, I think Israel Cawley set it up for them. He probably had the butcher's wagon there on the place – a perfect dodge. Men wearing aprons and paper caps – who would arrest them?' He hesitated. 'Do you have to tell the police their true identities and this connection with Israel Cawley now?'

'I'm supposed to. Why?'

'I bought a gun from the kid – an excuse to go back and talk to him again. But if all this gets in the papers, there will be cops and reporters all over the place. And suppose I'm right in thinking the kid wasn't in on it, and he suddenly discovers who Cawley's visitors were, that his own brother was one of the fugitives . . .' Bassett shrugged again and spread his hands.

'They have already flown the coop,' Havenhurst said slowly. 'I can't see that it will hinder the police if I hold the information a few more hours, at least long enough so that it won't make tomorrow's papers.' Suddenly his hand slapped down on the table and he swung to face Bassett squarely. 'Bought a gun, you say? With whose money? If you think the company will foot the bill for it, you're mistaken.'

CHAPTER IV

Cassie carried a big pot of coffee into the shop at three o'clock in the afternoon, as always, and the men stopped work to have a cup. Walter Hoag, the foreman, opened the top of the pot and looked inside.

'Cassie, see here what I found floating in your coffee,' he said, and appeared to withdraw a horseshoe from the pot. He held it up to show her. She laughed and covered her face with her apron, then said, 'Next time, I fill it with skunk juice, see if I don't.'

'What's happened with them guys that bust jail?' Augie said, as Cassie left the room.

Hoag produced a morning paper with cutaway drawings of the jail showing how the men had broken through the skylight.

Dotted lines sketched the escape path. The bearded, scorched faces of the fugitives stared woodenly off the page in halftone cuts. 'They got clean away,' he said. 'Slickest thing I ever saw.'

'But where would they go?' Blue said. He glanced over Hoag's shoulder at the paper as Hoag's finger traced the dotted line. He saw the sullen faces in the photographs with the names Mullins and Burrows beneath them.

'Railroad yards is only two blocks from the Four Courts,' Augie said, 'Me, I'd hole up in a boxcar.'

'First place the coppers looked,' Hoag said. 'I came past there this morning and they were still looking.'

Augie clenched battered fists. 'Nen I'd gemme a boat and cross the river, grab a freight onna other side.' He looked worried. In the shop it was generally understood that Augie had killed a man with a billiard ball back in Bridgeport, Connecticut.

'Cross the river and you'd be right out in plain sight on the water, with no way to run,' Hoag said. 'Even at night that would be taking an awful chance.'

'Best to haff friends to go to,' Axel said. 'Stay a vhile, change clothes, change everyting, ja?'

'I hope the bastards make it,' Augie said fervently.

Blue was alone in the shop, sweeping up after quitting time, when Israel drove his buggy into the stable yard, careening through the gate. Blue left his broom and went out to attend to the horse.

'Where's Axel?' Israel demanded. His face was flushed.

'Gone home. It's past quitting time.'

Israel swore under his breath and wrenched a heavy gear wheel from the back of the buggy. 'Here is a gear wheel from old man Stossel's big cutter – got jammed, he says. The spoke is cracked and two teeth are busted out of it. I told him it would be fixed before morning.'

'I can do it,' Blue said. 'Axel has been breakin me in on the carbide blowpipe.'

'Who told him to do that?' Israel growled. Blue waited, knowing Israel could not let a word go by without finding fault in it. 'All right, no matter – but see you do it proper, hear?' He went into the house, shaking his head and mumbling.

Blue unharnessed the horse, gave him a quick rub and put him in his stall; then he took the broken gear wheel into the shop, fastened it in a vise and prepared the fractured surfaces. The carbide blowpipe was a new development in metalwork, in which acetylene gas and oxygen were mixed to provide a welding flame of very high temperature. Blue turned on the generator, a tank device where the acetylene was made from carbide granules and water. He slipped on dark goggles, then popped the torch alight with a flint striker and began melting bronze rod where the broken teeth had been, building up the surface in layers. When sufficient metal had been laid down, he welded the broken spoke. With the goggles shielding his eyes and the torch roaring, he did not see movement or hear footsteps.

'Whatever you're doin, it's terrible hard on the eyes,' the voice said. A girl's voice. Blue jumped, then turned to look at her. He touched his goggles.

'You don't want to look directly at it.' He turned off the blow-pipe and pushed up the goggles. The girl had freckles across her nose and red hair coiled untidily on top of her head. She was wearing a print dress and a shawl. The same girl he had seen last night at the window – and memory of what he had seen caused him now to be acutely uneasy, as if she might somehow know what he had seen. But he was curious, too. He wet a rag in a bucket of water and cooled the gear wheeel, then began dressing the teeth with a file.

'I spect you will be Blue,' she said.

'That's right, but who told you?'

'I been talkin to Cassie in the kitchen.' She walked along the aisle between the banks of machinery, whirled and turned back, holding the shawl close with a small frown of distaste.

'For a shop, it's clean,' Blue said. 'You came last night with Israel's friends, didn't you?'

'What friends?'

'I saw you. In fact, I thought you went on with them when they left.'

She shrugged slightly. 'I know what a shop is like. My daddy used to work in the Katy shops – Parsons, Kansas, that was. I would carry his lunch to him, sometimes.'

'Is that where you met the people you are ... traveling with?'

'No. That was – it don't matter where it was, does it?' She was smiling now, mischief showing in the curl of her lip.

'Who were they?' Blue continued filing.

'My name is India. India Wood. No jokes, if you please.'

'No, I mean the men you came with. Who were they?'

'You might have said "Peased to meet you." ' She was looking a little annoyed. 'Didn't anybody ever tell you it aint polite to —'

Heavy footsteps sounded in the hallway, then Israel entered the room. 'If you will just pause to remember, young woman, you promised to stay in the other part of the house.'

'Is this some kind of jail?' she flared.

'You'd know about that, wouldn't you? You wasn't so fresh last night when you —' Israel caught himself, turned on Blue. 'And you had a job to do, by god. Jawing with her aint getting it done.' The girl went furiously to the door and stopped there, looking back, her face pale under the freckles.

'It's all finished,' Blue said. He held up the gear wheel.

Israel took it angrily, his hands quivering. He started to say something; then he saw on the bench a two-foot-long contraption made of bundled copper tubes. 'What is that thing?'

'It's a new kind of blowpipe Axel made – for cutting, though. See here, he cut a piece of half-inch steel with it, in just a particle of the time it would take to saw it.' Blue showed Israel a heavy slab of steel with a long cut running through it, the edges of the cut beaded where the metal had melted.

'He's messing with this stuff on my time, is he?' Israel snarled. 'My time and my stock?'

'Well, it's the same as with the welding blowpipe,' Blue said. 'We can do cutting with this that no one else in this part of the country can handle —'

Israel slammed the heavy slab of steel down across the blowpipe, inches from Blue's fingers. The tubes were smashed and bent. Blue did not flinch. He deliberately left his hand where it was on the bench. 'I spect Axel can make another one,' he said softly.

Israel's eyes glared beneath the thick brows. He had been drinking and he needed a shave and a bath. Blue had never seen him so filled with – what? Fury? Not alone. More like *fear*. 'Damn you, Blue,' Israel said. 'It's that stinkin Russell blood of yours again. By god and what you need —' He drew back his arm for a backhand blow. Instantly, Blue caught his wrist. Israel strained against his own arm. He was twisted back over the bench, off balance and unable to kick or strike. 'By god, Blue —' he panted through clenched teeth.

'No,' Blue whispered. 'Don't try it. Not ever again.' For a long moment Israel's arm and body strained back against him like a massive, quivering spring, his red-rimmed eyes squinting and blinking above flared nostrils. Blue increased his pressure. Suddenly, the tension went out of Israel. He nodded, a slight jerk of his head. Blue released him carefully and stepped back.

Israel stood rigid. A long moment passed; then he let his breath out slowly, turned and stalked through the door. The girl watched him defiantly as he brushed past her. They heard a door open and close down the hall. She looked at Blue with a quirky smile.

'He's a pet, all right,' she said.

Blue was shaken. It was the first time he had ever openly defied Israel. He fingered the ruined blowpipe, then said awkwardly, 'It's something he can't help.'

'Like a skunk, you mean?' When he did not answer, she said, 'I wondered what you would be like.'

'Why?' Blue was startled.

She shrugged, still smiling.

'Well, did you decide anything?' he said.

'Hardly had time. You're a foot or two taller than I expected, and – not near as nasty.'

Blue laughed. 'It's been a while since I was that size. Who have you been talking to? Cassie again, I guess.'

'Maybe.'

She did seem bent on teasing him, Blue thought. It was as if she knew him or something about him that he did not know himself, but ought to know – something elusive and shadowy.

'How long are you going to be staying?' he said.

'I don't know for sure.'

'Do you know where you'll be going?'

'Don't know that either. West, someplace. Soon as ... they get settled, they'll send for me. It could be some little time.'

'I'll likely be gone myself before long,' Blue said.

She frowned. 'And leave me here alone?'

'You couldn't have counted on me.' Blue grinned. 'You'll have Israel for company.'

'I never counted on that, either.' She bit her lip. A tear suddenly spilled onto her cheek and she brushed it away angrily. 'Not *knowing* nothing – it's as bad as being scared.'

'Scared of what?'

'Oh, of where we're goin, of what's goin to happen ...'

'If you knew all that ahead, you might not want to make the trip,' Blue said, grinning again.

'That's what I'm afraid of. Nothing is ever the way it starts out to be. What happens to it?'

In the morning Axel came to Blue holding the ruined blowpipe. 'He do this ting, Blue?' he said softly. Blue nodded unhappily. Axel thrust a short mechanic's hammer into the pocket of his baggy overalls, then went purposefully into Israel's office. Blue heard the murmur of voices, Israel protesting, Axel saying simply, 'Give me my time.' Silence then, and minutes later Axel came out, his plump cheeks pale. He threw the hammer on the bench and gathered up his tools. Leaving, he roughed Blue's hair and said, 'Don't forget Axel, Blue – he try to make you a first-class mechanic, ja?'

Bassett spent the morning nosing around the railroad yards, talking to trainmen and bums, trying to get a lead on the yeggs he had followed across Indiana and Illinois. He left the yards and followed the Frisco tracks along the levee, questioning freight handlers, brakemen, work gangs. Several were convinced they had seen the escaped Four Courts prisoners, but there was no trace of the yeggs.

In midafternoon he decided that he would pick up his new gun. But Bassett thought he had better not see Cawley and the Russell kid at the same time, since he had let the kid think that he, as Wagenbach, had supplied Cawley with some sides of meat. If the matter arose in Cawley's presence, Bassett would be undone.

He walked into Zumbach's, saw the little waiter with the splendid red mustache and said, 'Aint seen Cawley, have you?'

The waiter nodded toward a corner table. Basset turned and saw a big, bearded man sitting alone, glowering into a half-empty glass. 'Good,' Bassett said and turned away toward the door. The waiter blinked. 'You don't vant to see him?'

'Not for a while – I owe him money,' Bassett said in a low voice, touching the side of his nose and winking at the little man. He left then and walked to the old house, Cawley's shop. Inside, the big motor was running and belts were slapping, that sound in turn lost in the chittering and burring sounds of lathe and shaper. He recognized Augie, who was standing at a gas stove near the forge, suspending a long gun barrel in a shallow tank – probably a bluing set-up, Bassett thought. The Russell kid came in from the shed and said something to Augie, who laughed. The the kid saw Bassett and walked over to greet him.

'You've missed Mr Cawley again,' he said, 'But your gun is ready for you.' He led Bassett into the gun room, where he opened a box and took out the pistol in its new holster. Bassett saw the initial *W* worked into the leather and ran his fingers over it. 'Your initial, Mr Wagenbach,' the kid said. 'That's to make you feel that two dollars for this outfit was well spent.'

Bassett laughed. 'I didn't see Axel out there. Have you hung him up to dry again?' He slipped out of his coat and pulled on the holster rig.

The kid frowned. 'Axel aint here anymore.' He looked troubled.

'How about the people who went off with them hog sides of mine? You seen anything of them?' Bassett said. The kid adjusted the straps for him and the gun settled flat against his ribs on the left side.

'Not a thing,' the kid said. 'I didn't see them in the first place. Not their faces, anyway. That gun is a lot flatter than a revolver. Under a coat, it won't even show.'

'They stayed the night though?' Bassett said.

'I never said that,' the kid said. 'You'll want some bullets too, won't you?'

'A couple of boxes. Smokeless.'

'Smokeless costs twice as much, did you know that? Two boxes would run you two fourteen.'

'That's more than two cents a shot,' Bassett protested.

'Everything's going up, all right.'

They just drove in here in their butcher's van and spent the night, is that it?' Bassett said.

'No, we had the van, the kid said. He was adding figures in pencil on the side of the box.

'You mean they walked here?'

'No, they – a girl brought th—' The kid caught himself.

'A girl?' Bassett pressed on. 'Was her name Helen?'

The kid looked up, frowning again. 'Her name is India. That adds up to twenty-two dollars and sixty-four cents, Mr Wagenbach.'

Bassett winced. 'At your prices, it will cost me too much to shoot the bastards who are trying to rob me.'

The kid grinned. He opened another box and showed Bassett a cased Colt revolver. It had carved ivory grips and the metal was crusty with engraving and gold inlay. 'You could have this one for eight hundred dollars, if you'd rather.'

'All the robbers aint in jail,' Bassett said. Out of the corner of his eye he saw movement through the door at the rear of the room, behind the desk. A woman – a girl, really, he thought – had started to enter but then pulled back into the hall. 'So,' Bassett said, 'She didn't go with them . . .' He left the words hanging, not quite a question, his voice low.

Flustered, the kid said, 'No.'

'Supposing I was to talk to her,' Bassett said. 'She might be able to tell me —'

They heard sudden heavy footsteps down the hall and a thick, snarling voice. 'Sniffin around again, is that it? You and the kid, messin around – don't try to tell me different, by god.' There were sounds of scuffling and the girl's voice hissing, fierce in protest, but lost under the man's. '. . . so you mean to play the tart here, too. No? All innocence, is it?' There was the sound of a slap, then Israel's sudden grunt of pain, and he backed into the gun room holding the girl's wrist, dragging her with him. He pulled her close, pinning her arms to her sides, but the look he saw on her face caused him to turn. Startled and confused to see Blue and a stranger in the office, his grip loosened. The girl pulled free and darted out of the room.

'Mr Wagenbach has bought one of our self-loaders,' the kid said evenly. 'He has been wanting to ask you about —'

Bassett bumped him, cut him off. 'Some other time, maybe. The young feller has done a job of selling on me – I best be on my way while I still have a nickel in my pocket.'

Israel tried to speak, grunted something that sounded like 'Good,' flashed his teeth in a grimace, then swung stiffly around and stalked out of the room.

Bassett gave the kid a one-sided, wry smile. 'You want me to get my head chewed off?'

In the agency office, Bassett pulled the folder marked *Mullins – Burrows* from the file. He saw that a line had been struck through those names and *Murdock – Russell* written after them. Among the notes and reports from various operatives who had worked on the case, he found one report filed in Carthage, Missouri, following the train holdup and shooting near there which had ultimately landed the two robbers in the Four Courts jail. The operative had established that the two robbers had stayed in a boardinghouse for several weeks prior to the crime, that the boardinghouse had a shady reputation locally and that two of the female tenants had disappeared the day before the robbery, possibly, suggested the operative, to set up housekeeping for the robbers elsewhere. The names of the two women were Millie Dorton and India Wood.

Bassett went in to see the super, Havenhurst. 'I figure,' he said, 'that the girl was on hand to meet them at the time of the jailbreak and that she took them to Cawley's, where they left her behind when they left the next morning. Chances are good that she will be in touch with them again, so keeping tabs on her could give us our lead.'

Havenhurst nodded. 'We can watch the girl, but right now I want you to get a shave and make yourself presentable. We have what appears to be an insurance swindle in Memphis —'

'If there is any bookkeeping in it . . .' Bassett shook his head.

'Nonsense, Bassett,' Havenhurst said firmly. 'Now listen to me . . .'

After Wagenbach left, Blue went back to the kitchen. Cassie was there, cutting up squash for baking. 'Where is India?' Blue asked.

'Gone to her room. Did she have a argument with you Uncle Israel?'

Blue nodded. 'You could call it that.'

'Same as last night,' Cassie said. 'It near killin that man to have a young female in the house, is what Cassie thinkin.' She looked up grimly. 'Specially one like her.'

'What do you mean?'

'Trashy, is what I mean. You keep away from that girl, hear?'

'Who is she, Cassie? Who did she come here with?'

Cassie bore down on the big butcher knife and the blade bit into the tough squash. She did not answer.

'I think you know,' Blue said. 'Why won't you tell me?'

'You won't hear nothin from Cassie. Not a word.' She pressed her lips tightly together and turned her back on him, putting the pieces of squash into a baking pan. Blue had to grin. He squeezed her shoulder. 'Not a word,' she said. Shaking his head, Blue left the room and went back to the shop.

Walter Hoag, the foreman, saw him and beckoned him over to the power hacksaw, where he showed him a heavy piece of steel on the saw table. The steel was marked with a chalk line. 'This is a job of cutting Axel was going to do with his blowpipe,' Hoag said. Blue nodded. With the wooden fork lever overhead he moved the leather drive belt onto the power wheel; then he oiled the blade and began to cut. The steel was thick and the cutting was slow. The rest of the men had left by the time he finished.

He put the steeel on the bench where Hoag would find it in the morning. The ruined copper blowpipe was still lying there, pushed back under the tool rack. Blue pulled it out and looked at it, seeing from the arrangement of tubes how Axel had meant for it to work. On sudden impulse he went to the bins and found the stock of tubing Axel had drawn from to make the blowpipe. He took the pieces to the bench and began to cut them to length, matching them to the ruined ones. But even concentrating on the work could not push India from his thoughts – not just that she was pretty and that she had been teasing him a little, but the strangeness of her coming there at all. There was something nagging at Blue and he could not place it.

He was still working when Cassie called him to supper. She had set a place for him at the kitchen table. Alone. 'Where is India?' Blue said.

'She won't come down,' Cassie said. 'She fraid you Uncle Israel gawn come back. I don't blame her none, the way he done her. She tell me she aim to take the morning train to Kansas City, stay with her girl friend. With her gone, maybe trouble crawl back in the hole. Now you eat, Blue.'

Blue ate quickly, scarcely tasting, then went back to work in the shop. He salvaged a valve for the oxygen jet from Axel's torch and drilled out a block of copper to make another mixing chamber and nozzle. Cutting, fitting, he saw the torch grow under his hands. It was late when he put it down, finished except for the threaded fittings where the hoses would be connected. He heard thunder rumble outside, then the rattle of rain on the iron shed roof.

He went into the shed, pulled off his shirt and washed up in the trough. Bent over, dipping up water with his hands, he saw the stable yard light up in a flash of lightning; through the slanting rain he saw the light farm wagon that India and the two men had arrived in. He stared then, after the lightning faded and while the thunder rolled, at the patch of dark where the wagon sat. He thought of how the wagon had rolled in that other night – it had been raining then, too. Except for that wagon, by now he could have been aboard a freight train, and almost to Denver. After what happened with Israel, he thought, it's time to go for sure. Now.

He turned and looked up at the house, icy rain stinging his bare shoulders. There was a light in the kitchen and there was a dim light in India's room upstairs. In his mind he saw her, the untidy coil of red-dark hair, the freckled nose and teasing smile, and he heard her again, *I wondered what you would be like.* The words echoed in memory. And, *You're a foot or two taller than I expected, and – not near as nasty.* Blue stiffened. At the time he had taken it for granted that India and Cassie had been gossiping about him in the kitchen, but it was suddenly clear to him that Cassie would not have said anything about his size – he had been over six feet since he was fifteen and Cassie was used to that. No. India had to have talked to someone who still thought of Blue as a little kid. Clay?

Blue ducked back under the shed, caught up his flannel shirt and mopped himself with it. He pulled it on again as he went back into the shop. He turned off the Edison lights and went down the long hall, past the stairway to the kitchen

Cassie looked up from the table. She was fixing a tray of food – hot biscuits, soup and a glass of milk. 'You're soaked, Blue!' she scolded. 'How come you aint wear no slicker? You want somethin to eat?'

He shook his head. 'I want to talk to her – did Israel come back?'

'I don't know. He maybe come in his own street door. I fixed her somethin to eat.' She touched the tray.

'Let me take it to her,' Blue said.

'Cassie hopin you keep away from that girl.' Her voice was low, troubled. 'We both stayed too long, Blue. Too long.'

'I'm leavin, Cassie – tonight, but after I talk to her.'

He lifted the tray of food from the table and slipped into the hall as Cassie went back into her own room and closed the door. The steamy fragrance of her biscuits was in his nostrils as he climbed the stairs. He turned left at the top. A dim bar of light glowed under the door ahead. A door closed downstairs – Israel? No way now to know. He balanced the tray on one hand and scratched at the door panel with his nails. Waited, then scratched again. He put his ear close to the door and thought he could hear her breathing on the other side, but his own heart began thudding wildly and he could not be sure.

'It's Blue.' He breathed the words, almost without sound.

After a moment he heard the click of the key in the lock. The door opened a crack. The crack widened and India stood dark against the dim glow of light from a gas lamp on the wall behind her.

'I brought you some supper,' Blue said.

Instead of answering, she caught his sleeve, pulled him into the room and closed the door behind, her hair brushing his chin as she did so. He heard the key grate again, then she took the tray from him and put it on the chest of drawers. Her lamp was turned down so far the flame was nearly gone and the dim yellow light pulsed and flickered on the wall.

'I want to know —' Blue started to say, but she put her lips close to his ear and whispered, '*Shush*, Blue.' She was so close to him that Blue felt the soft touch of her breast against his ribs. There was not room for him to step back, as good manners told him he ought, so he stood politely still, yet unable to close his mind against the gentle nudging. Nor did she step back. She appeared to be listening. Somewhere a board creaked. She flinched at the sound. The nudging softness against Blue's ribs stirred. He licked his lips uneasily, not daring to move. His ears roared and he suddenly realized he was holding his breath. He gasped and inhaled deeply. The warmth stirred against him, then she stepped back and it was gone.

'I have to talk to you,' he said.

She hissed at him and touched fingers to his lips. 'Can't it wait?'

'You're awful jumpy.'

'You didn't hear everything he said to me – if he finds out you're here, he'll *murder* us. He was in a terrible fury anyway, because of us.' She shivered. 'I'm glad you came, though. Bein alone in this house is miserable.'

'I'm fixin to leave here. I aimed to be gone before now.'

'What stopped you?'

'Same thing that's stoppin me now. I want to know who it was you come here with.'

'You're talkin too loud again.'

'Who were they, India? Tell me. I've just got to know.'

Her lips twisted in a little smile. She put one finger across his lips, her forearm resting gently on his chest. Her eyes gleamed, framed in the tumbled darkness of her hair, 'Why should it matter to you? It was just my ... my gentleman friend and his partner. They trade in horses.'

There's more to it than that – the way they left, in that butcher's wagon.'

'There's nothing wrong in that.' The smile teased him.

'And there's been a gent here, calls himself Wagenbach. He's asking questions, too.'

She let her hand trail across his cheek. Her fingers touched his ear lobe, toyed with it. He shook his head, annoyed, wanting her to answer. A low laugh escaped her. 'Don't you dare to try to shake India loose,' she scolded. She took his face between both her hands and pulled his head down to meet hers, and Blue was astonished to find her soft lips planted firmly and moistly on his own. For a moment he was rigid, then his hands caught her shoulders. She leaned back, smiling, letting him hold her.

'You didn't answer me,' he gasped. The way she lay back with the weight of her upper body on his hands caused her hips to press against him. She stirred knowingly.

He swallowed and tried again, desperately. 'Tell me, India. Was it – my brother Clay?'

Her mouth quivered again in that teasing smile. 'No,' she breathed, 'no, no,' shaking her head slightly, insistently, and he felt the slight movement run through her body like a shiver. He tried again to speak. 'No, no, no . . .' She would not let him say the words. They melted in his throat, became an aching knot lodged there. The pale downy sheen of light along the edge of her cheek blurred close. Then the light was lost and he felt her soft darting tongue.

In his innermost self Blue seethed with disbelief that this could be happening to him. A part of him seemed to slide away, out of himself, and hover weightless in the gloom, peering down, dimly seeing the two of them there locked close. Under his hands, thin cotton skidded on her skin. He felt the fragile spine dip into the hollow of her back and touched a dimple there through the cloth; then she twisted against him and their lips parted and warm breath flowed along his jaw.

He drew a deep, shuddering breath. 'I didn't believe it.' His voice was a shaky whisper.

'Do you now?' It was breath, not sound.

'I – I ain't sure.' He felt her shake and knew she was laughing at him. His eyes, clamped shut, felt gluey. It would take all his strength to open them. He did not want to try. Not yet.

'Here now, you're all damp.' She murmured the complaint and pushed away his shirt; then she was turning, sinking with him onto the loose softness of feather quilts, lips searching again and clinging. Blue was lost in the long passing seconds until sudden disbelief that was like panic shot through him again. With an effort, he pulled away and opened his eyes. Inches away, he saw India's eyes peering at him through a fallen lock of red-dark hair.

'Time you looked,' she whispered tartly. 'You afraid of India? I spect you meant to go now.' Breathy-soft voice, yet taunting. She pulled the gown snugly across herself. Blue peeled her fingers away from the cloth and let it fall. Her skin was pale in the faint yellow light, the lines and mounds and valleys blurred and flowing away into distance, Blue thought, like a mysterious country, hazy amber under a dim sun.

'Well then . . .' she breathed.

CHAPTER V

The sound of the rain was a steady, soft roar on the roof and in the gutters. Blue lay watching the wire-thin edge of flame in the lamp. India made a little snuffling sound, her breath hot against his shoulder under the edge of the quilt. Somewhere a dog began to bark. She stirred, then stretched, a long, shivering stretch, and murmured something, the sound lost against his shoulder as he turned to her. Then her hand was against his chest.

'I said you best shoo. Git now, Blue.' She yawned.

Stung, he got an elbow under him and leaned over her, but she did not move. Her face and eyes were without expression. Then she shook her head. Her whispered voice was crisp. 'It's like money – you spend it all now, you won't have none for later. Git, now. I mean to be up at the crack of day to catch a train.'

Blue bit his lip, then sat up abruptly and fumbled for his

shirt where it had been thrown across the ladder back of the chair. He slipped into it, thinking that she would reach out and pull him back to her. She stretched again and yawned. Blue reached for his britches. They had fallen across her valise, sitting on the splinted seat of the ladder back, the belt buckle caught in the jaws of the valise. Blue pulled sharply and the valise toppled to the floor with a thud and chink of buckles.

'Clumsy,' she said. 'See what you done.'

Blue pulled the trousers on and buttoned them; then he bent and lifted the valise back onto the chair, stuffing folds of cloth back into it. 'You're messin up my things,' she scolded and came across the bed on hands and knees, the quilt falling aside, her skin amber in the faint light. She snatched the cloth, a dress or petticoat, from him and began to fold it, sitting back on her heels in the tumbled quilt, her breasts quivering as she turned the ruffled cloth. Watching her, Blue felt himself grinning. She looked up, saw him looking at her. 'Oh, *you!*' she snapped and turned to feel in the bed for her dressing gown.

Still grinning, Blue bent, found a shoe and felt for the other. His fingers touched cloth. A scarf. And something else. A hairbrush. And a piece of cardboard. He lifted them. India suddenly bent forward and snatched at the things in his hand, pulling away the scarf and brush. Blue glanced at the piece of cardboard. It was a photograph, several people sitting stiffly, glaring back at him from the sepia paper. India's hand darted for it and her nails raked Blue's hand. 'It's mine! Give it to me, Blue.' A sharp whisper.

'Hold on,' Blue said, half turning to let the dim lamplight fall on the picture. His skin turned prickly and cold as he stared. They sat against a painted woodland framed by tasseled drapes, a plaster column holding a plaster urn next to the gaunt woman, the hard-jawed young man in his stiff collar, with an improbable umbrella furled across his knees. And sitting cross-legged at their feet, the small boy. Himself, forever frozen in that moment, peering up from beneath wet-combed hair. India caught a corner of the photograph and he let her have it.

'You should have give it to me when I asked for it,' she said.

'Why wouldn't you tell me? Why wouldn't *he* tell me?' Blue sank back on the edge of the bed, pulled on and laced his shoes. 'My own brother. I haven't set eyes on him since I was nine years old.'

'They were in a hurry – to close a business deal. I don't know more than that.'

'You've been with them.' Blue took her by the arms. 'You must know more than that. What kind of business would make him sneak away from here without saying a solitary word?'

'Let me go.' She pulled at his fingers. 'If he had wanted you to know about it, he would have told you. And I haven't been with them – I just met them at the train, is all, so don't ask me what I can't tell you.'

Blue looked around the room. 'This, tonight, it was just to shut me up, wasn't it?'

The quirky smile played again on her lips. 'Don't go making too much of something, one way or another, hear? What happened to us was better than bein alone on a dark and rainy night, wasn't it?'

'If you leave here, how will you get along?'

She regarded him for a moment, her head cocked, and the smile tugged at her lips. 'India will get along, Blue. Don't you worry none about that.'

'How will Clay get in touch with you?'

'My girl friend, Millie – he'll know where we are.'

'Tell me where that is. I mean to find Clay – he'll let me work with him, horses or whatever he's doin.'

She shook her head. 'Don't try it. His partner – you wouldn't want to mess with him. He's every bit as mean as Israel. Clay wouldn't want —'

'He's my own brother,' Blue said stubbornly. A tiny sound, like mice scratching, came to his ears. He stopped breathing and listened, suddenly aware of where he was. Her hand went to his arm, the nails raking lightly.

'There, it's nothin,' she whispered, 'but you best get out of here. Shoo, now.'

'Wait – we could go together, India. I could get work, then when Clay —'

'No. No such thing. Not with me. Blue, you go now, this minute.' Her hand pressed against his chest with sudden strength, pushing, turning him toward the door.

Blue felt a sudden rush of helpless misery. 'At least tell me where to find you.'

For a moment she pushed, and then she reached up and kissed his cheek, letting her lips nibble at his ear lobe. She whispered, the breathy giggle back in her voice, 'You ask around for Miss Francie's. It's a boardin house.' The latch clicked under her hand and she pushed him through the door.

Blue half turned, resisting, then something struck him on the side of the head and knocked him against the wall. A moment later he found himself on his hands and knees by the top of the stairs, not remembering how he came to be there He saw Israel standing by India's door glaring down at him, legs apart, heavy hands hanging, lips moving fiercely in the twisted, bearded face. Blue struggled to hear through the vast roaring that filled his head. He knew he should speak to Israel, yet his tongue felt rough and huge in his mouth and his words would not take shape. He tried desperately to remember what he wanted to say. Then he saw India, her eyes wide and glistening in the pale light, her mouth open against the spread fingers of her hand in a silent scream. Or was it silent? Blue wagged his head, puzzled, while the roaring gusted in his skull, and then suddenly he was hearing Israel's words.

'... bastardly jailbirds, the whole damned outfit, and you're no better, by god, sneakin up the backstairs to that slut and by god, Blue, I'll tear the hide off your back. You hear me, Blue? Count on it – you count on it ...' And he was advancing on Blue, who felt the floor spring beneath his hands from Israel's weight, yet could not move himself even when he saw the kick coming. The heavy boot missed his jaw and thudded into his chest, the shin smashing against Blue's face and nose. Pain flashed bright behind his eyes and Blue distinctly heard bone crack as the kick spun him rolling onto the stairs in a shower of splintering spindles. Lying on his back on the landing, Blue looked past his own sprawled and strangely distant legs and saw Israel clutch the rail and start down, and then hot wetness flooded his eyes. He rolled and blew salty spray from his nose and mouth. Israel tried to swing another kick but stumbled on the cramped landing and lurched into him. Blue caught the thick leg and heaved. Israel flailed his arms and cried out and they both toppled in a long slow arc into the yellow fan of light that streamed from the kitchen.

Israel landed on his back on the walnut-planked floor, the wind driven from his lungs in a mighty grunt. Blue felt Israel's body go slack beneath him. He crawled up and looked into Israel's glaring eyes, saw the mouth open, gasping like a beached fish. Israel's arms lay at his sides, palms up, the fingers twitching. Blood dripped in a steady stream onto his shirt front from Blue's smashed nose and gashed head. Blue tried again to speak, an earnest, reasonable thought, but only bubbles formed on his lips. Israel sucked a deep, shuddering breath through his clenched teeth. Blue crawled on, antlike. Before him, down the length of the hall, he saw the heavy paneled door to the shop.

Behind him, Israel rolled over and worked himself to his feet, staggering against the wall so that plates fell from a high plate rail to crash at his feet. He gasped, clutching at his belly, unable yet to take a step as India scuttled down the stairs and darted past him into the kitchen. She had her traveling cloak around her shoulders and both arms were wrapped about her carpetbag. He glared at her in helpless fury.

India backed away from him. She turned to run and stumbled into Cassie. She screamed in sudden fright, then caught herself. 'Cassie! It's Israel – he's killin Blue!'

Cassie put out an arm and swept India toward the back door. 'You go on – git, and keep a-goin. Cassie see to this.' Her eyes on Israel, she heard the whisper of the girl's footsteps and the click of the door latch.

Israel swayed, his breath coming in short quick gasps. 'You stay clear of this, Cassie, hear me? By God, I'll skin that kid.' He blinked and turned away, dragging his feet unsteadily.

Her own voice was shaky. Israel looked drunk and crazy-mad to her. 'Mist' Israel, I cain see that boy hurt – leave be, now.'

'Shut up, Cassie.'

She peered around the doorframe and saw Israel stagger against the big double door that led into the shop. The door opened and he half fell through into the dark room. Cassie gnawed on a knuckle, looking about the kitchen. Her big cleaver lay on the kitchen table, the blue-gray blade glinting dullly. She stepped to it and moved to pick it up, but could not close her fingers around the brown handle. She heard a crash as Israel stumbled over something in the shop. It was nothing to parcel out a mess of ribs with that cleaver, but the thought of swinging it on a man was too much for her. But *there* – next to the big black iron stove – she bent and caught up a piece of stove wood. Hickory, rough and splintery, heavy in her hand. She ran down the hall and through the door into darkness, ran hard into Israel's thick-muscled arm. He smelled of whiskey and sweat.

'Tole you, stay clear, woman.' He twisted the stick of wood from her hands. 'Jus' what I need, by god —'

She squirmed, tried to duck under the heavy arm, but she was held fast. 'Where *is* that kid?' Israel snarled in her ear, his breath a sour wash of air. Half-choked, frantic, Cassie remembered something – had a bunioned foot on him, Israel did. Cassie stamped down hard with her heel. Israel bawled like a stuck bull and hurled her against the wall. Cassie bounced back against him, clawing now for his eyes, then Israel felt her knee jab into his thigh.

'Black bitch!' he grunted and brought his elbow hard across her face. Cassie slid down the wall and lay still.

Blue was on his hands and knees beneath the big rifling machine. Blood dripped steadily from the end of his smashed nose onto puddled oil and steel shavings. He wiped his eyes on his sleeve and felt his nose move, the bone grating noisily. A faint spray of light from the kitchen fanned through the doorway and Blue saw it break as Israel walked through it. In a moment he would turn down the aisle between the long workbench and the bank of belt-driven machinery.

Footsteps whispered in sawdust, then Israel's foot struck something. He grunted and swore, the sound of his voice instantly lost in a great whirring racket of spinning shafts and slapping leather drive belts. He had fallen against the wooden-handled knife switch that controlled the two banks of machinery, all belt-driven by the big Monarch motor. The floor throbbed.

Blue waited for the machinery to stop. When it kept running, he decided that Israel could not find the handle in the dark

– and he knew that Israel would have to go back to the door, to the wall switch there, to turn on the Edison lights. A man scarcely dared move among all those chattering drive belts in the dark. Blue's arms quivered under him.

Light flared and he was blinking against the sudden glare of naked hanging bulbs. He crawled back into the aisle between the two banks of machinery and tried to get his feet under him. Israel lurched into the end of the aisle, a dozen feet away.

'Get ready, Blue!' he shouted. 'You won't be nothing but a smear, by god, when I'm done with you. Hear?' Swinging the piece of stove wood, he stalked toward Blue, ignoring the chattering belts. Blue heaved himself to his feet, reeled against the lathe bed. Israel wagged the raw-splintered hickory at him and swung it, feinting. Blue flinched and Israel drove the butt of the stick into his ribs. Blue skidded along the bed of the lathe and Israel sprang forward, caught him by the front of his shirt and bent him back. Blue looked up through blood-smeared eyes. Israel's face was a contorted blur against the glaring light as he lifted the piece of stove wood. The slapping leather belt running from the power shaft overhead down to the lathe was twisted a half-turn to control the direction of rotation of the lathe's spindle. Israel's hickory club thrust up and back. Instantly, it was caught and whipped around by the twist of belt in a short sharp arc; it struck Israel just over the ear with a solid *chunk* as the club was snatched against the idler wheel and the belt snapped.

Israel toppled onto Blue and bore him down, his jaw sagging aslant, his eyes staring, the club clattering down with them in a tangle of leather belting. Blue lay in the sawdust, Israel's heavy body pinning him down, pain from his cracked ribs tearing through him. He squirmed, gasping, then twisted and rolled Israel off of him. On hands and knees, his senses spinning, he contemplated the bearded face and tried to comprehend what had happened. Blue slapped at the bearded jaw. Israel's head lolled loosely. Blue saw a glimmer of white through parted eyelids, saw blood puddling in the sawdust below Israel's ear. His arms buckled. He caught himself falling, and when he looked down and saw Israel's face again, it seemed hours that he had been looking at it.

He turned and began to crawl, seeing brightly beading blood splatter between his hands. He reached the forge and rested; then he hauled himself up, tottered to the shed door and fell through, not seeing Cassie, who still lay where she had dropped at the far end of the room. Blue moved like a fighter bare-knuckled down, smashed loose from his senses. He hitched himself up again, the thrumming of rain on the iron roof a meaningless roar in his ears as he staggered out into the night. He kept moving, stumbled over a wagon axle protruding from the great pile of scrap iron, and came then to the tall board fence. He unlatched the gate, slipped through and began to walk along the dark cobbled street in the slanting rain.

CHAPTER VI

Blue staggered out of the canyon of six-storied warehouses onto the open levee facing the vast rain-shrouded river, and into the sudden glare of night lights from the big slumbering sternwheeler *Bluff City* tied silent at the levee. Numbed instincts urged him to run, to get out of the light. Blue's feet dragged in a shambling run. He crossed the railroad tracks, threading between tarp-covered mounds of freight, stacked timbers, coiled hawsers, empty wagons. A match sputtered alight on the boiler deck of the *Bluff City* and a watchman sucked fire into rain-damp tobacco. The sternwheeler's bow line caught Blue across the chest. He ducked under it, tripped and fell hard across the wooden thwarts of a rowboat, drawn up under the broad bow.

'Who's yonder?' the watchman barked, peering now through red and green flashes in his eyeballs from the sudden flare of match light. He grabbed his Winchester and levered a cartridge into the chamber. 'Speak up, by god, I see you!' Sparks gusted from his pipe. He cocked his head and listened. The *Bluff City* lifted gently to the current and her hawsers groaned. The watchman mumbled to himself, thumbed the tobacco in his pipe to pack it tighter and settled back into his slat-back chair.

A sharp-edged wooden thwart cut into Blue's ribs. Pain goaded him. He rolled over. When his weight rocked back into the stern, the rowboat's bow lifted, her bottom skidded – a gritty whisper. She floated and swung into the current.

Blue's head and one shoulder were wedged into the sharp angle of the bow, his body awash in the half-swamped boat as she spun away in the rain.

A cabin door swung open. Packard Disbrow stepped out onto the lofty texas deck of the side-wheeler *Shawnee Princess*. He looked down with pleasure on the rushing waters of the river; then he stepped to a ladder and descended to the covered promenade of the passenger deck. Morning mist swept in drifting wisps over the water and myriad droplets hung from the Gothic gingerbread openwork of the long promenade. The sun, rising red beyond the trees on the far shore, struck brilliant sparks from the droplets.

Disbrow, who was known in his circle of friends as Packy, hooked an arm around a chamfered pillar to steady himself and added his own small stream to the vast river. He sighed contentedly as the sun burst free of the trees and brushed him with warmth. He turned aft and made his way toward a deck bench, moving with some difficulty because he was crippled and because the rail was slanting, wobbly and broken away entirely for part of its length. The deck itself was tilted, spongy with rot, treacherous with broken boards and open holes. Farther forward, the roof of the promenade was collapsed under a fallen smokestack. The *Princess* was a hulk, hard aground and half-buried in silt.

She was an Anchor-line side-wheeler built in 1886 at Howard's yard in Jeffersonville, Indiana, for the Mississippi passenger trade. She was 294 feet long, with a beam of 49 feet and a draft of nine and a half feet, and she was powered by two Schoellhorn-Albrecht slide-valve steam engines fed by eight great boilers. When the great tornado of 1896 struck the St Louis waterfront, the *Princess* had been directly in the path of the storm. The wind scattered coals from an iron stove, and the *Princess* caught fire and was cut loose. Out in the river, she was ripped by the winds and crushed between other drifting wrecks. Twelve people perished in her, her share of the two hundred and twenty-five all told who died in the storm. The swollen river dumped her miles downstream onto a desolate sand spit known as Cogson's Bar. After the bodies were removed, she was stripped of engines and furnishings.

Now on her sloping promenade deck, Packy Disbrow settled onto the bench, then straightened abruptly as a drifting rowboat caught his eye – his one good eye, for the other was hidden under a tattered flap of bandanna held in place by a dented derby hat. The bow of the drifting skiff ticked the steamer's crushed wheelhouse and spun. The boat was full of water, close to foundering. As it passed beneath him, he saw a body lying awash in its bottom. The current sucked the skiff away from the *Princess* in an arc that would carry it on around the bar. A few yards away the branches of a downed willow hung into the water, clawing at brown scum and trash. The boat drifted against the branches and clung there.

Holding the trembling rail, Disbrow scuttled along the steep slope of the passenger deck. Beneath it, the main deck disappeared in silt and tangled scrub. The broken passenger deck sank sloping, almost to the level of the bar. Disbrow came to a break in the rail and jumped down. He kicked free of the scrub and hobbled through damp silt toward the skiff.

Just then a second man appeared beneath the slanting passenger deck, a scrawny and ragged wraith with flushed, sunken cheeks, a wool cap set crookedly on his head. 'Leave him be. I seen the son of a bitch first,' he snarled.

Packy Disbrow leaned down and wrenched a spindle from a length of deck railing embedded in the silt. He twirled the spindle, smiling agreeably at the other man, but he continued walking. At the water's edge, he caught the skiff's rail and grounded it against the bank.

'He's mine, I tell ye,' the scrawny man said.

'I don't see no bill of lading pinned to him.' Kneeling by the boat, Disbrow put the spindle where he could reach it, then pushed one sleeve up and dipped a hand into the water, where he proceeded to fish for pockets. Except for quick glances, he kept his one eye on the other man, who glared furiously at him, inching closer for a better look into the skiff.

'Clean as a whistle.' Disbrow raised his dripping hand to show it was empty. 'Somebody else glommed him first, before or after they worked him over.'

The scrawny man's shoulders slumped a little. 'By god, you needn't think you're the man to do me out of my rights.'

'Not atall, amigo – that aint my style.' Disbrow reached back into the water, caught a hip pocket and pulled, the better to get at it. The body rolled. Face and nose went under water. A moment later the shoulders heaved and a blast of air burst from mouth and nostrils. Disbrow caught a handful of hair and lifted the head clear of the water. Spray blew from mouth and nose in feeble, racking coughs. For the first time, Disbrow had a good look at the face. He winced at what he saw.

'Jesus! I thought he was a stiff,' the scrawny man blurted.

'So did I.' Disbrow felt the limp wrist for a pulse, shook his head and tried the neck. He grunted then and said, 'He's close to cashing in – before the sun sets, is my guess. Shame, too. Been beat severe, he has.' Packy Disbrow thought a moment. 'Terrible severe.'

'Push him off.' The other man was suddenly irate. 'I mean it. Get shut of him. The bastard's likely wanted. Here, by god, I'll give you a hand.'

He scrambled forward, but Disbrow reached down and picked up the spindle. He held it up and sighted along it, tried it for heft, looked please. Then he said, 'When he breathes his last is soon enough. No more than you would want done for you, pal.'

'You'll have the law on our necks, hear?' The scrawny man dug a finger nervously into one nostril and twisted it fiercely.

'He left no tracks,' Disbrow said mildly.

'He come downstream, didn't he? The river is tracks enough.'

Disbrow squatted on the rail of the boat and regarded the battered body. 'I judge the bulls will be chasin after the other feller. This one is the dismalest piece of goods I ever set eyes on. There won't be nothing after him but a flock of buzzards.'

'No? Hell they won't. I say get shut of him and quick, or we're in trouble, betcher ass.' The finger dug again. 'Give the goddam boat a shove.'

Packy Disbrow sighed. 'No, I won't spring the trap on a man. After he cashes in, it won't matter. You can move on if you're nervous, pal – the landlord will give you a refund.' He slapped his knee and laughed.

The scrawny man withdrew his finger and glared. 'Hell with him! Hell with you both!' He coughed and spat and stomped away furiously through the silt and scrub, pausing once to blow his nose between his fingers and glare back at Disbrow; then he crawled back under the folded-down passenger deck into his own hole, wherever it was in the half-buried caverns of the main deck

Packy Disbrow twisted the fingers of one hand in the battered youngster's collar and pulled. The collar tore. Disbrow's right hand, in its ragged cotton glove, was distorted and nearly useless, but he got around behind the limp body, hooked his wrists under the arms and pulled. The body skidded out of the skiff and Disbrow sat down hard in the sand under it. He rested, breathing hard, then squirmed free and rose to his feet.

A steam whistle hooted shrilly. Disbrow squatted quickly and crawled back into the brush to hunker there, peering uneasily through the branches. Out on the river, a double-hulled government snag boat steamed upstream, her great iron beak held fiercely aloft by a spidery maze of tackle. Disbrow saw a flash of sun on brass buttons. He glanced over at the body in the sand, wondering if it was sufficiently hidden from view by the fallen tree and the grounded skiff. It did not occur to him to seek help from the crew of the snag boat, which now whistled again.

When she was well upstream, Packy Disbrow ventured out of the willows and continued his prowl. He discovered two planks half-buried in the silt. The planks were cleated together. He tied the skiff's frayed painter to the planks to make a kind of sled, then he rolled the limp body onto the boards. A shadow passed over the bar. The warmth of the sun on his back was suddenly gone. He looked up and saw a bank of thickening clouds driving in from the west.

'Before you turned up, pal, there wasn't a damned thing on my mind,' he said. When he had rested a moment, he hooked an arm through the rope harness and dragged his burden across the bar to where the fallen passenger deck angled into the bank. On down the deck from where he stood yawned the broad doorway to the grand cabin, a tongue of silt licking from the gloom within, half filling the opening.

Packy Disbrow skidded his sled of planks in through the doorway and collapsed to catch his wind. He rubbed sweat from his eyes and looked around, the smell of smoke in his nostrils. A cloud must have passed, for sunlight suddenly streamed down through broken stained-glass clerestory windows. It slanted in many-colored beams through shifting layers of smoke to puddle the colors in the floor of silt, as if it were molten. And as he looked, figures stirred all down the giddy length of the cabin – men painted in those hellish colors, sitting up or turning to have a look at him, their movements repeated scores of times in broken fragments of the *Princess*' great shattered mirrors. He blinked, not knowing if there were fifty men there or a hundred, then decided as his eyes adjusted that the number was nearer ten. A few yards away several of the men were clustered around a nickel-trimmed stove bedded in the sand, smoke leaking from the cracked iron potbelly, a stewpot steaming on top. The men looked suspiciously at the one-eyed man and his burden.

Packy Disbrow grinned and lifted his gloved hand. 'My partner is just a touch under the weather, gents – a little rest will set him right again.'

He skidded the planks across the silty floor to a tilted alcove that was partly screened by the wilted yellow fingers of a dead potted palm. There he sank into the sand, easing his crippled leg out before him. 'What the hell,' he sighed.

Blue's eyes fluttered, opened slowly. Above him in the dim light – vast and distant, it seemed – he saw sweeping interlocked arches, lacy-white with delicate scrollwork, and he marveled. Now where's India? he thought. She ought to see that. No, she's gone with Clay. He traced an arm of soaring arch, up and up, through the firmament. No, that aint right – she was with me, just this minute, she was.

'India?' He was surprised at the sound he made. A raw

whisper, not his own voice. 'India?'

There was movement in that vast firmament. A face swam into view. Purple and orange light licked at the gaunt jaw, glinted in the one eye. 'India, you say? So that's where you've been. Time you was back, boy. I didn't think you'd make it.'

'Where's India?'

'Yonder,' said the face. 'Way yonder.'

Blue puzzled. The face moved away and his eyes wandered along that soaring arch again, so vast his eyes ached with the strain of it. Then it drifted away and he lost it.

'No,' Blue said firmly. 'I aint hungry.'

'No? Aint hungry won't do, my boy. The bill of fare is a can of beans, like it or not, but eat you must and will or by god, I'll choke you with it.'

The spoon clicked on Blue's teeth and he grunted with pain, but the beans were warm in his mouth and suddenly he was ravenous. He licked fiercely at the spoon, tried to follow it when it went away, but when he moved, tearing pain ripped through his body. His startled cry caught in his throat and tears squirted onto his cheeks. The bright fire of pain licked through him, then sank, and he was left floating in the murk. The gaunt face misted again before his flooded eyes, the long jaw warped to emit a barking laugh. 'Hurts, does it? Shouldn't wonder.'

After a moment Blue dared to swallow. The spoon went in again. Blue thought his jaw would come off, it hurt so, but he sucked greedily at the beans. Then he stopped suddenly. 'How long have I—'

'A considerable time.' The spoon prodded and Blue ate. His eyes wandered. He admired the lacework arches that converged in the ceiling. Turning his head a little, very carefully, he looked through the lank fronds of a potted palm, down the enormous length of the grand cabin. He frowned at the room's giddy slope, the wildly pooled colors, and looked again at the gaunt face of the man who was feeding him. The face was in shadow, but he saw that one eye was covered by a corner of bandanna that hung down below a battered derby hat. The man shoved the last of the beans into Blue's mouth.

'You're a tolerable sight better company now than while you were out.' The man set the can down, took off the dented hat and wiped his face and forehead on his sleeve. Blue had turned the other way and suddenly saw himself, broken in the fragments of a shattered wall mirror. *Himself?* That knotted nose, both eyes blackened, peering through puffy slits, a scabby jaw and thickened pulp of lip. His fingers crept up to touch the mirror-broken pieces of his face.

At that instant Packy Disbrow looked up, saw the fear and reached out to put a hand on Blue's shoulder. In the broken mirror, Blue saw a face appear behind him – purple, green and orange light caught the shaggy thatch of rumpled hair and the empty eye socket glaring wildly over a twisted scar and gap-toothed mouth.

Blue sucked in his breath, turned and stared into the face. A single eye blinked at him. The other was an empty, red-rimmed hole. Disbrow ducked back into the shadows and settled his hat and its attached scrap of bandanna back on his head.

'A body forgets,' Disbrow murmured. 'You may take comfort, for your face will get better. Mine won't.' His wry grin exposed missing teeth again, but with the flap of bandanna covering his empty eye socket and the hat cocked, he now looked merely raffish. He observed himself in the broken mirror. 'Meet Packy Disbrow, chum. He aint much to look at now, but time was when Packy Disbrow was reckoned a dead game sport. Yep, cards, dice or the wheel, and waiter, fetch the wine list. A sport all the way, my boy.' He sighed, wagged his head mournfully. 'Oh, how the girls at Miss Francie's would shriek and holler when Packy showed up.'

Staring, Blue stammered, 'M-miss Francie's?'

Packy Disbrow took his spoon from the empty can, polished it on the sleeve of his coat and slipped it into his pocket. 'Yes. A little establishment I once frequented. For a trifle of gambling, mostly.'

'Not a boardinghouse?'

Packy Disbrow considered, then shrugged. 'Call it such if you will.'

Blue shivered, looked again down the tilted, vaulted grand

cabin. Saw the wretches stirring heavily in the strangely molten sand. Panic squirmed against his ribs. 'For God's sake, mister – what in hell is happening to me?'

CHAPTER VII

Blue dreamed that he swung down from the hayloft on his rope. He could hear Israel bawling after him, *'You there, Blue!'* Then the rope ran free in the pulley. Blue fell in the darkness, down and down.

'Hold on, chum,' the voice was saying. A dark figure leaned over him in the gloom.

'No, I let the fire go out again,' Blue said. 'He'll skin me alive.'

'What fire is that?'

'In the forge.' Blue was sweating, cold. His ribs hurt. Suddenly he knew. 'It's you, isn't it?'

'Packy. That's right, chum,' A match flared and Packy lighted a stub of candle set in a broken saucer. 'Who was fixing to skin you alive?'

Blue suddenly saw Israel's face – the jaw hanging aslant and the eyes glimmering white behind slitted lids. 'No one,' he said. 'It was only a dream.'

'All right.' Packy had an open sardine can in his hand. 'You heard the dinner gong, no doubt.' He tipped the sardine can and a dusty stream of sand ran out, and Blue saw then that the can was red and flaky with rust. Packy tossed the can away.

'Eating regular is only a worrisome habit anyway. Any man of substance would do well to rise above it. What am I to call you, chum?'

'Blue —' He stopped, seeing Israel's bloody head again in memory.

'Blue. Not much of a handle. What's the rest of it?' Blue squirmed but did not answer. 'Cat got your tongue?' Packy said. 'Or maybe you are a wanted man, desperate and notorious. Would that be it? Is the law after you?'

'I don't know,' Blue said, after a moment. 'But if they aint, they will be.' I'll say no more about it, he thought.

‘Did you shoot somebody? A party named Israel, maybe? Or was it Clay?’

‘Startled, Blue said, ‘How did you —’

‘You’ve been chatty in your sleep.’

‘It was Israel, but I didn’t shoot him. I don’t think so, anyway. I can’t remember nothing much after the first lick he give me, except —’ Blue hesitated. He had not meant to say anything more about it, but it spilled out, unbidden. ‘I’m certain I saw him dead. I see him now, right before my eyes. He’s dead, all right.’ He swallowed. ‘Russell is the rest of it – my name, I mean.’

Packy grinned. ‘Your secret is safe with me, chum. Disbrow and the law are not speaking.’

‘What is this place?’

Packy told him about the *Shawnee Princess*. ‘The Frisco line tracks run close along the river here, just yonder on the bluffs, they are. I happened to be riding south and a brakeman put me off. I could see the *Princess* from the tracks – figured a river voyage would do me good.’ With his thumb he pointed down the grand cabin. ‘Others have the same idea, it seems. The old *Princess* has turned into a hotel for bums. A poor class of trade.’ He shook his head, looking sadly at the broken fretwork, then leaned forward and tapped Blue on the knee. ‘I tell you, kid, being on the bum is no life for Packy. A man with a bad hand can’t chop wood to earn a handout, and with a gimp leg he can’t run from the dogs, so he dares not steal a chicken. She’s uphill all the way. One eye, one ear, one hand and one leg – Packy aint but half the man he used to be.’ He laughed. ‘Maybe less.’

Blue looked at the rusty sardine can, suddenly aware that he was ferociously hungry. ‘What are we – I mean, what are you gonna do?’

‘About eating, you mean? In my present debilitated condition, I spect I will starve to death almost immediately.’ He sniffed, turned. Down the grand cabin, twenty yards away or more, half a dozen men huddled close to the nickel-trimmed stove, their dark shapes edged with flickering light from the little window in the stove’s fire door. One of the men stirred a pot. Blue smelled it then too, mingled with the sharp scent of wood smoke. Stew. Packy climbed slowly to his feet, cleared his throat nervously, then fished his spoon from one pocket and a tin mess plate from another. He limped toward the stove. One of the men saw him coming, nudged the big man next to him. The murmur of talk around the stove died.

Packy stopped short of the stove. 'Boys, we are just the least bit short of grub. If you would let us share a meal . . .'

'Not a god damn lick,' the big man said, 'without you put something in the pot.'

The man next to him shifted uneasily. 'Hell, Anse . . .'

'Not a god damn lick,' the big man said again.

'The kid who is with me – you saw the shape he is . . .' Packy's voice trailed off as the big man turned his back. The other man shook his head slightly at Packy, lifting his shoulders.

'Fair enough, gents,' Packy said. He limped back to Blue and eased himself back down. 'Well, kid, I don't suppose this is the first time you've went to bed without your supper – it was a regular thing at the Newsboys' Home when I was a pup.'

'When I was a little shaver,' Blue said, 'after my brother left the farm, we fell on hard times. But we always ate and we ate good. Cassie saw to that – she was the colored woman who looked after us. We ate grits and greens, and possum and woodchuck . . . and catfish . . . and crawdads . . .' Blue yawned. Talk of food was making him sleepy. 'Course Ma didn't like it. She said it wasn't decent. Nothing would do for her but we must go to stay with her brother . . .' His voice died away. He was remembering the dismal night ride to St Louis on the coach, the clicking of the rails and his gritty eyes, the vast, hollow, echoing train station and the great tall, bearded man looking down at him.

'A likely boy, sister,' Israel was saying. 'A learner, is my judgment.'

In the morning when Blue opened his eyes, Packy was nowhere to be seen. Down the grand cabin, a few men here and there were still sleeping, or stirring, crawling from their beds of silt like locusts. Only two men now tended the nickel-trimmed stove, and as Blue watched, one of the men walked across the cabin to the wall nearest the river. He scuffed at the sand with a foot and turned up an ear of canvas. He pulled it back, looked at something that was buried against the wall; then, appearing to be satisfied, he turned the canvas down again and covered it over before returning to the stove.

'What in hell are you nervous about?' Blue heard the other man say.

'Cause we'd ought to be hightailin south this very minute, is why.'

'You caint tell Anse nothin.'

'He say when they gawn be back?'

'I don't tell him nothin, he don't tell me nothin.'

'By god, we better git movin south, is what I say.'

One of the men saw Blue and nudged the other. The two men turned away, their voices dropping to a low mumble of sound. Blue struggled slowly to his feet and stood clutching the carved pillar as dizziness swept over him in waves; then he hobbled toward the patch of sunlight framed by the tilted doorway, tottered through on tingling feet and stood blinking in the sun. Packy was coming toward him through the willow scrub. A chill wind made sawing noises in the ship's fretwork. Blue clutched his ribs and shivered, but looking up he saw white clouds scudding low past the pilothouse, and suddenly the *Princess* appeared to him to be speeding downriver.

'Full speed ahead!' Blue shouted. 'Look at her fly!'

'She'll make Memphis tomorrow,' Packy agreed glumly, 'but they will disembark my dead carcass in a wheelbarrow if we don't get some grub.'

Blue saw a rowboat grounded on the bank next to a fallen tree. 'You arrived here in that boat,' Packy said. 'Don't you remember anything about it?'

Blue shook his head. The boat was half full of water. Clear water. The river was muddy yellow. He sagged down onto his knees and took a long drink from the water in the boat. His nose felt huge and thick and hot. He cupped water in his hands and sloshed his face with it. 'That takes the fire out of it.'

'It was all over your face when I found you,' Packy said. 'I pushed it back where it belonged, before you woke up.'

Somewhere a frog croaked, deep and resonant. 'Now I hear it,' Blue said.

'Hear what?'

Blue picked a stick out of the sand. Nails spiked from one end of the stick. Blue took it by the other end and swung it, swatting the nail end down onto a scrap of wood. The nails skewered the wood and Blue grinned. 'The dinner gong,' he said.

Later – it was past midday – they went downstream a few hundred yards and built a little fire on a creek bank and boiled frogs' legs over it in an old lard can while they fished. The fire felt good, for Blue was soaked and shivering from wading after frogs in the boggy pond enclosed by Cogson's Bar and the hulk of the *Princess*.

Packy sucked a fragile bone clean and tossed it away. 'Now in N'Orleans,' he said, 'I would order a French wine with these. A Chablis would do the job. The snails was first-rate there, too – maybe we could find some snails.' He nibbled on another leg. 'Hell, I always had a cast-iron stomach. Damn good thing, too – some of the grub I've sat down to in stir would make a buzzard sick.' He licked his fingers clean, then looked up. 'That slipped out – about the pen, I mean. Old Packy has done his stretch, all right. About a year of it was in the hospital. Lucky it wasn't the boneyard, the shape I was in. They picked me up with a spoon. And once in Texas, I ate armadillo – that's a kind of anteater with scaly armor on him like the knights of old, that Round Table crowd. Baked right in the armor, see?'

'Hold on. What *happened?*'

'A business meeting.' Packy wrapped his arms around his knees and stared at the water in the creek. 'With Leo Birdsong, a gent I used to work with. There was a band concert in the evening, in the square. Cornets and Mexican march pieces —'

'No, wait. You said they picked you up with a spoon.'

Packy looked startled. 'So I did, but that was a long time later. Maybe he just jogged his elbow – Birdsong, see? *Poof!* There is no more to be said about it.' He jogged his willow fishing pole and water rippled around the line, kinky wire Blue had torn from the engine room of the *Princess*. 'You want to hunt some more frogs?'

'Something exploded, is that it?'

'Nitro. Puff, Birdsong called it.' He lifted his maimed hand in its tattered glove and squinted at it. 'Yes, I hated the stuff and I told him so, but Birdsong, he could laugh a hangman out of his job. It blew me to rags. And there wasn't nothing left of Birdsong but a smear.'

Blue baited the hooks – made from fine wire nails – with more scraps of frog flesh. The afternoon wore on. Sunlight crept up the bank. Dry leaves rattle in a sudden gust of cold wind.

'So this is fishing,' Packy said. 'There was boys in the pen who could talk fishing from dawn to dusk. I can't deny it's restful, but I don't see the charm in it. Give me a run at faro —'

Blue suddenly held up a hand. Underbrush twitched a few yards back from the creek bank. He crawled toward it, stalking. Behind him, Packy climbed uneasily to his feet, elevating in lanky sections like a heron. Blue laughed shakily. 'Look, a turtle. Bring the cookin can.'

The turtle was a snapper, eight or nine inches wide across the humped shell. Blue carried it by a hind leg as they went back along the brush-hung riverbank to the *Shawnee Princess*. Cogson's Bar was separated from the mainland by a muddy channel bridged by a fallen tree. They climbed across the tree. The *Shawnee Princess* lay some forty yards distant, scarcely visible through a dense jungle of willows.

The path was like a tunnel. Blue ducked into it, hearing only Packy's breathing behind him and their soft footsteps on the muddy ground. The frog pond was on their left and open ground lay ahead, bone-pale in thickening dusk, when a hoarse shout split the silence like an ax. '*Yonder one runs! Roust the bastards, boys!*'

From the direction of the *Princess*, other voices shouted now, back and forth.

'Quick!' Packy plunged off the path into the willows bordering the pond. Blue clutched the turtle to his ribs and dived after him, fighting the branches. The branches released him and he fell face down into the water. Gasping, he tried to get up, but Packy held him down.

'It's me they're after!' Blue said in sudden dread.

'Hush now – don't move.'

A running man appeared around the bow of the *Princess* and pounded across the sand. Behind him ran four or five shouting men – farmers, Blue thought as he watched their baggy overalls slapping as they ran. The man darted for the tunnel through the willows. One of the farmers cut him off and the runner turned and plunged toward the river. For a moment he was lost to sight, then Blue glimpsed his sprawling dive into the water.

'Ketch im, Ben!' a man bawled. Shouts and sounds of running men echoed around the *Princess*; then a stream of men returned from the river, clustered around two sodden figures. One was holding his head and staggering. The other, a tall, skinny man with lank black hair plastered to his skull, had the runner collared and he was grinning fiercely.

'I aint done nothin to y'all,' the prisoner said, and Blue recognized him as one of the men camped by the nickel-trimmed stove in the *Princess*' grand cabin.

'That's right, bum. None of you bastards done nothin.' One of the farmers punched the bum between the shoulder blades with a grub hoe handle.

Other farmers were dragging prisoners out of the *Princess* and into the open area around the ship's broad bow, holding them there in a sullen huddled cluster. Close to the willows where Blue and Packy crouched, one of the farmers produced a flannel-wrapped package from beneath the bib of his overalls. Blue saw him peel away the flannel and screw the lid off a zinc-capped fruit jar. The man took a long drink. *'Whoo-ee!'* he shuddered and passed the jar to the man next to him, who drank and handed it back.

'Now we gawn whup us some bums, Morg,' the man said.

A voice, nasal and querulous, rang out near the bow of the *Princess*. 'Got no *call*, you say? No *call*?' The others fell silent. The man speaking was thin as a slat, hatchet-faced, with a wagging chin-whisker and an upper lip that sucked into a gap left by missing teeth. He glared at the big hobo named Anse, whose back was jammed hard against the bow of the *Princess*.

'Got no call?' he said again. 'When you son of a bitches is stealin us blind? And bad-mouthin our women? I god and you gawn find out what decent folks think of trash. Leroy! Now whurve you went to, boy? Git out here!' The farmer turned and caught a boy by the arm and wrenched him around to face the prisoners – a red-nosed boy with hair like a forkful of straw, his sharp shoulders jutting from the frayed bib of his overalls.

'Now, by god, Leroy, you point to the man who said them things to your mama, hear?' The farmer turned the malarial heat of his stare on the prisoners, one by one.

Close to Blue, the man with the fruit jar nudged his friend Morg. 'By Christ, Peebles' old woman skeers me half to death jess to look at her, let alone git fresh.' Morg whinnied a spray of corn whiskey and doubled over, holding his ribs.

'Point him out, Leroy!'

Shivering, Leroy drew his nose along his sleeve, then stabbed a finger at Anse. He ducked back as Anse furiously tried to tear himself loose. The men holding him wrestled him around and trussed his arms to wooden-horned cleats on the ship's rail.

'What you aim to do?' Anse said. Looking back at them over his shoulder made big cords stand out in his neck.

Peebles handed his shotgun to Leroy and took a coiled stock whip off his shoulder. He shook it out and the lash slithered in the sand like a snake. 'I god and what I'd oughta do is make a steer out of ye.'

'Go ahead and do it, Henry!' a man shouted. 'We'll ear the sumbitch down for you.'

'No,' Peebles said, 'what I'm gawn do, I'm gawn print some gospel on your hide, bum. And when the other bums see it, they gawn know to steer clear of this county.' He reared back suddenly and sent the lash crackling about the man's ribs. Anse stiffened and sucked in his breath. Peebles shook out the lash and struck again. The straw-haired boy, Leroy, pulled back, fear and horror on his face. Hugging the shotgun, he sidled around the edge of the crowd. When the whip cracked again, he ducked and ran into the willow thicket.

At that instant the turtle clamped its jaws on Blue's thumb. Blue choked back a cry and thrashed to his feet, directly in

Leroy's path. The boy stopped, his jaw aslant in terror. He swung up the shotgun, clicked back the mule-ear hammers. He tried to call out, but his voice was a dry bleat – '*Pa-a-a*...'

Blue thrust the turtle at him, its beak grinding stubbornly into his bloody thumb. 'Don't say nothin. *Help* me!'

The whip hissed and popped. Anse moaned, Leroy uncocked the shotgun and leaned it against a branch, then picked up a stick as Blue climbed out of the water. Leroy jammed the stick in behind Blue's thumb and bore down, his breath snuffling. 'You won't say nothin, will you?' Blue whispered. The thumb came loose. Leroy left the stick between the turtle's jaws and backed away, shivering. 'Oh god,' he croaked, 'I wisht I hadn't of came.'

The whip cracked again and Anse's bawl scaled into a startled shriek. 'Look'ee yonder,' said the man with the fruit jar. 'Henry has gotched the bum's ear.'

'Peel it off, Henry!' another man shouted.

Blue held the turtle under his arm and wrapped a corner of shirttail around his thumb. 'We aint bums like that bunch, understand? Now get on back there before they come lookin for you – but keep quiet, hear?' Leroy stared at him for a moment, then he snatched the shotgun and scuttled back through the willows.

Blue and Packy crept along the edge of the pond to the fallen tree. Henry Peebles' querulous voice drifted to them. That'll do. He's had a plateful, but I god, there's a-plenty more if any other tramp wants a taste.'

'She's near dark, Henry,' another farmer said. 'Let's not leave the bastards sleep this side of the county line.'

Prodding and shoving, the farmers herded the tramps into a shuffling line and marched them into the willow path. Blue and Packy sank down, neck-deep in water under the clawed roots of the fallen tree. Blue felt the turtle swimming lustily against his ribs. The tree sprang and bucked as the men passed over it.

Suddenly Blue sniffed. A thin curl of blue smoke drifted across the pond through the scraggly willows. A muffled *boom* sounded and a ball of flame burst from the boiler deck of the *Shawnee Princess*. In seconds the flames crackled along the sagging gingerbread work, then her whole forward superstructure ignited with a roar. Above Blue and Packy, on the log bridge, the farmer Henry Peebles laughed and pounded the shoulder of the man next to him.

'Take away their bed and board,' he cackled, 'and I god I garntee the sumbitches won't be back.' Flames engulfed the hurricane deck and the row of texas cabins, licking at the pilothouse above.

The men stopped briefly on the high ground above the riverbank to watch the fire, and then they were gone, hurrying into the dusk. Blue and Packy crouched low in the water, hiding now from the furnace heat of the fire as they watched the *Princess* burn. When the pilothouse and texas deck fell in upon the lower decks, a great tongue of flame *whoosh*ed out across the bar and licked through the willows like a huge blowtorch, crisping the leaves in one mighty breath.

At daybreak Blue and Packy crept from the shelter of the tree and the fire-warmed pond. Scorched leaves rattled in the morning breeze. The *Shawnee Princess* was a smoldering mound, her entrails skewered by wilted lengths of pipe, her eight great boilers lying like blackened eggs. Beyond her the river and the distant Illinois shore shimmered through a vast column of heat waves that roiled skyward from the burned hulk.

Blue regarded his turtle. Its legs clawed for a purchase and its jaws were still clamped on Leroy's stick. 'At least we can build a little cooking fire without the smoke drawing that bunch of farmers down on us.'

The heat from the wreck drove them to the lower end of the bar, to the shelter of a low bank. They gathered driftwood and built up a fire with coals from the *Princess*.

Blue laid the turtle on a plank then grasped the stick between its jaws and pulled its head free of the shell. He stabbed down with Packy's knife, through the neck and into the plank. The turtle struggled on vigorously, apparently merely annoyed by the knife. 'Cassie says a turtle don't know when the game is up.' Blue said. 'He will just go on and on like that.' He put the turtle into the hot water and stirred up the fire. When it had boiled for some time, the turtle ceased quivering, the muscles relaxed enough for Blue to finish cutting it up. He put all the pieces back into fresh boiling water and threw in a handful of scorched wild onion for seasoning.

Long before it was done, they began to fish out the small chunks and eat them. They ate silently, too hungry and exhausted from the long night for talk. Through the day, they stayed out of sight in the lee of the bank, resting and watching occasional passing boats through the screen of scorched brush. At sundown they ate the last of the turtle and finished the soup.

'If this fails at all—' Packy said, 'which I am not saying it does – it is only for want of a dash of salt and pepper to go with it. But there is none left for tomorrow and we must think ahead to tomorrow, and beyond.'

'We ought to be able to make up some better hooks,' Blue said.

'No doubt. But I mean beyond that, too. We are working awful hard for what we eat and not eating too often, either. A few frogs and a turtle. Next it will be snakes, or worms. And without the *Princess* to shelter us, we can't stay here.'

Blue stared at the river and gnawed his lip.

Packy laughed. 'You mean to grow old here, do you? What will you do when the frogs are gone and the snow is piled up?'

'The law will be lookin for me,' Blue said. 'How come you're willin to travel with me?'

'I'm no stranger to the way the law operates. You would do better with me than fumbling around alone.'

'But why?'

'It's not just that a man craves company on the road. I admit it. The thing is, old Packy has come to look a little scary.' He touched the flap of cloth that covered his empty eye socket. 'Spose you go up to a house, knock at the kitchen door, say, and ask the folks for a bite to eat – they will feed a youngster like you, see what I mean?'

'I never begged for nothing in my life,' Blue said.

'You've never been down and out, either.'

The idea of begging for food at back doors made Blue's stomach churn. 'I figured maybe I would locate my brother

Clay and go to work for him. He is . . . he is doing a little horse-trading down in Indian territory.'

'If the law is looking for you, that would be the first lead they would follow. Let some time slide by, kid. Move on south while the snow flies. Time enough to find your brother in the spring.'

Blue was silent for a time. He watched a rickety sternwheeler with streaked paint churn upstream on the Illinois side of the river. 'But what would we *do*?'

'Do?' Packy spread his hands, laughed helplessly. 'Do? By god, I don't know – we would just *go*.'

'That bunch of farmers – I wouldn't want to run into them.'

'No . . .' Packy suddenly rose to his knees and peered back over the bank upstream, squinting against a swirl of blown ashes. 'Do you suppose? . . .' He scrambled up and began to run in his one-sided, hitching gait. Blue hesitated uncertainly, then followed slowly, as Packy reached the rowboat.

It had burned down to the line of the water that sat in it, and since it was drawn against the bank at a slight angle, part of the stem and bow were charred away, but she was still holding water.

'We'll want the can for bailing,' Blue said, 'and maybe a couple of boards for paddles.' Turning, he saw a windblown swirl of ashes where the wall of the *Princess*' grand cabin had been. Sand once held inside the cabin by the wall had spilled down, exposing blackened metal. Blue kicked an unburned plank free of the sand, went closer and prodded with it. Metal chinked. He shoveled up a piece of iron with the board. 'It's some kind of wedge.' He scooped away the sand.

'More wedges – a whole set,' Packy said. 'And screw jacks and there's a B and O punch, with the handle burned off. Cold chisels . . . a drill . . .'

'I saw one of the bums from the bunch around the stove go look at this stuff,' Blue said. 'He had it buried.'

'No wonder. So they weren't even honest bums. They were yeggs.'

'You mean those are burglar's tools?'

'To be exact, they are safe-cracker's tools. I spect the yeggs were casing the town when something happened to put the farmers on the prod. That big gent, Anse – he was lucky to get away with a horsewhipping. Just getting caught with a mess of tools like this is enough to put a man in jail.'

CHAPTER VIII

Shortly after midnight that same night, a westbound freight train stopped at the cattle pens in Pawnee Rock, Kansas. A string of empty cattle cars was uncoupled and left on a siding, then the train rolled on west. A few minutes later Clay Russell and Zack Murdock slipped from one of the cars where they had clawed a hiding place in a pile of manure-matted straw.

It was a dark and moonless night. Clay Russell led the way across the tracks and climbed onto the loading platform at the rear of a frame store building, Hilbrich's Feed and General Merchandise. Clay touched a tall stack of sacked grain.

'I bet I slung a million of them sacks,' he whispered. 'Fifty cents a day is what the old fart paid me. Here —' With the heel of his hand, he struck upward against a window sash. The catch tore loose and they climbed through. Clay Russell struck a match, found a small lantern hanging on a nail and lighted it, the lantern tucked in close under his jacket to shield the light.

'Hurry,' Murdock said, 'I could eat a skunk, raw.'

In the faint glow of light they scuttled along the floor to the grocery shelves. For a time there was heard only the sounds of ravenous men eating – crackers, cheese, canned beans, fruit, sardines. Then Russell crept along the counter to where a barrel stood. He lifted the lid and felt inside. Flour. With the metal scoop, he dug deep and brought up a tin box.

'I used to watch the old boy put the cashbox away,' he whispered, 'and when I quit, I tapped him for sixteen dollars.' He took a handful of bills and some change from the box and crammed the money into his pockets. Leaving the box open and empty on the floor behind them, he led Murdock into the dry goods section of the store, where they clothed themselves – hats, flannel shirts, wool britches, canvas jackets. They stuffed shirts, socks and canned goods into a satchel. Just before dawn another train stopped in Pawnee Rock. When it pulled out, they were settled in a boxcar, opening canned peaches for breakfast.

The river was black dark. Blue held a length of broken board off the stern of the skiff as a steering oar, but the skiff wanted to spin as it drifted on the current, and after a time Blue withdrew the oar and let it. And watching a yellow light on shore as the skiff swung, he suddenly became certain that the boat was running straight and true, that it was the light out there that was moving.

Then he must have dozed, for he blinked awake to see a vast bank of lights circling around the skiff with a great thrashing and clanking of machinery. Packy came awake with a startled squawk as the thing sped closer, tightening its circle, and suddenly it was upon them and Blue saw that it was a great steamboat, that it was the skiff that had been turning, not the steamboat. The skiff grated and bumped along its rail. A man's voice shouted down from between blazing lights. Blue pushed off with the board and paddled frantically as white water gushed over them from beneath the huge wheelhouse. The skiff swung away, wheeling slowly in the choppy wake of the steamboat.

'A citizen has no rights anymore, Packy said shakily. 'There is no place the common man can turn for redress of wrongs.'

'We're about to go under,' Blue said. 'Don't move.' He bailed gently with the lard can. Slowly the boat rose in the water. After that it began to rain and they took turns bailing. A cold wind cut through Blue's soaked shirt. He was racked with shivering, but then his mind wandered and he was startled to find himself suddenly weak from the violent shaking of his muscles.

The night stretched away in the endless dark, like the black river itself. A great time passed; then movement shook him awake.

'Awake, are you?' Packy said, bailing.

'Yes.' Blue hugged his ribs and shuddered.

'Well get out then. We're close enough to wade in.'

Blue looked and after a moment made out the shape of a tree against the dark sky. He rolled over the side, the boat went under and Blue crawled ashore on hands and knees.

'We could bail her out, pull her up into the bushes —'

'No,' Blue said. 'No more.' He could see his hands in the sand. Gray light oozed into the sodden sky through mizzling rain.

Blue leaned against a rain-slick cypress tree. Before him the water-filled ruts of a muddy road mirrored the gray sky and the scrubby growth. On the far side of the road a few yards away, a rickety wagon sat aslant over a broken wheel. A tarp had been stretched from the roof canopy and tied off to trees, forming a lean-to. Smoke curled up from a small fire. A tiny old woman wearing a man's hat and a piece of oilcloth draped shawl-like about her shoulders tended an iron kettle set on stones at the edge of the fire.

Packy hobbled up to join Blue beneath the tree. 'See there,' Blue said, 'I told you I smelled smoke.' Packy nodded, wheezing. They stepped out onto the road, sodden shoes making squelching sounds as they walked. Packy sneezed. The old woman settled the lid of the kettle and turned to face them. In the crook of her arm was a gun – a long barreled pistol with a wire-frame stock, Blue saw.

'I knowed ye was a-comin,' she said in a voice like the screech of a pulled nail. 'Heerd ye, thrashin about in the swamp.' Blue stopped uncertainly. His teeth were chattering. She regarded them for a moment, then said, 'Aint a thing here would look good to no tramp – jess me and Daddy, and he is tolerable nasty to tramps.' With a jerk of her head she indicated the wagon. Its side curtains were tied up, and from the gloom of the wagon Blue saw a white-haired man staring at him fixedly.

Packy touched his hat brim and water ran out in a small stream. 'Madam, you have the advantage of us. We are not tramps, but we are fairly lost and near to perishin for want of a cup of coffee. You see, we snagged our skiff on the river —'

'Hawshot!' The single strange, sharp word sounded from the dark wagon.

'I'm a-watchin em, Daddy,' the old woman said.

'How do you aim to travel, lady, with your wagon broke down?' Blue said.

'Don't you worry none. Daddy is a-goin to fix her.'

Shivering, Blue studied the wheel. Spokes and felloes, free of the iron tire, had fallen like an armload of kindling. He spoke through chattering teeth. 'If you will give us a cup of coffee, we will fix her good enough to roll.'

The old woman looked into the wagon. Inside, the old man's staring eyes glittered. 'On account of the rain, Daddy was jess turble stiff this morning, or he would have had it all fixed by now.'

'Some bailing wire would help,' Blue said.

She shook her head. Blue moved closer to the fire. Even the skin over his ribs was sore from shivering. A breath of white steam escaped from the coffeepot and fragrance filled the air. Abruptly, she put the gun in the wagon box; then she poured coffee into a tin cup and placed it in his hands. He held it under his chin and let the steam curl against his face. She gave Packy coffee in a chipped granite cup. *'Hawshot!'* the old man said.

Standing in under the lean-to to catch the warmth of the fire, Blue saw a small wooden trunk behind the wagon seat. It was homemade, with rawhide-bound corners. 'Will you be travelin far?' he asked the old woman.

'Six-eight mile.'

'Rawhide would hold the tire on, long enough to get you home,' Blue said. He nodded at the little trunk.

She pursed her lips, then touched the iron kettle with the toe of her shoe. 'Corn bread is most done. You boys eat first.'

She gave them corn bread buttered with bacon fat, along with more coffee. Then Blue took her hatchet and cut a small, straight oak and used it to lever up the wagon axle. He peeled the strips of rawhide off the little trunk and put them in a bucket of water to soak, then began to reassemble the wagon wheel, the wet wood squealing as the pieces went together. He slipped the iron tire on over the felloes, bound it with strips of the slick and gluey rawhide, then drove wedges under the tire all around to tighten it. 'That tire is just a sight too big,' he said. 'It ought to be cut down and shrunk on, hot.'

'Hit's been a-gettin worse right along,' she agreed.

Gently they let the weight of the wagon settle down onto the wheel. The rain had stopped falling. Steam misted from the sodden ground where sun touched it. The old woman led her mule out of the brush and backed him between the shafts.

'So-o-o, Dick,' she screeched softly. Settled on the wagon seat, the reins in her hands, she looked straight ahead and said, 'You boys could go along home with me and Daddy, if it aint out of your way none and if you've a mind to.'

It was near dusk when they reached the farm. Leaving the swamp at last, the road wound up into rocky hill country, a hard pull for the old mule. The house was built of logs hewn flat, with dovetailed corners, and was covered with weathered clapboards, many of which were now missing. The shake roof sloped out to cover a porch which rested precariously on posts. A big iron kettle, good for scalding hogs or making soap, sat on smoke-blackened stones in the yard. Off to one side beneath a broken-limbed black oak sat a railed stock pen, a shed and a smokehouse. A few acres of cleared ground bore a sorry crop of weedy scrub, except for one corner near the house where a few rows of corn struggled among squash and beans.

Blue and Packy slept warm in the shed on a bed of sacking and corn shucks and two tattered blankets given them by the old woman.

Her name was Serena, she told them. She put a breakfast of fried grits, bacon and coffee before them on a pine table in the kitchen. While cakes of grits sizzled in an iron skillet, she stood looking out the small window. 'It were a tolable little farm once,' she said, 'but then Daddy went to the war. Twice shot, he was. He never was strong after. They was just a heap of things I weren't big enough to do, so the place run downhill. And the stroke hit Daddy, left him a child, poor soul.' Abruptly, she filled a wooden plate and carried it into the bedroom. They could hear her chiding the old man to eat, clucking and scolding.

'You see, don't you,' Packy said, 'that she's feeding us the best she's got. If we stay long, they'll go hungry. And how will they ever get through the winter?'

Blue nodded. Shortly she returned with a faded blue flannel shirt and an ancient round-skirted coat. She handed them to Blue. 'Bare ribs is a poor sight, boy. These will kiver ye.'

At the door Blue said, 'We could lay in some firewood, if that's agreeable.' Humming a tuneless, scratchy sound, she seemed not to hear.

For two days, Blue cut and hauled wood, using the mule, Dick, to skid logs in from the woods. Packy could not swing an ax, but he split kindling with a hatchet and stacked wood. The first morning, working in the sun, he put his still-damp coat out on some tall grass to dry. From the lining he took a number of flat oilskin packets of papers and examined them for signs of dampness. Later, when the coat was dry, he slipped all the packets back into the coat.

Looking for a maul and wedges to split the tough black oak, Blue found a battered block of iron in the shed, along with a hammer and a couple of rusty pairs of tongs. Looking further, he found a crude and dilapidated bellows resting on boards up in the crossbeams of the shed. In the twilight after supper he cleaned and tallowed the stiff leather. He tried it and heard the click of wooden valves on the air holes inside. Air gushed from the nozzle. 'It will work if we don't push it too hard,' he said. 'There's an old stone hearth out back of the shed and a few tools. The old man must have done some smithing before he got sick.'

'You mean to tell me you're going to try to get the stuff working?' Packy said.

'If I can fix her wagon wheel, at least we won't leave her afoot.'

Blue set up the forge in the morning. He made a frame to support the bellows and rigged a spring pole overhead to help him pump them. He blew out the rusty blowpipe in the hearth and connected the bellows nozzle to it. There was no coal or even charcoal. He packed the hearth with heavy chips of oak from the woodcutting and with corncobs from a pile back of the shed.

'You talked about a forge fire when you were light in the head,' Packy said. 'I never thought to see you work at it.'

'Guns, locks and fine smithing – that was Israel's line,' Blue said. 'Take this wagon wheel – a loose tire is the commonest thing to go wrong. It comes of the wood drying out and shrinking away from the tire with age, or maybe it was fitted on a damp day in the first place. The wheel has dried out good now, so it's a good time to fix it.'

Packy watched intently as Blue heated a portion of the iron tire in the forge, then cut it at the anvil with hammer and chisel and beveled the edges for the new joint. He watched him heat the beveled ends once more, bringing them to the blistering yellow welding heat before joining them with light ringing blows of the hammer.

Blue looked up for an instant and saw the one eye staring fiercely at him. He thought of a hawk he had seen his brother Clay shoot – years ago, it was – and he remembered the glare of its golden eye fixed on him as its horny talons convulsed on twigs and branches in the brush where it had fallen.

Blue dug a shallow circular trench the size of the wagon tire and shoveled burning chips and corncobs into it from the hearth. He set the tire in the trench and added fuel to cover it. Again he felt the force of Packy's watchful stare. 'You could help me fan the fire,' he said, a little annoyed.

Packy held up a small sliver of iron. 'I found this in the shed, amongst the trash. No doubt you could bend a little prong on the end of it, like this —' He sketched in the dirt with the piece of iron.

Blue took the sliver of metal and put it in the coals. He pumped air to it and heated it cherry-red in seconds, then quickly hammered, bent and cooled it. 'You'd want it tempered, I spect.'

'How did you know?' Packy said, startled.

'I know a lock pick when I see one.' Blue grinned, then shook his head. 'To do it right, I would use tool steel and a brine bath or oil for quenching – but that ought to get you through a door if the lock aint stuck.'

When the iron tire was hot, he lifted it with tongs and placed it over the wooden wheel. Smoke curled up from the scorched felloes. Blue went quickly around the wheel, tapping, driving the tire down, then he doused it with water. Steam roiled up in clouds and spokes squealed as shrinking iron drew them tight.

'Tell you one thing,' Blue said suddenly. 'I aint making any more lock picks.'

Supper was a squirrel stew, mostly gravy, spread over grits, with corn bread and greens Serena had found on the hillside.

Later in the shed with evening light filtering through the trees, Blue said, 'Dirt poor – I had near forgot what it's like to be dirt poor.'

'As a condition,' Packy said, 'I don't claim to admire it. It's time for us to move on. But the question is, do we mean to better our condition, or will we be happy sleeping in sheds and eating handouts?'

'Where were you bound?' Blue said. 'I mean when you found me, back yonder at the *Shawnee Princess*. You must have been headed someplace.'

'A man on the bum is just going,' Packy said. 'He don't have to be headed any place in particular.'

'Maybe not, but now you're talking of bettering our condition. That is not the talk of a drifter. Something is eating you.'

Packy stiffened. 'All right,' he said, suddenly decisive. 'Look here, kid. Until today, I was just playing out my cards, and a hell of a hand it was, too.' He looked at his warped hand in its tattered glove and smiled bleakly. 'It was the soup kitchen for Packy. What else? Until today, by god. I think I've drawn a card, Disbrow is back in the game.'

Blue stirred uneasily. 'Don't think you're going to make a holdup man out of me,' he blurted.

'*Holdup?* I never carried a cannon in my life. Disbrow is no common saloon crook.'

'You went to jail.'

Packy sighed. 'It's easy enough to go to jail – bank presidents and mayors make a regular thing of it. And don't forget you're a wanted man yourself.' Packy pointed his clawed fingers at Blue. 'Up there on that scaffold with the black hood over your head and that hairy rope all prickly under your ear, jail would just look mighty sweet to a man.'

The skin of Blue's neck prickled suddenly and his bowels felt sick and watery. He thought of the black hood dropping over his head and shuddered.

'That's right, Blue. The prospect is not a dainty one. Any man who thinks of it is bound to wonder if it wouldn't all just run down his leg when the time came to stand up there and take the drop . . .' Packy let his voice trail off. After a moment he went on softly, 'Blue, what I'm talking about is a way out for both of us. Just one score, see? I could live like a human again, instead of a wharf rat – maybe down in Old Mexico. You could go west and set yourself up on a ranch and never have to look crossways at the law again. One score, see, Blue? One score is all I'm talking about.'

Blue shook his head. He wrenched his eyes away from Packy's and stared at his own two fists, knotted on his knees. 'I want no part of it,' he whispered.

'Just think on it, Blue. It don't cost you a dime to think.' Packy reached into his coat and brought out one of the oilskin-wrapped packets. He tapped the dented crown of his derby with it. 'It's all here, Blue, just waitin for us – all it needs is your hands and eyes. It was seeing the way you worked with tools that put me onto it.'

Packy pulled his shirttail out and fumbled at what appeared to be a money belt. From a pocket in the belt, he took four silver dollars and threw them on the blanket. Blue saw that they had holes drilled in their centers and each was notched on its outer edge. Packy went through his pockets – along with his razor, spoon, burning glass and broken comb were various oddly shaped small pieces of brass and bone, a number of screws and a wooden soapbox.

'You could have took up with that bunch of yeggs back on the *Princess*,' Blue said. 'They had a mess of tools.'

'I would as soon take up with the Dalton gang.' Packy began to assemble within the soapbox some of the pieces of bone and brass. 'Amongst your back-alley trash, your pimps and skull-busters and shooters, yeggs are maybe worst of the lot. Heavy grift, see? But Disbrow, he was a *class* thief, Blue, an artist. You could ask . . . anyone.' His voice hushed reverently. 'Slick as a pearl . . .'

He dropped the silver dollars over a brass post in the soap-box, then turned a spindle on the back of the box which caused the coins to turn within, clicking softly. Then he put the box in Blue's hands. 'What would you guess this is?'

'I know what it is,' Blue said uneasily. 'It's a combination safe lock. Israel would get one in the shop from time to time.

But this couldn't lock anything, with these wooden parts. Why—'

'Because I made it in stir, is why. There I was, blown up, crippled and in the jug, see? In the hospital, I could get opium. So the time passed. But after I was patched up, I couldn't get at the opium anymore. I woke up in the hole, in a strait jacket, bawling like a baby, with snot all over me. But a man's got to take hold, get me? The ones who don't – I saw em, Blue, crawling around in their own dung and chewing one another's ears off. What I did, I began to take locks apart, see, all in my head. By the time I got out of the hole, I was still crazy, I admit it, but I was crazy on locks and I went on making them, like this one, out of anything that came to hand.'

Blue turned the spindle and saw how dialing the proper combination aligned the silver dollars and allowed a lever to drop and the bolt to slide. The useless lock, brass glinting against wood and polished bone, was a thing of beauty.

'An ocean of time lay before me, understand? I began to work out the jobs I had entertained doing in the old days. In stir, a lot of this kind of information was circulating – even plan drawings of banks and express offices, all cased by experts. I collected it, all the time I was in there.' Packy slapped the oilskin-wrapped paper. 'Here, my boy, is the biggest collection of unopened safes in America. It's worth millions.'

'It's nothing but paper,' Blue protested.

'No, not just paper – Cape Girardeau is where I was headed,' Packy whispered, 'if you want to know. Just to take a look at it, see? Alone and crippled, I couldn't have tackled it, but looking at it was better than nothing. Cape Girardeau is less than forty miles from here, kid.' Packy sat up and looked sharply at Blue. 'Look here, the first thing we must do is get a little scratch together and make ourselves presentable, traveling men, see, but not too flashy—'

Blue swallowed hard. 'I never said I'd do it.'

CHAPTER IX

They rode into Cape Girardeau on a farm wagon loaded with pigs. The town lay on the bluffs of the Mississippi overlooking a broad bend in the river. The farmer drove along Water Street, above the sloping cobbled levee, and stopped near the Frisco railroad station, where numbers of other farmers were pulling in with grain, calves, hogs and chickens to sell.

Blue slid down from his perch on the slatted crates, grateful to be free of the smell of the pigs. A whistle shrilled in the bright morning air. White water gushed under a steamboat's wheelhouses and she backed into the current.

'One thing about being on the bum,' Packy said, 'a man appreciates his grub.'

'Grub? We aint had a bite since yesterday noon.'

'That's what I mean, and it was good, wasn't it? Panhandling will build you an appetite, see if it don't.'

Blue's belly rumbled with hunger. Still, he protested. 'Not me – I aint —'

Packy nudged him, motioned with his jaw toward the railroad station and the untidy row of farm wagons. 'Do you see the two-bit skin game?'

Three or four of the farmers were clustered next to a wagon full of crated chickens. They were flipping coins and betting, laughing and punching one another on the arm as they won or lost. A beefy farmer with a red stubble of whiskers and a red thatch curling up above the bib of his overalls held up a coin. 'Call,' he said. But then he feinted slightly with the coin, so that it was not in the air as the man called 'Tails.' The big man caught the coin and slapped it onto his cuff. 'Gotcha, Tom.' He laughed and raked the coins off the wagon bed.

'He didn't flip it,' Packy said. 'He just wobbled it. See, he heard the call first, then tossed it so it stayed face up, the way he wanted it. That is some line of grift. I learned it when I was eight years old.' He looked sharply at Blue. 'Kid, I think we are in the way of making ourselves a dollar or two eating money.'

Blue winced. 'I don't want to rob nobody.'

'I didn't say anything about robbing. His own greed will do the job. When he sees a chance to beat me, he will be putting down money with both hands. Now, here is what you do ...' Packy quickly told him the part he was to play. Listening, Blue felt an uneasy tremor beneath his ribs, yet as he listened he realized with a start that he was going to do it and he felt suddenly reckless and daring. He strained not to laugh aloud.

Quickly, Packy said, 'Just remember, you don't know me – and when it's over, you go on around the block there and wait for me.' And before Blue could speak, Packy sidled into the crowd. Blue moved away a few yards and stood at the corner of the brick depot. Another farmer was in the game, a skinny man whose overalls swung loose on his body. He had a jersey heifer on the end of a short length of frayed rope and the calf nuzzled him as he slapped his dollar down on the wagon bed. To quiet her, he offered his thumb, which the calf then sucked noisily, ropes of foam swinging from its jaws.

The big farmer won again. 'One more, Tom,' he said. 'Just one. Git a dollar down, Nat. You aint in.'

The other farmers looked uneasily at each other. Tom shook his head. 'I don't want to go her no more, Orv.'

Packy suddenly walked between them and stopped next to the wagon. He was gnawing his lip, frowning unhappily as he craned his neck to search the faces of people gathered near the wagons. He had some cards in one hand.

'Say, boys,' he said, 'did you happen to see a big tall feller with slick hair – kinder ugly, but a sharp dresser?'

The farmers shook their heads.

Packy slapped the wagon bed. 'Well, let me tell you, you want to steer clear of him if you do. He just took me for a hundred dollars at cards.' His shoulders slumped and he wagged his head slowly. There was a little catch in his voice. 'Hell, boys, I don't know nothing about cards. My old lady will rip me to pieces now. I just sold my little trotting mare, see? Got a dandy price for her, too.' He looked sadly at them. 'Dumb as I was, I'm just mighty lucky he didn't get all of it.' He shook a pocket and a metallic chinking noise was heard.

'What game did you play?' the big man, Orv, asked.

'There wasn't but three cards,' Packy said. 'Here, let me show you.' He threw three cards on the wagon, face up, a deuce, a seven and the queen of spades. 'Now spose I turn em over and mix em up, then the idy is, you pick the old woman.'

'*Shew*, there ain't nothing to that,' the big man said.

'Well how come he beat me so bad then?' Packy mixed the three cards face down, then picked one. The queen. He laughed. 'The old woman herself. Ugly as my mother-in-law. Now why couldn't I do that when there was money on the table?'

At the corner of the depot, Blue swallowed nervously, then stepped briskly around the corner of the wagon. He saw the game, stopped short, and then shouldered in to watch as Packy turned up the queen again.

'You pick the queen, hunh?' Blue said. 'Is that all? I betcha I could do it.'

'Damn if he don't sound just like me, boys.' Packy grinned. No bets, kid. Once burned, twice shy.'

'Come on – a dollar,' Blue said.

'I already lost a hundred.' Packy said. 'My woman will murder me if I don't bring the other fifty home.' He danced a little step to make the chinking noise in his pocket again, then dealt himself another hand.

'That one!' Blue stabbed a finger at one of the cards.

'There was no need of your butting in,' Packy grumbled. He turned up the card, a deuce, and slapped it down, laughing. 'You lost, kid.'

Blue held up two of the silver dollars from Packy's lock. His thumb covered the notch in the edge and the hole in the center. 'Two bucks, mister. All I've got – I'm game to bet. How come there is no sand in your craw?'

Packy frowned. No need to get snotty, either.' He hesitated. 'All right, I'll go you for your two dollars – but only one bet. If I lose, I'm through. It's only to please you, see?'

Quickly, he mixed the cards. Blue studied them intently, then reached out and turned one up. The seven. He threw it down angrily. Packy rocked back on his heels, laughing.

'*Hoo!* That done it!' He held out his hand and Blue slapped the coins into it. Packy's elbow brushed the seven off the wagon as he pocketed the coins. Still laughing, he bent to look for it.

Blue nudged the big farmer, Orv, and winked, then reached out and nicked a corner of the queen card with his thumbnail as Packy straightened. Blue nudged Orv again, and nodded his head slightly at the cards. Orv's freckled, red-bristly cheeks spread in a slow grin. Next to him, Tom and the skinny man, Nat, smirked at each other.

'Hell,' Orv said, 'I'm good for a hand.' He slapped a dollar down.

Packy brushed the dollar back. 'No, I meant it. You heard me say I wasn't going to play.'

'Well, by god, you took the kid's money quick enough.' Orv's grin was gone. Nat and Tom nodded.

'That was just to teach the kid some manners.'

'Well, my manners has went a little sour, too,' Orv said. 'Now goddammit, I'll go you one hand for five dollars. You goin to crawfish on me?' His face was now brick-red.

Packy sighed. 'Boys, I never meant for this to happen.' He looked up at the other two. 'I spose you want in, too.'

Tom and Nat fished money from their pockets and put it down. 'Betcher life,' Nat said, his eyes riveted on the nicked queen.

'All right, then,' Packy said. He started to mix the cards, but suddenly he gathered them together and started to put them in his shirt pocket. He shook his head. 'Boys, I changed my mind. I just can't do it.'

Orv glared at him and caught his wrist. 'By god, mister, you caint back down. We aint gawn let you back down, are we, boys?' Both of the others agreed vigorously. 'We put our money down in good faith. You can do the same. We're holdin you to it.'

Packy slumped for a moment. Then he straightened, squared his shoulders and thrust his jaw out and returned Orv's stare. 'Gents, you have struck me where it hurts. No man ever said yours truly showed the white feather and made it stick. I'm slow to ketch fire, but fast to burn. This was none of my idy, but if you aim to bet' – he glared at all three – 'then by god, let's make her a good one. I'll bet every cent I've got on me – the fifty from selling my little mare, and the two I won from the kid, and since he started the whole thing, he can hold the stakes. And any man whose nerve fails him now can walk away, no shame to him.'

Orv inhaled deeply. His eyes were shining and his mouth twisted in a reckless grin. 'Goddammit, I'll just take twenty-five of that and you boys can cut the rest up any way it suits you.' He pulled a roll of dirty bills from his bib pocket and peeled off twenty-five dollars in fives and ones, then caught Blue's hand and slapped the bills into it. Both Nat and Tom quickly dug down and pieced out their bets in small bills and silver, both straining to keep from grinning openly. Blue took the money and nodded. 'She's all here, mister. Play cards.'

Packy grunted and slapped the cards onto the wagon, saying 'Remember, now – one bet. Who's going to pick the card?'

'I will, goddammit,' Orv said. 'Get on with it.'

Packy mixed the cards. Tom and Nat looked at each other and Tom's body twisted in a frozen jig step.

'Play,' Packy said.

The three bent forward, peering at the cards. Orv's wind made a snoring noise in this throat. He poised one thick, freckled hand over a card, then looked at his partners. Almost imperceptibly, they nodded. Orv turned the card.

It was the deuce.

'Shee-e-it!' Tom moaned. Orv's breath whistled out. 'I don't know what happened to the sumbitch,' he said. He reached out and turned over the seven and the queen.

'Fair and square,' Blue said. He handed the money to Packy, then turned and slipped away through the people who had gathered to watch. In a moment he had disappeared.

'I just don't hardly believe it,' Packy said, licking a thumb and counting.

Orv picked up the queen and examined it, then threw it down, shaking his head. He picked up the deuce and felt the little nick on one corner, His teeth were clenched and his face was purple. He started to speak, thought better of it and slammed the card down with all his strength.

'*Hey!*' Packy said. He looked up, holding the money up in

his hand. 'That fresh kid – where is he? Look here, boys – he held out on me. He kept half the money! By god, his life won't be worth a nickel when I —' He broke off, glared furiously about him and scuttled away through the crowd.

Orv, Tom and Nat stared after him. A purple vein stood dark on Orv's thick neck. His nostrils fluttered and a trickle of tobacco juice ran from the corner of his mouth into his whiskers.

'*Shee-e-it!*' Tom said again. He turned and kicked the wagon tire.

Blue inhaled deeply. The smell of steak and potatoes frying in the cafe behind him was almost more then he could bear. He had crossed Water Street, which fronted the levee and the river, and walked a block west on Good Hope Street to Main. The cafe was just around the corner on Main. Across the street from him, Good Hope Street climbed steeply as it mounted the bluffs, its painted brick buildings stair-stepping up the incline. A farmer driving a loaded wagon down the hill leaned back in the seat and sawed on the reins to keep his mules squatting low in the traces. Their iron shoes struck sparks from the cobbles.

Blue was shocked at himself. He was still feeling the thrill and excitement of it. He had done it well. That was the trouble. But now he was not sure what might have happened after he left. He stood next to a lamppost and idly looked both ways along the street for Packy.

Behind him, the etched glass door of the cafe swung open and a heavy man in a gray suit stepped through onto the sidewalk. Blue turned slightly to watch. The man finished sharpening a match with a jackknife, clicked the knife shut and thrust the match through the mustache that bushed beneath his red-veined nose. His meaty hand brushed back the skirt of his coat to pocket the knife. Blue saw a shield on the big man's vest and in the same instant he saw the birdhead handle of a double-action Colt protruding from a holster high on the man's right hip.

Blue's belly sucked flat with dread. His skin felt icy. The policeman probed with the match, spearing vigorously as he rocked on his heels. His eyes were pale beneath the brim of the square-set gray hat. Blue felt them stop and bore into him – felt his own eyes lock frozen in their sockets. Suddenly the door opened again and a tall bald man with a drooping black mustache joined the policeman, who belched and said to him, 'Spose you leave me a list of what the bastards took, Hardie. I'll look into it.'

The man mopped the top of his bald head nervously with a blue bandanna. There was white dust in the seams of his dark suit. 'It aint the tools, John. A few quarry tools don't matter none. But who would bust in and take a hundred sticks of sixty percent? That is just a hell of a mess of powder.'

Blue's legs felt like sticks of dead wood. He forced one knee to bend and let himself sag against the lamppost, turning in what he hoped was a casual disregard of the officer. But looking away was worse than feeling the man's cat-eyed glare. He wrenched himself upright and looked at the two again. The officer suddenly bit his match in two and spat out the pieces.

'That it is, Hardie. No use guessin what it could be, but leave me a list all the same.' He grunted sociably and strode away, setting off across the street. The other man clipped the end off a cigar and lighted it, mumbling to himself, and then he too walked away. Across the street Blue saw a small man appear at the corner, having just come down the Good Hope Street hill. The small man ducked furtively when he saw the police officer, then quartered away with his chin tucked down against his shoulder. Blue had seen the small man before, among the bums back on the *Shawnee Princess*.

The thought skidded away from him. Suppose something had gone wrong and Packy was in trouble? His fingers plucked nervously at the buttons of his ancient coat. Something touched his back. Startled, he turned. It was Packy, grinning, trying to catch his breath. Blue's heart pounded. He looked back across the street, but the policeman was gone.

'There's a second-hand store just down the street,' Packy said. 'In twenty minutes, you and me will look like two different men.'

A block south, the policeman climbed the courthouse steps and entered police department offices. He grunted at the desk man and went to his own big roll-top desk, where a small sign read CHIEF OF POLICE – JOHN DOANE. He eased his weight into the swivel chair and for a moment studied the telephone set hanging on the wall next to a sepia-toned photograph of a Confederate infantry company, himself in the first row, lean and sunburned, a chew of tobacco bulging his cheek, staring back at him across the years.

He cranked the phone, heard the operator's voice through what sounded like the crackle of small arms fire, then gave her the number of the Pinkerton office in St Louis.

A man's voice sounded on the other end. The chief bellowed, 'How do?' When they had identified one another, he said. 'This might not mean nothin atall to you people, understand, but a quarry shed was broke into here last night. A mess of tools was took. Drills and such. And a hundred sticks of dynamite from the powder house . . . Yes, I suspicion it was yeggmen. Now, spose that's so – I spect we will handle it here all right, but if you knowed some other places you could connect me with on the map, then maybe you could get an idy which way they was headed, say maybe it was New Madrid or Memphis or maybe north. It might help them people to know . . . Paoli, you say?' He listened intently, then said, 'If he wants to stop, he will be made welcome.'

Pleased, he hung up. He was sweating from the strain. After a moment he went out and stopped at the duty desk. 'Milt, I blieve I'll go get me a piece of pie and a glass of milk.' At the door, he stopped, frowning. 'I want to set a watch on the bank for the next two-three nights. Look at the roster and see who we can put on it.'

CHAPTER X

Mrs Clellan's boardinghouse was on the steepest part of Good Hope Street, where it climbed the bluff. Built by a prosperous trader in the years before the war when steamship traffic on the river was flourishing, it was of rose-colored brick, with a handsome, gingerbread-trimmed veranda. A flight of stone steps flanked by an iron railing led down to the street. Above, its steep mansard roof followed the intricate jogs and offsets of the building. On the uphill side of the house there was a spacious lawn and gazebo, with a garden at the rear. A two-story commercial building was snugged close on the downhill side.

Up under the mansard roof, the third floor was mostly attic, but in the rear there were two small rooms, servants' quarters in the old days, which Mrs Clellan now kept for gentlemen boarders. In one of these rooms, the one on the uphill side, Packy stood awkwardly bending his knees in order to study the cut of his blue suit in the mottled mirror over a rickety wash-stand. Blue was stretched out on the bed with his fingers laced behind his head.

'Middling fair goods, for secondhand,' Packy said, squinting down at his lapel, 'but the gent who owned this was better fed than me.'

Blue glanced at him over the brass-framed foot of the bed. Seeing just the unscarred side of Packy's face, the dark hair damply combed, Blue glimpsed for an instant what Packy had looked like before he was mangled by the explosion – a fine-looking man, he thought, no doubt more than a trifle on the rake-hell side. Then Packy stepped back from the mirror and faced him, his empty eye socket now covered by a plain black patch.

'It's near time for supper,' Packy said. 'Spose I see you downstairs.' Without waiting for a reply, he left, closing the door behind him. Now he was in a small corridor at the top of the stairs. There were two other doors. One, on his left, bore a thumb-tacked card which read, in Mrs Clellan's copperplate, *Mr Hardie Foulkes*. Packy hesitated, touched the knob, then recoiled, thinking he had heard a noise within. He listened, but he could not be sure. He turned to the third door, opened it.

He found himself in the attic. It was dusty, hung with cobwebs, stuffed with the trash of three generations of life in the house, all sprayed with light from the gable windows that pierced the mansard roof. He moved quickly to his left, to the first window. It was opaque with dust. He rubbed a peephole and looked out. A few feet away, say seven or eight, was the roof of the commercial building next door – a few feet away and slightly lower. He grinned with pleasure, then took hold of the sash and tried to raise the window. It would not budge. 'Damn,' he murmured. He felt along the frame. Nails. Heavy nails.

Packy shook his head in disgust; then, from an inside pocket, he took one of his oilskin-wrapped packets. He opened it, shook out the flimsy tissue and spread it on top of a steamer trunk where he studied it intently, from time to time peering through the dusty peephole to compare what he saw there with the drawing. An hour earlier on the street, as he approached the boardinghouse with Blue, he had observed that the street floor of the building was occupied by the Girardeau Suit & Pants Company, with an entrance on the side next to the boardinghouse that led upstairs to the office of the County Treasurer. Now he looked down upon the roof over that office. He saw the low parapet around the roof, a chimney with several tiled flues projecting from it, a plumbing vent. A slant-topped skylight. No stairwell. All neatly and accurately depicted on the tissue, along with copious information written in fine, spidery script.

He folded the drawing and put it away. The nailed windows were the only hitch. He went back out into the corridor and confronted Foulkes' door again – clearly, it was the only way to gain access to the building next door. He cupped a hand to his ear and listened, close to the door. Hearing nothing, he reached for the doorknob. Suddenly the door swung open and he was confronted by a tall, mustached bald man in a dark suit. The tall man, seeing his hand thrust out, grabbed it and shook it. 'Neighbors, are we? I'm Foulkes.'

'Bristol,' Packy said, letting his hand be pumped. Just then Blue opened his own door. 'My partner, Adams,' Packy said. Blue blinked at him, startled to hear himself given a false name and to see that the man who now grunted sociably and shook his hand was the same man he had seen talking to the police officer earlier in the day.

'Let's see what the old lady has throwed in the trough,' Foulkes said, and led the way down.

The stiff white collar rasped at the raw flesh of Blue's neck. He thought it would draw blood. The seams of his cheap blue-striped shirt sawed under his arms as he finished a second helping of fried eggplant, potatoes and milk gravy, the few pork-chops having disappeared early from the table.

In his advanced state of hunger, he had scarcely taken note of the other faces around the big oval table. Now Blue took a deep breath and watched the potato bowl as it moved from hand to hand toward him, but he was not prepared for the swiftness of its passage. He reached, but saw it deftly whisked away in the hairy hand of Mr Foulkes, who promptly scraped it clean. Blue stared at it, frowning.

'Mercy, Mr Adams,' Mrs Clellan said to him from the head of the table, 'we didn't reckon on such an appetite, but there now, we do have a lovely cobbler coming.'

Confused to hear himself addressed again by his assumed name, Blue bobbed his head and mumbled thanks. Mrs Clellan rang a small silver bell and nodded to the colored hired girl who appeared from the kitchen. 'That will do, Eula,' and to Blue, 'You are very young to be established in business, Mr Adams. In what line are you traveling?'

Blue gulped, unable to find words.

'Mr Bristol said you were in sales, I believe,' Mrs Clellan prompted. She was passing pressed glass dishes of apple cobbler.

'Vaults, ma'am,' Packy said quickly. 'Vaults, caskets and funerary supplies. I am fixing to train Mr Adams in sales. He worked up his appetite loading a shipment for me onto a boxcar at our home office this week, before we set out on the road. And heavy work it was, too.'

Blue ducked his head, flinching. Mrs Clellan blinked behind her spectacles. 'Yes, heavy work, indeed. One is not prepared to think of caskets in carload lots.'

'Extry heavy work, in fact,' Packy persisted. His collar and tie and well-used dark suit gave him now an air of shoddy sobriety. 'All on account of our casket having a one-piece liner of sheet plumbium, with all corners doubled and turned.'

Mr Foulkes stiffened, next to Blue. 'Plumbium – that aint nothing but plumber's lead,' he growled.

'Double refined for purity,' Packy said.

'Lead is lead,' Foulkes snapped.

'Others have tried copper and zinc,' Packy went on, ignoring him, 'but our plumbium can't be beat, especially in a country like this with your high water table.' Packy turned back to Mrs Clellan. 'As you no doubt know, ma'am, below ground level, water seepage is the enemy of flesh. We contend that not a drop of water can touch the loved one through our plumbium liner, providing especially you order the torch-weld closure.'

'Soldered, I spect you mean,' Foulkes said. 'That's no job with lead. Not that it matters a whole lot.' He barked a short laugh and splashed thick cream on his cobbler.

'We call that model the Eternal Slumber,' Packy said.

'Well, I do see why you weren't packing the usual run of salesmen's sample cases,' Mrs Clellan said, her voice sounding faint against the chink of dessert spoons.

'We also carry a product called Egyptian Balm,' Packy went on relentlessly, his voice firm with earnestness as he turned to Mrs Tolliver, the pretty young widow on his right. Blue nervously dropped his napkin; when he bent to retrieve it, he saw that Miss Brenner, the young lady on his left, was touching ankles with Mr Adderly across from her, a slender young man with thinning blond hair combed in a curved wing over his brow. 'Egyptian Balm,' Packy repeated. 'This product injected into the veins of your cadav – your dear one – will preserve it in tone and texture and absolute fidelity to life. A thousand years of time don't mean a thing to this product.' Packy thumped the table.

'How you going to prove that?' Foulkes said. He was finely powdered with white dust, Blue saw, even to the hairs in his ears, and Blue remembered suddenly something about a quarry, the theft of some tools.

'We have a sample,' Packy said, 'which was donated to us by a medical college strictly for scientific purposes and which we prepared in this fashion. And let me tell you, folks, except for the absence of a heartbeat, it cannot be told from life.'

Miss Brenner stopped eating, a spoonful of cobbler half-way to her mouth.

'Where is your thousand years in that?' Foulkes said.

'Many a time I've sat there for an hour or two,' Packy said. He held his gloved right hand before Mrs Tolliver and with his other hand gently sketched on its palm an almost palpable presence. Mrs Tolliver stared raptly at it. 'Yes, and held the little thing's hand in my own. Why, there was times' – Packy allowed his voice to break as he held out the imagined hand and looked solemnly from one face to another around the table – 'when I'm certain the little darling's hand turned in my own, as —'

'*Shew!*' Foulkes exploded and his spoon clattered into his cobbler dish.

'– as much as to say she knew I was setting there with her.' Packy's voice was low and vibrant. 'As much as to say —'

'No, you don't, by god!' Foulkes rumbled. Mrs Clellan gave a startled gasp. A low sob escaped the young lady, Miss Brenner, on Blue's left.

'– to say she was grateful —'

'Hear that, goddammit?' Foulkes cried, lunging to his feet so that his chair fell over with a crash. 'Hear that, now? I *knowed* he would say that, and by god I'll thank you to tell me what that's got to do with your thousand-year garntee.'

Blue felt his insides cringe. Packy looked at Foulkes in stony dignity. 'There are believers and there are scoffers. If you cared to come to our home office in Terre Haute, your doubts would be laid to rest soon enough.'

'By god, if you think —'

'Please, Mr Foulkes,' Mrs Clellan said.

'It's easy to scorn the reverence of others,' Miss Brenner said in a choked voice.

'But *he said a thousand years*!' Foulkes shrieked. Then he flung out his arm. 'And that business about the little hand turning ...' His face was patchy-red as he mocked Packy.

'It don't seem incumbent upon me to have to defend our product when you have not so much as placed an order,' Packy said in an injured tone.

'No, and you can bet your —' Foulkes caught himself. 'They can turn me under with a grub hoe, by god! It won't matter none!'

'Perhaps you are not giving sufficient thought to our high

water table,' Mrs Tolliver said sweetly. Foulkes threw down his napkin and stalked from the room.

'I think we might go into the parlor now,' Mrs Clellan said dazedly.

Blue caught up to Packy as they filed past the end of the table. Packy smiled affably. Ahead, Mrs Tolliver turned under a beaded curtain that hung in the arched doorway leading to the parlor. Just then Foulkes stamped out, slamming the front door behind him. The beaded curtain danced with concussion. Mrs Tolliver shrugged slightly and returned Packy's smile. 'A choleric disposition, has Hardie Foulkes. A thousand years, indeed, Mr Bristol.' A dimple deepened in her cheek.

'My oath on it,' Packy said. 'What does a body find to do here of an evening, ma'am?'

'Speaking for myself, a good book is my best friend – but sometimes a hand or two of whist is congenial. Or double sol. Mrs Clellan doesn't favor gambling, of course.'

'Naturally not. Perhaps you would sit down to a hand with me,' Packy said.

'I did promise Mr Foulkes a game, but since he has gone off in such a fret —' She inclined her head and turned to a small game table with an inlaid checkerboard top and a leaded glass-shaded lamp, at the base of which reclined a nude shepherdess in bronze. 'Will you join us, Mr Adams?' she said to Blue.

'He has some letters to write,' Packy said. 'Mr Adams is soon to be married.'

Blue winced again at Packy's bland and easy fibbing, but he was relieved to be able to get away. He said he thought he would turn in early and he went on through the parlor to the front hall and the stairs.

Packy seated the widow at the game table. He noticed that Mrs Clellan had settled down with some knitting, and that Miss Brenner was seated at one end of the sofa, crocheting a wool afghan. Next to her sat Mr Adderly, who was looking at stereopticon views.

Mrs Tolliver held out a deck of cards as Packy sat down. She held on to the deck as he went to take it, so that for a moment her hand rested in his. A slow smile warmed her face. 'How did it go, Mr Bristol? "... the little darling's hand turned in my own?"' Her shoulders shook slightly.

She released the deck. Packy spread the cards. 'High card deals? No, we both deal, don't we?'

She opened the table drawer and found another deck, which she shuffled smoothly; then she began to lay out her hand of solitaire as Packy, on his side, did the same. As he dealt, he admired the gracefulness of her hands. The cards appeared to flow from her slender fingers. They finished dealing and began to play. Packy was distracted by her presence. He studied the lamplit richness of her brown hair, the gentle planes of her nose and chin and particularly he admired the delicate way she had of nibbling a moist lip as she concentrated.

Her white lawn blouse was trimly fitted and buttoned up to a lace-edged bosom of eyelet embroidery, which rose to a high ruffled collar held close under her chin by a black ribbon tie. Since only the ribbon held it closed, it had a way of parting slightly as she moved to play her cards and Packy was unable to avoid noticing the splendid curving swell of flesh beneath.

'You're not playing, Mr Bristol.' She reached across and played a couple of his cards for him. 'See there, now.'

He forced himself to follow the game. 'Poker is my game ordinarily, stud or draw,' he said.

'No doubt for high stakes. I simply wouldn't dare.'

'A few coins put at hazard do give the game a lift.'

She quickly played several more of his cards, as well as her own. 'Of course, even in a game like this, the stakes are high, so to speak.'

'How do you mean?'

'The way we play tells us so much about one another, doesn't it? You, for example, would shortly know so much about me ...'

'Such as what?'

'Oh, you know – a widow, too young to be left a widow, not uncomely, and one having known the warmth, let us say, the *comfort* of marriage, who would perhaps be ... vulnerable. Surely some of this must have passed through your mind.'

'Um ... some, maybe.'

'*There*. You do see.' She tilted her head and looked intently at him. 'Now you do know far too much about me. I feel stripped ... stripped simply *naked* before you now.' Her voice had fallen to a husky whisper. She was playing the cards again, both her own and his, quickly building on the aces between them.

'Not atall,' Packy said.

'Yes, I do, though. *Naked*.' She savored the word. 'High stakes indeed, Mr Bristol – it's as if my ... my *virtue* were at stake, isn't it?'

'I think I'd like that very much,' Packy said.

'You *are* a tease,' she laughed. 'And look – you've won the game. Imagine if we had made such a bet.' She gestured at the cards. 'What would you do?'

'I hold gambling debts to be debts of honor. I would endeavor to ... collect.'

She laughed again and touched his hand. 'You are much too bold. Shall we play again, or is the game too dull for you?'

'For the stakes you have suggested?'

'Really! You will force me to scold you.' She deftly separated the cards and handed Packy his deck. She shuffled and began to lay out the cards again. Watching her, Packy's left hand strayed absently to the small bronze figure beneath the lamp. His fingers traced gently up the polished leg, slowly moved up across the finely-wrought hip to the two gleaming, superbly plump little breasts.

She swiftly set out the columns of cards, but her lashes fluttered and her hand faltered as she saw his fingers. She took a deep breath and went on dealing. The blouse parted fetchingly as her hands moved across the files of cards. Mesmerized, Packy was unaware that his fingers were touching the tiny bronze breasts. Darting occasional glances at his fingers, she continued to deal, then stopped. His fingers explored delicately.

'High stakes indeed. Aren't you playing?' She looked pointedly at his left hand.

Packy saw where his fingers had strayed. He snatched his hand back and began quickly to lay out his cards.

Glancing back at the little bronze figure, she moistened her lips with the tip of her tongue, then daintily loosened the ribbon which held the frothy lace close around her throat, and with her fingers spread back the lace. Her own breasts swelled richly into view, barely contained by the confining garments below.

'My land and nation, it is warm, isn't it?' she breathed. 'I see you have the instincts of a . . . betting man,' she said lightly, and a little bet does add spice to the game, doesn't it?'

'Beyond question, it does.'

She leaned forward slightly. 'In the game as it now stands, we have identified my – shall we call it bankroll? But what are you putting up?'

Packy passed a shaking hand across his brow. He was not at all certain how seriously to take her. 'My capital is tied up in stock just now, but I'm expecting to close a very handsome deal in a day or so, perhaps even by tomorrow evening.' The cards were now all laid out.

'Well, then, we might look forward to sweetening the pot a trifle, mightn't we?' She leaned forward again to straighten his files of cards. The curving tide of flesh flowed, threatening the fragile dam. 'I mean, *both* of us,' she said.

'But what about Mrs Clellan?' Packy said lifting his gaze with difficulty to meet hers.

She nodded at the cards and said, 'Let's start, shall we?'

Packy bent forward to move a black four to a red five on her side. At the same moment, she saw a ten on his side waiting for her nine and leaned forward to play it. For an instant their cheeks nearly touched and Packy was staring down into the pale smooth depths of what appeared to his single myopic eye at such close range to be a vast canyon. She breathed warmly on his neck as she appeared to have some difficulty playing the card. A delicate feminine fragrance came to Packy's nostrils. The she sat back. Packy reluctantly dropped his card and withdrew.

'You say she does not care for gambling,' he said.

'Indeed not.' She leaned forward again to move a card on his side and Packy saw a place for his black trey at the end of a long file descending on her side. Gratefully, he leaned forward and whipped his trey across the table, but as he placed the card on her red four, which lay close to the edge of the table, she shifted slightly and Packy's fingers were firmly pinned by the weight of her bosom, which swelled perilously. For an instant he fancied that a pink blush of color had risen to wink at him.

'She needn't know, need she? And for the present, at least, we're only playing with ... promises, aren't we? Here now' – she sat back, and as Packy reluctantly withdrew his liberated hand, she opened a small matchbox and shook out some matches, which she then broke in half – 'let's consider the plain end to be a one and the red end to be a five.' For a moment, she held the red of the match close to her lips. 'And let's say that whoever has cards remaining in front of him at the end will owe the other the face value of those cards.' Her moist lips caressed the end of the match. 'We can just keep track with the matches, can't we?'

'I spect we could,' Packy said hoarsely.

'Or possibly that's too rich ...' She leaned forward to play.

'No, no, not atall.'

Mrs Clellan's needles clicked away the minutes to the steady tick of the mantel clock and the soft slap of the cards. After a time Miss Brenner folded up her afghan, murmured a good night and left the room, followed shortly by Mr Adderly.

Packy played automatically, captivated at once by the intimate murmuring of Mrs Tolliver's liquid voice and by the dangerously swelling curves of flesh. He learned that she was merely stopping here a few days, that she was on her way to Memphis to visit her sister, that her husband Thomas had been gone now almost a year. The soft eyes flashed at Packy and the little frown of concentration vanished as she leaned forward intently. 'Even now, I can scarcely credit it – his going, I mean. He was so ... vigorous ...' Her nostrils flared and she licked her lips. 'One is so unutterably lonely.'

Promptly at ten-thirty, the clicking of Mrs Clellan's needles stopped. She rose from her chair and began pointedly turning out the lamps. She compared her lapel watch with the mantel clock. 'Early to bed, Mr Bristol, is the rule of the house – sleep is your great restorative. But I see Mr Foulkes is late again.' She frowned. 'He has just five minutes or he sleeps tonight on the levee.' She gathered her skirts and moved about busily.

Mrs Tolliver quickly counted the considerable stack of matches before her, totaling under her breath. Wide-eyed, she covered her mouth with her fingers. 'I never would have dreamed it could add up so. Over a hundred dollars, Mr Bristol.'

Packy smiled wanly. 'I told you my game is stud.'

'Yes, I'm certain of that.'. She opened the drawer and raked the matches into it. Packy blinked, not certain he had actually seen a great many broken matches already in the drawer. 'A hundred and eight dollars, to be exact,' she said.

'Yes, well . . . I only have a few dollars' traveling money with me', Packy said. 'Thirty or so.'

'But there – it was only a game, wasn't it? We needn't take it seriously.'

Nettled, Packy said, 'Nothing of the sort. I spect I'm good for it, soon as I clear up my business.'

A single lamp was still burning across the room. The light was very dim. She lifted her arms to tuck up a stray lock of hair. Then she delicately took hold of the lower edge of the lace-trimmed blouse and the bodice beneath it, pulled them gently free of herself and shook her shoulders slightly as if to settle their burden, and for a stunning instant the burden bobbled without restraint.

'You could just win everything back tomorrow evening,' she said, smoothing the collar. Heavy footsteps sounded on the front porch. She led the way to the stairs.

Packy hesitated. His pulse was thundering. 'Maybe the night after – me and Blue, I mean the kid, we'll no doubt be talking with my principals tomorrow night.' He followed her up the stairs to the second floor and walked with her to her door, which was nearest the rear of the house. It was quite dark in the hallway. Packy stepped close to her and slipped a hand around her waist. For a moment she leaned close to him, her cheek brushing his own, her lips close to his ear.

'You are a dead game sport, Mr Bristol,' she breathed, but as he moved to kiss her, she put a finger over his lips and shook her head. 'A dead game sport . . . but you *lost*.' She twisted away with a little laugh and slipped through her door into her room.

Packy tried the knob just as the key turned. A bolt clicked softly.

'Early to bed, Mr Bristol – early to bed,' Mrs Clellan caroled from the head of the stairs. She had Foulkes firmly by the elbow, and now she gave him a push toward the back stairs, 'Mr Foulkes, I shall hope this will mark an end to your coming in late, most particularly with the reek of spirits on your person.'

Foulkes brushed past Packy and mounted the stairs to their third-floor rooms, stumbling and reeling against the wall as he climbed. At the top of the stairs, Foulkes turned and waited for Packy, who shrank from his steaming breath as Foulkes stuck a finger in his chest.

'You and your goddam ... thousand-year ... garntee!' Foulkes blurted, then he staggered through the door of his room and fell across the bed with a crash.

Packy followed him into the room and pulled him around on the bed, then unlaced and pulled off the enormous shoes. In the dim light from the small bulb hanging at the top of the stairs, he saw the powdery stone dust in the seams of the shoes. He drew a blanket over the big man, then quickly scuttled to the gable window and looked down.

A couple of feet lower and six or seven feet away lay the roof of the building that housed the Girardeau Suit & Pants Company, and the County Treasury.

A glow of light from Mrs Tolliver's window played on the brick wall opposite. Then the light went out. Darkness yawned below and he looked again at the roof across from him. He pulled back in sudden cold fear. It would have been easy in the old days, but not now. He shook his head. But that was what the kid was for.

Behind him, Foulkes moaned and rolled over. Packy took one more quick look, then ran the window down. He stepped around the bed and left the room, closing the door behind him, then he turned off the hall light and entered their own room. A single lamp was on. Blue was intently manipulating the silver wheels in Packy's prison-made combination lock. He looked up at Packy and said, 'What was all that racket?'

'Foulkes. He came in with a skinful. I just finished a few

hands of cards with the little widow lady.' Packy could not bring himself to tell Blue that he had lost their bankroll, plus eighty dollars they didn't have. 'I thought you would be asleep.'

'No. I couldn't sleep.' Blue frowned. 'I'm tryin to figure out what we're doin here, and where we —'

'A few days ago you were eating frogs and turtles. Now fortune has taken you by the hand. Are you squawking?'

'No, I don't mind to eat now and then, but why here? You've got something up your sleeve.'

Packy pulled the tissue from his pocket and shook it out. 'Blue, this is the building next door. The County Treasurer's office is in there, about ten feet from Foulkes' window. There's a skylight —'

Blue put up his hand, started to protest.

'Kid, it's a *stake*,' Packy said. 'Where is a wanted man going to get without a stake? Some rube cop will collar you for panhandling and before you know it they will be fitting you for a black hood.'

Blue flinched. After a moment, he said, 'I been thinkin about it – somebody could get hurt.'

'Nip in, nip out – that's the trick. Nobody gets hurt.'

'We don't have no tools.'

'Tools! You're thinking of that bunch on the *Princess*. It would take a four-horse team to carry a mess of junk like that.' Packy took the combination lock from Blue's hands and twirled the silver dollars. 'Disbrow was a fingers man.'

Blue's laugh was caustic. 'I've worked with lock men – they say it can't be done.'

'Sure they do – but every deck has its aces. Oh, I wouldn't claim to open everything with fingers alone. Locks . . . they're like pieces of music, see? Your fingers man learns them, one at a time, and he sticks with the ones he knows. Blue, it's all here, right down to the hinge pins. We'll pull out of here in style.'

'I don't care about style. Are you . . . certain?'

'Like shooting fish in a rain barrel.'

Blue took a deep breath. 'It's hard to choke down the idea of stealin.'

'Stealin? *shew!* It's *tax* money, Blue. Squeezed out of the farmers.' Packy sensed that Blue was leaning, close to toppling. He said, 'Tonight – we'll take it tonight.'

'Tonight!' Blue sat up and bedsprings squalled.

'It's the waiting that's eating you up. Now's the time – Foulkes is out like a light.'

'Foulkes?'

'The only way across is through his room, and you couldn't wake him up with a cannon. We won't get another chance like this.'

Blue did not answer for a long time. Fragmented thoughts spun in his mind. Israel's bloody head. Thick, smothering folds of black cloth dropping over his face. He shivered.

'A man needs a stake,' he said.

CHAPTER XI

Blue felt reckless and bold, slipping around the foot of Foulkes' bed in the darkness. He smelled stone dust, sweat and whiskey. The bubbly sound of the big man's snoring made him want to laugh. Suddenly Foulkes coughed, mumbled a threatening curse and thundered a fist into his pillow. Blued clung to the window sill, his boldness dribbling away like wet sand. Foulkes slowly subsided, grinding his teeth. Blue took a deep breath and skinned out the window onto the guttered cornice.

He stood, leaning back against the steep slope of the mansard roof. The parapet of the building across from him was a soft blur in the darkness. Below, between the two buildings, emptiness yawned – it might have been a thousand feet down to the cobbles. He was suddenly giddy. His ears roared and terror licked through him. *Stop it, Blue – take hold.* His nails dug into the shingles at his back, then he gathered himself and jumped. He landed rolling on the tarred roof and lay there on his back for a moment wanting to laugh aloud into the night.

Low clouds reflected faint light onto the roof. The air was damp and smelled of rain. Blue crawled to the skylight. He felt along under the lip until he found the butts of the hinges. Brass pins, Packy had said. Blue felt the burred end. He took Packy's file from his pocket and dressed the end, then put the sharp tang of the file against the pin and pushed. The pin slipped on through and he pulled it loose. Another minute and the second pin was out.

Blue lifted and the skylight grated upward, the padlocked hasp inside serving as a loose hinge. He stuck the file on end to prop it, then he snaked through, swung down and hung by his hands in pitch darkness. *Maybe the ladder isn't there anymore*. Panic fluttered again. He made himself let go and landed crouching. *It will be a toilet room and mop closet,* was what Packy had told him. He put his hands out, touched the cold slick bowl, smelled it. Turned right and felt along the wall, past the corner. Mop handles rattled. There, the ladder. Carefully, he set it up beneath the skylight and the narrow slit of faintly luminous darkness that was the sky. Climbed out. Pulled the ladder up after him, collapsing the legs as he hauled it through.

He lugged it to the parapet. Packy's face was at Foulkes' window, a pale blur. He stood the folded ladder on the parapet, let it topple. Packy caught the other end, eased it to the sill, then scrambled across, the ladder springing beneath him. Together they carried the ladder back to the skylight, slipped it through and climbed down.

Packy struck a match, lighted a stub of candle. 'Put the ladder away now,' he whispered. 'When we leave, we'll let ourselves out the back door and in through Mrs Clellan's kitchen door.'

'Won't it be locked?'

He heard an amused grunt from Packy, but no answer. Packy opened the door and slipped out into a corridor. They crossed to a doorway. A small sign next to the door read TREASURER, GIRARDEAU COUNTY, and beneath that, URBAN D. WHITTLE. Packy knelt at the door and Blue heard the snick of metal. Then the door swung open.

Before them, in the faint, shaded light from the bull's-eye lamp, Blue saw a long narrow office room, with a half counter across the middle. To his right as Packy went in, he glimpsed an enormous leather sofa with rolled arms and tufted back, and portraits of bearded presidents in a sepia row above. There were two windows on the left, the side next to the boarding-house. And at the far end of the room, the safe.

Packy nudged Blue and played the faint beam of light on it. It squatted against the back near the center of the room, and stood about four feet high on its heavy casters. Above the door on the upper rim was lettered STANDFAST SAFE & LOCK CO., CINCINNATI, O. Above the dial on the door, Blue read GIRARDEAU COUNTY set in painted tendrils of ivy.

Blue's heart thudded against his ribs and his tongue was dry as a stick of wood. Packy jerked a thumb at the window. Blue, fumbling with shaky hands, drew the green-black roller blinds. Packy thrust the lamp into his hands and knelt before the safe. He twirled the dial to the right with the fingers of his left hand.

'First you locate the cam gate,' he whispered. His voice sounded dry and breathy. 'It will have a spread of seven or eight points of the dial, see? Then start around the dial looking for your first wheel gate —'

'Don't tell me now,' Blue croaked, 'just do it.'

'Then hold the lamp still!' A whispered shriek.

Blue was startled to discover that Packy was jumpy too. He jammed his shaking wrist tight against a bent knee to steady the lamp. In the tiny puddle of light, Packy's fingers slowly turned the dial. 'There's the gate, see? Between six and fourteen. You can even hear it.'

'Never mind telling —'

'Hush. *Hush!* I've got to talk. Got to.'

Blue saw the fingers tremble. Packy's breathing was ragged and Blue was suddenly aware of his own pulse battering beneath his jaw. His ears roared with it. Packy grunted, swore under his breath and wrenched Blue's hand closer. 'Need light. More light.' His head was cocked, his one eye peering down from scarcely six inches away.

'There's a number now. See what happens at the cam gate.'

'I don't see nothing,' Blue said through clamped jaws. 'Not a thing.'

'It's there. You got to look close. It don't take much. Make that sixty-eight. We'll need three more wheels now – oh, lord, for a right hand and two good eyes.' He stopped, pressed his forehead against the cold metal for long seconds and sat back again, turning the dial, murmuring.

Blue strained to follow his movements with the dial, but his mind seemed to have shrunk back inside a great, raw, pulsing, sweaty-slick skin of fear. He rubbed his eyes and swallowed hard. Time was a senseless mumbling voice, a blur of fingers in quivering light – time was smells of dust and metal, wood, ink and musty paper and the rank tobacco stink of the spittoon under the counter. Blue stirred, shuddering. Packy hissed at him.

A crack sounded. Sharp and splintery. Blue's head snapped around. Had he really heard it? Packy hissed at him again. Blue said, 'Didn't you hear that?'

'Hold the light.'

But Packy was half deaf. There – a chunking sound, a clink, something sliding. Downstairs, somewhere. He gripped Packy's arm.

'No – I'm almost there,' Packy said. Footsteps sounded, gritty on uncarpeted stair treads. Another sharp crack of tearing wood. Blue scrambled to the door. A faint glow of light moved up the stairwell. He closed the door and bolted it, then scuttled back to Packy and doused the candle.

'It's no watchman,' he breathed. 'They busted something to get in – I heard it.'

Light glowed faintly under the door. The knob rattled.

'The sofa.' Packy thrust him toward it. Blue pushed a small table aside, steered Packy in under the high sloping back of the sofa, followed squirming and sank onto Packy's legs as the door gave way with a splintering crack. Blue's nose was jammed against the bottom of the sofa. With his left eye, he saw light spray across the floor, saw heavy shoes, a long canvas-wrapped bundle tied with rope.

'Yonder is the son of a bitch,' a voice growled.

'By god, she's big. You won't peel that bastard.'

'Not waggin our goddam jaws we won't. Where in hell is Hub?'

'I tole you – him and Monk is carryin up bolts of yard goods to pad her with.'

They shuffled back to the safe, dropped the bundle and Blue heard the chinking sound again. By tucking his chin in hard against his chest he could see their legs and the lower half of the safe. They untied the bundle, laid out tools. A heavy sledge, some hand drills. Tongs. A gallon can with a lid on it. A long-handled punch with a bottle-shaped head that was like a sledge on one face, with the long snout of the punch on the other. One of the men put down an oilcan, well to one side.

'Look at that sumbitchin door,' the nasal voice whined. 'Caint punch her nowhere – she's solid plate and tempered like a butcher's knife, I betcha. Wisht I had my tools – by god, I would put a blister on her lip with them little wedges and screw jacks.'

'Forget your goddam tools, Artie. We got to snuff the bastard anyway.'

Blue felt Packy's legs convulse beneath him.

'We still got to start the lip, Anse, so's she will dreen. The soup won't do no good if it runs down the front.'

Packy's legs jerked again when the man's name, *Anse*, was spoken. At that moment, the two bent over the tools and their faces were clearly etched in the light. Blue was sick with shock and fright. Anse, the big stubble-bearded one, was the man the farmers horsewhipped back at the *Shawnee Princess*. And the other one was the man Blue had seen coming down the Good Hope Street hill yesterday. And forgotten to mention it to Packy. The *tools* – Blue saw again the blackened set of tools left behind in the charred ruin of the *Princess*. So the tools they had with them now were the ones stolen from the quarry where Foulkes was foreman.

Footsteps rasped again in the doorway. Two or three men, breathing heavily, came into the room and heavy burdens thudded softly onto the floor and sofa.

'Go back for more,' Anse said. 'All you can get. We will drop that door without a sound.'

The men left. Blue saw piled bolts of woolen goods. The small man, Artie, kicked at the long-handled drill. 'This here B and O is too blunt to start the lip – she is too snug a seam.'

'Use the bull-prick then,' Anse said, 'but get a move on so's we can soap her up. And wrap it good.' Anse was opening the gallon can. Blue smelled linseed oil. Artie tore off strips of woolen fabric and began wrapping the head of the big sledge. Blue could hear the other men returning with more bolt goods.

Artie coughed and said, 'Wisht I had m'own wedges.'

'Shut up about the wedges and hold the drill,' Anse said.

Offended, the small man said, 'Git one of them bastards to hold it. I'm gawn putty the door, see the sumbitch is done right.' He clawed a gob of putty from the can and began to roll it out between his palms.

Anse swore under his breath. The other men were dropping bolts of cloth. 'Hub! Take a holt of this drill – hold the sumbitch right there.'

The man called Hub shambled over and took the drill. Blue dug his chin deeper, saw the wrapped sledge swing. It struck with a muffled *thunk*. Hub flinched. 'Jesus! She stung me!'

'Hold er straight.' Anse swung again.

'Anse! That sumbitch hurt!' The man shook his hand.

Anse merely grunted, drew back. Swung. Blue saw Hub flinch and jerk the drill, heard the *chunk* as the hammer skidded down the shaft of the drill and pulped the man's hand against the steel door of the safe, saw Hub's jaw hang down in stunned shock as he stared at the stump that had been a hand. He sank to his knees and sucked in a lungful of air.

Anse let go of the hammer handle, snatched up blood-spattered woolen cloth and jammed it between Hub's jaws, clamping it there with a hand and an armlock around the man's head. Hub's scream was a muffled whinny. He clawed at Anse with the good hand, then with the stump itself, flailing, but Anse bore him backward over his knee and held him there as his body arched and bucked.

The small man was frozen at the safe door with a snaky length of putty swinging from his hands. *'Git his legs!'* Anse snarled, and the man dropped the snake of putty and sprawled, hugging Hub's feet and ankles, his eyes fixed on the flailing stump. 'Oh, goddammit, Anse – oh, goddammit, goddammit, ...' he moaned over and over as the now feebly waving stump slowly dropped. 'Anse – he's out. Let him go.'

Anse held him a moment longer. 'By god, I told him to hold

still. I *told* him.' He got his hands under the man's limp arms and dragged him back away from the safe, dropped him in front of the sofa. Scarcely four feet away, Blue could see Hub's upturned face, the cloth still wadded into his mouth. 'He can bite on that till we're done,' Anse said. 'You *heard* me tell him.' He swung back to the safe, snatched up some putty and began viciously slapping it onto the seam around the safe door. On his knees, he glared suddenly at the small man.

'The son of a bitch had it comin. I *told* him.'

Four blocks away, in the bedroom of a small brick house on a side street, the chief sat up on the edge of his bed. His wife murmured a question.

'I'm hungry, my feet are cold and I caint sleep – that is about the substance of it,' he said.

'A hot water bottle is what you want. Spose I cut you a nice piece of rhubarb pie and put a kettle on?' She put a hand on his back and rubbed gently.

'Tickle me near to death,' he said.

Three minutes later, sitting at the kitchen table with a robe over his nightshirt and a forkful of pie in his hand, he said, 'You could let the kettle go for now – I just thought of somethin.'

It was a five-minute walk to his office. The night was dampish, a trifle raw. He tugged the collar of his flannel nightshirt up under his chin. He had just pulled his britches on over it, and put on coat, shoes and hat.

What he had thought of was simple enough. Theft of the dynamite and quarry tools pointed to safe men. The bank was covered, and that was good, but his officers made their foot patrols around town so as to pass most other places of business only every hour or so. Yeggs could crack a safe in as little as fifteen minutes – two minutes would do for the smaller ones with their straight-through spindles, like the one in the hardware store. So he was not really covering five or six other safes – of course, most of them wouldn't give up enough money to pay slave wages for busting them.

But would the yeggs know that? He thought they would. They worked like a foraging party of soldiers, with scouts out to locate the chicken houses – the safes. Yeggs called their scouts gay cats. The chief could not figure the name, but that did not matter. That was the way they worked. In two-three days, their gay cat could probably know near as much about cash receipts as the bank teller. All right, three or four safes right here in town were apt to be carrying a fair amount of cash. And tax money was piling up in the County Treasury this time of year.

A young officer named Hollis had the night desk. He was nodding when the chief walked in. He snapped alert.

The chief grunted. 'Anything doin?'

'No sir. Elwood is sitting in the storeroom at the bank and Clinefelter made his two o'clock check-in on time and went out again.' He indicated a town map on the wall. 'He will be over on Broadway by now. And Hugo is clear out by the gristmill and the brickyard. Hawes is due any minute.'

'Tell you what, then. You go find Clinefelter and the two of you stay together and check these places' – he pointed them out on the map – 'front and rear. Keep moving so you get each one every ten, fifteen minutes. On your way.' The chief moved behind the desk and sat down as Hollis left.

Hollis was glad to get away from the night desk. To intercept Clinefelter, all he had to do was get over on Broadway and stand under a streetlight. Top of the hill would be best and the alley was the quickest way to get there. He passed between high board fences, parked dray wagons, trash barrels.

Hollis stopped. Cocked his head. There it was again. A faint, metallic chinking sound. Muffled thuds. His heartbeats quickened.

Blue heard footsteps pounding up the stairs, A hoarse, gasping whisper. 'Anse! I just slugged a copper – at the back door!'

'Anybody with him?' Anse was draping bolt goods over the safe. The small man was gently squirting liquid from the oilcan into a puttied lip in the top seam of the door. 'No? Then he won't be missed for a few minutes. We're near done. You git on back.' Anse turned and suddenly peeled the oilcan from the small man's hand. 'Give me the goddam soup.'

'*Anse!* Watch it!'

'There aint *time* to pussyfoot. Get the rope on her.'

Blue felt the tremors in Packy's legs quicken. Working furiously, the small man tied several turns of the stout rope around the safe and knotted them. He scurried to the sofa, stepped over Hub's sprawled body and took the seat cushions and spread them on the floor in front of the safe. Then he piled more bolts of material on top of the safe and pulled the cloth down around it in thick-draped folds. He suddenly stopped. 'Judas, Anse, don't use it *all*!'

'Shut up. Git back out of the way now.' Anse handed him the oilcan and waved him back.

'What about Hub?'

'Hell with him – just git back.' Anse pushed the folds of cloth aside to clear a small space near the center of the safe door and then stepped off a pace to one side and lifted the sledge. Packy's legs convulsed under Blue. He kicked, tried to scramble up. Blue caught his legs and held him down.

The chief looked up when Clinefelter walked in. 'Where's Hollis?'

Clinefelter, a wiry, middle-aged man, was startled to see the chief. He looked around the office. 'Aint he here?'

'I sent him after you.'

'He could hardly have missed me.'

The chief sucked on his mustache for a moment. Then he got up and took a sawed-off shotgun from the wall rack, tossed it to Clinefelter and took another for himself, stuffing shells into his pocket. Clinefelter caught a bull's-eye lamp off a shelf as they ran out the door and turned toward Good Hope Street. Another officer, Hawes, coming to the station from the direction of the levee, saw them and called out from across the street. 'Come on with us,' the chief called.

Anse swung the twelve-pound hammer against the safe door. Shock traveled up his arms and he was thrown back against the wall, the hammer ripped from his grasp, as the explosion blew the safe door outward with a deep, soft-muffled *whump*. Trailing streamers of woolen yard goods and raveled ends of manila rope, and paper from within the safe itself, the door fell face downward onto the thick pile of cushions and bolts of fabric. The air was thick with blown dust, bits of paper and the sharp reek of fumes.

It was almost soundless. A few feet away, through two brick walls, Mrs Clellan stirred slightly, then resumed her steady snoring. Mrs Tolliver sat up for a moment, then turned onto her other side and went back to sleep. Foulkes did not stir.

Blue gripped Packy's legs with all his strength as the door blew off. He felt a great breath of wind and the floor seemed to slap them solidly. He peered back through the swirling, murky clouds, and in the glow from the bull's-eye lamp, he saw Anse on hands and knees, clawing through a pile of tumbled ledgers and torn paper. Anse snatched up a tin box, wrenched open the battered lid, clapped it shut and plunged for the door. He tripped once over the fabric and the door itself, then tripped again over Hub's body and fell solidly, the tin box clattering from his hand and spilling a shower of greenbacks across the body. With his breath sawing in his throat, Anse stuffed bills back into the box and bounded again for the door.

Blue shouldered the sofa aside, crawled over Packy and scrambled on all fours to the head of the stairs. He heard footsteps going out the back way, then the sounds of bodies colliding, with grunts and blows and Anse's deep growl. 'I've got the stuff – scatter!'

Packy crawled around the end of the sofa on hands and knees. He felt something under his fingers. Paper. He looked down. Loose bills. He stuffed them into his coat pocket. There were more, scattered. He scrambled after them, found himself peering down into Hub's staring eyes. Packy recoiled, snatched up another handful of bills and turned, just as Blue clutched his shoulder.

'They ran into that cop down there,' Blue whispered. Sounds of the fight carried up the stairwell.

'The roof – quick!' Packy said.

They ran into the utility room and set up the ladder under the skylight in the dark, climbed up and pulled the ladder after them. Blue ran to the rear parapet and looked down as Anse staggered into the yard with Officer Hollis clinging to his legs. Artie followed, kicking the officer. Anse struck Hollis with the tin box and knocked him among the packing cases. Both men ran through the gate in the high board fence. Hollis struggled up and followed, running off downhill in the alley. Blue was certain one of the robbers turned and ran uphill. He realized then that it was raining.

Packy hissed at him. Blue ran back and together they carried the ladder to the parapet opposite Foulkes' window. They extended it out over the gap between the two buildings and let the upper end down gently onto the window sill. Blue settled it so that the feet rested very close to the edge of the parapet, to keep it from sliding back on the wet tile. 'What are we going to do with the ladder?' he whispered.

'Have to pull it across after us,' Packy said. He scrambled out onto the ladder. It sprang and bucked under him. As he cleared the parapet, for an instant all his weight was on one rung under his knee. The ladder was ancient and had seen hard service. The rung broke. With a strangled bleat, Packy slipped through, carrying with him the ladder's back supporting legs, which now hung almost straight down between the buildings. Blue desperately held the feet of the ladder as they skittered on the wet parapet.

The rung in Packy's hands made cracking noises. He hooked the hanging rear support legs with his feet, let go up above with one hand, dropped down and caught a rear leg just as the rung broke away. Now he was far below the sill of Foulkes' window, clinging desperately with his one good arm and his legs to the flimsy rear legs of the ladder, which swung him from side to side like a pendulum with every move.

The chief reached the corner of Good Hope Street and Main and pulled up, puffing. 'The bank looks quiet – spose you two go up the street. I'll take the alley.' Hawes and Clinefelter set off at a run. The chief crossed the street, passed the dark, silent bank and rounded the corner of the alley. In the light from the streetlamp behind him, he saw a man running toward him. A small man.

'Hold it right there,' he barked.

The man tried to dodge him, skidded on the wet cobbles and slipped down, but came up instantly, circling now. The chief heard a click and saw the glint of a knife blade. 'One of them, hunh?' he said. He feinted with the shotgun barrel, then swung the butt of the gun around hard against the side of the man's head and dropped him like a bundle of sticks, the knife chittering away on the stones.

The chief heard footsteps again. Another man running down the alley. He stepped back into the shadows, and as the man came abreast of him, the chief stepped out and drove the shotgun butt solidly into his belly, then slapped him above the ear with it as he dropped. The chief bent down and turned the man over. It was Hollis. At that moment, he heard the alley window of the bank open behind him. 'Don't move or you're a dead man,' a voice said.

'Goddammit, Elwood, it's me. I just hit Hollis. Christ, what a lick I give him.'

'What the hell is going on?' Elwood said.

Just then Clinefelter ran into the alley from the street. 'We caught one out on the street – Hawes run off up the hill after another one.' He saw Hollis, stretched out on the cobbles. 'By god, I'd like to ketch the bastard that done that to pore Hollis.'

The chief sighed, then said, 'They've scattered all over hell-and-gone. Must've got into the County Treasury. Cuff that one to the railing yonder and let's go see.'

Inside her room in the boardinghouse, Mrs Tolliver awoke and sat up in bed. She thought she had heard a man's voice say, 'Don't let me drop.' Part of a dream, no doubt, but she could not recall the rest of the dream. She puffed her pillow and started to stretch out again when the same voice said, 'My god, Blue, hold on to it.'

There was nothing outside her window but a straight two-story drop to a cobbled walkway. Perplexed, she swung her feet to the floor and stepped to the window. It was raining lightly. She heard a slight rustling, scratching, a faint creak. She knelt close to the window and looked up.

The faintest of lights reflected off low clouds. Against this light she saw what appeared to be a man swinging by his hands from something. Yes, a ladder. Or what was left of one. She was not alarmed when she recognized the voice – Mr Bristol, the man she had played cards with after supper. And he had called the other one Blue.

She wrapped a shawl around her shoulders, then pulled a footstool over close to the window to sit on while she watched.

Clutching with hands, elbows and knees, Packy hitched himself up the quivering support legs of the ladder a little at a time; then hugging the legs, he got a foot over a cross brace and from there reached up and caught the side rail with his good hand. A moment later he had an arm and shoulder over the rail and was climbing up through the rungs, taking great care not to put his weight on them When he had himself lying out flat, he snaked forward, lifted the window a trifle and slithered into the room headfirst, where he lay for a few seconds shuddering and gasping. When his breathing and thundering pulse had calmed a little, he turned to steady the ladder for Blue.

A glow of light played suddenly on the high board fence across the alley. It moved away, then streamed back, moving closer. Rain slanted, glistening against the light. The rungs quivered under Blue's hands. As he reached the middle of the ladder, he distinctly heard a voice below, just around the rear corner of the building from him. 'Chief, here it is. The back door is busted in.'

Footsteps sounded close. The light swung back and forth. Blue saw Packy's face staring at him from the window. He was certain now that he would be found – he saw in his mind a policeman rounding the corner of the building and shooting him off the ladder, and he flinched at the imagined shot. A dry croak came from his throat. Then the light snuffed out as the men went into the building.

Blue hitched forward. Packy caught his shoulders and eased him to the floor. He heard Foulkes' bubbly snore again. Together they leaned out the window and pulled the ladder across and into the room. For a moment it was directly over the snoring man, then Packy slipped around and opened the door. Seconds later they were in their own room, with the ladder on the floor against the wall.

Blue sank onto the bed in the dark and covered his face with his hands. Only a minute earlier he was certain he was going to die. Now a strange ecstasy welled in his throat. He had to clamp his jaws together to keep from shouting.

'One thing we should have done,' Packy whispered, 'we should have put the pins back in the hinges on the skylight.'

CHAPTER XII

Bassett and the chief and the two officers, Clinefelter and Hawes, climbed down from the chief's canopy-topped rig. In the gray morning light, Bassett saw open fields puddled with rain stretching away on both sides of the road, and the road itself was congested at one point with buggies and wagons and a clustered knot of people. They walked over and stood in the rain at the side of the road, looking down at a pair of feet protruding from a culvert.

The chief grunted, then turned to the several children who watched both him and the protruding feet in silent awe. 'You chillern get on to school, hear?'

A small boy spoke up. 'We tried to pull him out.'

'I know. You done just right. Hurry now, you'll be late.' He frowned and stared hard at them, letting the force of his stare start them moving away toward town and school, something over half a mile distant. Then he said to Bassett, 'We was closer to catchin him than we thought, but in the dark and the rain and all, we figured we had lost him. He must have been right underfoot, too.'

A trickle of water was coming through the culvert around the dirty, wet trouser legs and enormous shoes. Across the road, the water was backed up, flooding over the top of the culvert. The chief climbed down the bank and straddled the ditch.

'Feet on the pore son of a bitch like the *Robert E. Lee*. You want to give me a hand, Mr Bassett?'

Bassett slid down next to him. The two men set themselves and pulled. The body moved slightly. The flow of water quickened. 'Once more,' the chief said. They both hauled at once. The body squirted from the culvert, propelled by a milky gush of water – free of the culvert, it rolled once and lay still, grotesquely sprawled.

Both men were wet to the knees. Bassett unstraddled himself from the ditch and turned the body face up. There was a metallic noise. Caught under the body was a badly mauled and dented tin box. Bassett handed the box to the chief, then looked at the purple-lipped, dark-stubbled, wet face.

'Yes, his name is Anson,' Bassett said. 'Anse for short. He's wanted for murder and escape from the Ohio pen.'

'A man his size —' the chief said softly, 'reckon what he thought when he knowed he was stuck and the water commenced to come up around his chin?' He looked into the box, saw the mass of sodden bills and closed it again. 'That's about the size of it – two dead, two in jail, and maybe one or two got away. Hardly worth your time, Mr Bassett.'

'Not atall,' Bassett said. His lips twitched in what might have been a smile. 'I was in Memphis on another matter and was told last night about your call, so it was a simple matter to stop off here. This is the same outfit that hit the Adams Express office in Paoli. Killed the night man. They're Cincinnati yeggs, a damned nasty bunch. No, you did right to call us.'

The chief looked pleased. He turned to Clinefelter and Hawes. 'Spose you boys borrow a wagon and take him to Doc Jeffers.' To Bassett he said, 'Long as you're here, you might want to take a look at the safe, too.'

'Educational,' Bassett said.

The two men walked back to the buggy and climbed in. The chief shook out the lines and turned his chestnut mare toward town. Shortly, they were back on Good Hope Street, shouldering through a knot of people gathered around the street door of the County Treasury. They had to stand back to let two men through, bearing a covered body on a litter.

Upstairs nothing had been touched except for the removal of the body. An elderly colored man was sweeping the hall. Inside the office, the County Treasurer, Urban Whittle, a small man with wisps of lank hair combed across his skull, stood ankle-deep in blood-spattered yard goods staring numbly at the wreckage of his safe. He was making clucking noises with his tongue. A plump man wearing glasses and a gray hat held a length of woolen material up, wringing the cloth between his hands. 'Who is going to pay for my goods?' he pleaded.

The chief touched Whittle's arm and gave him the box. 'Will you give us a count on it, quick as you can, Urban?' Whittle took the box as if he had never seen it before. He started to answer, then clucked his tongue again and turned back to staring at the safe.

The chief looked around for Bassett, saw him in the door of the utility room, across the hall. He was looking up at the skylight. The chief walked over to stand next to him. He pointed to the padlocked hasp. 'The lock wasn't touched, Mr Bassett. No need. They come along the alley – jimmied the back door, the door to the tailor shop and this door.'

Bassett nodded, started to turn away.

The black man stopped sweeping and leaned on his broom. 'Somebody taken my laddah, cap'n.' He pointed at the corner of the room. 'She gone, see?'

Bassett reached out, frowning. 'Let me borrow your broom, old-timer.' He put the end of the broom against the frame of the skylight, on the side opposite the padlock, and pushed. The skylight rose, exposing the dripping lower edge of the frame. They could just see the unmated butts of two hinges.

Dark fatigue smudges under Blue's puffy eyes gave his face a battered look. Watching Packy brush his suit coat with a damp folded towel, he could not stop yawning. For no reason, he suddenly remembered what he had intended to ask Packy.

'What would it mean if you heard that someone stole a hundred sticks of sixty percent?'

Packy turned slowly, fumbling with his glasses to straighten them on his nose. His hand trembled and his face wore a stricken look. 'Where did you hear such a thing?'

Blue bit off a yawn. 'Yesterday, when I was waiting for you in front of the cafe, I saw a man – some kind of cop or sheriff, he was – come out of the cafe with Foulkes, and Foulkes told him that someone had broken into the shed at the quarry and took some tools and a hundred sticks of sixty percent. And a little later I saw one of the bums from the *Princess* – just for a second, see. I meant to tell you, but I forgot.'

'You . . . forgot,' Packy's voice was weak. 'You knew the bums were yeggmen, dammit.'

'I just saw the one – the little guy – and he wasn't nothing but a bum to me.'

'The sixty percent means dynamite,' Packy whispered, wagging his head. 'Straight dynamite. It comes in different grades. Fifteen percent, forty, sixty, like that. The little guy was their scout and the rest of them were probably in some shack somewhere a mile or two from town, cooking the dynamite down to get the nitro out of it. My god, Blue, should have told me.'

'I didn't make the connection.'

'Let me tell you, if I had known someone stole a hundred sticks of dynamite in this town, and a mess of tools, I would not have ventured within a hundred miles of that safe, or any other.'

'How was I to know it was safe blowers that done it?'

Packy ran a comb through his damp hair, frowned at himself in the spotted mirror, then shrugged into the coat. 'It's done. There is no calling it back. But we aren't clear yet – I keep thinking of those blasted hinge pins. We've got to go eat breakfast as if nothing has happened, and leave when everyone else goes to work. Only we won't be back for supper.' With a pang, he thought of the little widow and saw again the way she tugged at her blouse and shivered her shoulders in the dusky light.

At the breakfast table, Mrs Clellan pushed a great ironstone bowl of oatmeal toward Blue. 'Oats will stick to your ribs, young man. You look like you never slept a wink. A plate of cakes will be along directly. And some eggs. I see you folks have heard about the dreadful business next door.' She passed a pitcher of milk and the butter plate, 'I slept right through the whole thing.'

'I thought it was the bank that was robbed,' Miss Brenner said. Both Mrs Clellan and Adderly spoke at once to correct her. Foulkes hunched over his bowl of oats, eating with glowering concentration. Mrs Clellan rang her silver bell.

Mrs Tolliver had managed to ignore Foulkes' offer of the chair next to him and allowed Packy to seat her next to himself. She leaned close to Packy. 'A terrible thing,' she murmured, her shoulder brushing his. Packy nodded, pleased at the intimacy she accorded him. She wore a pale-blue high-necked blouse this morning, which still managed to excite his memory, and he found something captivating in her profile and the damp tendrils of hair that curled at her temples.

'It will go hard with them when they're caught, won't it?' she said.

'Deed it will,' Packy said. 'Yeggs like that are the lowest stamp of crook in my estimation.' Her sudden answering smile warmed him.

Mrs Clellan rang her bell again and looked distractedly at the kitchen door. 'Where is that Eula? I spect she ducked next door again to rubberneck. She watched them take away the body and said it – was that the back door?' She rang her bell again.

Mrs Tolliver leaned close to Packy again. 'Might we look forward to another hand of cards this evening?'

Packy hesitated. 'We just may be detained too late.'

'What a shame.' When she smiled, he admired the way the corners of her eyes crinkled. 'Well then, do you suppose – I mean, I have some shopping to do this morning. Did you ... one hates to come right out boldly with it. There is a class of people that thinks gambling debts are not to be honored.' She laughed merrily. 'Even the innocent little ones like ours.'

'You won't count me among them,' Packy said, a little stung.

'Oh, of course not.' Her hand closed for an instant over his own.

'As a matter of fact, my wallet with my traveling funds in it just happened to be in my other suit, or I would have —'

'After breakfast then,' she said softly. 'Out by the stairs.' For a moment, her knee touched his under the table.

Eula came into the room with a big Staffordshire platter of fried eggs and bacon. She put the platter down, then bent and whispered into Mrs Clellan's ear.

'They recovered all but how much?' Mrs Clellan said.

'They find another dead man,' Eula said, 'and they git back all but four hundred and thirty some dollars, and they is a Pinkerton man with the chief this minute.'

Packy felt Mrs Tolliver's eyes on him. He peeled his lips

back in what was intended to be an amiable grin, then as Mrs Clellan offered the platter of eggs, he quickly lifted a hand. 'No thank you. No eggs, please.'

'You *are* in a hurry, Mr Bristol,' Mrs Tolliver said, her voice suddenly tart. Packy rose and bent to help her with her chair. She led him through the parlor to the foot of the stairs, where she turned to meet him, her eyes crinkling again in a smile.

'I thought we might take care of this before the kid gets away from the table,' Packy said. He fumbled in his trouser pocket and brought out a few bills and some silver. She leaned forward and rested a hand on his arm. Her smile broadened as she cocked her head and waited. He swallowed. 'I did tell you that I only had thirty dollars or so, but I will pay you out of company funds – it was a hundred and eight dollars, am I right?'

'Oh,' she laughed lightly. 'Surely you're not forgetting so soon?' The fingers of the hand touching his arm strayed to his breast pocket, a gentle caress. 'It was four hundred thirty ... some odd. Counting the thirty you already had, shall we make it an even four sixty?'

Packy's grin faded. His spine felt suddenly cold. He tried to speak, but no words came.

'I could have leaned out my window and touched the ladder,' she whispered. The corners of her eyes continued to crinkle cheerily at him. Packy saw that Blue was finishing his eggs, was pushing back his chair. Her hand stroked the pocket.

'Won't you even leave us eating money?' Packy croaked.

The tip of her tongue moved delicately along her lips. 'A girl has to get along, but I won't be a monster. Keep twenty.'

Packy peeled off two tens, handed the rest of the folded bills to her and saw them disappear into a small bag that swung from her wrist. She touched his cheek lightly and breathed, 'I do love a good loser.' Then she put her hand around the back of his neck, pulled his head suddenly down and kissed him, and for an instant her lips parted and he felt her darting tongue. Stepping back then, she turned to go up the stairs. He caught her hand. Blue was coming.

'If you want to hold on to that,' he nodded at the bag,

'there's one thing you can do for me – for both of us —'

As Blue entered the hall, he saw Packy say something to the widow in a voice too low for him to catch, and then she smiled and went on up the stairs.

'What was that all about?' Blue said.

'Mary, now think about it,' the chief said. 'Is there nothin more you can tell us about them?'

It was an hour later in the morning. Mrs Clellan was back in the kitchen with Eula, the other boarders had all gone to work, and Mary Tolliver was the only one now in the parlor with Bassett and the chief. They had already looked through the attic and the two upstairs bedrooms, with Mrs Clellan's co-operation.

'Can you give us a first name?' Bassett said.

She hesitated. 'I did hear Mr Bristol, the older man, call Mr Adams "Blue." Will that help? It's not atall a common name.'

'It might,' the chief said. 'There is precious little to go on.' He put aside the remains of a dish of bread pudding and thick cream from Mrs Clellan's kitchen, and he and Bassett rose to leave. The chief let Bassett go through the front door, then turned and looked at her squarely, though a little uneasily. 'Mary, I thought me and you had a little understanding, after last time. You *promised* me you would not work your boarding-house card game another time in this town. Now tell me if that aint true?'

'So I did, Chief – and truly, I'm just passing through. Mrs Clellan will attest to that. Aren't you glad to see me?'

'Always,' the chief conceded. 'I wisht you would find yourself a decent man and marry him.'

She laughed. 'And only have one chump to trim?'

He winced. 'You mind that promise now. It aint fair to Mrs Clellan, for one thing. She as much as told me your card games was an embarrassment to her and a blot on her house.' He went on through the front door.

As Mary watched the chief and Bassett go down the front steps, Mrs Clellan came out of the parlor and stood next to her. 'Do you believe I said such a thing, hon?'

'Of course I do, but I don't think you meant it, after all the business we have done together. In fact, as long as we're on it, I might as well give you your house cut for last night.' She counted some bills and silver dollars into Mrs Clellan's hand. 'I took Bristol for ... a hundred and eight dollars, so that's twenty-seven for you. It's just too bad I couldn't have gotten him into a game *after* the safe was blown open – if indeed he is the one who made off with that money.'

'Oh, my stars!' Mrs Clellan said. Both women laughed merrily, then Mary Tolliver went up the stairs and along the hall to her own room. She did a waltz step and pirouette going through the door, then sank gracefully into a chair. A small frown line appeared between her brows.

'Now what am I going to do with *you*?' she said softly to the broken-runged ladder lying on the floor of her room.

Bassett's train arrived in St Louis early enough for him to walk from Union Station to the Wainwright Building and arrive there well before the six o'clock closing time. He reported immediately to Havenhurst and told him what he had done in Memphis, answering a staccato fire of questions as he went along.

Havenhurst noticed the dried mud on Bassett's shoes, the bedraggled lower legs of his trousers. 'Did the Cape Girardeau thing have anything to do with our yeggmen?'

Bassett said it did and explained at length, telling finally about finding the big yegg's body jammed in the culvert. Then he said, 'What would you say if somebody told you that Packy Disbrow was back in business?'

'Are you telling me that yourself?'

'Not exactly. But a one-eyed crippled man was involved in this affair in Cape Girardeau.' He told him about the mysterious tenants in Mrs Clellan's boardinghouse.

Havenhurst thought about it, then shook his head. 'Disbrow is too broken up for second-story work, or for any kind of hard work, and safe-busting can be hard work.'

'What if he had a sturdy-built young buck to help him get around and to do anything that called for muscle?'

'No. Too chancy. Disbrow was bold as brass, but he never

took foolish chances and he was fussy about who he worked with.'

'Does that include Birdsong?'

'Of course – the Birdsong thing was an accident, a bolt of lightning, a —' The super stopped with the sudden embarrassment of a man who catches himself with a tear in his eye over an ancient and foolish memory.

'What if,' Bassett went on, 'the kid just happened to be a first-class mechanic himself?'

'Maybe – all right. That would help, wouldn't it? I take it you have someone in mind.'

'The one-eyed man in Cape Girardeau was heard to call the younger man Blue.'

'That was the name of Clay Russell's kid brother, wasn't it?'

Bassett nodded. Havenhurst drummed on the desk. Then he suddenly said, 'Some say otherwise, but a man could be tempted to say that blood will tell.'

'I don't know about that,' Bassett said, 'but I can find out if the kid is still at Cawley's place.'

Bassett walked to his hotel. In his room, he opened his grip on the bed and made a bundle of his laundry. He changed into the same stained and shapeless suit he had worn as Wagenbach, slaughterhouse proprietor, then he left the hotel and boarded a southbound trolley. Twenty minutes later he was standing at the street door of the splendid, decrepit old house with the big carved Dragoon Colt hanging over the door.

It was locked. No lights showed inside, though it was long after dark. Bassett walked on to the levee and turned the corner to Zumbach's Saloon. Except for a little dish of bread pudding at Mrs Clellan's, he had not eaten since daybreak. He took a corner table and ordered a workingman's supper – knockwurst and sauerkraut, bratkartoffeln and a five-cent beer. The waiter brought the beer right away – he was the same small man with the great red mustache.

'I aint seen Cawley for a while,' Bassett said.

'You aint know his head vas broke?' the waiter said.

'You mean he's dead?' Bassett was startled.

'Pretty tamm close. Dot kid in der shop vas give him a lick and der son of a bitch, his head vas broke and good job. too.

Two-tree days he's oudt. Not long enough, you ask me.' A look of alarm crossed his face. 'You friends of him?'

'Oh, hell no,' Bassett said. 'I been in his shop, is all. And just now I seen it was locked up tight and dark. What happened to the kid?'

'He schkinned oudt. Vere? Christ, who knows?'

In the morning, Bassett returned to the agency office. He told the super what he had learned.

'So, it appears to confirm that Blue Russell has taken up with a safe-breaker,' Havenhurst said. 'What did I tell you? Blood will tell – it was in the kid's nature to turn to crime. There is no other explanation for it.'

Havenhurst leaned down and took a paper-wrapped bundle from the floor. He shook a filthy denim jacket from it. The jacket smelled of cow manure. 'A railroad dick found this under a culvert in a burg called Pawnee Rock, which is near Great Bend, in Kansas. See the stencil on it – the jacket was issued in the Four Courts lock-up. The dick says a general store was robbed there two-three nights ago, clothes and a couple hundred in cash.'

The file labeled *Murdock – Russell* was lying open on the super's desk. Bassett touched it.'They're moving west. They enlisted in Denver. The file shows that a lot of the men in their regiment were from the back country of Utah and Wyoming.'

'You're looking for old connections?' the super said. 'We know that there are warrants out on half a dozen men who served with the Studs – staying out of jail is as good a reason as any for enlisting, right? In fact' – the super pawed through the file – 'the two men who were with them when they robbed the army paymaster in Florida both did time in the Wyoming pen and had connections with the Wild Bunch. Yes, here it is – their names are Carver and Naylor.'

'After the robbery in Florida,' Bassett said, 'they naturally split up. I'm betting they aimed to get together again.'

'But Murdock and Russell were waylaid by Kruger's Invincible and wound up in the Four Courts jail, is that it?'

'Yes, but once they get together again, they won't be just two fugitives running scared – they'll be a *gang*, operating in country they know, able to move almost without restraint a thousand miles or more north and south on the outlaw trail in the badlands along the Green and the Colorado.'

'What are you getting at?'

'You'll never catch them by ordinary means in that country. If they do a job, they'll have relays of fresh horses for their getaway, the way Cassidy works. The law can't duplicate that.'

The super smiled slightly. 'I never said it would be easy to put the collar on them. All right, assume they do turn up as you say, a train robbery no doubt – they will just butt their heads against Kruger's Invincible again. And we'll be after them.'

'It wouldn't stop me,' Bassett said. 'Maybe once it might, the way it stopped them, but if it was me, I would find a way to crack that box.'

The super's smile faded. 'I helped sell the express companies on that safe, and now you're telling me —'

'If it took a year, or ten years, by god I would break it.'

The super frowned and suppressed an angry retort. At length he said, 'Yes, maybe you would.' He turned his chair. From an oval mahogany frame on the wall, a bearded face glared sternly at him. The super drummed his fingers on the desk. 'You know what the old man always claimed, don't you, Bassett? – that there was one thing no criminal organization could withstand ...'

'The inside man,' Bassett whispered.

'Infiltrate, infiltrate, infiltrate.' The super's big fist thudded onto the arm of his chair. He turned back and looked hard at Bassett. 'That was where we found you, wasn't it? Eighty-eight, I believe.'

Bassett nodded. 'The year after the big blizzard wiped out my cow outfit. I was cutting and hauling timber for railroad ties near Rifle, Colorado. Yes, I know the country, all right.'

'It's the cut nearest the bone,' the super said.

And Clay Russell was saying, 'Owlhead, you'll fall into that thing and drownd yourself.'

Byron Carver, known as Owlhead, held a whiskey glass on his forearm and peered at the tattooed horse through it, as through a lens. 'Member that ol' spic in Gitmo that done the tatooes? He cackled like a chicken when I made him savvy he was to put that big whang on the horse —'

'Never mind that,' Zack Murdock said. 'What was it you said about your brother-in-law?'

Owlhead blinked. It was his banjo eyes and sharp, bent-down nose that gave him his name. He was seated with Murdock, Clay Russell and Cape Naylor at a stained table in a decrepit saloon near the railroad stockyards in Alamosa, Colorado. 'Don't rush me now, Zack. Always rushin a man. You boys are the ones who're late, not ol' Owlhead.' He laughed explosively. 'Damn near six months late, aint that right, Cape? Me and Cape, soon as we hear you busted out, we come a-runnin, same as we said we would, didn't we, Cape?'

Cape Naylor grinned past a week's growth of beard. 'Sure as hell did.'

'And don' forget, you owe us for the horses,' Owlhead said. 'We *paid* for the bastards.'

'We won't forget. Now tell us about the train, dammit,' Russell said.

Carver took another drink. 'Yes. My brother-in-law Jared is assistant yardmaster in Durango. All us Carvers is railroad people. Me, I was station agent two years on the Colorado Midland —'

'We heard about that twenty times,' Russell prodded. 'Durango, you said . . .'

'That's Denver and Rya Grande, see? There is a train there, it don't run but once ever week or ten days, see? – the one they call the Shotgun Run – but when it does, it carries near a quarter million in payroll for the mines. And my brother-in-law Jared, he can tell us which train is the Shotgun, see? He is just nearabout burned up, the way the line passed him over for yardmaster. He —'

'And you know for damn sure we can count on him?' Clay Russell said,

'For a cut,' Owlhead said.

'How do they carry the money?' Murdock said.

'In a spr . . . spress car, a safe, bout like the one the paymaster had down there in Florida. And a hell of a mess of shotgun guards.'

'You blow the face off one or two of them guards,' Murdock said, 'the rest will just by god eat their shotguns.'

'Say we nail it then,' Russell said, 'how do we get away? I packed ore in those mountains. A horse don't last long, running straight up.'

'Strings of horses,' Naylor said, 'running west, to the badlands. A Mex named Chavez will set em up, relays, ever fifteen, twenty mile. He done the same for Cassidy in June when he hit the UP train at Wilcox.'

'But it's gawn take time to get the horses together,' the Owlhead said, 'and we got to rustle money to pay Chavez.'

'He can wait, same as us,' Murdock said.

'No, Chavez gets paid first, a hundred dollars a head. Even Cassidy had to pay him,' Naylor said.

'A hundred a head – that's two or three thousand dollars!' Clay Russell said. 'And hell, we don't even get to keep the horses.'

'Where we going to get the scratch?' Murdock said.

The Owlhead and Naylor grinned at each other. 'From a Methodist mine foreman,' the Owlhead said, still grinning.

Russell grinned back. 'Go on.'

'He runs the Yellow Rose – it aint too big, see, maybe forty men, two shifts. It's eighteen miles from right here. This foreman, he comes down hard on booze, see, so he don't want his men runnin off to saloons to cash their checks. He pays cash, and ever two weeks, he takes the cash to the mine in a buckboard.'

'How come you know all this?' Clay Russell demanded.

'Hell, I told you we ben waitin for you – we run into one of the miners right here. He was cussin because his ol' woman showed up at payday and got her hands on most of his wages and he couldn't hardly work up a decent drunk. Me and Cape, we shared a cup of skullbust with him and he told us all about it . . .'

Only two days later, on a rutted wagon track through the brushy hills north of Alamosa Creek, Henry Garringer, boss of the Yellow Rose and dedicated temperance man, was stretched out on the ground next to his buckboard, bleeding from a four-inch scalp wound put there by a pistol barrel in the hands of one of the four men who had ridden suddenly out of the brush and stopped him. Lying there, he was dazed and unable to move, except for his eyes. He was later able to give meticulous descriptions of three of the men to the county sheriff, notwithstanding the bandannas they wore to cover their faces – one of them, he said, had peculiar pop eyes and his mask kept slipping down off his small, bent nose. And when one of the others, a heavy-shouldered man with black crinkly hair, leaned down out of the saddle to snatch Garringer's valise, the turned-back cuff of his flannel shirt exposed part of a tattoo. 'I took it to be a horse,' Garringer said, 'with an unholy big *thingum* on him, if you know what I mean ...'

CHAPTER XIII

The *Judith Quennell* tied up on the New Orleans levee at four-thirty in the afternoon after a run of four days from Cape Girardeau. Blue followed Packy off the ramp. The broad levee was choked with people, wagons, animals and cargo. The moist air was heavy with the stench of fish, garbage and manure. They threaded their way among stacked cotton bales and great dray wagons. A stake-bodied wagon filled with butchered beef carcasses rumbled past, trailed by a dense cloud of flies. From the back of the load a jiggling steer head stared down at Blue with sightless eyes, the long pale tongue swinging slack from the jaws.

They crossed railroad tracks. 'Decatur Street is right over there,' Packy said. 'I know where we can get a bed for ten cents apiece.'

'That's mighty rich living, aint it?' Blue said. Having learned of the loss of their stake, he had grown a barbed tongue.

An aged black man in a straw hat shouted from behind a rickety cart. '*Baton amandes,* cap'n.' Blue smelled sugar and almonds. Saliva gushed in his mouth.

'You could let me have my share of what's left,' he said to Packy. 'I'm near starved.'

Packy counted the change in his pocket. 'We're down to sixty cents – let's see that we have a bed first, then we'll get something to eat.'

'I'm caught up on sleep, but I'm way behind on eating.'

Packy led him a short block from the waterfront, turning left on a narrow crowded street flanked with low brick and plaster buildings, with iron balconies overhanging the sidewalk. 'The last time I was here,' Packy said, 'I had over ten thousand dollars in my kick.' Instantly he regretted saying it, fearing that he was leaving himself open for another prickly comment from Blue. But Blue, subdued by hunger, merely smiled frostily and said, 'Only ten?' What happened?'

'I managed to run through most of it in four or five days, then I caught a boat upriver to meet Birdsong.'

He turned into a cobbled alley that smelled of damp and decay, and entered a low, arched doorway. Blue followed, nearly blind in the gloom. A swarthy fat man wearing a stained linen coat over a collarless blue-striped shirt sat at a table eating fried shrimp from a cracked plate. He spat tails and shucks onto the floor and grunted at Packy and Blue. Behind him on the cracked plaster wall, a small sign said SEAMEN'S REST – BEDS 25C. Through another doorway, Blue glimpsed rows of iron cots. A barefoot man sat cross-legged on one of the cots, scraping his nails with a long dirk. He was pock-marked, hollow-cheeked, dark as a gypsy. He grinned at Blue, showing a broken row of snaggy teeth.

'The price has gone up,' Packy said. 'It's too much.'

'I'm all broken up,' Blue said. 'Really disappointed.'

They went back out into the alley and turned toward Decatur Street again. A woman's voice shrieked at Blue from a window, hoarse words in a strange language. He saw a flash of earrings swinging beneath tousled ringlets, a thin black cigar in the painted mouth, her orange wrapper half open down the front. She laughed and held it open. Blue stumbled on the cobbles, fled after Packy.

At the corner Packy stopped before a window and studied his rippling reflection in the glass. He brushed his hat on a coat sleeve, set it on his head again and looked at himself critically. 'How do I look?' he said suddenly.

'Wonderful,' Blue said. 'Very classy.'

'No. I mean really. Would you take me for a businessman?'

'The way the widow took you?'

'There is no need to get mouthy. I have an idea, is all, and you stand to profit by it, too.'

Blue laughed. 'You mean like in Cape Girardeau?'

Packy stiffened. His nostrils flared. 'All right,' Blue said. He looked at the shoddy blue suit. There was a small tear in one knee from the ladder and Packy's shirt and collar were peppered with cinder marks from the *Quennell*'s stacks. His shoes were cracked and scuffed. Blue shook his head. 'Packy, you don't look too good.'

'It will have to do. Come on.' Packy set off again, walking rapidly in his peculiar hitching gait. At the next corner he stopped at a vendor's high-wheeled cart. It was filled with trays of cakes and breads, shrimp and crab. 'Can't work on an empty belly,' Packy said. 'It's going to be a long night, where we're going.'

'*Pain-patate*, gent'men?' the black man said, gesturing.

The mingled fragrant odors from the cart made Blue giddy. Packy ordered from the trays and the black man wrapped the food in twists of newspaper. Packy paid the man and they went on a few yards; then Packy stopped next to an iron-grilled gate and opened one of the packets. 'It's a kind of bread made out of sweet potatoes —'

Blue took a piece gratefully and bit off a corner. His eyes fell on the twisted paper in Packy's hand. 'Clay!' he muttered and snatched it. Boldface headline type read: DARING CRIMINALS IDENTIFIED. *Zachary Murdock and Clay Russell Named – Escaped Four Courts Jail.*

Blue's voice shook. 'That's why Clay wouldn't make himself known to me.'

Packy looked at the paper. He frowned; but the pain and shock on Blue's face kept him from speaking. After a minute he touched Blue's shoulder. 'Come on, Blue.'

'He was supposed to be trading horses – that was all I ever knew,' Blue said dully. Packy tugged at his sleeve. Blue put one foot before the other and walked. Packy gave him a piece of the sweet potato bread and he ate, walking, without tasting it. They came to a broad cobbled street. Trolley cars rumbled, bells clanging and sparks crackling from the little wheels on the overhead wires.

'A man turns his head and everything changes,' Packy said. 'Last time I was on Canal Street, horses pulled the trolleys.' Blue stared at him. 'Look here, kid, I don't know what is going through your mind, his being your brother and all, but you are well off not being with them. Stickup is a wrong grift.'

'Wrong grift!' Blue flared. 'Mighty pious, aren't you?'

Packy sniffed. 'There is wrong grift and there is class grift, and the sooner you learn it, the better. Now we've got to get a little scratch together before we starve to death, but we can't do it if you don't take hold and pull your end.'

Packy shook him gently, then set out up Canal Street through the busy afternoon traffic. After a moment, Blue followed, his mind seething with hurt and sick comprehension. He had no idea where Packy was leading him. They crossed Canal Street, turned into a side street, and shortly came to an alley corner where a teamster was backing a four-mule dray wagon into a loading area on the alley side of the building.

'This is it,' Packy said. Three husky black men swung down the wagon's tailgate and began wrestling a big two-door safe off the wagon and onto a loading platform. A sign over the street door read LATOURETTE SAFE & LOCK COMPANY under a painted visored helmet and the slogan *Security is our Trade.*

'I'll do the talking,' Packy said. Blue followed him up some steps and into a large oak-paneled display room. New safes of different sizes and designs stood on either side of the room, all with doors open to display the interiors. Four desks were arranged behind a counter, and beyond through a large, arched doorway, Blue saw a big service shop and storage area, with light from the loading ramp spilling in.

A man with a pipe and sleeve garters shouted orders to the black men, directing them where to trundle the huge safe. From where he stood, Blue could see at least a dozen safes and five or six overalled men working at benches. A man wearing an eyeshade and a business suit left a desk and approached them. 'Hep you gentlemen?' His eyes roved quickly over them.

'Of a certainty,' Packy said, and Blue turned to stare at him because the word came out sounding like *sut'n'teh*. 'My name is Bristol – f'm Santone?' Packy went on in the altered accents. 'You must excuse my appea'ance – we have but just now got off the boat f'm Gavveston and she was a rough crossin.'

The man relaxed against the counter with a confidential smile. 'Thirty years in this business, suh, have taught me that it's what's in the wallet that counts, not what the wallet's in.'

Packy threw back his head and laughed, and punched Blue. 'Too clevah by hayf. Well, you doubtless wondrin why'm heah. Weah in the way of handling a little piece of change off'n'on – cattle, hawgs and cotton – and by god, suh, m' safe was broke open, *smaished* open is more like it. The scounnels cleaned me out. Ennaways, we needin a safe, and not a *sig*gar box this time.'

A well-dressed man with curled gray sidewhiskers and a silk hat entered behind them and walked straight to the counter. He rapped on it with a gold-headed cane. 'I want a word with you, Sage. I'm sure these men won't mind.' He glared at Packy and Blue.

Sage set his jaw and started to retort. Packy touched his sleeve and almost imperceptibly shook his head. 'Plenty time,' he murmured. Gratefully, Sage walked to the irate customer. The man said between his teeth, 'I've told you the damned machine was misbehavin. Now it's locked me out and I want to know what you are going to do about it. We caint shet down the Cotton Exchange on account of that misable box. That's where the cash is, man.'

'It is nothing more than a malfunction,' Sage said. 'I know we can put it to rights —'

'Well, goddammit, let's get on with it.'

'You understand, suh, we may have to drill, in order to penetrate the safe?'

'Drill? After the price we paid you for the son of a bitch?' The man's face was mauve. 'If you drill or otherwise mutilate that piece of propitty, you will have a summons pinned on your shirtfront. I will expect a man there first thing in the mornin!' He turned to go.

'Tomorrow afternoon is the soonest we can handle it,' Sage said grimly. 'Our chief mechanic is in Mobile tonight.'

'Nevertheless,' the man snarled, 'eight o'clock.' He strode away without a backward glance.

When Sage stepped back to Blue and Packy, his face was white and he was trembling. 'I deeply regret, gentlemen —'

'It don't matter none,' Packy said. 'Hell, us boys know a wrong card when it's cut.' Sage was writing on a card.

'Your safe then, Mr Bristol,' Sage said. He turned for a moment and put the card on a corner of his own desk. He swept his arm out at the display. 'We represent the leading companies. Here, in fact, is Kruger's great three-door Invincible, the very model that caused the capture of Murdock and Russell, the train robbers. Bad job they escaped the rope —' His face darkened. Blue's skin prickled. In sudden fascination, he stared at the massive safe, at the glittering boltwork and the terraced edges of the steel doors.

'Kruger's own mechanics were unable to break the Invincible,' Sage went on. 'Three sets of doors, you see, each designed differently, to foil the most diligent thief – the inner is a *ground* fit, like a watch case. Say your nitro-man got so far as the inner door. His soup would simply not flow into the seams.' He pushed back the two thick sets of outer doors and swung open the chunky door to the inner chest. A mischievous laugh bubbled in his throat. 'Supposing Russell and Murdock had bungled their way to the inner door – supposing they had somehow acquired the *combination*, itself. The time lock would have still prevented the door's being opened until the time set by the express people!'

'Mr Sage, I had in mind somethin ever bit as *stout*,' Packy said, 'only maybe not quite so *grand*. Our place in Santone, it's near the stockyards and the safe is gawn stand a foot deep in cow dab ennaways. Reckon you could show us something with the new wore off? Somethin yonder?' He nodded at the back room.

'Say no more,' Sage said. He opened a gate in the counter and motioned them toward the back room. 'We have the best line of safes and strongboxes built since the war —' In the doorway he stopped and looked intently at Packy. 'Mr Bristol, it seems to me that we have met before.'

'Not hardly,' Packy said.

'I never forget a face. It could have been years ago.' He tapped his teeth with a pencil.

'I went to Louisville once,' Packy said, 'on a Diamond Jo Line boat. Buried my old mother – look here, Mr Sage,' he interrupted himself, 'I see it's close on to quittin time. You got your desk to tidy up – spose you could let us poke around a few minutes? We can skin out the alley door thout bothern you, and be back first thing in the mornin. Don't have a red cent on me now, ennaways,' Packy grinned an ingratiating apology. 'Cross my heart, I won't carry one off in my hip pocket.' He nodded at the Kruger Invincible.

'Good enough,' Sage laughed. 'Make yourselves at home, gentlemen – I will see you in the morning.' He turned away, spoke to the foreman, nodding at Packy and Blue, then went on back to his desk in the front office.

A long double row of safes was banked along the side wall on the right, stretching to the far end of the long room, and many strongboxes of various sizes and designs were stacked among them. On the other wall were workbenches, racks of tools, boards covered with thousands of blank keys, and floor-to-ceiling shelves filled with locks and parts. Overhead, a big chain hoist rode an I-beam track.

Packy strolled negligently down the aisle between the rows of safes, stopping to try a door or to peer into the cabinetwork inside. Blue heard a rumbling noise. One of the black laborers drew a huge rolling door shut across the loading platform. He threw over a big iron handle to dog it shut. The foreman clamped a hasp over it and locked it with a padlock.

Blue and Packy came abreast of a door at the end of the room. Packy darted a glance back toward the foreman, opened the door suddenly and slipped through, pulling Blue with him. A dim bulb hanging from a dropcord lighted a row of lockers, a long sink and toilet booths, a closet filled with coats and coveralls and stacks of accumulated trash. Packy pushed aside some coats and steered Blue in behind them, then ducked in himself.

'What are we —' Blue said. Packy jerked his sleeve. They

heard voices. The door swung open and men entered.

'Did them customers leave all right?' one said, grunting as he climbed free of his coveralls. 'Must've. They aint here no more, the other said. 'Let's go lap up a leetle dish of beer, what say?' They hung up the coveralls and took out their coats. 'I'm your man,' the first one said. The light switch clicked and the door swung shut.

'Not a word,' Packy breathed. 'We'll give them a half hour, to make sure the place is empty, then go to work. Here —' Blue heard of soft crackle of newspaper and smelled *pain-patate*. They waited silently, eating sweet potato bread. Cold shrimp. Crab. Minutes passing.

'But the safes are all empty,' was the first thing Blue said.

'They are full of what you've got to learn,' Packy said, 'and that's all we're going to steal here. "The proper study of mankind is man." Did you ever hear that? No? I read that in the library in stir. You want to know something about safes, this is the place to come.'

'So Mr Sage did remember you.'

'Yes, but it was a long time ago and I looked different then. I used to come here to study my locks before a score, or a place like it in Cincinnati, if I was up north.'

A dim night light burned over the service door, but Packy found and lighted a lantern, after first taping all but a narrow slit of the glass. He took a labeled key off the wall over the foreman's desk, then turned to the racks of blank keys and quickly located a matching blank. He handed them to Blue.

'If you make us up our own key, we won't have to trouble Mr Sage again.'

Blue clamped the keys into a key-duplicating machine on the bench and began to crank. The cutting wheel bit into the brass blank. It was work he had done often in Israel's shop and it jogged bitter memory. 'Israel *told* me the Russells was crooks, thieves and jailbirds,' he blurted. 'I hated him for it, but now it turns out he was right – about me and Clay both.'

Packy examined a lock, whistling soundlessly. 'We are all put on earth for a purpose, only some people live all their lives and don't know what they're cut out for. Me, I was hooking pocketbooks from suckers on the horsecars when I was eight years old, so I was lucky enough to learn the game early and profit by it.'

'Lucky to be a thief?'

'A *class* thief,' Packy snapped. 'An artist. Not stickup trash—'

'Like my brother, is that it? You're talking about class but what I see in front of me is a tacky old jailbird.'

Packy's lips drew into a thin white line, then he sighed. 'You would break it right off in a man's gizzard, wouldn't you, Blue? If a suit of clothes is all you're bitching about, by tomorrow you and me both will look like Diamond Jim Brady.'

'What do you mean, tomorrow?' Blue said.

'The score stood right in front of you and you didn't tumble?' Packy grinned. 'The nasty gent in the silk hat – he wants someone to open his safe at eight o'clock in the morning. Mr Sage's man can't be there until after lunch. That gives us four hours. Look here.' He walked into the front office and took a card off Sage's desk. He returned, reading from it.

'Here is the job ticket. The nasty gent is named Ashburn. Ashburn, Tufts and LeBlanc, Cotton Brokers. Here is the number at the Exchange. The safe is a Heimlich Burglarproof. The malfunction is, he says here, a sticking dial, probably a broken fly.'

'Sage said it would have to be drilled.'

'We'll see about that,' Packy said. 'Get a screwdriver.' He took the card across the room to the rows of safes, stopping in front of one. 'Here is one, exactly the same. Take the backplate off the lock.'

Blue removed four screws from the plate on the lockbox set on the back of the safe door. Packy turned the wheels on the spindle. 'The fly is the little nub that sticks off each wheel, so that the wheel next to it will catch it and turn it when you turn the dial. Now, if that little nub should break off and get jammed between the wheels, you can't work the combination.'

'Then you're locked out,' Blue said. 'You do have to drill, the way Sage said.'

'Maybe.' Packy aligned the wheels with the tip of his screwdriver and watched the brass finger fall into the notches. A twist of the dial caused the bolt to slide back, freeing the handle to move the door bolts. He reached into a pocket and took out one of his silver dollar wheels. He held the screwdriver out straight and slipped the wheel over it – the notch in the edge of the dollar was nearly all the way down.

Packy gently tapped the screwdriver with a fingernail. The dollar moved slightly. He tapped again and the notch moved past the quarter, or three-o'clock position and stopped almost straight up. 'That wheel is trying to tell us something,' he said.

'The side with the notch is lighter,' Blue whispered. 'It wants to rise.'

'You have gone straight to the kernel of the matter,' Packy said. He turned the rearmost lock wheel until the notch was out to one side in the three o'clock position, then he tapped the side of the lockbox with the screwdriver handle. 'Birdsong,' he said, 'used to tell me about an express agent, Ohio, I think it was, or maybe Kentucky, who would show up for work at seven o'clock in the morning and find his safe door unlocked. But nothing was taken. Not a dime missing.' He continued tapping. Slowly the notch rose. 'It scared him half to death to think someone was opening that box every night. He loaded his shotgun with double-ought buck and planted himself next to the safe to spend the night. The trains rolled through – the ten o'clock, the midnight mail, and then at three in the morning, a long freight, and those trains fairly rattled his teeth. As that long freight pulled away, the feller heard a click. He tried the handle and the safe door opened. It was the trains, you see, rumbling through there, vibrating the wheels in the lock, just the way we're doing – the trains dialed the combination.'

As he tapped, the notch rose and reached the top, then stopped. The fence, the metal finger, did not fall.

'Maybe it worked on that one,' Blue said, 'but it won't work here.'

'In this lock, the fence doesn't fall quite straight down. It's a few degrees off. Now spose we were to tilt the lock? Stick a timber under the edge of the safe and lift her a trifle ...' Blue found a two-by-four and another short block of timber near the loading area. He put the block down as a fulcrum and levered the safe over at an angle. Packy tapped at the lock. 'More.' He went on tapping. 'More. More.'

The fence dropped with a firm click.

Packy laughed aloud. 'There! What did I tell y—'

But Blue had turned away. He was staring fixedly at the great Kruger Invincible squatting a few feet away massive, malevolent – the safe that had caused his brother to go to jail.

'You want to stay away from that one,' Packy said.

Blue gave a nervous start. 'Why? You claimed you could open anything.'

'And vanity and greed, I said, will put you away – stay away from it.'

'You mean you can't open it? Say you had plenty of tools and me to do the heavy work —'

Packy's face darkened. 'A man sticks with what he can handle,' he said lamely. 'I'd have to study it —'

'I could do it,' Blue said suddenly.

'You're a fresh kid, too,' Packy snapped.

'No, I mean it. I'm a smith, not a safe-breaker, but I could open it.' Blue's voice quickened with excitement. He knelt before the safe. 'What I would do is, first —'

'Come away from that damned thing!' Packy said.

'I think you're scared of it,' Blue said.

'Think what you please. I have stole a million dollars in my time, doing it my way, and I never took a fall until I was blown to pieces, and that wasn't my doing.'

Blue grinned. 'You want to make a small-time crook out of me, is that it? Where is the class in that?'

'You can wag your jaw all night if you want —' Packy huffed, then broke off and frowned curiously at Blue, for it suddenly came to him that the kid had swung around in his thinking. Absurdly pleased, Packy struck at the wheels of the lock. Clicking, they spun.

THE THIEF

New Orleans
November, 1899

CHAPTER XIV

They let themselves out with their own key a few minutes before seven o'clock in the morning. They wore cotton shop coats and Blue carried a long heavy toolbox. A light rain had fallen in the night and the streets were damp and fresh. On Canal Street, loaded trolley cars clanged and buggy tires hissed through puddles. Voices babbled in strange tongues.

They had worked at the locks for hours. Packy was a stern master – Blue could assemble that Heimlich lock blindfolded if need be. And working again, feeling the cold-slick polished metal under his fingers, with the smell of machine oil in his nostrils, Blue felt a curious, fierce excitement.

Now, lugging the toolbox in the bright morning light, he thought again of Clay – the very idea of a jailbreak, of a brother wanted for train robbery, took some getting used to. Blue shivered, yet the first chilling shock was gone – along with his own oppressive and haunting burden of dread. Walking, he felt his cheeks stretch in a foolish, elated grin.

Packy spent their last six cents at a street hawker's cart. They each had a piece of hot fried rice cake and a cup of *cafe au lait*, lingering over it on the crowded sidewalk before moving on. Off Canal Street, they found the Thibault Building, a splendid rococo structure in the financial district, near the Cotton Exchange.

They entered the echoing marble-and-tile lobby. A uniformed floor man intercepted them and Blue shuddered, but the man merely directed them to the service elevator. At eight o'clock they entered the glass-partitioned offices of Ashburn, Tufts and LeBlanc, on the fourth floor. Blue's pulse thundered. He glanced at Packy, who seemed utterly at ease. A young man wearing black sleeve guards over his cuffs and an eyeshade on his narrow skull left a desk to meet them.

'Latourette Comp'ny,' Packy said languidly. 'We heah to look at yoah safe.'

'Bout time,' the man sniffed. He was thin and the front of his starched white shirt crackled when he moved. 'Mist' Ashburn was fixin to *chew* the doah off.' He led them through a maze of cubicles separated by glass-topped partitions, to a handsomely carpeted area where mahogany-shuttered doors stood ajar to reveal carved lounge chairs and ornate desks, with oil portraits of past partners on the walls.

The clerk opened a door on which *Zenas Nesbitt, Cashier,* was lettered in gold leaf. There were two desks inside the paneled office. A young woman in a pale dress was just sitting down to the smaller of the two, inside the door on the right. A large carved mahogany desk stood across the room, and behind it in the corner was the safe. Lacquered a Chinese red with gold striping, it was bigger than the County Treasurer's safe in Cape Girardeau. On the door the firm's name was lettered in an arc of gold over an ornate cartouche framing an oil painting, an ante-bellum scene in which mountains of cotton bales were being loaded aboard a riverboat by files of smiling slaves, with hoop-skirted ladies and gentlemen in tall hats looking on.

'Miss Kirby will look after you,' the clerk said. He smirked at the girl. 'These men aim to fix the safe. Maybe we should call in a squad of Pinkertons to keep y'all company.'

'That does not strike me as amusing, Mr Dabney,' she said, with a prim smile at Packy. The clerk left, still smirking.

'In ouah line of work,' Packy said, 'we do get ribbed, but of course you know weah bonded.' He motioned Blue to the safe. 'But that is not to say weah not *human* – if there's a sack of diamonds in the thing, praps you'd consider runnin off to Bonas Aires with me.'

'What a divine idea,' she laughed. 'It does have a considerable sum of cash in it, I think. You will need to know the combination, I suppose. Unfortunately, Mr Nesbitt is not in yet.'

Packy took a card from his pocket. 'No, I have it right here. Kep it on file. I do spect its gawn be necessary to drill, though.'

She looked worried. 'Mr Ashburn will have apoplexy.'

'We will have to see how the patient responds.' He knelt before the safe and began to dial, referring to the combination written on the card. Miss Kirby left them and returned to her desk. Packy noted that she could see him perfectly well from her desk, as could anyone at the door; however, Mr Nesbitt's tall-backed swivel chair could be swung around to cover, at least partly, should he need it.

Miss Kirby swung around and saw him looking at her. She tapped a paper on her desk. 'Shipping news – I think you should know that a fast steam packet is leaving this afternoon for Brazil and the Argentine.'

'I declare, Miss Kirby, you will have me wrestling with the devil,' Packy said, turning the dial, feeling and listening. To Blue, he said, 'Two of the wheels are not picking up. Let's tip it up.'

Blue handed him a piece of cardboard from the toolbox, which had a penciled line on it marking the exact angle at which they had inclined the Heimlich safe in the Latourette shop in order to open it. Packy held the cardboard against the floor at the back corner of the safe while Blue levered the other side up with a pinch bar. When the safe met the penciled line, they slipped blocks under it to hold it.

'But what if the wheels won't turn now?' Blue whispered.

'Then of course it will have to be drilled.'

'By us?' Blue was astonished to feel that his fear had receded and that he was thinking now of the job itself, as a mechanical matter.

'Maybe,' Packy was answering, 'but Ashburn may squawk and we are likely to run out of time before the Latourette man gets here.' He handed Blue a four-pound smith's hammer and took a lighter one himself. He pointed to the several places along the side of the safe, on the forward edge, where Blue was to hit. 'Start now, as fast and steady as you can keep it up, and I'll work it on this side.'

Light, chinking blows. Bottom to top, steady as the ticking of the office clock. Miss Kirby looked alarmed at first, then she got up and closed the door, returned to her desk with a helpless shrug and a smile. Suddenly the door was thrown open.

'What in blazes is goin on in heah?' It was Ashburn, his pomaded sidewhiskers quivering. Then he saw Blue and Packy. He frowned. 'It's you, is it? I thought you were . . . customers.'

'Not atall,' Packy said. 'Mist' Sage was jess layin out some work for us. You said eight o'clock, so he put us on it.'

'Must you make that infernal racket?'

'Drillin would certainly be less noisy and maybe faster. We would weld the hole – plug it near good as new.'

'By god, I'll not have it! The heat would spoil my oil painting. Now, how long is this goin to take?'

Packy shrugged. 'No tellin, suh.'

Just then a small, fretful-looking man with spectacles pinching his thin nose and a gray derby hat in his hand came to the door. 'Ah, Zenas,' Ashburn said. 'Just in time for a meetin in my office, while these people pound on our safe. Damned place sounds like a stamp mill.' He started to turn, then stopped. 'Miss Kirby, you will stay here, of course. It would not do to leave the ... ah ...' He nodded slightly at Packy and Blue and the safe.

'One of yoah gentlemen suggested callin a squad of Pinkertons,' Packy said brightly. 'Possibly a depitty would serve as well. We would be glad of the rest if you want to call —'

'Officers will not be necessary.' Miss Kirby smiled capably. 'I have my shipping schedules to keep me busy here.'

Ashburn glowered at Packy. 'Your impertinence is misplaced.'

'I merely aimed to make light of the situation, suh,' Packy said earnestly. 'You realize, suh, weah *bonded*.'

Ashburn sniffed, then took the cashier's arm and left.

Miss Kirby closed the door and leaned back against it. Sighed deeply. 'No one joshes Mr Ashburn. Humility is the rule, gentlemen.' Suddenly she crossed her eyes and stuck out her tongue, rustled her skirts once in a little can-can step; then her prim office self returned and she sat down again at her desk.

Two blows a second, one hundred and twenty a minute, up the edge of the safe and back again. The four-pound hammer fused to Blue's hand, seemed after a time to move of its own accord and he watched his hand as if it had become a machine. Sweat ran into his eyes and soaked through his shop coat.

Packy stopped him, checked his dial readings. 'If I'm right, three of the notches are lined up and the other one is creeping around. Of course, it might just be stuck . . .'

Blue hammered. For a while he counted the blows, then lost track when he was up into the thousands. His mind wandered. He thought of Clay again and the blows faltered. Packy nudged him. Hammering, he thought of Cape Girardeau, realized that the fear was gone. For now.

Packy's left hand was on the dial as he rapped with the hammer with his right. The dial clicked solidly under his fingers. Startled, he put down the hammer, twisted the locking handle. It turned – the safe was unlocked, but he dared not open it. Blue stopped hammering. Packy motioned to him to continue, leaned close. 'Keep it up until we can be alone with it for a minute.'

Blue hammered. His arm glowed with hot, aching fatigue. Miss Kirby looked at them once, covered her ears with her hands and smiled gamely, then turned back to her work. Blue thought he could not go on. The door opened and Ashburn stood there glaring and furiously chewing a cigar. Packy touched Blue's arm.

'You people have driven me plumb to the verge of despair,' Ashburn said around his cigar. 'How do you spect us to conduct business when we caint heah one another?'

'Praps it ought to be done at night,' Packy said. 'But I'm afraid we will have to recommend to Mr Sage that drillin is the only course. Our chief mechanic will be here directly, and he can confirm my judgment, as I believe he will.'

'The whole affair confirms *my* judgment,' Ashburn snarled, 'that the country has fallen into an advanced state of *dee*-cay. The workin class has altogethah abandoned doin an honest day's work, by god if it isn't the truth! Now you men pack up this rubbish and leave the premises.' Ashburn's face was liver-colored. He turned to Miss Kirby. 'Bring your book into my office at once, Miss Kirby. And I think you can return to your desk now, Zenas.'

Packy inclined his head humbly. Blue felt an ecstatic shout gurgling around under his ribs, trying to get out. Mr Nesbitt went uneasily to his desk as Ashburn and Miss Kirby left, she with a fleeting backward glance. Of shared sorrow, Blue thought. Nesbitt looked unhappily at the safe and the tools spread out on the dropcloth. 'Mr Ashburn does cherish that painting,' he said, nodding at the safe door.

'The old home place, no doubt,' Packy said.

'Actually no – he would not like this noised about, but Mr Ashburn is from Philadelphia. He married into – ouah people.' Nesbitt sighed and began making entries in a ledger.

Packy and Blue knelt, began picking up tools. Packy pointed to the dropcloth, pantomimed holding it spread wide, like a curtain. 'Here, now, Adams,' he said gruffly, 'fold the tarp. I will get the rest of the tools.' He shook a handful of wrenches, made them chink. Blue stood with his back to the safe and spread the canvas wide, as if to fold it. Behind this curtain, Packy swung the safe door open. Inside were stacked ledgers and letter files and a bank of brass-knobbed, rosewood drawers. Blue shook the canvas. Packy began opening drawers. Found stock certificates, other documents. Small bills in the fourth drawer. Large bills in the fifth.

Zenas Nesbitt pushed back his chair, swiveled to see what they were doing. He frowned up at Blue, who looked innocently back at him over the edge of canvas that he held stretched taut under his chin.

'Whatever are you doin?' Nesbitt said.

'I was about to fold this, sir, but you have rolled your chair onto it.' Blue nodded down. Nesbitt muttered an apology and rolled his chair back, then returned to his ledger as Blue heard the faint whisper of paper behind him and vigorously shook the tarp to produce crackling noises.

'That appeahs to be the lot,' Packy said. Blue folded the canvas, his throat swelling again with that joyful bubbling. He made a snug square of the canvas and stuffed it in on top of the tools. Packy negligently reached out and twirled the dial. Zenas Nesbitt did not look up as they left.

Miss Kirby met them in the carpeted hallway. She rolled her eyes ever so slightly. 'I do hope you gentlemen were not offended by the show of temper this morning.' She smiled. 'Actually, most days, it's much worse.'

'Then you are well-prepared to see it erupt again this afternoon after our chief mechanic renders his own diagnosis,' Packy said. 'It grieves me to say goodbye to you, howevah. Praps another time?'

'In Bonas Aires?' she said, walking with them. 'I don't think you can know how much I'd love to.' And at the door she looked down the corridor to see if anyone was watching, then blew them a kiss and whispered, 'Come back, hear?'

They put the toolbox down in the outer corridor and slipped out of their shop coats. 'We can just leave the tools by the door for the chief mechanic,' Packy said. He rang for the elevator, folding his own coat into a tidy bundle, the stuffed pockets turned inside, and tucked it under his arm. Machinery whirred within the elevator shaft. Looking down through the painted grillwork, Blue saw the cage rising. Then it was there, the door opening. Among the passengers was a large man wearing a tan cotton shop coat and carrying a heavy toolbox with 'Latourette Safe Co.' stenciled on the side of it. Blue and Packy stood aside to let him out, then entered the cage and the grilled door closed. As the cage started down, they saw the man stop in the corridor, his head cocked curiously as he looked at the toolbox sitting by the door of Ashburn, Tufts and LeBlanc, which also bore the stenciled words, 'Latourette Safe Co.' Then the cage dropped and he was gone.

They left the elevator on the ground floor and went out onto the street, turning back toward Canal Street. Choking sounds of joy burbled from Blue's throat.

Packy grinned back. 'The mechanic already knows something is haywire. That gives us a few minutes before they get into the cash drawer – let's make ourselves scarce.'

A trolley approached from the direction of the river. They hurried to catch it. Packy deftly extracted a dollar bill from his folded coat and paid the fare as they boarded. They settled into a cane-backed seat.

'We'll ride the cars for a while, changing now and then,' Packy said, 'then we'll work over toward Prytania Street. There used to be an eye doctor there, a yellow house it was, with an iron fence out front. I remember he was considered to be a magician when it came to fitting a glass eye.'

CHAPTER XV

Only a few hours after the temperance-minded foreman of the Yellow Rose Mining Company had his scalp split open by a pistol barrel, and the payroll removed from his keeping, a telegraphed report describing the incident was on Havenhurst's desk in St Louis. He called Bassett into his office and showed him the report. Bassett read it and nodded. 'It's Russell and Murdock, no question about it.'

'I spoke to the chief in the Chicago office,' the super said. 'He reluctantly approved your assignment, on the basis that we receive some kind of proof that Murdock and Russell have indeed joined forces with other outlaws in such a way that they appear to be headed for something big. They have connected with their old pals, all right, but notice that the haul was only a little over three thousand.'

Bassett shrugged. 'It's grocery money. They'll need time to set up a big one.'

'Supposing you take a day or two to clear up your affairs here —'

'To write my will, you mean?'

'— while I scrape up some money to bankroll you.'

Blue's first glimpse of Maison Lafitte came as he turned their hired buggy off the river road and into the long lane of moss-hung oaks. There it sat, a grand old house squatting in the embrace of its Corinthian columns.

'Crooks, sports or senators,' Packy said, 'they all meet up here.'

'What about the law?' Blue said.

'Shew! When it suits the politicians and the rich sporting crowd to hobnob with crooks, the law stays away, you bet. Pretty near any town of substance has its Lafitte House, where a roving man can get his tea leaves read and catch up on his mail or play a hand of cards.'

'Mail?'

Packy laughed. 'You think I'm going to step up and sing out my name at the General Delivery window? When a man changes his monicker as often as his shirt, this is the only way to reach him. Or it could be at Fanny Porter's in Fort Worth, or maybe Miss Francie's in Kansas City, see?'

Even after a week, Blue was not used to having Packy look at him with two eyes, the second bright blue like the first though not moving in perfect concert with it. A touch of make-up served to reduce the scar on his face, and where before his leanness had made him look half-starved and scrawny, he now appeared lithe and elegant in a suit of fine blue worsted. Blue himself felt dashing and reckless in charcoal cheviot and high-heeled Cuban boots as they swung up before the regal entry and left their rig in the care of a silk-turbaned black boy.

And Blue, seeing how Packy was embraced at the door by an aged and saintly-looking man in evening dress, was impressed to see tears in the old man's eyes. Shortly then, in a richly carpeted, walnut-paneled dining room, Blue was eating what he took to be a rare and succulent steak, though it was called *Boeuf Châteaubriand*. The same old gentleman brought Packy an envelope. 'You see, my boy, we 'ave keep your mail for you, as always.' And he swept out again, snapping his fingers at more turbaned boys. Reading from the yellowed paper, Packy began silently to laugh. Unable to speak, he dabbed at his eyes with his napkin – tears sprang from the glass eye as well as the good one – and handed Blue the letter.

Dere Packey – Sence I knowe you do not Like Puff May Be you wold as soon Pass on this One it is a Kruger & I have to Snuff it Your roll is putt away Safe Give the girls a Kiss for me See you In KC next Month – Leo

'This must have got here a day or two after I left,' Packy gasped. 'I caught a boat upriver to meet Birdsong, and when I saw him, he said to me, "Didn't you get my letter? – well nevermind, you're here now, let's go." So we did, and we got ourselves blown up.' The laughter was gone and Packy wagged his head bleakly.

'What's this about your roll?' Blue's eyes stung too as he sipped his drink – a Sazerac, it was called, swirling amber in the candelight, fuming in his gullet.

'When we left Texas, I had over a hundred thousand dollars and I meant to set some aside for a rainy day. But money had a way of slipping through my fingers in those days, so I kept a few thousand for table money and told Birdsong to keep the rest for me until our next score. I figured to quit the game, see, and take my girl to Paris, or maybe Mexico. It's there yet, Blue, wherever he put it.'

After they had eaten, they went into the gaming parlor. Great crystal chandeliers glittered above the tables. The room hummed with sound. Blue noted with interest that most of the ladies were very young and daringly gowned. He was unused to such opulence, and for a moment he hung back in the doorway. Packy gave him a little push. 'You aint shoeing horses anymore, Blue. Try to show a little style – you don't want to look like a rube.'

Packy's voice had taken on a buzzing quality and seemed slightly muffled. Blue's mouth was dry, his lips feverish. A waiter appeared holding a silver tray and Blue took a stemmed glass of something pale and frosty with bubbles rising in it. It cooled his lips. He drank gratefully.

Before them was a roulette table ringed by people in evening clothes. A space opened at the rail and Packy moved into it. Double eagles glinted, slipping from his fingertips onto the marked squares. Blue flinched at the spray of wealth, but the wheel was already spinning. He felt his wrist clutched. Looking down, he saw an old woman with diamonds in her hair, the nose on her like the bright cutting edge of a hatchet. She wore a monocle and smoked a thin black cheroot. 'For luck, sweet darlin,' she croaked. Then the stick man pushed chips across the table. She cawed a laugh and her talons raked Blue's wrist.

Blue tipped up his glass and drank. Through the crystal, the figure of a girl across the table from him shimmered, her dress of pale amber silk miraculously blending into the amber of the wine in his glass so that she appeared to be hovering naked in a golden bubbly sea. Pleased with the effect, he peered intently at her. At that instant she looked up, and through his glass he saw her smile. He looked over the glass. She inclined her head to acknowledge his apparent salute. Startled, Blue grinned uncertainly. She nodded at the elderly man beside her and shrugged, pouting a little.

Packy pushed chips into Blue's hand. 'Play red or black, either one, until you get the hang of it. The odds are even up, see?'

Someone refilled Blue's glass. Packy was gone. Blue set his jaw and stepped up to the table. When the wheel spun, his head seemed to spin with it, but the wine was refreshing. He put two chips on the black. The ball spun, clicked in the wheel slots, stopped. Black. The stick man paid him. The old woman caught his arm again. By the time he squirmed free, he saw that he had won again. 'Darlin boy,' she croaked.

Blue felt movement on his left. It was the girl in the amber silk dress. Negligently, she placed chips here and there on the table. Her eyes flickered at Blue. She wore a single pale amber stone hanging from her neck on a thin gold chain. When she moved to place her bets, the stone rolled in and out of its deep nest. Blue realized that he had forgotten the game. He wrenched his eyes away and saw that his stack had doubled, then doubled again. Dazed, he drank from his glass, which unaccountably was still full. He held back chips, moved the rest to black.

The girl laughed, moved her chips next to his as the wheel spun. They both won. Looking now at his chips, Blue could not remember how much they represented – they were hard to count anyway, appearing to divide before his eyes as he watched. He moved back to red and the girl followed, murmuring, 'Next time ask for Nicole.' *Ask who?* he thought.

The stick man called for bets. A heavy dark hand reached from Blue's right to place chips close to his stack. The thick hand hovered for a moment, then drew back. Blue shook his head and blinked – his stack appeared to be shorter. He could not be sure because he could not remember how much he had let ride. He bent forward, looking for the owner of the hand. The old woman leered, blew cigar smoke at him. Next to her stood a powerfully built dark man, with scar tissue glistening in his heavy brows and lumping his cheeks. The ball spun, fell, paying 23 red. Blue and the girl lost. It stung him to lose. Blue frowned and doubled his bet, a tall stack, and the girl matched it.

The dark man played again. The big hand hovered, moved across Blue's stack to drop chips beyond, then withdrew. Blue blinked and rubbed his eyes.

'What the hell,' Nicole said. Then her voice shrilled. 'Did you see that?' And Blue, unable to stop himself, caught the thick hand and twisted. Chips, pinched into the palm at the base of the man's thumb, spilled onto the table.

The dark man wrenched his hand away. Rage warped his jaw. 'You son of a bitch – you want your ears chewed off?' The old woman's cheroot fell from her lips and she backed away.

'What's this now?' the stick man said.

'That ape is palming checks,' the girl said. The topaz stone rolled free of its nest and quivered, then fell back.

'You going to listen to that tart?' the dark man snarled.

'I'm the one that hobbled you,' Blue said.

The dark man made a gargling noise in his throat and lifted his right hand like a maul. He was seized on both sides. Two big men in evening clothes had materialized and now held him fast. Around them stepped a dwarf, a squat chunky little man with the head of a giant and diamond studs glittering on his shirt front. His black mustache hung in waxed spikes around his cigar.

'Keep you shirt on, Jamie,' he said to the dark man, then grinned at Blue. There was no warmth in the grin. 'I de proprietor here – call me Rosario, kid. You going to prove this?'

'I saw it. He topped my stack – I know because this lady here had bet the same amount.' Blue pointed. The girl's stack was four or five chips taller.

Rosario rocked on three-inch heels. 'Easy to make a little mistake, when you playin, don' you think?'

'They were in his hand,' Blue said.

Rosario reached out, touched Blue's hand. Blue opened it and saw that he was holding a dozen checks. Rosario gestured around the table. 'Everybody here holdin de checks, kid. It ain mean nothin. How else to bet?' He squinted through cigar smoke, grinning. 'Spose you gents shook hands, we all go back to playin. De table top off you stack, kid. What say, gents?'

'Not me,' growled the dark man. 'By god, I will see his teeth on the ground before I'm done.'

Blue saw Packy staring at him, white-faced. The girl caught at his sleeve. 'That ape, he called me a tart,' she pouted. The table and the people around it seemed to Blue to dip suddenly, then take a great swooping turn. Rosario sucked on his cigar.

Blue was trapped. Behind him, a man whispered, 'Look at the shoulders on the kid – he would go one-ninety easy.' And another voice said, 'Hell, Jamie would eat him up.'

'Are you talkin two to one?' the first voice said.

'All right – two to one if the kid don't eat crow.'

'Save me a hundred of that,' the old woman hissed.

Rosario rapped the table with his knuckles. 'Say de word, kid. We trow him out and he don' bother you no more. Is you play.'

Blue swallowed. The room dipped again. He saw Packy shake his head slightly. *How did I get into this?* he thought. A voice said, 'I don't need you to throw him out.' His own voice. Excited babble rose around him. *What did I say?* Blue thought. Packy looked sick.

'Then maybe we step out into de garden, gents,' Rosario said, and Blue found himself caught in a warm, babbling tide, swept dizzily through great French doors into a lantern-lit garden. Beyond a brick-paved patio was a square plot of grass roofed by the moss-hung branches of a great live oak.

Someone was pulling at Blue's coat, peeling it off. Packy. 'What the hell got into you?' he snarled in Blue's ear. The girl stripped off his tie. A few feet away, Jamie Dakin shrugged out of his ruffled shirt and turned, working his heavy shoulders. His hard belly shuddered with muscle under a crinkly black thatch.

Packy pushed Nicole's hands away and tugged at Blue's shirt. 'Hey,' Blue said, 'be careful of my new shirt.'

'Shut up and listen to me. The thing for you to do is bite the dirt, get me?'

Voices clamored, making bets. Packy turned away suddenly,

saying, 'I'll cover that. Make it five hundred?' Blue was absurdly pleased.

Blue's heart pounded. 'Ends only one way—' Rosario was saying, 'when de man don' get up. No argument then, see?'

The noise of voices was swallowed by the thudding in Blue's ears. He was alone on the grass facing the other man, the faces melting into a blur, a ring of color splashed against the darkness, and Dakin was grinning and moving in, working his shoulders and making snuffling noises. The left hand darted, struck like a snake and Blue's head snapped back. He tasted a raw lip, salt. The hand darted. Blue could not get out of its way. Stabbing, it struck his ear, his cheek, eye – the ear again, and Blue felt a warm trickle down his neck.

Knuckles chunked against his nose and Blue's head whirled. He stumbled, ducked and covered up with elbows and forearms. The hand hooked across his shoulder and caught his ear again. Panic fluttered through him, but at that moment someone laughed. He looked past Dakin's grinning face and saw the old woman. She cawed around her cheroot. Blue's panic congealed into rage. He bulled in under Dakin's arms and pumped solid blows to his belly and ribs, drove him back gasping.

The grin was gone. Dakin cocked the heavy right hand, ready now to tear his head off. Blue crouched, his body bent far forward, his head and shoulders thrusting, feinting. *And he was back now at the forge, fourteen, sixteen years old, the smiths putting aside dinner pails to watch Augie roughouse him, bullet-headed Augie with arms like tattooed nail kegs saying kid, it's awright, you moving like Corbett, but gim a shot adda head, see? and lem bust a duke on it . . .*

And Dakin, now furious, swung at the offered head. Blue heard through his own skull the crunch of knucklebones. Found himself on one knee, blinking, but rose and saw Dakin's jaw hanging open, the eyes squinched with shock and agony, the shattered hand puffing like a squash. Dakin held the hand before him, crooning to it, and kicked at Blue's crotch. Blue twisted away, ducked his head and butted. Dakin caught him and hung on with the good hand. Blue felt the fingers clawing for his eyes. In horror, he uncoiled and the back of his head caught Dakin in the mouth and nose. Timbery cracking sounds filled Blue's head.

Swaying, Blue looked for Dakin through the mist. He shook his head, found him. Dakin was on his back in the grass, his face, neck and chest spattered with blood. His lips puffed around broken teeth and his nose was flat with his face. Blood leaked from his ears into the grass. Blut contemplated him at a time, then turned and shambled with great concentration toward the fountain. People moved away to let him pass. It was a long, long walk. He reached the fountain and studied the sparkling lights caught in the falling water. Then he fell in.

Blue felt stinging slaps, and then cold water was dashed in his face. Sputtering, he pawed at the hands. 'You there now, Blue?' Packy's voice, a long way off. 'Stay with it, Blue – hang on.' Water dashed again, trickled down his neck in icy runlets. He opened his eyes and light exploded into his brain. He blinked, cowering. It was sunlight, streaming through the branches of a tree. He was on his hands and knees on a muddy creek bank by the roadside. His fine charcoal suit was a stained ruin. Blue shuddered. After a moment, he allowed himself to be led up the creek bank. He recognized their hired buggy and the gray horse. With a great effort he climbed into the buggy. Packy shook out the lines and the horse broke into a trot. Blue's head thundered. Looking back along the river road, he saw the great old plantation house squatting in the embrace of its colonnade among the live oaks. Somewhere ahead was the Canal Street ferry that would take them back to New Orleans.

Packy appeared determined to devote himself to his driving, though a corner of his mouth twitched suspiciously. Blue started to speak, then stopped, helpless. His tongue was a shapeless mass, glued to the roof of his mouth. In place of memory, he sensed a vast aching void behind his eyes. The buggy tires lisped. Patches of sunlight whirled past. He strained to pull fragments of memory from the void.

He remembered Dakin, bloody, stretched out in the grass. Then hands carrying him, and the face of the dwarf, Rosario, grinning down at him and waving the cheroot. Drifting away then, and Blue was floating in the billows of a great canopied bed and the two of them, Nicole and the little dark one, Lola – was that it? – were tearing at his sodden clothes. The amber stone spun close over his face and Nicole poured fiery brandy into his mouth. Choking, he rolled off the bed into deep carpeting and tried to crawl away, but they grappled with him on the floor, shrieking and squealing, and he was hobbled by the trailing legs of his britches. Bearing them both with him, he crept snakelike through a doorway. Steam roiled in his face. An enormous black woman loomed out of the steam. With hands like bear traps, she caught his arms and skidded him across wet marble into a great sunken tub. He surfaced blowing and flailing and saw her disappear into the steam carrying his clothes, then ice water poured onto his skull – it was Nicole, kneeling above him on the marble with a pitcher upended, and Lola, the dark one, next to her. Blue swept them both screeching into the water. He remembered slick wet softness and damp coils of hair falling about his face and warm wash of breath and tangled limbs. *Both of them?* He marveled. But that was later. And the gambling room again, and more drinks, money, wads of it, Dakin, his face masked under sticking plaster, shaking hands, pawing him, hugging him. Somewhere the memory stopped.

Blue squirmed on the seat of the buggy. 'Don't fret,' Packy said. 'You'll be back, soon enough.'

Blue shuddered. 'Not me. I've had enough.'

'There is no such thing as enough,' Packy said, 'though a man could almost get caught up for a little while at a time.'

'Work – that's something I know about. What I want is to get back to work.'

'There is a place in Baton Rouge, on the river. Let me tell you about it . . .'

CHAPTER XVI

'It's a rare thing,' the super said to Bassett, 'to watch the development of a criminal from the very beginning.'

'Meaning?'

'Blue Russell, of course.' The super waved sheets of the agency's yellow report paper. 'After that peculiar business in Cape Girardeau, I sent a bulletin to our branch offices asking to be informed of anything involving a man of Disbrow's description and a youthful accomplice. Now here is a response from New Orleans. It appears your one-eyed cripple and the kid cleaned out a cotton broker's safe in broad daylight – during business hours, in fact. The safe was out of whack and they claimed to be mechanics from the safe company.'

Bassett laughed. 'Did they make wages?'

'Something on the order of eighty-seven hundred dollars – and the operative reports that the two of them embarked on a glorious spree in a palace of sin called the Lafitte House, where the kid mopped up a tough named Dakin. The New Orleans sporting crowd is full of gossip about it.'

'Are we on the case?'

'We are now. The brokerage house has called us in on it. Foolish of Disbrow to show himself that way – they will be in the bag inside a month, my word on it. These old crooks – they lose something in stir.'

'A genius with safes, though,' Bassett said. 'What do you reckon he would do with the Kruger Invincible?'

'He would know enough to stay away from it.' The super laughed. 'Hell, it was a Kruger that got him blown up.' He hesitated, looking speculatively at Bassett. 'You're ready to go, are you?'

'If you've got my bankroll,' Bassett said.

The super opened a drawer and took from it a packet of bills. He riffled through them, then tossed the packet to Bassett. 'All thousands. Unsigned bank notes, so don't go trying to spend any of it.'

'A train robber would be an idiot to try passing a thousand-dollar bill.'

'But he would be too greedy to throw the stuff away, right?' The super set out a smaller stack of bills and some gold coins. 'And here is a thousand in legitimate money. You will owe us an accounting.' He glared at Bassett, who sorted the money and grinned wryly at him. It seemed to the super that Bassett did not always feel the weight of his responsibility. A little annoyed, he went on. 'And what name have you given our train robber?'

'I was born in Bucklin, a little town over on the Mussel fork of the Missouri – let's call him Bucklin. Preacher Bucklin.' Bassett pocketed coins and paper money.

The super nodded, then smiled acidly. 'In truth, I have wondered if Bassett disguised were not closer to the real Bassett.'

'Whoever *that* is – when I look in the mirror, I aint sure anymore.'

'You already sound like him.' The super glowered. He was always nettled at Bassett's disconcerting way of shedding his identity – it made the super want some affirmation of loyalty, which in turn made him feel foolish. 'This Bucklin will be out of touch with us for a long time —'

Bassett appeared to read his mind. 'It could be mighty hard to come back to this. I never minded sand in my beans or sleepin on the ground.'

The super stirred. Was Bassett pulling his leg? 'I'll be damned if I'll offer you more money,' he blurted.

Bassett laughed sardonically. 'If I was in it for the money, Bucklin would never come home.'

The super fumed inwardly and changed the subject. 'Even though you'll be working out of the Denver office, I'll want copies of your reports – getting the collar on Russell and Murdock again is important to me. If *Bucklin* has to get in touch with me, he can use Neilsen's Saloon as an address.'

Bassett nodded. A thought struck him. 'Let me know, will you, if you get any word on Blue Russell or Disbrow. I'm curious to see how long the kid can hack it.'

Two hours later Bassett boarded a train for Denver.

As Bassett's train rolled west through Kansas, Packy and Blue were in their hotel room on Royal Street. The floor, two beds and a table were covered with Packy's paper collection of unopened safes, all unwrapped and spread out. He walked among them, picking out one, then another, setting them aside. At length, he put away all but those few.

'These six,' he said to Blue, 'are all in this part of the country.

Here's a Pierce-Stahl in Shreveport, another Heimlich in Alexandria, a Hall in Baton Rouge. The Pierce-Stahl will have to be drilled. With some practice working on the lock, we can probably finger the Heimlich. The others —'

'Baton Rouge is closest,' Blue said.

'Right, and I cased that one myself – it's in a factory building on the river front —'

'Then why didn't you —'

'Because Birdsong thought we ought to work north for a while. I never got back to it. But I figured a way to take it, if you're game.'

'You know I'm game.'

Packy laughed. 'You'll see. If you want to take it first, we'll need a few pieces of equipment.'

'I want to take them all,' Blue said.

Packy stared at him. 'Could it be that your eyes are bigger than your belly? Remember what I said, greed and vanity —'

'It aint greed. If safe-breaking is going to be my line of work, I ain't going to go at it the way my brother and Zack Murdock did, like a couple of rubes with their shoelaces tied together.'

'You've got to know your locks then. Look here, we'll pick up one or two at Latourette's for you to work on, and put em back when we're through – that way no one is wise to us and we'll be able to go again, when we need to for another job.'

At about the time Bassett was alighting in Denver's Union Station, Blue and Packy, soberly dressed in well-cut dark suits, were ushered into the office of the president of Louisiana Gum Distillers in Baton Rouge. It was an airy, high-ceilinged room, balconied, on the upper floor of a great old brick river-front factory where once black powder had been manufactured to repel Grant. Now it smelled of turpentine.

'You might have give me some notice.' The president, whose name was Callard, did not rise or offer to shake hands.

'Surely, suh,' Packy said, 'you recall Mr Sage explaining our obligation to you at the time you purchased the safe – that we would clean and adjust the works of the lock at intervals —'

'But that was ten years ago!'

Packy smiled. 'Yes, suh, that's the interval. Caint hardly nothin go wrong with em, you know. Now the way we work, we will ask you to open the safe and we will leave the room while you do it. Weah bonded, of course, but that way you can feel see-cure.'

Thus disarmed, Callard shortly had the safe open, both the outer door and the smaller inner door to the burglarproof chest. 'I spect I best remove the money, too,' he said. Bulbous pockets on either side of his thin, curved nose seemed to impart a nasal whinny to his voice. 'Naturally, I know to the penny what's in the box anyways.'

'As you wish,' Packy said. Callard shrugged and sat back to watch, his close-set eyes narrowed under his frown. Blue had opened a handsome fitted toolcase and was expertly removing the backplate of the door lock. He flicked dust away from the lockbox with a camel-hair brush, then dampened a piece of flannel with solvent and wiped the gleaming brass parts. He removed and cleaned the wheels – each with its inner disc, by means of which the combination was set or changed. He oiled them and replaced them on the post. 'Pretty as a handmade watch,' he said.

'Yes,' Callard said, pleased, 'but I was never certain we needed it – we run dawgs in the yard, you know, and gents, them bastards are big as lions.'

Packy laughed warmly and stepped through French doors onto the iron blacony where he could look down into the narrow, brick-paved yard, three floors down. 'I see the rascals,' he said. 'They would make a meal of a man, if ever he was to get over that wall first.'

'The broken glass on top was my idee,' Callard said. 'More than one son of a bitch has left his guts hangin on that glass.' Packy nodded judiciously, noting how the brick steeple of the old church across the narrow street rose beyond the wall.

Blue finished the second lock, then wiped off the locking bars and tested their articulation by working the handle. 'Smooth as silk – you want me to close her up?' he asked and when Callard nodded, he closed the doors in order, spinning the dials to lock them.

Outside on the sidewalk three minutes later, Blue took pencil and paper from his pocket and wrote down two sets of numbers. 'You sure he didn't know I could read the combinations off the wheels?'

'He watched and didn't say a word – a man who knows something *secret* likes to show it off. And he was getting something for nothing. He didn't want to miss that.'

They ate supper at an excellent restaurant and afterward attended a repertory company production of *Macbeth*. Back in their hotel room, Blue practiced manipulating the Heimlich lock – whenever he successfully fingered it open, Packy would reset the combination. At 3 A.M., they left the hotel by the service entrance and walked three blocks to the factory. Streets along the waterfront were poorly lighted and they were not seen. Packy paused by the glass-topped wall near where he had seen the dogs. He threw five pounds of beef, cut into small chunks and laced with chloral hydrate, over the wall, a few pieces at a time. He heard a tentative bark on the other side, then snuffling and snorting and low growls. Waiting, he shortly heard a soft, drawn-out whine, then one or more deep sighs. He *meow*ed, listened and walked on.

Above him, Blue, having slipped into the church and climbed the stairs to the bell tower, heard the *meow* and crawled out onto the narrow parapet of the steeple. Crouching there, he swung a small, sheepskin-wrapped iron grapnel on the end of a light rope and loosed it in the direction of Callard's balcony. On the second cast, it hooked on to the balcony rail with a muffled *thunk*. He ran the rope through a small pulley and tied it off at the steeple, then took a firm grip on a strap suspended from the pulley and launched himself into the darkness. Silently, he sped across the sixty feet of space above the narrow street and bricked factory yard to the balcony. The French doors were not even locked. In less than three minutes he was back on the balcony. He dropped the grapnel into a canvas bag under his coat, then retied the rope to the balcony rail using a simple slipped hitch. Among the strands of the silk rope was a fishing line. Blue tied the end of the line to the end of the rope where it was tucked through his hitch knot, then he took the rope again, hand over hand this time because it was slightly uphill. When he was halfway across, three drunken roustabouts passed beneath him on the street, singing a bawdy saloon song. Grinning to himself, Blue hung there until their backs were to him, then made his way hand over hand to the steeple. There he untied his rope, located the fishing line within its strands and pulled the distant loop of knot loose, the fishing line sliding easily within the rope. He retrieved the rope and coiled it. A block from the church, Packy stepped out from behind a parked wagon to meet him.

'Slick as a pearl,' Packy said.

When they were in their hotel room, Blue took off his coat and shook it upside down. Packets of money fell from inside pockets, spilling onto the bed. Blue threw himself into a chair, laughing. 'Going across there on the rope – I never wanted it to end. Do you know what I mean?'

Packy stared at the money. 'I know,' he said softly. 'You want to count it?'

Blue waved a hand. 'You count it if you want, I don't care – I'm too fired up.'

'Cool off on the train. We'll have supper at the Lafitte House.'

'No, I don't want to cool off, Packy. I want to go on to Natchez – today.'

'Without a break?' Packy looked troubled. 'A man can get careless, Blue.'

Blue reached over and took the brass Heimlich safe lock from his grip and gently turned the dial, listening to the faint clicks and whispers within the box. He shook his head. 'I'm ready to go. If I put it off, I'll start thinkin about it.'

Late in the morning, Harlan Sage, manager of Latourette Safe Company, was called to the telephone. 'Pinkertons, you say? – I was fixin to call you people anyway.' He listened intently, then said, 'well, damn it all – this business of burglars using our name at the Cotton Exchange has worried me half to death, and now you say they have done the same thing in Baton Rouge? This caint go on, you know! Yes . . . well, here is why I aimed to call you. One of our shop men has found a couple of safe locks missing – maybe more, we don't know, they are just odd parts. Now who would steal a lock without the safe? I wouldn't even mention it, except that the same thing happened ten or twelve years ago ... No, we never put a guard on – they only amounted to a couple of brass boxes, and that would have been like locking the barn door after the horse was stole, wouldn't it? So there wasn't no *need*, but later, they turned up again ... No, there was no chance we simply mislaid them. And this is what I'm getting at – there was a string of safe-breakings then, too ... Suspicions? Well, there was a man in here about the time of that mess at the Cotton Exchange. I know I've seen him before – I never forget a face, see – and I think it was back around the time I told you about ... You damned right we will this time. As for warning all the customers with those types of safes, I don't hardly think it's possible, less we take a year to do it ... Yes, and you let me know, hear?'

In Natchez, some two and a half days after Harlan Sage's telephone call from the Pinkerton man, Blue Russell climbed to the roof of a three-story building by means of a drainpipe; then he went from roof to roof almost the length of the block and entered an office building after picking the lock on the stairwell door. On the floor below, the door of E-Z-Way Trading Co. – Mortgages Our Specialty – yielded to his pick. He fingered the Heimlich safe open in nine minutes. But except for a few scraps of paper, the safe was empty. Blue stifled a desire to laugh, then cautiously played his shrouded lamp about the room. The wall calendar read July, 1898. The desk was littered with paper. Blue ran a finger through a thick coating of dust. The front page headline of a crumpled newspaper read SPANISH FORCES IN SANTIAGO SURRENDER. An item near the bottom of the page caught his eye – *Local Land Dealers Cited in Swindle.* The lead paragraph mentioned two firms, Golden Rule and E-Z-Way. Blue did not read on. Going back across the roofs, he wondered if E-Z-Way had escaped the law. He would never know.

Packy was waiting for him in their hotel room. He laughed when Blue told him about the empty safe. 'Pickpocket's luck – a fin or a c-note or a handful of air, a dip never knows what's in a pocketbook until he goes to cut up the touch. Now I'm thinking, it's a roundabout way to Shreveport from here – we had best take these locks back to Latourette's before they're missed.'

'I've been thinkin about that big Kruger,' Blue said. 'When we get there, I've got something to show you.'

Packy glared at him. 'Just because you fingered an old bucket like the Heimlich, don't think you can get into the Kruger.'

'Don't you ever want to hear about it?'

'It was a Kruger that got me blown up,' Packy said. 'I didn't want to touch it, but Birdsong, he said a little snifter of soup was all it —' He broke off. 'No, by god, I don't want to hear about it.'

CHAPTER XVII

Blue and Packy arrived back in New Orleans at eight o'clock in the evening. They checked into a small hotel in the French Quarter, then ate a late supper in a restaurant on Royal Street, where they lingered another hour listening to a black piano player finger ragtime tunes. It was past midnight when they left the restaurant. Blue carried the two borrowed safe locks in a cigar box wrapped in brown paper. The streets were far from deserted, but no one actually saw them slip into the alley next to the Latourette Safe Company. They climbed the steps onto the loading dock and Blue turned the key in the lock.

Inside, a big man named Hutch was leaning back in his chair against the far rear wall of the shop, out of the night lamp's circle of light. He knew better than to smoke on night guard, but he liked to eat, and his shirt front and the floor around him were covered with crumbs and scraps of food. He weighed 260 pounds, not including the .44 S & W in his shoulder holster. When he heard the faint sound of the key grating in the lock, he put down his paper of fried shrimp and lifted the 10-gauge sawed-off from his lap. He slipped off the safety.

Hutch saw two men enter the service door. He waited to see

if they were alone. The first, a big kid, went along the workbench to a bank of shelves containing crates of locks and parts, tearing paper wrapping from a cigar box as he walked. The skinny dude behind him closed and locked the door. So they were alone. Hutch swung the sawed-off toward the kid – the paper sack of fried shrimp under his right elbow crackled as his finger curled on the trigger.

Blue heard the paper crackle and he dropped as the gun went off. Above him, the wooden crate exploded in pieces under the charge of double-ought buck. Locks and parts and scraps of metal rained down on him. Packy saw Blue fall. Among the several safes on the shop floor was a big Heimlich, standing open-doored, yawning, empty of cabinetwork. A startled leap put Packy in the shelter of the safe, squatting in the protective embrace of the open door as Hutch swung on him and fired. The charge struck the massive door and drove it against Packy's side. He fell half in the safe and clung there, panting and scared. He heard the shotgun break, and the *tonk* sound as the shells were ejected. There was no place for him to go – the man with the shotgun would flush him like a rabbit and blow him in two. Packy shuddered. The shotgun snapped shut. Packy saw then that the backplate of the lockbox was gone. He skinned into the open safe and pulled the door closed just as Hutch jumped around the corner of the safe, the shotgun leveled. Packy turned the cam wheel that ran the lock bars into their sockets, and spun the wheels of the lock. Hutch wrenched at the handle. The safe was locked. He said, 'Shit!' and kicked at the safe.

Blue had fallen to the floor between the bench and a heavy wheeled cart of welding equipment. Flattening close to the floor, he saw the shotgun man's heavy shoes a few yards away. A smoking shotgun shell rolled into sight as the man reloaded. Blue reached up and took down the coiled double hose and torch. The flint striker was hanging with the torch. He reached again and opened tank valves. When the gas hissed he popped the torch alight just as Hutch kicked at the door of the safe. Hearing the slight scuffing noises, Hutch turned. A weird glow of light appeared behind the cart.

Blue turned up the torch, then hurled the coiled hoses,

torch and all, over the top of the cart. Hutch grunted in sudden panic at the whirling coil and fired as it came down on him. The shotgun blast cut through loops of hose, igniting acetylene with a sharp clap, and bright tongues of flame seared tracks across his jaw and neck and down his great belly. Then he was tangled in it and the sooty yellow flame from the cut hose gushed down his leg, igniting the filthy linen. Hutch staggered, bawled and flailed at the hose.

Blue bounded onto the cart and dived headlong at him – the shotgun went off and blew out a skylight, and Blue and Hutch rolled on the floor, grappling. Hutch battered Blue's jaw with an elbow, kicked free and pulled his .44. Blue caught up the hose and stabbed the flame at him as Hutch fired once – the bullet hit Blue on the left side just over his hip and turned him half around. Hutch squalled as the flame washed over his gun hand and the gun skittered away. Blue held a hand over the gunshot wound. Hutch saw blood leaking through the fingers and grinned.

'Ol' Hutch punched your ticket, did'n'e, boy? Now I god he's gawn shove that hose up your butt. He's comin for ye, boy.'

And Hutch picked a fire ax off a wall hook. At that moment two blocks away, a policeman, having heard shots, ran down Canal Street and encountered a frightened elderly couple who completed incoherently in telling him where the shots came from. He blew his whistle and set off at a run.

Hutch feinted with the fire ax. Blue wagged the hose at him, cobwebs of sooty carbon drifting from the thick flame. Then Hutch rushed, swinging – Blue stepped aside and the ax slammed into a five-gallon can behind him, crushing it and bursting seams. Blue jammed the flame at Hutch's face and scorched his ear. Hutch cried out and swung sideways with the ax. Blue dropped the hose and caught the ax as it swung out, then he hit Hutch in the belly with his right hand. Behind him, the flame ignited kerosene from the smashed can and fire ran along the floor among the safes. Paint blistered on the safe that held Packy. Heat soaked into the metal.

Hutch kicked at Blue, who caught the foot and heaved – Hutch was dumped on his back with a mighty grunt. One leg of his baggy trousers sopped up flaming kerosene. Hutch rolled away and climbed to his feet, frantically slapping at the patch of flame on his leg, and Blue stepped in close and hit him just below the ear with his right hand. Hutch wobbled and went down. He came to his knees and Blue hit him again. Stretched out on his back, Hutch watched flames creep closer. His mouth opened and closed and he pleaded with his eyes. Blue stepped in close to pull him away from the fire and Hutch caught him, pulled him down and clubbed him, then kicked him in the ribs. On his knees and dazed, Blue saw Hutch come for him again. He dodged the kick aimed for his jaw and swung his own elbow into Hutch's belly. When the meaty hands came down, Blue hit him on the Adam's apple. Hutch dropped, making gagging noises in his throat. Blue stepped in again and Hutch put up his hands. 'Don' hit ol' Hutch no more, boy,' he mumbled. Blue hit him anyway. Hutch went down on his face and lay still.

The pain in Blue's side was suddenly monstrous. He turned dizzily and peered through the flames and smoke to find Packy – he had not seen him since the first shotgun blast.

Inside the safe, Hutch's shots sounded to Packy like twigs snapping, and the sound of the fire ax hitting the can came to him as a tinny *thunk*. He had no way of knowing if Blue had survived the shotgun blasts. He knew that he would suffocate if he stayed too long inside, but he thought dazedly that he would rather suffocate than be cut in two by a sawed-off. It seemed to him then that the safe was very warm – as seconds passed, it seemed hot, then very hot, and Packy realized he was sweating. He sniffed hot metal – no, not sweating. *Frying*. To suffocate was one thing – to *fry* was another. Packy felt for the lockbox on the door. He turned the tumbler wheels, five of them, lining up the notches. The fence fell. He turned the cam wheel, retracting the bars. Was Hutch waiting? Goaded by the smell of hot metal, Packy gave the door a little push. Bright flame licked up from the floor. Packy squawked and threw open the door, then sprang out of the safe and through the flames like a terrified heron, trailing his game leg. He heard shouts outside, then saw Blue tottering toward him, bloody and scorched. Someone pounded on the door.

In spite of his sojourn crammed into the safe, Packy's suit was unmarred. He saw a big revolver on the floor, lying where it had skidded from Hutch's hand. Packy snatched it up, jammed it in Blue's ribs and unlocked the door. A police officer almost fell through.

'By god, it's time you was here!' Packy scolded. 'I'll handle this one – you put the irons on that fat bastard back yonder before he barbecues, then see if you can't do somethin to put the fire out.' And pushing Blue ahead of him, he marched past the officer, who said, 'Yes, sir!' and sprinted in to put the cuffs on Hutch.

Late afternoon sun streaming through the hotel room's tall window threw shadows of grillwork across Blue's bed. Blue stirred, then woke as Packy entered the room with an armload of packages in a string bag and a small chipped graniteware pail with a lid on it. In his gray suit, Packy looked like a prosperous businessman. He put down his hat and silver-headed stick along with the other things and stepped over to the bed. Blue flinched when Packy pulled back the edge of his gauze bandage and looked under. 'Um,' Packy said.

'Um?' Blue was pale, dry-lipped, listless.

'Ugly is what I mean, but the edges are stuck together so I spect it's mending. I brought you some grub.' He lifted the lid of the little pail and steam curled up. 'See? Gumbo from the Creole joint down the street.'

'I ain't hungry. Did you bring the papers?'

Packy took newspapers from the bag and tossed them on the bed. He watched Blue scan the pages. 'How could we know they had put on a shotgun guard at Latourette's?'

Blue frowned and looked up. 'Your brain must have gone soft in stir.'

'What the hell is that supposed to mean?'

'That guard was put there to kill *us*. Not just any thief off the street. Look, twice we've used the Latourette name, so a description of us has got back to them – and don't forget, Sage recognized you from the old days.' He hesitated. 'They must have caught on to the missing locks, too. Anyway, we're *known*, Packy.'

Packy peered past a sagging louvered shutter into the patio, a faint, bemused smile tugging at the corner of his mouth.

'You know something?' Blue said. 'I think you like that – letting em all know Disbrow is back in the game again. You and your flashy con rips. Didn't anybody ever tell you you were a show-off.'

Startled, Packy tried to protest. 'What gives you the right to —'

'Because I'm the one that got shot and I aim to stop it now before it gets to be a habit.'

After a moment, Packy shrugged. 'Birdsong told me the some thing once. But —'

Blue, looking at the paper, interrupted him. 'Here it is. "Veteran Guard Savagely Beaten by Four Assailants." Four?' Blue laughed. ' "Nothing of value was taken as the thieves were frightened off, one with a pistol ball in his body. Mr Hutchins was able to describe two of the intruders. Police believe they are the daring criminals who robbed the safe of a cotton brokerage in broad daylight earlier this month, using the names Bristol and Adams. Police are investigating a possible connection with a safe burglary in Baton Rouge. Mr Hutchins, known along Decatur Street as 'Scattergun,' killed eight men in as many years on the force before his dismissal last year on a charge of taking bribes . . ." ' The paper drooped in Blue's hands.

'Go on,' Packy said. The paper slipped to the floor. He saw that Blue's face had gone waxy-pale, his upper lip glistening with moisture.

'Packy, I don't . . . feel too good.' The fiber was gone from Blue's voice. His eyelids drooped. Packy touched his forehead. The skin was hot. Packy turned away. He was going to have to get the kid a doctor, but not just any doctor, now that they were fugitives. Damn me for getting careless, he thought. It was all going too easy. He turned to the window again. Below, a little girl of about eight was sitting on the rim of the fountain, playing with a doll, carefully putting its bandaged arm into a sling. He had seen her before – she was the child of the Creole woman who ran the hotel's kitchen. Packy took a ten-dollar bill from his pocket. He hissed and the little girl looked up, her dark eyes huge in her honey-colored face. Packy folded the bill and tossed it down.

'Sweetheart, you take that to your mama real quick. Tell her I need to see her. Tell her the man says no monkey business. All right?' The little girl picked up the bill, looked at him again, then ran, clutching the doll. Packy was remembering the wagons and carts that stopped in the alley through the week, unloading vegetables, fish, chickens and hams.

The next morning near dawn, a rickety wagon drawn by a blind white mule was stopped at the hotel's alley entrance by its driver, a hawk-nosed woman of middle age wearing a spangled turban. Trussed chickens and splint baskets of vegetables were unloaded. Then Blue, feverish and half-conscious, was taken from his room down to the wagon by Packy and the mother of the little girl, his arms about their shoulders, and put aboard the wagon on a bed of straw, among splint baskets, feed sacks and chicken feathers. They covered him with the sacks. With Packy on the seat beside her, his elegant suit shrouded under a tattered shawl, the turbaned woman drove away, moving west and south through the city, then out of it and onto a narrow, muddy, puddled track that took them deeper and deeper into the country of the swamp people.

CHAPTER XVIII

The humming in Blue's ears became voices. He heaved against the great weight of his eyelids and the face of the hawk-nosed turbaned woman glimmered over him. The glimmer divided and he saw that with her was an aged black man with a milky eye and a crinkly white poll, and the old man was digging then into the hole in Blue's side, probing and stirring down through him and far into the void that was him and yet beyond him. Pain flared outward, like a wave of bright light. Blue watched it coming for him, but before it reached his eyes he was gone.

He was next aware, dimly, of light as a motionless earthen

blur of random puddled shapes and it came to him that he had been studying a patch of vermilion floating there for a very long time before he even knew he was awake. He blinked. The vermilion stirred and he saw smooth long brown legs stretching before it, and hands moving, a basket, the hands sorting, tossing, peas or okra, he did not know, and her face was a child's face until she looked up and saw him looking at her; then a frown cracked its serenity, and she put the basket aside, rose from her seat on the wooden doorsill and hurried away, tall and leggy. I'm going to have to start thinkin about this, Blue told himself, and he was drifting again.

Clay Russell and Zack Murdock, wearing heavy sheepskin coats against the winter cold, followed Owl Carver and Cape Naylor into the Durango railroad depot. Passing the grilled ticket window, they went down a corridor to the office of the yardmaster. Carver took a quick look inside. 'He's alone,' he muttered and beckoned them to follow him with a jerk of his head. Moments later, his shadow fell across the desk of his brother-in-law, Assistant Yardmaster Jared Crenshaw.

Crenshaw peered past his celluloid eyeshade, then flinched. 'I told you never to come here!' he screeched softly.

'I made sure you was alone. What we want is a look at the car and the safe.'

'I figured you had give up on the thing. It's been months!'

'I was waitin for my partners.'

'By god, you've waited *too* long!'

'What do you mean by that?'

Crenshaw rose. 'Come with me. If anyone else comes, you are looking for some lost baggage, all right?' He peeked into the hall, then led them briskly down the hall and through a door that read FREIGHT & BAGGAGE.

Murdock swore under his breath when he saw the safe. Massive, hulking, somehow malevolent, it squatted next to a stack of fresh timbers. INVINCIBLE, proclaimed the glittering arc of gold leaf on the black-painted door. The dial stared solemnly.

'Solid as a cannonball,' Crenshaw said. 'Three sets of doors. There aint a way in the world that box can be broke. By tomorrow, it will be installed in the express car that makes the Shotgun Run. That's what I mean – you've waited too long.'

The four men rode out of Durango, following the winding tracks of the railroad for a time, then climbing onto open sage- and juniper-studded benchland, the snowy peaks of the San Juans glistening to the north. Wind sighed through the junipers and snow swirled, sparkling in the sun. For a time they rode silently; then Russell spoke. 'This aint gettin us out of the country.'

'We've got the relays of horses all set and ready,' Owlhead said. 'We could have tapped the train and been across the Colorado and headed for Mexico by now, if you hadn't wasted time getting the girls out here and all —'

'What might have been don't matter now,' Murdock said flatly.

'I mean, me and Cape, if we hurtin bad for a piece, we jess buy us some in town, like it was candy, don't we, Cape?'

Cape did not answer. Murdock said, 'Shut up about it.'

'What we're hurtin bad for,' Clay Russell said, 'is a *strike* – our money is all tied up in the damned horses.'

'That's right,' Naylor said. 'We paid for em – we could still use em to hit the Union Pacific. I know a sheepherder shack on Bitter Crick —'

'Hell, that's three hundred miles north of here,' Murdock said.

'Chavez could stake out the horses running south along the Green, toward the Roost or the Whiskey Hole,' Owlhead said.

'Could make the Whiskey Hole in two days,' Naylor said, 'same as Cassidy done after he hit the train at Wilcox. Rest up a day or two and head back here, or anything we wanted.'

'We wouldn't have a man on the inside,' Russell pointed out.

'Take our chances,' Naylor said. 'Cassidy done all right that way – I never said it was the big one, like the Shotgun Run.'

'Bound to carry *something*,' Owlhead said.

'All right. We've got no selection,' Murdock said.

Riding on, they talked about it, their horses snorting plumes of frost smoke in the cold air. A long-unused wagon track scarring the sage wound toward a clump of cottonwoods where a weathered shack of a house sat among collapsing outbuildings.

They reached the place, turned their horses out and went into the house, still talking.

'We've got no selection,' Murdock said again, 'but we'll have to wait for a thaw.'

'I don't know,' Russell said, 'damned hard to track horses on frozen ground.'

'But spose it snows —' Murdock said, 'snows deep, so's to break down the horses? We need a thaw.'

The wood stove in the littered parlor was smoking. Clay Russell kicked at the iron door and soot drifted down from the seams of the smokepipe. He opened the draft a little and the stove began to draw. A hoarse bray of female laughter sounded in the kitchen, then a plump, orange-haired girl entered, followed by India Wood. The girl, whose name was Millie Dorton, grinned and put a big granite coffeepot on the stove. She looked at Owlhead's muddy boots.

'Hereafter stomp your feet clean before you track up my floor,' she said. 'I'd sooner slop the hogs on Daddy's farm than clean up after this bunch.'

Murdock caught her and squeezed her waist. 'Maybe you'd rather go back to work,' he said.

'Haw – it's no different here, sweet baby, with you tryin to make up for lost time.' She brayed again and mussed his hair.

Wind sighed. Boards creaked in the house and sand sifted under the door. India hugged her arms and shivered. 'I'll tell you one thing, Clay Russell, we was doing all right at Francie's place. We could have stayed on a while longer. There was no need of your bringing us to a rattrap like this, after all you promised.'

'By god, my folks homesteaded here!' Owlhead said.

'They drove stakes in a manure pile, then!' India snapped.

'Oh, hell, honey,' Clay Russell said, 'it ain't for long. Just till we get this thing strung out.'

'And don't think, by god, you're goin to leave us here alone,' Millie said. 'I heard you talkin —' Murdock pushed her away. 'I mean it,' she said. 'We'll stay in a hotel in town, is what we'll do.' She gave Murdock a crooked grin.

Murdock slapped her, hard, and knocked her against the wall. After a moment she shook herself and went into the other room without looking at him again or saying another word. India followed her. As if nothing had happened, Murdock said, 'Owlhead, you and Cape go find Chavez and help get the horses strung out. Time you're done, me and Russ will meet you on Bitter Crick, ready to go. Now how do we find the shack?'

Blue could not take hold of time. Sunlight wheeled through moss-hung trees, spilled through the doorway onto the dirt floor, fanned slowly and was gone. Rain drummed down. Chickens strutted aimlessly in and out. A spotted pig minced in stately grace across the dirt floor and sawed its larded ribs against the iron frame of Blue's bed; the heaving bed squalled under him. For a time he did not eat at all, then she fed him, lifting his head, spooning in grits. Her name was Ginnie, or maybe Jena. Now and then a small child was with her, winding her skirts about her legs, peering at him. Packy was gone by then. Blue could not remember his leaving.

Blue tottered out for the first time, saw the place, not a village, a *settlement,* five or six scattered houses, sheds and shacks, two or three wagons, gardens set out here and there to catch the sun, chickens, pigs, two cows, water glinting through the trees. Through his window – the open side of the shed – he watched the women build up a fire under a blackened tank, then the hawk-nosed woman shot the spotted pig in the ear with a little octagon-barreled .22. The pig dropped to its knees with a thud. Jena ran the short blade straight in at the base of the throat, twitched the knife and caught the artery; blood spurted, pulsing. She looked at Blue at that moment, laughed and covered her face. They hauled the pig up, dropped it into the scald water, and when the hair slipped, they hauled it up again and scraped it. It hung there white and slick.

Walking, Blue heard metal ring. He rounded a cluster of sheds and saw the old man with the milky eye struggling at a crude forge, his palsied hands quivering on the tongs. Blue took the broken-eyed grub hoe from him and with heart-bursting effort fought it to the fire. Together they pumped, and through streaming sweat Blue saw the old man grinning at him. He set his jaw and heaved the hoe to the anvil and hammered the weld, his heart battering against his ribs, and tubbed it. Then he fell back against the split-log wall, laughing, the wind sighing out of him. The old man gave him a drink of white lightning from a medicine bottle. And that night Jena stopped at his door, her wet hair caught up in a turban of flour sacking. He smelled soap and damp cloth. She stepped close, bent, tugging at the thin blanket. The red dress was still unfastened after her bath. Blue's hand went out. Her still-damp skin was chilled. Her breath quickened, caught in a little gasp. His hand slipped up, pushed the cloth off her shoulder. 'Don't go,' he whispered. Seconds spun away, then she shrugged and the red dress collapsed at her feet.

CHAPTER XIX

Working out of the Denver office, Bassett was scarcely ever in Denver. He traveled endless railroad miles and filed his reports, copies to go to Havenhurst in the St Louis office. In Alamosa, he talked to railroad men, bartenders, drifters – yes, the four men in his photographs had been there, but where did they go? The Yellow Rose robbery seemed an ending rather than a beginning. South of Alamosa, in Antonito, a room clerk in a shabby railroad hotel scratched his memory and recalled four men passing through a couple of weeks earlier, headed south. Bassett followed them aboard a creaking Chili Line coach.

In Española, he learned that they were spending plenty of money. A Mexican chambermaid in a hotel there, eager to please, positively identified Clay Russell from his photograph. Bassett pressed on south, considering how he was going to make his approach. A packet of mail had been forwarded to him in Santa Fe, including an envelope from Havenhurst. In it were copies of reports on Packy Disbrow and Blue Russell with Havenhurst's own penciled comments in the margins.

How in hell did they get in? he wrote next to an account of the safe burglary in Baton Rouge. Reading, Bassett laughed, remembering how the kid had strung up the mechanic, Axel, by his heels that day in the stable yard.

Bassett caught up with the four men in a saloon in Socorro, New Mexico. They were well-dressed, spending freely and having fun, and one of them did look something like Clay Russell, but they were not the Gitmo Studs. Bassett made their acquaintance and the once who looked like Russell tried to sell him shares in a mining development scheme, so that was where the money was coming from. Bassett had a drink with them and left.

Back in Denver, he went through his mail and read a bundle of reports and newspaper clippings about the battle between the shotgun guard, Hutchins, and his assailants. Havenhurst wrote, *We think the Russell kid is probably dead*, and Bassett felt a sudden sharp pang. Surprised at himself, he slipped a hand under his coat and touched the Browning. Maybe I could have turned the kid around some way, he thought, but then he caught himself, shook his head and put it out of his mind. Or tried. It subsided, but would not quit.

Where, Bassett asked himself, could Murdock and Russell hole up for the winter? It occurred to him that railroad people often homesteaded land near their jobs. The Owlhead was from a railroad family. Bassett went to the personnel offices of railroad companies in Denever – Union Pacific, Burlington, D & RG – and there he discovered that Solomon Carver, a brakeman of the D & RG, had spent seven years beginning in 1882 working out of Durango. Bassett went to the government land office and found that Solomon Carver and spouse, Effie, had filed on 160 acres near Durango in 1883.

Bassett packed his saddlebags, tied up a bedroll and made ready to leave for Durango. At the office, he found that a telegraphed report had been passed on to him. McFadden, the chief of the Denver office, had underlined one sentence: BARTENDER CLAIMS OWLHEAD CARVER BOUGHT ONE CASE WHISKEY HERE. The report had been filed in Rock Springs, Wyoming, a town on the Union Pacific line some 300 miles northwest of Denver, and it had been sent by a Pinkerton operative named Costello, who was working with railroad detectives tracking down members of the Wild Bunch and the Hole-in-the-Wall gang in Wyoming. Bassett arranged to meet Costello in Rawlins, which was 100 miles east of Rock Springs on the Union Pacific, and caught a train within the hour.

On the station platform in Rawlins, with a cold wind whipping the snow in gusting clouds, Bassett was accosted by a wiry, dirty, unshaven, derelict cowhand. It was Costello. Over eggs and fried potatoes in a cafe across the street from the depot, Bassett learned that Costello's cover was riding the grub line – drifting from ranch to ranch through the winter, staying a few days, then riding on before the welcome soured, the winter practice of out-of-work cowboys in the high plains and mountain country.

'Tell me about the Owlhead,' Bassett said.

'I was grub-linin south along the Green, toward the Uintahs and Brown's Hole, and I camped one night with a sheep-herder' – Bassett nodded, for that was along the outlaw trail where it disappeared into the badlands south of the Union Pacific and Rock Springs – 'and he don't have much to say, but he tells me he seen Owlhead Carver and a Mexican and another feller drivin a bunch of horses, maybe fifteen or twenty. When I got to Rock Springs, I asked around. A barkeep tells me the Owlhead bought a case of whiskey from him.'

'If he bought a case, then he's quit moving,' Bassett said.

'Pushing horses this time of year is mighty cold work,' Costello said. 'Me, I'd hole up until the weather breaks.'

'I think you've hit it,' Bassett said.

'Hit what?'

'He's got a string of horses and a case of whiskey, which tells us he's also got a place to hole up in. But the Owlhead is no horse trader. The horses are for relays. How long before he uses em?'

'How long is a case of whiskey?' Costello grinned.

'Not long for the Owlhead.'

'Say until the weather breaks?'

'All right. Say it thaws, say they've got their horses strung out in relays, and say they knock over a train and ride south – it would be south, wouldn't it?'

'It would have to be, this time of year.'

'Yes. Where would they stop?'

'I'd say they would follow the outlaw trail – same as Cassidy's bunch last June after the Wilcox train robbery – and they wouldn't stop till they hit the Dirty Devil, or Robbers' Roost, or even Poison Springs. The law couldn't find em there – no one could find em.'

'Maybe not,' Bassett said, 'but by then the Owlhead would be just about desperate for a drink of whiskey. Where would he get it?'

Costello thought a moment. 'The Whiskey Hole. It's a ranch on the slopes of the Henry mountains, not far from the Roost. A Swede runs the place —'

'How come Whiskey Hole?'

'The Swede is a Mormon. Had hisself two wives, see? When they outlawed plural marriages in '96, he wouldn't give up neither one of his women. He moved down to the badlands where they couldn't touch him. He stocks whiskey on the place – the outlaws know they can always get a drink there, so they leave him, his cattle and his women alone. If it was me, I'd try the Whiskey Hole.'

Bassett returned to Denver. He passed word to Union Pacific people that he suspected a train robbery attempt shortly in the vicinity of Rock Springs. With nothing more to go on, there was little they could do except to alert flying squads of deputies in Rawlins and Rock Springs, who could be dispatched, horses and all, by boxcar, the moment there was trouble. Bassett settled down to wait. The next mail brought another message from Havenhurst: *The kid and Disbrow were traced to a Creole hotel, but the trail ends there – I am inclined to think they must have found a place to hide out in while the kid gets patched up.* Bassett felt unaccountably elated.

CHAPTER XX

Thirty miles east of Rock Springs, Wyoming, The Union Pacific railroad swung in a long southerly loop to skirt a spine of rocky hills. And there ran Bitter Creek, now milky-white with runoff from melting snow as it coursed west through desolate sage. The railroad tracks bridged the swollen creek over a low wooden trestle. The engineer of the westbound run saw timbers cocked up at odd angles and thought the bridge had broken up in the flood. He hit the brakes. Seconds later, he was feeling the ice-cold muzzle of a .44 New Service Colt under his ear.

The train was uncoupled between the express car and first coach. 'Run her acrost the crick,' the engineer was told. The big locomotive pushed aside the stacked timbers, pulling its tender, the mail car and the express car. When a rash conductor climbed down and ran after it, one of the four masked robbers shot him in the leg and left him struggling on the trestle. As the express car cleared the trestle, the robber jumped down and lighted a fuse, then ran on. Some forty seconds later a dynamite charge exploded and destroyed the near end of the trestle. The injured conductor, crawling, had reached the far end. He was knocked flat again, but shortly stirred and crawled on. The engine was halted a couple of hundred yards past the trestle.

'Run the damned door back if you want to live!' a masked man shouted through the door of the express car. Locks rattled. The door rolled back. The agent elected to leave his shotgun where it sat. Blinking in sudden light, he thrust his hands skyward. Zack Murdock and Clay Russell vaulted onto the floor of the car. Owl Carver heaved a heavy canvas satchel up after them.

'*Russ!*' Murdock choked. 'Oh, dammit, no!'

Together they stared at the massive safe in its crib of timbers, at the glistening arc of gold leaf on its door. INVINCIBLE, it read.

Shivering, the agent said, 'I caint open it – what do you want me to do?' He should not have spoken – Murdock chopped at him with his pistol and the agent dropped with a broken jaw.

Furious, Murdock tore open the satchel and began making up a dynamite charge. A little more than twenty minutes later, the safe lay on its side, intact, in a deep crater blasted through the roadbed into the red Wyoming earth. The express car was matchwood and the rear half of the mail car was also blown to pieces, with scraps of mail blowing away through the sage. The outlaws were scorched and deafened and their clothes hung in tatters. Murdock was making animal noises in his throat. Across the creek, a traveling drummer had alighted from a coach and begun taking potshots at the bandits with a flimsy five-shot .22 pistol (*Bad News for Tramps*, advertised the pistol's manufacturer). The bandits scarcely noticed at first, but then Murdock's face was stung with grit from a near miss. He emptied his heavy Colt and drove the salesman back aboard the train. Standing up on the embankment to fire, he saw at last the smoke of a following train. The engine was just nosing to a halt behind the stopped coaches. Men were alighting, running along the roadbed toward the creek.

Murdock, unable in his fury to speak, kicked at Naylor. A moment later the outlaws were running for their horses. Behind them, a final charge exploded. Kruger's Invincible sank a little deeper into its crater.

As soon as the news reached Denver, Bassett boarded a westbound Denver & Rio Grande coach, ticketed for Green River, Utah. His luggage consisted of saddlebags, bedroll and a saddle checked through in the baggage car. In his bedroll was a copy of a newspaper – especially made up for Bassett by a Denver printer, it carried stories of another train robbery. A Colorado Southern train was said to have been robbed near Cimarron Canyon in northeast New Mexico, by one Preacher Bucklin and several unnamed accomplices. Bucklin appeared to have escaped dressed as a preacher and driving a buggy – officers reported that such a man stopped them during the ensuing manhunt and asked them what the fuss was all about.

Bassett looked out the coach window and saw reflected there the gaunt stranger's face under the severe black hat. No, I don't know you anymore, he thought. Somewhere back there among the drifters, cowhands yes, and solemn country preachers he had been or pretended to be, he had lost track of that clean-jawed young Holcomb Bassett who once had been, in his own mind's eye, himself, You're Bucklin now anyway, remember? I don't know him, either. You'd better get to knowin him – he is just that same drifter, Bassett, with a few more years on him now and full of poison. He almost went Bucklin's way. Could have, easy. The super was not far from the mark. He shook his head and the head in the glass shook back at him. I still don't know you, Bucklin, but I will.

At Green River, Utah, he grasped the iron handrail and swung down, his boots crunching onto ocher sand as he collected his saddle and bedroll at the open door of the baggage car. A scruffy dog, lean and gray as a lizard, observed Bassett with yellow eyes and lifted its leg languidly on the journal box of the car's wheel trucks. A trainman bawled, the engine chuffed, snorting black smoke, and in moments, it seemed to Bassett, she was diminished, snaking west through the sage, leaving in her wake a dust-devil.

Turning, Bassett saw a few weathered frame buildings scattered along the tracks near the Green River Bridge, and beyond, a great escarpment reared above the sweeping flats, washed in early morning light. Bassett tucked the bedroll under his arm, swung the saddle to his shoulder. Walking, he felt himself settle into the name and the man. He saw black letters in peeling paint on the building's false front – GENERAL MERCHANDISE–PROVISIONS AND DRY GOODS. The tall, gaunt hard-faced man who entered the door was Preacher Bucklin.

Four mules were tethered before the forge, waiting to be shod. Blue had the hind foot of another on his leather-aproned thigh and a hammer in his hand when Packy drove up in a buggy. Blue grinned around a mouthful of nails and finished nailing the shoe.

'I thought maybe you had gone to China,' he said. Packy's

suit was rumpled and there was a gray stubble on his jaw.

'I couldn't hardly stay here,' Packy said. 'No, I've just been here and there, cutting up touches – staying out of sight, to tell the truth, until I could guess you were well enough to move.' He climbed down from the buggy.

Instead of answering, Blue took hold of the anvil, heel and horn, and lifted it, stump and all, clear of the ground and held it there easily, then set it back. Packy laughed. 'You're ready to go then?'

Blue clucked at the mule, picked up the other hind foot and began paring the hoof. He nodded at the tehered mules and at a bent axle and a number of tools sitting nearby. 'I've got work stacked up.'

Packy frowned.

Blue touched the puckered scar on his side. 'Maybe old Hutch did us a favor – we could have been locked up, or dead, by now, if he hadn't put us wise.'

'We need to move on, all right. I think San Antone —'

Blue shook his head. 'We're too easy to spot now. I figure it's time for us to split up, Packy.'

'You'd quit on me now, after what you've learned from me?' Packy's voice was tinny and querulous with shock. 'You know I can't go it alone. A few more tricks —'

'We'd be rich as Midas.' Blue grinned. 'You're not fixed too bad now.'

'You think you can shed it all, stay on here poundin horseshoes, is that it?'

'No, this is too close to New Orleans. They'd find me here. Horseshoes or not, I'll have to move on west.'

Packy turned back to the buggy and pulled a thick bundle of newspapers from the seat and tossed them onto Blue's bench. 'The law knows about the Russells out there, too,' he said.

Blue put down the mule's foot, stepped to the bench and leafed through the papers. They were filled with front-page headline stories about the Bitter Creek robbery attempt. There were photos of four men, including one Blue remembered seeing at the time of the jailbreak – it looked nothing like the Clay that Blue remembered – and there were other photos of the Kruger Invincible and the wrecked express car. The names of Clay Russell and Zack Murdock were repeated many times.

'Well, it's nothing to do with you or me,' Blue said.

'Come to San Antone with me, Blue. We could ease up there. I know a place me and Birdsong used to —'

'A few more hours and you could be in Mexico. That's where you wanted to go.'

'I only said that when I was desperate – before I had a taste of living decent again. And you know I wouldn't last long on what I've put by.'

'You would if you had to.'

Blue turned back to the mule. Packy caught his arm. 'No. Blue, my roll is all gone. Don't leave me broke.'

Blue stared at him in stunned disbelief.

'Every damned nickel of it,' Packy said. 'I went to the Lafitte House, see, and I got to playing . . .' He spread his hands.

'You crazy old thief!' Blue flared. 'So now you want mine, is that it?'

'You know me better than that!'

'Do I?'

'I could have taken it while you were flat on your back. Hell, Blue, I didn't set out to blow it.'

Blue picked up the mule's foot again and went to work on it with his knife. After a time he said, 'If we raised a good score in San Antone, would you go to Mexico?' Packy's face warped in a nervous grin. 'You could take it all,' Blue went on. 'Whatever the score turns out to be, it's yours.'

Packy frowned. 'Disbrow take his partner's cut?'

'It wouldn't be the first time.'

Packy opened his mouth to snap back, but the words would not come. Blue laughed and punched him on the arm. 'Give me a few days to finish up here —'

'We've got to stop at the Lafitte House first,' Packy said. 'That's where I got the buggy. And we'll have to pay off the thousand I still owe. Disbrow don't walk off from his debts, you know. That aint my style, amigo.'

CHAPTER XXI

The horse Bassett bought was a roan with one white eye, chunky, a good walker. On his right as he rode south Bassett saw the San Rafael reef beetling against the sky, the ridges dark with piñon and juniper. To the east, the Green was lost below the skyline in its labyrinth of canyons. He forded the shallow San Rafael before noon. After that, there was no water, only slowly rising sandy ground cut with washes and stippled with sage – a lost and lonely country. He had come this way once, but going north that time, trailing two brothers named Ferris. Caught them over a breakfast of wheat cakes in Rock Springs.

In the afternoon he guided on great flat-topped buttes, passing them one by one, the roan wading in drifted sand between chalky pleated badland bluffs, with the Henry mountains purple in the distance. Then the ground was breaking up into canyons, running down toward the Dirty Devil. He stayed just to the north, for the canyons were the back door to hell, and Robbers' Roost. Rounding a shoulder of sandstone at sundown, he found it, a narrow patch of bottomland where a few cattle grazed under clumped dusty cottonwoods. A trickle of water stained the sandy wash. A small stone house sat back among cottonwoods and there were scattered weathered sheds, a half-completed corral.

Bassett let the roan drink. Nailed to the trunk of a cottonwood was a scrap of board on which was daubed in red paint an arrow pointing to the stream, over the words *wAtER HoLE*. Beneath that, another arrow pointed toward one of the shacks, over the words *wHiSKEy HoLE*. Both *O*'s in the board were drilled out with bullet holes. Nearby stood a battered wagon with two horses standing in harness.

The shack was built of split log planks. An attached shed roof was supported by twisted posts. Under the roof, a plank set across two barrels served as a bar, tended now by a bald wiry man wearing a drooping sandy mustache. That would be the Swede, Olaf, Bassett thought. The other two were older, miners probably, from a placer diggings somewhere near. They watched him warily as he approached. One of them, toothless, whittled on a stick. Bassett nodded.

'Would've broke my heart to get here and find no company,' he said. 'I've come a hell of a long ways to see if I couldn't get someone to help me drink this up.' He put a bank note on the plank bar.

'Hell, mister,' one of the miners said, 'there aint but the two of us, but we'll help ye, won't we, Asa?'

'Do the best we can,' Asa agreed, folding his knife and slipping it into a pocket of his overalls.

The Swede set out three chipped glasses and a bottle, poured, then picked up the note. 'Vat t'hell! You try to fool with me, mister? A tousand-dollar bill. Ay von't live long enough to make change for it.'

Bassett took a twenty-dollar gold piece from his pocket and put it on the bar. 'This will give us a start then.' He took the thousand-dollar bill and spiked it on a nail sticking out of a log in the cabin wall. 'It's something to look at, anyway.'

Asa blew a gust of wind past his gums. 'Damfitaint.'

Later, after the miners had gone, falling over one another as they climbed into their wagon, Bassett put another gold piece on the bar and said he needed a place to sleep. Olaf pointed to an open-sided shed, half full of hay. 'Yust stay away from t'house, is all,' he said. Bassett was bedding down when a little towheaded, barefoot youngster came out, left a lard pail and ran back without a word. Bassett opened it, found hot beans and thick, white, buttered biscuits. He lifted a biscuit, sniffing the fragrance, caught the running butter with his tongue and began to eat.

The next day Bassett put another gold piece on the bar, but there was no one at the Whiskey Hole to help him drink it up. When the Swede offered to pour, Bassett shook his head and began to lay out a hand of solitaire. The Swede went down among the cottonwoods to where he had dropped a wagon-load of posts, and began to dig postholes. After a while Bassett put down the cards, walked to the water hole and went to work with a posthole digger.

The corral was nearly finished and he was digging holes for the gateposts three days later when four men rode into the Whiskey Hole from the south. They came slowly, spaced well apart, and sat their saddles some time before dismounting, watching Bassett and the Swede and looking around.

'Dose boys lookin tirsty,' Olaf said. 'You comin?'

'Soon as I set these posts.'

'Dey gone vant to know who you are.'

'Name's Bucklin. They don't need to know more than that.' He paused for a moment with his hands crossed on the double handles of the digger as Olaf walked toward the shack, and then he went back to work, thrusting the digger down, clamping the jaws on to a good mouthful of dirt, drawing it out. He took his time finishing the hole, glancing up once to see a couple of the men walking back around the shack – good, he thought, they had been around back taking a look at where he was bunking. He set the posts, filled in dirt around them and rammed it down good with the shovel handle. Then he stuck the shovel in the ground, walked to the water hole and rinsed off his hands and face. The water dried on his skin as he walked the forty yards to the Whiskey Hole shack. Three of the men were seated on rickety benches back under the shed roof, and a fourth stood at the end of the plank bar with two glasses before him. Approaching, Bassett recognized them from their identity cards in the agency files. He knew the man at the bar instantly from his banjo eyes and small, bent-down nose. Owl Carver. His hair stood out from his head in frizzy ringlets, except where a patch appeared to have been scorched away. Carver tossed off both drinks and motioned to the Swede to fill the glasses again. By then, Bassett was close enough to hear him mutter, 'Hell, he *looks* like a preacher, sure enough.'

The tall one, Clay Russell, laughed. 'You wouldn't know nothing about that, Owlhead.'

Carver mumbled something Bassett could not hear and tossed off another drink. Russell, who was leaning back with his long legs up on a bench, grinned easily at Bassett. Murdock merely stared, wordless, frowning. The men were dirty, their clothing scorched and brush-snagged. Naylor's eyebrows were singed off. He watched Carver pour down another drink. 'You gawn be embalmed, boy.'

'He's got to get ketched up,' Russell said. 'He aint had but three or four since breakfast.'

'Likes an early start on it, does he?' Bassett said.

Russell laughed again. 'The old Owlhead, he likes to eat a plate of whiskey for breakfast, but he run short this mornin.'

'And damn near starved to death,' Naylor said.

'Awright, you bastards,' Carver growled.

'It put a peeve on him, too,' Russell said.

'I hate to see a man in pain,' Bassett said, fishing a twenty-dollar gold piece out of his pocket and spinning it on the plank bar. 'Let me pay the doctor bill, boys.'

'I don't mind,' Russell said. Murdock said nothing. After a minute, Olaf set the bottle out on the plank.

'Ay got fence to build,' he said. 'You want someting, holler.'

When he was out of earshot, Russell said, 'Olaf tells me you're called Preacher Bucklin. How come Preacher?'

'Spect I look pious, is all. Course, I do take the golden rule serious.'

'You mean—'

'Do unto the sons of bitches as they done unto us,' Bassett said, allowing himself the ghost of a smile.

Russell laughed outright again and for a moment Bassett saw in his face, through the dynamite scorches and the stubble of beard, the face of the youngster he remembered, Blue Russell.

'D'you spose I could have read about you in the papers?' Russell said.

'I don't doubt it atall,' Bassett said. So Russell was just letting him know he had seen the newspaper in Bucklin's bedroll, and maybe the preacher's collar.

'You the one stuck that thousand-dollar bill on the wall?' Owl Carver said. His eyes roved, not quite holding on Bassett.

'It was me, all right.'

Carver snorted. His lips twitched. 'Damn if that aint the funniest thing I ever set eyes on – man with a thousand dollars he caint spend.'

'Hell, friend, I've had my money's worth out of it – it bought me a look at the rubes who blowed the hair off their heads with dynamite, but couldn't crack the cashbox.'

Murdock's feet thudded down. 'You've got a hell of a mouth on you.'

'*Cashbox?*' Carver said. 'You don't *know!*'

'I know, all right – I got into the one I went after and you boys come away without a dime.'

'You come here to laugh about, is that it?' Murdock said.

'No. To make a deal.'

Russell was grinning again. 'Is it true you left in a buggy wearin a preacher suit, drove through the posse and asked what all the fuss was about?'

Bassett nodded.

'What is this leading to?' Murdock persisted.

Bassett reached into his pocket, pulled out a sheaf of bills and slapped them down on the bar. 'These damn thousand-dollar bills. They're as good as worthless. We both come out short-changed.'

'We don't need nobody to tell us we're broke – and if you're broke too, it don't bother me none,' Murdock said.

'I got pocket money out of it, Bassett said, 'but I was shooting for the big one. I missed that. One big one is what I want, still – then quit the game. Quit the country.'

Russell laughed again. 'One big one – that's what we thought we had.'

'On Bitter Crick?'

'No. We only took that one on when the other folded.'

'What folded?'

'Don't say nothing about it, Russ,' Murdock snapped.

'Oh hell, it don't matter now, Zack,' Russell said, and then, to Bassett, 'we thought we was all set on the big one, a hell of a big payroll shipment, see? Me and Zack, we went and had a look at the safe in the railroad depot – and by god, it's that same black bastard of a safe that can't be broke.'

'How did you manage that? You mean to say you had help on the inside?' Bassett said.

'Shut up about it, Russ,' Murdock said again.

Bassett ignored him. 'Have you still got your man on the inside?'

Russell started to answer, but Murdock put his glass down with a thud and stood. 'This aint getting us nowheres. Let's get going.' He turned toward their horses. Owlhead caught the whiskey bottle by the neck, fumbled his hat on with a grin at Bassett and lurched after him. Russell followed.

Bassett walked out with them. I'm about to lose them, he thought. He caught up with Russell. 'One mistake is all you made – think about it. Say you've got a sore tooth, you go to a tooth doctor, aint that right?' Got to hold him, Bassett thought, and even as he spoke, something was taking shape in his mind.

Murdock swung onto a big sorrel. 'Don't tell him another god damn word, Russ.'

'Hold on Zack,' said Russell. 'A tooth doctor —' he frowned at Bassett, 'a man who opens safes, is that it? You?'

'Not me. But I can get one.' It was all there now in his mind – crazy, Bassett thought, but it's bait on the hook.

The big sorrel whirled under Murdock, skittish. He caught the rein close to the bit with both hands and leaned back, the horse's foaming jaws drawn tight to his left knee. 'Russ!' he barked.

Clay Russell mounted his own horse. 'Who? Who would you get?' Murdock released the sorrel's head and the horse plunged away. Clay's horse danced, trying to follow.

Got to hook him now, Bassett thought. He grinned slowly. 'Maybe you've heard of Blue Russell.'

Clay wheeled his horse in a spray of sand, his face a white blur of astonishment. 'Think about it,' Bassett said. 'I'll be here long enough to help Olaf finish his fence. When Zack cools off he'll listen to you – then come on back and we'll talk.'

Clay Russell stared at him for a moment, then reined his horse around and galloped slowly away, looking back once before the canyon swallowed him.

He took it, Bassett thought. The hook is in his jaw.

CHAPTER XXII

Bassett worked all day setting posts with Olaf. For supper, he ate what the Swede sent out to him. It was barely dark and Bassett was feeding sticks to a little fire when his roan horse nickered. He pushed his coffeepot closer to the fire and put his tin cup on a stone next to it. He put a bottle of whiskey next to the cup.

'Coffee,' he said into the dark, 'or a jolt. The one cup will have to do. It's about half clean.'

They stepped into the firelight then, and after a moment sat in the sand near the fire. Murdock sat cross-legged, his elbows on his knees, his heavy shoulders hunched. 'Comin here is no part of my idea, Bucklin,' he said.

'Did I hear you right?' Clay Russell said. 'Did I hear you say Blue Russell?' In the firelight, the reckless grin gone, he looked gaunt and worn.

'You did.'

'You know I've got a kid brother named Blue?'

'That's what the saloon talk says. I spent most of the winter in New Orleans and you can't hardly buy a glass of beer in New Orleans and not hear about Blue Russell.'

Russell shook his head. 'It couldn't be him. The kid was livin in St Louis with my uncle. He don't know nothing about safes.'

'What happened is, the kid and the old man had a battle and the kid run off. Some way or other, he took up with an old-timer named Disbrow. A safe-cracker. The best in the game, too, except he was all crippled up from an explosion, but with the kid to help him – well, hell, the kid and Disbrow cleaned out a cotton broker's safe in broad daylight. They went in posing as repairmen, see?'

Clay Russell laughed, wagging his head. 'Last I saw him, he was shoeing horses.'

'Maybe so, but he's a first-rate mechanic, too – between

them, the kid and Disbrow can open anything with locks on it.'

'Including that three-door Invincible safe?'

'Including that.'

Russell tossed a pebble into the fire and sparks showered up. 'Busting safes – I'm damned if I can believe it!' He hesitated. 'He always was a game little cuss.'

'He's game all right. And damn it, the kid and Disbrow are doing a whole lot better than we are. You can believe that.'

'Then what makes you think he would do this thing with us?' Murdock demanded.

'Because he's Clay Russell's brother,' Bassett snapped. There was conviction in his voice, but he was feeling his way, trying to hold the flimsy scheme together. He was thinking that if he could at least get Russell and Murdock to disclose the big strike they had planned and then go through the motions of bringing the kid and Disbrow in on it, they would have to get back into civilized country. Give him that much, Bassett thought, and he would somehow find a way to get in touch with the agency or local law, wherever it might turn out to be. And put the collar on them all.

'How would you get to the kid?' Russell said.

'I know a couple of the places he and Disbrow have been hanging out. We can start there. Hell, I found *you*, didn't I?'

Russell and Murdock looked at each other, the firelight flickering on their faces.

'I'll tell you this,' Bassett went on, 'you'll never do it without the kid. Never.'

Murdock grunted and slapped a hand down on his knee. 'All right. You come along with us in the morning. When we get where we're goin, and after you get the kid, that's when we talk. Not before.'

Riding east, the country was all sun-blasted red sandstone, hewn by wind and water into nightmarish forms. They forded the Colorado deep in a red canyon at the Dandy Crossing, long known as the rustlers' crossing because it was the only place in a hundred miles where stock could ford the river. Stolen stock, of course, or mounted men on the run from the law.

After the river there was no water except in the deepest

canyons, and the old rustlers' trail followed the canyons, so deep and narrow in places that the sky was narrowed to a ragged slit, high over their heads. Late in the day they came to Chavez' place. Within sight of a great natural arch of red stone, there was a stone hovel built against the canyon wall where Chavez lived with his woman and their small child. There was a water hole and a corral. And horses. Good horses, Bassett saw. A pair of slant-eyed yellow dogs loped out, barking at them.

'He knows me and the Owlhead,' Naylor said. 'We'll go in first and talk to him.' Then Bassett saw movement behind one of the twisted corral posts. A saddled horse. Near the horse, a man detached himself from the shadows, put aside a carbine and climbed to the top rail of the corral, where he sat waiting. Naylor and the Owlhead spoke to him, then beckoned to the others. Chavez was lean and sinewy as a lizard. Even his skin-tight leather britches, brush-scuffed and powdered with red dust, looked reptilian.

'Where you want the horses?' he said.

The Owlhead looked at Bassett. Murdock shook his head slightly. Bassett laughed. 'Hell, you've got to tell him *something.*'

'That's right,' Naylor said. 'He's got to steal em, then drive em, and stake em out where we want em.'

'Start em near Durango,' the Owlhead said. 'We aint sure where yet. Stake em out running back this way, toward the Dandy Crossing.' He waved at the corrals. 'One stop here maybe.'

Chavez rolled himself a cornhusk cigaret. 'When you know for sure, you come tell me? I need two weeks, maybe three. And the money, now.' Smoke streamed from his thin nostrils.

'Hell, we're broke now,' the Owlhead said. Chavez merely stared.

'He's got to get started on it,' Bassett said. 'Then if we get the kid, we're ready to go.' He dug a wallet from his coat pocket and counted out $500, which he gave to Chavez. 'This tells you one of us will be back with the rest of the money – he will help you move the horses to where we'll want em.'

The second day they put the red desert behind them. Ahead, the ground was rising steadily in a vast sweep toward the snow-blanketed San Juans. Riding hard, there was among them the usual joshing and banter, except for Murdock – scowling, dark, suspicious, a powder keg, Bassett thought, with a short fuse. Instead of camping at nightfall, they rode almost the night through. It was moonless, but the country was open, rolling, the mountains hulking dark to the north, and the wind carried the bite of snow mingled with the smell of sage. Bassett heard the distant whistle of a train. Near midnight they came to a house and sheds set among a few cottonwoods. Even in the dark, Bassett sensed the decay and desolation. He heard a woman's voice, sleepy, querulous. Murdock and Russell went on into the house, but the Owlhead told Bassett to follow him. They threw their bedrolls down in a shed, on hay. Bassett was remembering that he had set out to find a homestead – 160 acres filed on by Solomon Carver and spouse, Effie, in 1883. Now he had found it. The long way around, he thought. Then he was asleep.

The sun was high when Clay Russell stirred him with a boot and woke him. Grinning down, Russell handed him a pencil and paper. 'You can start writing that letter to my kid brother. I aint much for writing, but I'll put a note on the end of it when you're done.'

Groggy from sleep, Bassett sat cross-legged in the hay with the writing paper and box on one knee. During the ride, he had decided what to write. It would have to look good, but his main problem was to get a message to the agency. It could not be direct – the letter to Blue Russell would have to serve if he could get it through to Havenhurst, by way of Jake Neilsen's saloon. The message itself and the Durango postmark would give the super some idea of Bassett's situation. And the saloon address ought to be a good one. In the underworld, saloon-keepers and madams formed a grapevine postal service, unscheduled but reliable. It was only in such places, certain saloons or houses of pleasure, that fugitives from the law could move more or less freely, even under their own names – places like Miss Francie's in Kansas City or the Lafitte House outside of New Orleans. Bassett knew the Lafitte House. If

Blue Russell had been there once, he was likely to go again. All right, he thought – one letter to Neilsen's and one to the Lafitte House. But even as he wrote, he was asking himself, what's going to happen if this doesn't work?

He was folding the two letters when Clay Russell returned. Murdock was with him. Russell handed him a tin cup of coffee and Bassett gave him the two letters.

'Both the same,' he said. 'Better chance of reaching the kid.'

Clay Russell licked his pencil and began to scrawl his postscript to the first one. Murdock took the other and read it, then grunted. 'Where you going to send these?'

Bassett told him, then added, 'The kid don't even have to be there, see? A ten-dollar bill will get it forwarded, one way or another.'

'I don't like it,' Murdock said. 'We broke out of jail in St Louis. I don't want a trace of us closer than a thousand miles to St Louis. Hell, somebody else could be paying that bartender, for all we know. You claim the kid has been in New Orleans. Let's start there.' He tore up the letter.

Bassett shrugged. He took the other letter from Clay Russell, put it in an envelope and printed BLUE RUSSELL firmly on the face of it, then folded that envelope and put it into another, along with a ten-dollar bill. He licked the flap and sealed it, then addressed it to Sr Rosario, Prop., Lafitte House, New Orleans. Murdock and Russell took it and left him alone then. Bassett was finishing his cup of coffee a few minutes later when he saw two women come out of the house and get into a buggy. He recognized India Wood from his brief encounter with her in Israel Cawley's shop. She flicked a glance at him as he stood in the doorway of the shed watching her. Bassett returned the glance – even if she could have recognized Wagenbach after all this time, Wagenbach looked nothing at all like Preacher Bucklin.

She turned the horse, shook out the lines and set off smartly, headed for Durango to mail the letter. Bassett felt like a man who had just walked into quicksand.

CHAPTER XXIII

It was dark when Blue and Packy pulled up before the Lafitte House and turned the buggy over to a groom. Blue passed outside the door and took out his wallet. 'Here is enough to pay Rosario what you owe him.'

Packy sniffed and looked at Blue with cool disdain. 'Is this how it's going to be, now? Maybe you'll want to go along to make sure I deliver it, pardner.' He bore down heavily on the word *pardner*.

Stung, Blue realized that Packy's pride would suffer if he, Blue, went along with him on this errand. He counted out another $500 and put it into Packy's hand. 'You don't have to tell me we're pardners, Packy – when you see Rosario, will you ask him to fix us up with a ride to town to catch the midnight train?'

Packy folded the money and pocketed it with the somehow righteous air of a man collecting a long overdue debt. Blue watched him go, then walked into the gents' bar – a hand caught his shoulder and swung him around. It was Dakin.

'Kid, I heard you was croaked.' Dakin's broken-toothed grin was ghastly. He squeezed Blue's shoulders.

'Not so's you'd notice,' Blue said. Behind Dakin in the dimly lighted barroom, he saw a number of Dakin's crowd of sports and gamblers. One of them spoke up.

'Dake, here's a hundred that says the kid can put your knucks on the table.' His friends were putting out a table and chairs before he finished speaking. Dakin grinned and rubbed his hands together. Blue shrugged, laughing, and sat.

'I'm on my last twenty,' Dakin said.

'Taken,' the sport said. 'You want to bet, kid?'

More people were drifting in to watch. 'I'll go twenty with anyone who wants it.' He had to put up $220, and he thought, this is how it is with Packy, money doesn't mean anything until it's gone.

Right hands clasped, elbows planted on the table. 'Gentlemen, commence,' the sport said, and their arms were locked and straining. Dakin's arm was like an oak branch. Blue's mind fled. He thought of Jena, then of Hutch, then he saw the great Kruger Invincible sitting before him. Staring into Dakin's squinting eyes, vaguely hearing breath snuffle through his flattened nose, Blue was opening the Kruger in his mind – he was turning the dial, feeling for the minute change of pressure, watching for the infinitesimal shift in the dial reading that told him he was on a number. He found it and went on around the dial looking for the next and then the next. The tumbler was turning, the notch rising toward the fence – in his mind's eye, he could see through the lock and watch every part of it – the fence dropped. The wind went out of Dakin with a sudden rushing sigh and his arm slammed to the table.

'Kid, you breakin my heart,' Dakin said. 'By god, I cut me a club next time.'

'Seventeen minutes,' the sport said.

Blue grinned and picked up his winnings. He saw that Dakin was broke. He peeled off some bills and threw them onto the table, then looked around at the faces of the betting sports. 'Dake ought to make something out of this, too,' he said. He waited. After a moment, money began to flutter down in front of Dakin. Blue turned to go and Rosario was there, teetering on his three-inch heels, grinning at Blue through the smoke from his cheroot. He tucked an envelope in Blue's pocket, winked and said, 'Kid, you partner talkin to me about a ride to town. Cost you five hundred, is what I tell him.' He waited. Blue thought, they're all that way – money doesn't mean anything. He paid Rosario. Just then, a black servant pushed a wheelchair into the hallway. In the chair was an aged man, his palsied hands shaking before him on the head of his stick. A shawl was draped over his thin shoulders.

'We better hurry,' Blue said. 'Where is —' The old man lifted his stick and punched Blue in the ribs with it. *'He-hee,'* the old man cackled, and then Blue knew him.

The letter Rosario had given Blue remained in his pocket.

Their train was the Gulf Special, the night run to Houston and

San Antonio. Blue, wearing eyeglasses and a black hat and coat, pushed Packy through the station in the wheelchair. A porter led with their grips. Blue thought, *How many of those people are police*? He was aware of scores of pairs of eyes, all, he thought, boring into him. The porter led them to their compartment. When they were alone, Packy climbed out of the chair. He caught sight of himself in a mirror and shuddered, then peeled off his scraggly white wig and mustache and threw them aside.

'Blue, I've been thinking about this.' Packy took a bottle from his grip and poured himself a drink. 'We could do our trick in San Antone, then move on – maybe to Frisco. Out there, we could —'

'Stop it, Packy! I aint a rube kid anymore. It's catching up with us – don't you see that?'

'The wheelchair is a good dodge —'

'For how long? Once more? Twice?' Blue was shedding his clothes. The train was already rolling, its laminated paper wheels clicking softly beneath them, its bell sounding a steady *ding-ding* up ahead. Blue climbed into the upper berth. Propped on one elbow, he looked down at Packy. 'If we're lucky and don't do nothing foolish, we'll get you to Mexico.' A smile broke his frown. Then he thumped his pillow and rolled over.

Packy sat in a chair and finished his drink, then poured himself another. He turned down the lamp and watched the lights of the city spin past. He was filled with a sick, uneasy tension. Outside, the lights thinned. Soon the train was rolling through darkness. He saw faint starshine on bayou waters. After a time, he pulled off his collar and tie and stretched out on the berth. A pinpoint of yellow light from a distant lantern flickered through the trees. *I'm losing the kid.* The thought stung him. More, it frightened him. Suddenly the tiny room was suffocating – like waking up at night, knowing he was in the pen.

Packy sat up. Blue hadn't moved. He was a sound sleeper. Packy caught up his coat and shoes and slipped out the door. In the old days he had ridden this train many times. There was nearly always a game in the gents' smoking parlor, back in the rear car.

Blue dreamed that he saw Jena standing in her skiff, saying something to him that he could not hear. Then Hutch was beside him, saying earnestly, *I told ye, boy, he had it comin.* Blue strained to hear what Jena was saying and her voice slowly became the rushing sound of the train. Awake, Blue slipped out of his berth. He picked up his watch from the small night table and held it close to the dim light of the gas lamp. It was two-thirty in the morning. He yawned and put the watch back. His eye fell then upon the corner of an envelope sticking out of his coat pocket. Blue pulled the envelope out of the pocket and tore it open. He turned up the lamp a little. His skin prickled as he read.

Your brother is desperate to see you regarding a business venture calling for your line of work. Great mutual profit is certain. He would seek you out himself but travel is dangerous to his health. This is the one that will make you rich if you are man enough for it. We must have your answer now. Wire reply to me —

Rev. H. Bassett
Genl Delivery – Durango Colorado

And beneath that message, Blue recognized Clay's scrawl.

Hello Blue its time we got togather – Brothers need one another and I need you now – yr bro – Clay

Blue read both messages through twice. His mind was seething. On sudden impulse, he turned and reached out to shake Packy awake. The bed was empty. Startled, Blue pawed the bed. After a moment he opened the door into the corridor and looked out. Just as he started to turn back into the room, he saw the conductor round the bend of the corridor at the end of the car. The conductor nodded and smiled agreeably.

'You wouldn't – just by chance – know of a game somewhere on this train, would you?' Blue said.

The conductor placed a finger alongside his nose and winked. 'Aint nothing like a hand or two of cards when a man can't sleep,' he said. 'Try the gents' smoking parlor, rear car. Top caliber action.' He nodded again and moved on.

Blue closed the door after him. He was furious. I ought to just get off the train and keep on going, he thought. He read the letter again. *Brothers need one another and I need you now.* The train began to slow. Lights flashed past the window. Blue looked out. He saw some parked wagons and an old frame store building near a grade crossing. Seconds later, the train was rolling to a stop before a station. A night light flooded a sign, NEW IBERIA, and off to one side near a corner of the building, another sign read WESTERN UNION. Blue pounded his fist on the window sill, then turned suddenly, snatched up a pencil and began to write on the back of the envelope.

Housed in the 70-foot length of the rear car were an elegant lounge and buffet, trimmed in gold and claret drapes like opera boxes, and the gents' smoking parlor. The four card players in the smoker scarcely noticed when the train made its brief stop in New Iberia. Packy was a little ahead and holding a good hand. The two drummers, Gage and Barnes, were the big winners. The fourth man was J. B. Keeler, who thought he had a good hand, but was finding himself now short of cash.

'Table stakes, mister,' Barnes said to Keeler. 'If you're shy of money, you'll have to call her quits for this hand.'

Keeler bit down on his cigar. 'Hell, I'm good for it – anyone can tell you J. B. Keeler is good for it.' He was in fact more than two thousand dollars behind, as of that moment.

'You're five hundred shy, Mr Keeler,' said Gage. 'Me and Mr Barnes have folded. Mr Bristol is entitled to take the pot.'

Packy leaned back, holding his cards close to his good eye and at the same time catching light from the Pintsch gas wall lamp over his left shoulder.

'Hold on!' Keeler put his cards face down and his hand darted beneath his coat. Packy saw the flash of metal and froze, staring now at the pistol in Keeler's fist. Keeler laughed, then put the pistol down with the chips in the center of the table. It was a Smith & Wesson, gold-inlaid and engraved, with the figure of a mermaid carved in the ivory grips, her tiny breasts nippled with rubies.

'No offense, gents,' Keeler said. 'I didn't aim to startle you. Will you take a first-class handgun, Mr Bristol? Made up for me special by Israel Cawley in St Louis, and she run me seven-fifty. Two hundred alone for them little titties. What say, m' friend?'

Packy touched the weapon gingerly. He had a powerful aversion to firearms. On the other hand, it came from the shop where Blue had grown up. Was it some kind of sign? Packy was suddenly sure he ought not to let the gun get away.

Pleased, Keeler turned up a full house, sixes and queens. 'First decent cards I've touched all evenin.'

Packy spread out a straight in diamonds, ten high. Keeler's magenta jowls sagged. 'Hell. I'll just have to get Cawley to make me up another —'

Packy pulled the chips and gun toward himself. 'But Israel Cawley's dead!'

Keeler grunted. 'Not less he's croaked in the last month, he aint.' He grinned and made clucking sounds with his tongue. 'I caint shoot worth a damn, but I always fancied a good handgun and no one does a job on em like Cawley. A damned tacky old shop he runs, too. It's your luck you caught J. B. Keeler short of cash, friend. Now if you gents will let me raise a few hundred on my watch before the next hand, so's I can get back in the game, I'll buy the iron back from you, a few hands from now, what say?'

Packy felt suddenly dizzy. The murder charge – Blue was free of it. He felt honor-bound to give the gun to the kid now. He shook his head. 'I've took a fancy to the little sweetheart, myself – I believe I'll keep her.'

Keeler's jaw thrust forward. 'God damn. Give me a one-hour limit. That aint asking much.' Gage had already given him money on his watch, and was dealing another hand.

Packy frowned. 'It was your idea, Mr Keeler, and you lost it.' He picked up his new hand and leaned back to catch the light on his cards. Across from him, the drummer, Gage, saw the hand of cards reflected in the glassy varnish of the satin-wood marquetry wall paneling behind Packy. Keeler subsided, mumbling around his cigar, and looked at his new cards.

Gage studied the reflection of Packy's cards in the varnish, then scratched his head with two fingers, which told Barnes that Packy held two pair. The two men had been working the trains together for twenty years and communicated easily in a language of coughs, sniffs, sighs, blinks and scratches.

Unaccountably to Packy, his luck turned and he began to lose. He had always loved the easy talk of the tables and the undercurrent of suspense, the unfolding mysteries of each new hand, even when he lost, and he had left tens of thousands on the tables over the years with never a backward look – but now, watching his roll melt away was suddenly painful because of Blue's unreasonable and *foolish* stand. Packy squirmed, thinking of the thousands he had blown just since the day they cleaned out Ashburn's safe. How could they make enough back now in just one job – enough for him to live even halfway decent in Mexico, or anyplace?

And suddenly the gold-inlaid pistol that sagged in his pocket was nagging at him too – he wished he had not learned that Cawley was still alive and that Blue was free of the murder charge. Without that hanging over him, Blue might even back out of the score in San Antone. By three-thirty in the morning, Packy had lost every cent Blue had given him.

Packy pushed back his chair, grinning gamely. 'Boys, you could as well have sandbagged me.' He thought for a moment of raising fresh money on the gun. Packy believed in fresh money, but it came down to a simple matter of loyalty. He was going to have to tell Blue about the gun and what it meant to him. He could not bring himself to get rid of it now.

Blue found Packy on the observation platform of the the rear car. It was four o'clock in the morning. Packy was leaning on the railing, looking back, his shoulders hunched. Coal smoke mixed with salty air whipped away on rushing wind. Up ahead, the steam whistle wailed at a grade crossing.

'I woke up and found you gone,' Blue said. Packy did not answer. 'All right, I see – nothing good will come of my asking where you've been.' Blue was seething.

'Don't scold me till I get a cup of coffee down the stack,' Packy said.

'You lost, is that it?'

'I had those two drummers backed right up, and a good piece of J. B. Keeler, too, then the two of em started raising me, putting on the squeeze.'

'They could have been working together. Did you think of that?'

'Not soon enough,' Packy said reluctantly. 'And it's no good thinking about it now. We'll make it all up in San Antone,' – he swung and peered sharply at Blue – 'that is, if you're through talking foolishness, so we can go back to work.' Packy felt the weight of the gun in his side pocket. He grinned warmly. Interrupting Blue as he replied, he said, 'Look, kid, I want to show you something – it —' He stopped, blinking, not certain he had heard right.

'No, Packy,' Blue said again. 'San Antone is out.'

'You can't mean that!'

'I mean it.' Blue took the letter from his pocket and gave it to Packy. 'Rosario gave me this before we left.'

Packy held the letter to the light from the door window and read it. He wagged his head. 'Train robbery is what he's talking about. You know that, don't you?'

'It don't say train robbery. It says my line of work. They must have found out about me some way.'

Packy's laugh was bitter. 'Every crook and grifter in the country knows about Blue Russell by now. They mean to use you.'

'Clay is my own brother. He needs me – desperate, it says.'

'They're stickup trash, and you'll get the rope, same as they will.'

'I'll get it anyway.'

'No, Blue, that's not —'

Blue cut him off. 'You've told me so yourself, plenty of times. Look, Packy, I figured I owed you something, but I don't see no way to pay you more than I already have and make it stick – when I woke up and found you gone, I knew what you were up to. That made up my mind for me. I gave the conductor a telegram to send for me, back at the last stop. I said I would be in Durango in two days.'

'You'll pull out and leave me *broke?*' Packy's voice sounded thin and querulous. He pulled me out of the river, Blue thought, and saved my life – I can't dump him.

'Yes, broke,' he said. 'If you're broke, I'm thinkin there's a chance you'll throw in with me on this. You know I'll need you, same as you couldn't handle a safe without me. And you'll have your score. But either way, I'm going.'

Packy's hand closed on the gun in his pocket, tensed to draw it out – if I give it to the kid, he was thinking, and tell him Israel is alive, there won't be anything pushing him to go with Clay. Packy felt an instant of panic. He was certain that Blue would quit him now, too – that he would leave him finally and completely broke with no way left at all to get himself another stake. The moment skidded past. I'll tell him later, he thought.

'You said yourself I was a natural,' Blue said with a twisted grin. 'Now we'll find out what kind of a crook I was cut out to be. Will you come with me?'

Packy's mouth was dry as sand. He felt weak and sick. His voice was raw and hollow. 'Spose it got around that Disbrow let a man go it alone before he was ready? That aint my style, amigo.'

The train rumbled onto a bridge. Lights from a distant shore glistened on dark water. Packy slipped the gun from his pocket, his body half-turned to shield the move. He hesitated, then tossed the gun away, into the night and the river water.

CHAPTER XXIV

Blue and Packy were in Houston shortly after dawn, and Ft Worth by early evening. There they boarded a Ft Worth & Denver sleeper. North and west the train rolled through the Texas night, trailing her plume of coal smoke and cinders. Henrietta, Quanah, Amarillo – the conductor sang out the stations.

Back in New Iberia, when he gave the conductor his telegram to send for him, Blue had asked, 'Going from here to Colorado, can you give me the name of a place where a wire could catch me?' And the conductor had said, 'You can't miss if you make it Trinidad,' and he spelled it out. Blue signed the message Bill Cawley. Some seventeen hours out of Fort Worth, a telegram was waiting in the Trinidad station, addressed to one Bill Cawley.

> YOUR INTEREST OUR MISSION MOST WELCOME MEET YOU SAWMILL CREEK SIDING FIVE MILES DURANGO SIGNED REV H BASSETT

Night again. Waiting. Changing trains, boarding the narrow-gauge westbound Denver & Rio Grande. Grasping the night-cold iron of the handrail, with coal smoke from the hissing locomotive sharp in his nostrils, Blue thought, *What am I doing here?* He awoke once in the night and saw moonlight flash pale on white water in the canyon below the tracks. He heard the slow beat of the locomotive's pistons as she labored on a long mountain grade.

In the gray light of dawn, the train stopped and Blue saw two cowboys get off. It was high, open country, dotted with sage and juniper, not a road or building in sight. Looking out the window, Blue saw saddles and bedrolls tossed down to them from the baggage car, and he watched the two of them standing there, reeling a little, looking after the train as it pulled away in a gush of steam; then they picked up their saddles and started walking. They know who they are and where they're going, Blue thought. That's where I'm going – to *find out* who I am. Thinking of it that way gave him a sudden sharp surge of excitement and for a few seconds his heart pounded with it.

Shadows slanted on brushy hills. The conductor tapped him on the shoulder. 'Sawmill Crick, gents.' Blue shook Packy awake. The train rumbled to a stop at a siding, hissing. He saw a corral, a loading chute, and a horse and wagon facing the train near the corral. A tall man sat on the front seat of the wagon, a tall man in a black hat and suit with a preacher's collar, lifting his hand solemnly as they climbed down from the coach. The train chuffed, pulled away, rounding a juniper-studded hill, its plume of smoke breaking up and drifting.

The tall man reached up and pulled off the white collar and

its attached shirt front and put them on the seat beside him. It was the collar that had made him look solemn and pious – without it he looked hard. 'That was Reverend Bassett, come to meet you,' he said with a faint grin. 'I'm Preacher Bucklin.'

Another man came out from the brush behind the corrals. Tall, gaunt, sandy hair, a haunted look. Blue was puzzled. 'I figured to meet my brother here —' he said.

'Why dammit, Blue,' the sandy-haired man said, frowning, 'don't you know me?' Then he grinned, and it was Clay.

Brushy hills capped with ridges of red rock. Juniper, green-black and twisting. Topping a rise, Blue saw snow-capped mountains to the north, their lower slopes black with pine and cut with long scars of bare rock. Clay, sitting in the rear seat with Blue, laughed aloud once and clutched Blue's shoulder. 'By god, Blue – I don't believe it!'

Wind moaned in the sage. The house, flimsy and weathered, sat among dusty-leaved cottonwoods on an open and desolate slope of ground. A thin streamer of smoke curled up from a tin smoke pipe. A young woman with orange-blond hair was splitting wood with an ax, back of the house. The buggy rolled to a stop. Another young woman stepped out holding a chipped enamel dishpan. She threw water in a greasy splatter and turned.

Blue, startled, said, 'India!' She was thin and her blue cotton dress was faded and stained. Her reddish hair was twisted into a knot on her head and lank strands hung about her face. Her lips were parted, quivering, but Clay said, 'Never mind that now.' She bit her lip and went back through the kitchen door. Blue turned then and saw the men in the doorway of a shed – three of them, one now lowering a sawed-off shotgun, setting it back out of sight.

'There you are, Blue,' Packy murmured. 'That's the style here – you're doing business with gents who store their brains in shotgun barrels.' He shook with a silent laugh.

The blond woman carried an armload of wood into the kitchen and dropped it with a crash. She appeared at the door again, her face shiny and her mouth lopsided from the smeared red of her lips. 'You boys can eat or starve to death

– it don't matter a damn to me.'

They ate in a small room off the kitchen at a rough plank table – fried beef and potatoes, canned corn, biscuits dipped in the beef fat, coffee from a big granite pot. They ate almost without talking, Clay grinning when he caught Blue's eye. The one they called the Owlhead and the plump blond woman were both a little drunk. The Owlhead spilled food on his shirt front and rubbed it in with his hand. The heavy-shouldered man with black, crinkly hair, Zack Murdock, tore at his steak with square, stained teeth, eating rapidly and drinking his coffee in gulps. Still chewing, he grunted once at the blond woman and nodded at his plate, sucking his teeth noisily while she forked another piece of beef onto it. India stayed in the kitchen, eating standing up while she tended a big iron stove. She smiled once, nervously, at Blue through the door, then looked away.

Zack Murdock put his plate down abruptly and sat staring fixedly at Blue and Packy while they finished. Then he said, 'It's time we told you about the train.'

'The telegram said *our* line of work,' Blue said. 'What has a train got to do with it?'

'It's the one that runs from Durango to Telluride – the Shotgun Run, they call it, on account of all the mines yonder in the mountains. A couple of thousand miners, see? The payroll shipments into Telluride run between two and three hundred thousand.'

It was going too fast for Blue. Nothing was the way he had expected. He was sickened by the squalor of the place and it hurt him to see India looking shabby and worn and frightened. And he wanted to talk, to get acquainted again with his brother. Instead, Zack Murdock was talking trains and payrolls. Blue looked again at Packy, who smiled indulgently at him and said nothing. 'Trains – it appears we have came a long way for nothing,' Blue said after a moment. 'Holding up trains is not our —'

'We will take care of the train,' Murdock said. 'All you've got to do is open the safe in the express car.'

'It's still a holdup. You pull the trigger on someone and we would get the rope, same as you.'

'Well, goddamn —' Murdock started to say.

'Look, Blue,' Clay said quickly, 'what we aim to do is get aboard the train on the Telluride run, and stop it, see – uncouple the engine and express car and run em across the bridge at Lizard Crick, then blow the bridge.'

'Just like that? What about the express agent?' Blue said.

'I *told* you,' Murdock said. 'We'll handle all that, same as we would without you.'

'The real question is,' Bassett said, 'how much time will you need to open the express car safe?'

'We have to know what kind it is,' Blue said.

'We saw it – it says Invincible across the front,' Clay Russell said.

Packy laughed derisively and shot a knowing look at Blue. 'By god, it's no wonder you need help. That box is like a bank vault on wheels.'

Murdock swung on Bassett. 'Bringing in these clowns was your doing.'

'He didn't say it couldn't be done,' Bassett said mildly.

'How much *time*?' Murdock snarled.

'Any safe can be broke,' Packy said. 'A couple of days' hard work is what you're talking about. Twelve hours, tops, for firstclass men with the right tools and nothing going wrong.'

'Twelve hours,' Clay Russell said in disgust. 'It could as well be a hundred years.'

'Most jugs,' Packy said, 'are cracked between closing time Saturday and opening Monday morning, to give a man time.'

'What the hell are you going to be doing with all those shotgun guards for twelve hours?' Murdock raged.

'What shotgun guards?' Blue said. 'You mean you're not talking about just an express agent, or maybe one guard?' Next to him, Packy now fidgeted uneasily.

'An army of guards is what he means,' Clay Russell said. 'Hell, all over the train, like fleas on a dog's back.'

'It aint our style,' Packy said bluntly.

Blue leaned back and looked from one to the other. He was remembering his excitement when he first set eyes on the Kruger and had known instantly that he could crack it, even when Packy said it could not be done. He suddenly felt the same way about the train. He was seized by conviction, certain and reckless at once. This is why I'm here, he thought, to do something no other man in the country can do – but not the way they've got it figured.

'We can break the safe,' Blue said softly. Packy stared at him and half rose from his seat. Blue put out a hand and held him there. 'We can break it,' he said again, 'and do it in a lot less than twelve hours, but not while you're blowing the heads off the guards. What we have to do is figure a way to get at the safe that will give us the time we need. I want to see the train, the express car and every foot of track.'

'Any maybe you want to meet the president of the line, too,' Murdock said. 'He could write the combination down for you.'

'Any man who don't look over the ground first is a damn fool,' Bassett said. 'I watched my train for near a month before I tapped her. You told me you had a man on the inside. That ought to help.'

'The Owlhead's brother-in-law,' Clay said.

'That's another thing,' Owl Carver said, 'my brother-in-law, Jared – he aint doing a thing without he gets five thousand beforehand. Earnest money, is what he says, case somethin goes haywire.'

'We don't have five thousand,' Murdock said flatly. 'He will have to wait.'

'He says he won't – hell, he is risking his pension.'

'I'll talk to him,' Blue said, 'and pay him if I have to.'

There was a long silence. 'Damn,' Carver said, 'maybe we'd ought to leave the train alone and put the touch on you.'

'I don't like a slick-ear kid tellin me what to do,' Naylor said suddenly.

Blue faced him. 'Would it help you any to like it better if I was to break your jaw?'

Naylor stiffened. Clay Russell laughed. 'By god, Naylor, I would pay to see the kid do it. What the hell, you don't have to *like* nothing. If the kid set it up to crack the box and you get yours, you'll like it, all right.'

'We can travel as mining men,' Bassett said, 'mining men looking to buy a property – that will give us a good excuse to poke around the railroad and the mountains between Durango and Telluride.'

'If you're thinking about going in town with them, or anyplace else,' Murdock said, 'you can forget it, Preacher.'

'I figured by now I was in this thing,' Bassett said.

'You're wanted, same as we are. Russ can go with them if it has to be, but you stay out of sight, along with us. From now on until we're finished, I'm not letting you out of my sight. You and me are going to be like two pigs sucking side by side.'

Bassett frowned, staring back at Murdock, and then he shrugged. My foot is in the bear trap now, he thought.

A little later, Clay Russell showed them to the shed out back of the house. He lighted a stub of a candle on a broken saucer. The dim yellow light flickered on two rope-bound bunks, tattered blankets. Cold air gusted through the cracks. Packy looked around him and wagged his head, laughing helplessly. As soon as Clay left, he caught Blue's sleeve and swung him around. 'What's got into you, Blue? You don't have to prove nothing to a mess of gun sharks.'

'I told you that first night in Latourette's shop that I could bust the Kruger,' Blue said. 'Now I'm going to do it.'

'*Why*, Blue? On a train, with shotgun guards – it's suicide.'

Blue sank back on the bunk, his eyes fixed on the candle flame. 'Three sets of doors, off-set spindles, burglarproof locks ... we'll be the first ones to bust a Kruger Invincible. Think of it.' He suddenly looked squarely at Packy. 'Don't you want to know how I aim to do it?'

'I just want to know *why*.'

'No class thief would back down in front of that bunch,' Blue said.

CHAPTER XXV

In the morning, Blue and Packy and Clay Russell were driven into Durango by Naylor and let off near the railroad yards. 'We'll take the train to Telluride,' Blue said, 'to look over the ground, and rent some livery horses for the trip back, so you can expect to see us back at the farmhouse in about five days.' Naylor nodded and drove back the way he had come.

'You have seen Crenshaw,' Blue said to Clay. 'There's no need of your seeing him again, is there?'

Clay shook his head. 'The river runs through town, just yonder. I'll wait for you there.'

Jared Crenshaw, wearing a green eyeshade low over bloodshot eyes, scribbled on an order pad. Ink spattered from his pen nib. He sensed movement behind him and turned to face two well-dressed men. The younger of the two smiled affably.

'Mr Crenshaw? My name is Adams. My partner, Mr Bristol. We're mining men, interested in developing a property near here, and of course, we'll be transporting machinery and cash. Your brother-in-law, Mr Carver, suggested —'

Crenshaw flinched at the name and looked nervously about him. 'What the hell do you mean, coming here?' he mumbled through his teeth. 'I told that idiot no one was to come around here.'

'Praps you would show us how you transport cash?' the older man said.

Crenshaw's neck appeared to thicken and his hands made convulsive sawing motions. 'Not a word! You've got to show me ... a proper piece of paper first. I'll talk to you in the General Grant. In the bar. Thirty minutes.'

The General Grant Hotel was built of red sandstone, a block from the depot. In the paneled barroom, mounted heads of game animals peered from the walls. Blue and Packy took seats beneath an enormous bearded bull buffalo and waited. When Crenshaw hurried in a few minutes later, he was wearing a derby in place of his eyeshade. His black sleeve protectors showed beneath the cuffs of his coat. He went straight to the bar. The bartender automatically put out a shot glass, filled it with whiskey, then stood a foaming mug of beer next to it. Crenshaw threw the whiskey down at a gulp, chased it with a swallow of beer, then carried the mug to their table and sat down.

'Gents,' he said, his teeth bared. He was pale, his skin slick and moist.

'Just how often do these trains run, Mr Crenshaw?'

'Business first, goddammit. My pension is at stake.' He looked nervously behind him. 'I want five thousand.'

'I can give you twenty-five hundred right now in a money belt,' Blue said. 'The rest will have to wait until the job is done. 'We've got to be certain you'll go through with your end.'

'Show me,' Crenshaw said. Blue unbuttoned his shirt, lifted a flap on the belt and Crenshaw saw bank notes. He closed his eyes tightly for a moment, then nodded. 'Give it to me in the toilet when we leave.'

'The trains?' Packy said.

'Twice a month, but never the same days or times as before. I'm told just in time to alert the deputies and make up the train, so I couldn't tell you nothing much before the train pulls out.'

'Can you handle the telegraph machine?'

'Christ! Anything that goes out on the wire is heard all down the line.'

'Can you?'

'A little bit, but—'

'What about the safe? Do they just roll it on the car?'

'Hell, no. It weighs near four thousand pounds. If it ever got loose, it would tear the car to matchwood. It rides in a combine, meaning half baggage, half coach, centered over the trucks in the head end, the baggage end, on account of the weight. It's in a timber crib, braced four ways. The doors are metal-lined, solid, and the double-barred the whole trip.'

'Who rides with it?'

'Just the express agent and one deputy. No use everyone sitting, watching the box. It aint doing nothing.' He laughed, then caught himself quickly. 'But there are other officers in the coach part of the car, and one in the locomotive. They move around – even walk the roof from time to time. All with sawed-offs.' Crenshaw shook his head. 'You're crazy to try this—'

'What else goes in the car with the safe?'

'Not a damn thing. That's the rule, see? Any freight cars on the run have to be sealed, so no one can hide in em. And there are never any coaches or passengers on the train. To keep the bastards from buying a ticket —' He caught himself.

'What kind of gent is the express agent?'

'Kemp? Well, hell – he's got a temper on him, but then he's – yes, he's decent, God-fearing ... Methodists, just like us Crenshaws. A religious man. You caint bribe him —' He broke off, flushing darkly.

'Are the safe and combine car any place where we can see them?'

'The car is standing in the yards with an iron fence around it and the safe is kept locked, even when it's empty.'

'All right,' Blue said. 'Does the express car always have the same place in the train?'

'Almost always. The mail car, if there is one, goes behind the tender, then the combine with the safe. I make up the consist according to what gets dropped off along the run – we always drop a couple of ore cars and maybe a freight at Aguila, and other ore cars at different sidings for the mines. Look, I've got to get back.'

'Does the train make any other stops, except at stations and sidings?'

'No – well, yes, she takes on water to make the long grade before the summit. She's up over ten thousand feet there, see, and the grade is near about three hundred foot to the mile —' Crenshaw rose from his seat. 'I'm going into the gents' right now. Will you? —'

'Yes. I'll follow you. You'll hear from us again soon, Mr Crenshaw.'

On the street, a few minutes later, Packy caught Blue's sleeve. 'She's a wrong go, Blue.'

'Maybe you're right, But I just can't back off from it yet.'

Packy sighed. 'What I taught you was how to crack a jug on the sly – not go in against an army of dicks packing sawed-offs.' He hesitated. 'You heard what he said – we can't even got a close look at the car beforehand, or the safe.'

'We don't need to,' Blue said. 'We already know all we need to know about the safe. The cars are all alike anyway. What I want you to do is get yourself a tape and a notebook. Spend the next few days casing the train. We'll want to know the measurements of the cars, the couplings, the windows, the locomotives – everything. You can wait for us here at the General Grant.'

'I'm broke, remember?' Packy said.

Blue thumbed a hundred dollars from his wallet and handed the bills to Packy with a wry grin. 'We're near cleaned again.'

Packy took the money with a wink. 'If I see a three-card monte game, I'll steer clear of it. Count on it, Blue.'

Blue watched Packy turn away, into the General Grant, and then he went back to the D & RG station and bought two tickets for Telluride at the window. A few minutes remained before train time. He went into the La Plata County Mercantile Company, to the gents' furnishings department, and bought a plain gray Stetson, a couple of flannel shirts and a gray-green corduroy Norfolk jacket, all of the type worn by mining men. He left his other clothes to be picked up later, then went outside and walked the short distance to the river. Clay was waiting, sitting on the bank under a cottonwood, holding a willow pole with a length of line on it over the water. He put the pole down when he saw Blue. There was neither hook nor bait on the line. He was clean-shaven, wearing a dark suit coat and string tie, without the familiar gun belt, but carrying saddlebags over his shoulder like any cattleman come to town – his long-barreled Colt was in a pocket of the saddlebags. They went back to the station. The train was waiting, the Tuscan red of the coaches bright in the sun, steam hissing in clouds from the glistening locomotive. They boarded and a minute later it rolled.

For miles the railroad grade followed the flanks of grassy, rolling hills, climbing steadily through juniper and sage.

'First time we've had to talk,' Blue ventured.

'That's so, aint it, Blue? But hell, there aint much that will pay us to thrash over, is there?'

Beneath them, wheel flanges groaned on the curved rails. The conductor was at Clay's shoulder asking for tickets. Clay, looking out the window, did not see or hear him over the noise of the train. 'Tickets please, gents,' the conductor said again. When he touched Clay's shoulder, Clay jerked back and his hand flew beneath his coat. He caught himself, shook his head with a grin and the hand brought out his wallet with the ticket in it. 'Spect you thought I was your mother-in-law,' the conductor said. Clay grinned back and nodded, but there was a white line, like a stain, around his mouth and his lips were drawn tight. For a moment, he was a stranger again.

'What I remember,' Blue said, 'is that long train ride at night with Ma and Cassie when we left the farm and meeting Uncle Israel and bein scared half to death. And you not with us. All Ma would ever say is that you went to Kansas to work on a thrashin crew.'

Clay laughed. 'Well, I did. You know there wasn't a whole lot of excitement around home. Me and Tom Patton got lit up and went down around Sedalia and kind of robbed us a store – must have tapped it for five or six dollars, I can't remember – but there was an old geezer out on the street, had him a spotted dog on a string and he stood there and watched us come out, and he knew Tom, so we couldn't go back home. We caught a freight and rode her to Great Bend and went to thrashin – I remember when we got off the train, our shirts was crawlin with graybacks, you bet.' He laughed again, quick and short. 'I sent Mom ten dollars from there.'

'If you had come back, we wouldn't have had to go live with Israel.'

'Hell, Blue, there wasn't nothing I could do about it. After we left the thrashin outfit, we went down in the Indian nations and – I done a stretch in jail. Two years, it was. Time it was up, I couldn't hardly go back and do nothing for you and Mom. Things change, you know that. And Israel, he had told me not to come around, long before that. I spect you heard him go on about the Russells and their bad blood.'

'You come around last year all right, didn't you?'

'Yes, by god, and there wasn't nothing he could do to keep us out of there. Pious old bastard – who would have believed he wasn't in on it, my own uncle? Hell, he was handling stolen goods all that time.'

'I was right there and you didn't say a word.' Blue could not keep the hurt out of his voice.

'What the hell, Blue. One slip and we was goners. We broke

out of jail to beat the rope. Zack, he had to go and shoot that express agent in Neosho —'

'Had to?'

'The damn fool *made* him do it. Come down to it, that's why we're goin for the big one now, Blue – we've got to get out of the country. We started, you know, messin around and it was, hell, it was *fun*. But the fun has went out of it. I want to get through this thing and catch a steamer for South America. That's cattle country down there and beef is somethin I know about.' Clay turned in his seat and stared hard at Blue. 'Kid, you don't know what it's like, thinkin about that rope.'

Blue suddenly did not want to hear any more or say any more. About Israel, or himself, or anything.

Miles clicked away beneath the swaying train. It stopped at Mancos, Dolores – scattered buildings, ore cars, a work train on a siding. Then the steel swung north and east to follow the Dolores River. The valley narrowed rapidly. It seemed to Blue that the train plunged into the mountains. Cottonwood and willow thinned along the banks and rock ledge showed through the gravel. There was white water now, foaming and swirling. He left his seat and went out on the open platform between the rocking, pitching cars and leaned against the iron rail to look up at hulking peaks, with their patches of snow flashing white through the green-dark pelt of trees. Ropy gusts of blue coal smoke whipped past and cinders fell in gritty showers.

Clay joined him, stood silently as Blue peered around the corner of the car, squinting against the cinders. At last he said, 'Blue, what the hell are you lookin for?'

Blue, without turning his head, said, 'I don't know yet. I don't know, but I'll find it.'

Telluride lay in a narrow valley walled on three sides by towering mountain cliffs. It was dusk when the train arrived. Looking up at the cliffs, Blue saw waterfalls hanging there in long gauzy wisps. He could just make out the towers and the cable-hung ore buckets of an aerial tramway running ore down the mountain in a constant stream from the faraway mine portal.

They spent the night in a boardinghouse for mining men.

In the morning they rented horses from the livery stable and started back, now following trails along the flanks of the mountains high above the railroad grade, trails that dated back to the days before the railroad when ore was packed out of the mountains by muleback. Their progress was slow – from time to time, Blue descended to the railroad grade to look over the trackage, a siding or a bridge. In the afternoon they stopped at a mine called the San Ignacio, not far from Ophir. Blue told the mine manager that he was thinking of starting a smithing business – ironwork for mine operations – and the man said, 'Count me a customer, son. You would deliver me from the scoundrels in Durango.'

He took them on the aerial tramway, riding an ore bucket up the mountain to the upper mill and the mine proper, where the ore was brought out of the earth. Blue looked down hundreds of feet onto the spiky black pines bristling on the mountainside, the bucket swaying beneath him.

'She's self-powered,' the manager said. 'Twenty-four hours a day, the full buckets coming down pull the empties back up.' Hearing the sigh of wind in the cables, Blue marveled. The manager invited them to sleep in the bunkhouse. In the night, Blue lay awake listening to the thunder of the stamp mill and the high squeal of tram wheels on the cable.

The next morning they followed the tracks through the pass at the summit, at an altitude well over 10,000 feet. Before them, the tracks started on the long downgrade that would take them winding down out of the mountains to Durango. They followed a creek from its headwaters, and shortly the creek became a river, rushing, thundering, heavy with snow water. Then a vast red-walled cleft opened in the mountains. The river plunged over a series of falls, dropping hundreds of feet into the gorge. Above the gorge, a string of five or six weathered ore cars rested on a siding. The railroad tracks entered the gorge below the siding, clinging precariously to a narrow shelf cut along the sheer red wall on the east side of the canyon. Above the tracks, the cliffs went straight up for two and three hundred feet, then broke back onto a rounding shoulder of mountain.

'We're wasting time here,' Clay said. 'There's no way you

could get at the train on that ledge, and it's on the wrong side of the river. Wherever we set up to do the job, we've got to be able to head west in a hurry, across that ridge.' He pointed across the gorge to a great mountain ridge that ran parallel to the course of the river and the gorge. 'Once you cross that ridge,' Clay said, 'the mountains slope off fast. That's where we'll have the horses strung out.'

'An old wagon road takes off above the siding,' Blue said. 'Let's see where it goes first.' Dim and brush-grown, the road had not been used in years. It wound away through the pines, climbing toward timber line. Less than a mile from the gorge, though considerably higher, the old road rounded a jutting outcrop and brought them suddenly to the abandoned works of the Sheba.

Next to the trail, a weathered signboard lay where it had fallen from a dead pine. SHEBA MIN & DEV CO – EST 1874, it read in faded letters. Decrepit buildings of silvered wood stood here and there – a bunkhouse, toolsheds, cook shack, then the mill sheds stepping down the slope toward a stream.

In the open above the mill, a gallows frame of logs was set over a shaft opening. Steel cable spiraled in snarls from a heavy tackle suspended beneath the gallows. Blue followed the twisted rat's nest of cable and saw that it ran to a big geared drum mounted on iron side frames – the drum was meant to revolve, driven by a boom and geared wheel, but the boom was now broken off short.

'A damned old horse winch,' Clay said. 'You hitch a horse to the boom and he cranks her around.'

Blue kneed his horse closer to the old winch. At that moment they heard the faraway whistle of a train. 'Let's get down there where we can watch the train come through,' he said, and turned his horse back toward the red-walled gorge. Riding on, he was still thinking about the horse winch and the abandoned mine.

It was no more than half a mile to the brow of the cliff that walled the gorge. Blue and Clay sat out on a ledge of red rock and watched the train labor up the canyon grade; then it was into the gorge itself, close below. The locomotive snorted roiling clouds of blue-black smoke, and updrafts caught the smoke and whipped it in gusts up along the face of the cliff past the watching men. The train passed beneath them, lost to sight below the brow of the cliff. The *chuff-chuff* of the engine slowed. They heard the long sigh of steam escaping. The sound of voices drifted up.

Blue scuttled along the edge of the cliff, Clay following, past precariously clinging pines and scrub oak, until they could again look down upon the train through a narrow cleft in the rock. Three hundred feet below them, the locomotive sat next to a wooden water tank built into the foot of the cleft. Trainmen were swinging the big tank nozzle down to the mouth of the tank in the engine's tender. Water gushed. The train was almost touching the cliff on one side, and on the other, the cliff fell vertically for hundreds of feet to the blue depths of the gorge. There was not even room on that side for a man to stand.

Silently they watched. Filling the tender's tank took eight or ten minutes. At last, Clay suddenly blurted, 'Don't tell me you think you could stop her there.'

Blue did not answer. He jumped the narrow steam that fed the water tank below, and climbed up onto an outcrop. Below, a trainman shouted. The engine *chuff-chuffed* and slowly the train began to move, the cars rocking and clicking, until it was lost to view behind a bend in the cliff wall. Looking back the way it had come, down the long valley, Blue could now see from this vantage point the bridge downstream where the tracks crossed the river. And beyond that, four or five miles away in all, he saw the mills and sheds of another big mine like the San Ignacio. He remembered passing it on the train – it was called the Arapaho Girl. The towers of an aerial tramway stepped up the mountain from the mill sheds. The buckets, tiny at this distance, swung up along the cables from the mill sheds, on a climb that would take them thousands of feet up the mountainside.

'You hear me, Blue? There's no place to hide and no place to run to – if you stopped her here, the dicks would pick you off that shelf.'

'Not if they don't see you.'

'Hell, you're robbing their train – they'll *see* you, all right.'

Blue grinned at him. 'If there was no way to do this but a holdup, the way you and Zack have got it figured, I would just pull out. But we're going to put the touch on them like pick-pockets working a county fair. They'll think it was done by ghosts – there won't even be any tracks to follow. Only first, we've got to move everybody up here, to the Sheba. Including the women. And we've got tools to buy, and equipment. Before we're done, you're going to find out what a day's work is like.'

Blue found Packy watching a card game in the back room of the General Grant. As soon as Packy saw him, he started pulling bills from his pocket.

'Grub and a room is all I spent it on, Blue. Here is eighty dollars.'

Blue pushed his hand away. 'Let's go where we can talk.' They bought two mugs of beer at the bar and took a corner table beneath a stuffed mountain lion. The room was almost empty.

Packy listened intently as Blue told him about the gorge and the cliffs, about finding the abandoned Sheba and the horse winch, and the aerial tramway at the Arapaho Girl, a few miles downstream. 'There is no way any of us can work on the safe, as long as it's aboard the train,' Blue went on. 'What I aim to do is steal the safe right out of the car, without their knowing, when the train stops for water. It will take the train two hours to reach Telluride. Say they discover the safe is gone then, and head back with a trainload of deputies – we'll have four hours to work on the safe.'

Packy began to laugh silently when Blue said he meant to steal the safe. Now his face suddenly sobered. 'And you figure you'll have four hours for the safe. I'm telling you, it's not half enough time. The Kruger that got me blown up only had two doors. This one's got three. Say you do get through the first two. There's still the inner door. You can't drill or punch it, you can't finger it because of the time lock and you can't blow it because of the baffles . . .' He spread his hands on the table helplessly.

Blue grinned. 'Packy, I'm going to *burn* through the door.'

He went on to tell him about Axel's cutting torch, how the jet of flame, under pressure, would melt a channel through the hardest steel.

'I know more about breaking safes than any man in America,' Packy said, 'but I never heard of anything like that.'

'It's never been done before, that's why. Only half a dozen smiths or welders have the least idea of it yet. I can build the burning blowpipe myself. What do you say, Packy? Are you still afraid I can't handle it?'

It was a long time before Packy answered. 'No ... Now I think I'm afraid you can ...'

CHAPTER XXVI

Bassett caught hold of the the long timber, together with Blue, Owl Carver, Clay Russell and Zack Murdock. They lifted it and Blue guided it into the channeled socket on the drive shaft of the horse winch. Blue put a block of wood on it and hit it solidly with a sledge hammer. The timber sank into the socket, a long crossarm now, the ends springing gently.

Bassett looked back along the rugged slope of the mountain, seeing wagons tracks and twin skid marks twisting along toward the Sheba. The wagon itself stood nearby under a great yellow pine. It was filled with tools and equipment Blue had bought in Durango. Bassett could see the brass cylinder of the old pneumatic drill compressor Blue had picked up secondhand for sixty dollars. Steam-driven, it was. Air hoses with it, but no drill. Bassett was mystified. And the other stuff, copper pipe of all sorts, dynamite, the carbide generator tank, more tools, a reel of exploder wire – but no exploder. At first, Bassett figured they were going to blow the tracks, maybe even the train itself, and he resolved to slip away one night, try to get help to round them up. Of course they would spook and run if he did cut out, no doubt to rob another train someplace in a few weeks, so it would all go for nothing then. But then the kid explained to them how he meant to steal the safe, and one thing he said in the beginning made Bassett stay. He said, 'Forget you're carrying guns – one shot fired and we're finished.' Bassett thought, if that's how it is, I'll play the hand out.

Murdock bit at a splinter in his thumb. Spat it out fiercely. Blue nudged the crossarm. The drum turned a little, the cleaned and greased gears meshing softly. 'No noise,' Blue said. 'That's the whole idea – no noise, no tracks.' He turned and faced them. 'Now we've got to cut some more timbers, to make a frame.' He knelt and began to draw lines in the dirt with a stick.

Packy stood by, leaning on his silver-headed stick. 'By god, it wouldn't hurt you none to give us a hand,' Owl Carver suddenly snarled.

'Me and hard work are total strangers,' Packy grinned. 'You boys have the knack for it, though, a man can see that.' He strolled away swinging the stick.

'He'll have his turn,' Blue said. 'Let's get to cutting.'

It was night. A small fire burned in the cook shack stove. Bassett was playing cards with Clay Russell and Owl Carver. Packy was telling Millie's fortune with another deck of cards. Murdock sat on a packing crate, leaning back against the wall, cracking his knuckles and watching.

'He's a tall gent, speaking in a foreign tongue,' Packy was saying. 'Probably French. He has a brocade vest and medals across his chest and he is carrying a box filled with objects of great value, jewels no doubt. A present for you —'

Millie frowned. 'Where we going to meet gents like that?'

Packy shrugged, grinning. 'Ladies like yourselves, plenty of money and dressed to kill – the swells will flock around you, anyplace.'

Millie turned to Murdock, laughing. 'Aint the way I met you, sweet baby, is it? You never brought no box of jewels.'

'I got my money's worth though,' Murdock said.

'Ha! It was all on the cuff and you know it. But when we're done here, you can make it up to me – all the good times and all the promises.'

'We'll send for you, soon as we get located. You know that.'

Millie stared at him for a moment. 'Damn right,' she said.

There was a scratching noise at the window. Murdock came to his feet, a gun in his hand in that instant. Bassett touched his arm. 'It's the kid,' he said. A twist of double wire snaked across the sill and into the room. A moment later Blue entered. He picked up the wire stripped the ends with a pocketknife, then took an oak board from a box and fastened the ends of the wire to two terminals, part of the brass instrument mounted on the board. He put the instrument on the table.

'Where are the batteries?' Carver said.

'We don't need batteries,' Blue said, 'because we're not sending, only listening, right?'

Carver nodded. The instrument suddenly clattered. Millie jumped, with a small, nervous shriek. Carver took a pencil from his pocket, wrote rapidly as the telegraph sounder clattered. When it stopped, he said, 'This tells the agent at Ophir to have the southbound pick up two ore cars—' It clattered again.

'Turn it off!' Murdock said. 'Until we need it.'

Carver shrugged and disconnected one terminal. The clattering stopped. 'You'll listen every morning,' Blue said. 'Eight to eight-thirty. That's what Crenshaw told me.'

Blue found Packy in the bunkhouse. He was toying with the silver dollar wheels of his prison-made safe lock. He flicked a wheel into line and turned the spindle. The lock bolt slid smoothly back. Packy tossed the lock in its soapbox onto the bunk. 'Where are the others?'

'They're running through what they have to do,' Blue said.

'Shouldn't you be there?' Packy peered past a corner of bandanna that hung down over his bad eye – the eye had been bothering him and he had taken to wearing the bandanna again. His hat was dented now and his suit was stained and baggy and he needed a shave.

'It's all up to them,' Blue said. 'I won't be with them for that part, but it's time you and me cooked up the soup.'

Packy grimaced, but swung his feet to the floor and followed Blue to the toolshed. Blue took a wooden crate off a shelf. At the cook shack door, they heard India's soft voice, then Millie's brassy laugh. They pushed through.

'You could've knocked,' Millie said. She was seated at the sawbuck table with a flour sack around her shoulders, and India was winding a lock of her yellow hair on to a curling iron hot from the stove. A copper of water was heating on the stove and a wooden washtub filled with women's garments sat on the bench near Millie. When she saw the box, she said, 'What are you fixin to do, in my kitchen?'

'We only want to put on a kettle of soup,' Blue said.

'Our cooking don't suit your lordships?' India said.

'None better, ladies,' Packy said, 'but this is an old family recipe.'

Blue pried the box lid up with a hatchet. The waxy, paper-wrapped sticks, one and a quarter by eight inches each, lay in snug rows. India cocked her head to read the stenciled label. ' "Red Dot, Fifty Percent." *Dynamite*, Blue?' Smoke wisped up from the curler in her hand. Millie sniffed, then suddenly twisted away, clawing the curler out of her hair.

'What the hell, you want to brand me, honey?'

Fingering the scorched lock of hair, she watched Blue peel the paper off a stick with his pocketknife. Packy ladled part of the water out of the boiler with a cooking pot. 'That's my wash water,' Millie said unhappily. Packy merely smiled at her. Blue broke the stick over the boiler, crumbling it into small pieces. Looking up, he saw that Packy's smile had faded, that his face was pale and strained.

'I can't help it, Blue,' Packy said. 'I thought I was over all that, too.'

'Why don't you take Millie for a little walk?' Blue said. 'I know all I need to know about this.'

Packy hesitated, then pulled the flour sack off Millie's shoulders. 'You'll want this to strain it – and you'll want something to keep it in, something that won't spark.' He saw a small jar on the table, partly filled with fluid.

'Not my rose water,' Millie said. He nodded. She tipped the fluid into her hand and bathed her face with it, the rose water running down her forearms. 'Waste not, want not,' she said and gave him the jar. 'Only let me out of here first.' She left quickly with Packy.

Blue broke another stick over the boiler and crumbled it.

'Don't it scare you?' India said.

'Near to death,' Blue said. 'You don't have to stay, if you don't want to.'

She bit her lip and he thought of the night in the old house above Israel's shop, of how she had teased him, of how —

'I could as well help,' she said. 'It don't bother me. What do you want me to do?'

'You could stir it, easy, you know, with the wooden spoon.'

She thrust the long-handled spoon into the boiler water and stirred. 'Cornmeal mush, is what it looks like.' Her collarbones looked sharp as the hatchet blade. She hesitated. 'What is all this coming to?'

'Stir it easy, will you? You know as well as I do what we're doing here. We're waiting for a train.'

'I'm here to be with Clay, no other reason. I hope the train never comes.'

'When we're done, you and Clay can go anywhere in the world you want. All of us can.' He broke another stick into the boiler.

She shook her head, stirring, her face flushed from the heat. 'Wherever Clay goes, he means to go without me. He never said nothing, but I can tell. This is the end of it for me. That's why I don't want the damn train to come.' She looked around the cook shack and laughed. 'Funny, aint it? A girl not wanting to give this up? Believe me, this is nothing like what he promised, either. It's better than nothing, is all.' She stopped stirring. 'You never answered me – what is all this coming to? Will we get out of it alive?'

Blue took her hand with the spoon and moved it. 'Keep stirring, India. We'll get out of it.'

When he finished, the little jar was two-thirds full of clear, faintly syrupy liquid. Blue wiped it carefully and capped it. 'If I leave it here, something could happen,' he said, 'like closing the oven door with a bang. That's all it would take, so I want to wash it out.' He put the jar on the folded towel down in the boiler so it would not roll, then lifted the boiler by its wooden handles and carried it through the door and down the slope to the stream below the cook shack. Behind a big pine and some aspen trees, a broad flat rock overhung the water.

They pushed through between the trees. Blue knelt on the rock and washed the cloth and the boiler and set them in a patch of sunlight. India watched, sitting on the bank next to the rock, trailing her hand in rushing water. Blue saw a hollow under the roots of the big pine tree and put the little jar in it, well back out of sight. When he started to get up, India caught his arm.

'Where has all the fun went, Blue? Give me a little kiss, before I forget.' Her eyes glimmered close. Her mouth was soft and moist for a moment, then suddenly open and she was straining close, her nails sharp though his shirt. After long seconds, he turned his head to breathe.

'I thought Clay was all you wanted,' he whispered.

'I know what I said – I never did have good sense, Blue. Why else am I here?' She pulled him down with a soft laugh. 'Don't you dare try to shake India loose . . .'

When they got back to the cook shack, the sun was slanting low. Two saddled horses were tied by the toolshed.

'That's Naylor's horse,' Blue said. 'Chavez is with him, so the horses are all ready. We're ready too. We can go anytime. Anytime.'

THE TRAIN

Durango
June, 1900

CHAPTER XXVII

Dawn. The train stood in the yards, made up according to the yardmaster's orders and ready to roll. The engineer, Fred Olmstead, having received his order slip from the dispatcher, glanced down the length of the train as he walked to his locomotive. All freights and ore cars, except for the combine carrying the black box and the shotgun guards.

Long-nosed oiler in hand, the engineer went over the locomotive carefully – drivers, guide bars and linkage, forward to the steam chests on both sides. Her name, San Miguel, was emblazoned on the mahogany side panels of her cab in gold leaf. She was a diamond-stacked Baldwin 4-4-0 with 45-inch drive wheels and 12-by-18-inch cylinders, and she weighed almost 50,000 pounds. The domes atop her boiler glittered with gold striping. She wore fringed awnings over the cab windows and a splendid brace of elk antlers was mounted before the chimney of her headlamp.

The engineer mounted the gangway. The fireman clanged the fire door shut with his shovel and rapped a knuckle on the brass steam gauge. She was up to working pressure, 130 pounds. Olmstead looked at his big railroad watch, thumbed it back into his bib pocket and leaned out the cab window, waiting for the highball. He saw half a dozen men carrying shotguns and rifles standing back by the combine car. One of the guards, a stocky man named George Dillard, walked to the locomotive, swung up into the cab with a nod and a grunt and settled himself back out of the way on a stool, his sawed-off shotgun between his knees. 'They're feeding the black box,' he said.

Three cars back, in the baggage section of the combine, the express agent, Horace Kemp, was transferring thick packets of currency and wrapped stacks of gold coins into the inner chest of the Kruger Invincible. Two bank officers looked on.

'Two hundred sixty-one thousand, seven hundred and ten,'

Kemp said at last, 'a little more than usual.' He locked and dogged the door of the safe, then the two outer sets of doors, spinning the dials on each as tempered locking bolts thunked into their sockets. The bank officers marched out of the car.

Kemp and the guard who was riding with him, a man named Malone, swung a heavy timber across the front of the safe and set two braces slanting against it, so that the Invincible was timbered on four sides against the motion of the train.

'Time to crawl in the hole,' Kemp sighed. The two men ran the big sliding door across the side opening and locked it. Kemp lighted a little kerosene lamp over his table and took a pack of cards from a drawer. 'High card deals,' he said.

Outside on the platform, the conductor, Elvin Purdy, watched the shotgun guards climb aboard to take seats in the passenger section of the combine. The conductor and brakeman always walked the train at every stop, checking running gear, journal boxes and brake hoses. On the Shotgun Run, the armed guards also walked the train, including the tops of the cars.

'Boa-a-rd!' Conductor Purdy's melodious cry echoed through the yards. He raised his arm and waved. Steam burst from the brass whistle on the San Mig's steam dome, wailing, echoing off the hills. The locomotive chuffed. A ripple ran the length of the train as Olmstead shook the slack out of her and pointed her toward the mountains on the long curve of singing steel.

Assistant Yardmaster Jared Crenshaw watched the Shotgun Run rumble out of the yards at seven-fifty. He smelled coffee brewing on the stove in the dispatcher's office and he waited uneasily for Benson, the yardmaster, and Haugen, the telegrapher, to go in for their ritual morning cup, but Benson was fussing distractedly over a stack of papers on his desk, muttering to himself. The telegrapher looked over once or twice through the glass window in the door of his cubicle, but Benson did not notice him and he went back to pounding the brass key.

Crenshaw had known about the make-up of the train since the evening before, but had no way of getting to the telegrapher's set alone before this accustomed morning cup of coffee, and now it appeared that they were going to let it pass. Crenshaw shuffled papers and sharpened pencils, watching minutes tick away on the wall clock. He thought of his brother-in-law Owl Carver sitting next to a telegrapher's sounder out there in the mountains, somewhere north of Aguila – if they missed this train, it could be weeks before another with the right make-up came along. Crenshaw did not care about Owl Carver, but he was certain that he could not, himself, stand any more waiting.

At eight twenty-four Crenshaw suddenly blurted, 'I'd be glad to hold the place down, Mr Benson, if you and Mr Haugen was of a mind to have a cup of coffee.'

Benson stared for a moment, then said softly, 'Very kind of you to think of it, Crenshaw.' He left his desk and tapped the telegrapher's glass door window with a fingernail, then went across the hall to the dispatcher's office. Haugen finished tapping out a message, left his key and followed, leaving his door ajar so that Crenshaw could hear the sounder.

Fidgeting, Crenshaw waited a minute. The line was clear. All he had to do was send the three characters they had agreed upon, *R-I-C*, then a string of dits as if the sender had made a mistake. He walked into the telegrapher's cubicle. When he reached for the key, his hand was shaking.

Owl Carver sat in the cook shack at the Sheba, alone except for India, who was cleaning up the breakfast dishes. The sounder was on the table by his elbow. India leaned across the table and mopped the tattered oilcloth with a wet rag. Carver admired the way her skirt pulled snugly across her behind. A fantasy was building in his mind – the two of them together, and she —

He reached out and firmly squeezed her rump. She squealed and slashed at him with the rag. Soapy water stung his eyes and he caught her wrist. The telegraph sounder suddenly clattered. *R-I-C* ... then it stopped. Still holding her wrist, he stared at the sounder, his jaw hanging slack. The sounder rattled again, a string of dits as if the sender had made a mistake and elected to start over, and then it fell silent. Stayed silent.

Footsteps sounded at the door. Turning, Carver saw Blue Russell. India twisted her arm free.

Blue took two steps into the room and caught Carver by the front of his coat, but Carver, his arms limp, let himself be lifted free of the floor. 'That was it,' he said, pointing at the telegraph instrument. 'The train is on its way.'

CHAPTER XXVIII

The train rolled west from Durango, dropped a freight car at Mancos, then swung north. She dropped another freight car at Dolores and an ore car at Placitas. Her last station stop before the summit was Aguila, a five-hour run from Durango. There she would drop two ore cars.

The station agent in Aguila, whose name was Lander, was closing his dinner pail when he heard the steam whistle wail, down the valley. He hung a clipboard full of manifests on a hook by his desk and stepped out onto the platform.

A four-horse wagon was rumbling toward the station, passing now beneath a big cottonwood in front of a row of frame houses. What he noticed about it was the two black-shrouded female figures sitting next to the driver, a man with a bandaged face. Mighty grim, he thought. The plodding horses drew close, pulled up alongside the platform. Then Agent Lander saw the two rough-built coffins in the back of the wagon.

Except for the black veils, the women were dressed like miners' wives. Both wore tacky mail order print dresses and pancake hats sloping down over coiled hair. Their shoes were cracked and stained. The smaller of the two fingered her veil nervously. She was trembling and when she spoke, her voice was choked. 'Are we in time for the early train – to Telluride?' A movement of her quivering hand vaguely included the coffins.

'Yes, ma'am,' Lauder said uneasily – he was thinking of the consist of the train, as indicated in the dispatcher's message. It was the Shotgun Run, with that damned black box taking up all the baggage room and allowing no seats for passengers. 'I'm afraid there is no space on this train,' he said.

'Me and Mrs Connelly,' the woman said, 'we have . . . there was a cave-in at the mine and we lost our husbands. Now we have just got to get to Mr Brindley's place in Telluride.'

A sob broke from the stouter of the two women. Lander could see tears glistening on her cheek through the shoddy veil. Brindley was an undertaker in Telluride.

'There is another train this evening, late, a regular run,' he ventured.

'It's been over twenty-four hours already,' she said pointedly. 'Are you going to leave them setting in the sun this way?'

'Certainly not,' he said quickly. He trundled a high-wheeled baggage cart around to the rear of the wagon and the bandaged man climbed over the back seat and helped him skid the two coffins onto the cart. Lander wheeled the cart into the shade of the building. The women climbed down from the wagon.

'No need of your staying, Tom,' the slender woman said to the driver. 'We're much obliged to you.' The man grunted something through his bandages, climbed back onto the wagon and clucked his team into a trot, dust boiling up underfoot as the wagon turned and headed back the way it had come. The steam whistle sounded again, very close now. The women stood near the cart, the stouter one weeping noisily into her handkerchief. Lander walked to the tracks and checked to see that he had set the switch that would run the train through the siding, so as to shed the two cars ticketed for Aguila.

Thirty seconds later, the ground shuddered under his feet as Olmstead ran the sleek San Mig through the siding and stopped her on down the tracks. Trainmen climbed down and began to uncouple the two cars. Men with shotguns stepped out of the combine car and began to pace back and forth, weapons held at the ready. Lander approached the combine car as Conductor Purdy stepped down. The sound of the plump woman's weeping followed him.

'We've got two lady passengers for you, Elvin,' he said, 'with baggage.' He nodded guardedly at the coffins on the cart. 'Lost their men in a cave-in yesterday.'

The conductor blew through his mustache. 'We ain't *sposed* to do it – hell, we're carryin the black box, you *know* that!' He took off his cap and mopped his head with a blue bandanna. 'Christ! Maybe we could handle the ladies – you can put the baggage on the next train.'

Lander shook his head. 'It wouldn't matter none if it was January, but it's been *more than twenty-four hours*.' His voice became thin and reedy with anxiety. 'We've got to get em to Brindley's, see what I mean?'

Conductor Purdy's nostrils flared slightly. His sniff was barely audible. 'What do you think, Chet?' he asked Dolan, the chief of the railroad officers.

'You could ask Kemp,' Dolan said. 'Me, I'd say yes, but if he won't, you caint.'

Purdy turned to the train, cupped his hand around his mouth to funnel his voice through the crack at the edge of the door. 'Kemp! You hear me? We've got two pieces of baggage —' Kemp's protest cut him off. He tried again. 'No, listen – I know it aint regular, but these is *coffins*. We caint wait, understand? It's been *too long* already.'

'You're putting me in a hell of a fix for a Christian man,' the muffled voice said. 'Dolan, are you out there and is this what he says it is?'

'I am and it is,' Dolan said. They heard Kemp's key grate in the lock, and then the door was trundled back and the agent stood blinking against the sunlight. Behind him, Officer Malone held his shotgun at port arms. Lander was already running for the baggage cart. He caught the tongue and wheeled it around. The two women followed as he rolled the cart to the door of the combine car. Together, the men skidded the coffins through the door, angling them past the timbers that braced the massive safe.

'This is, by god, absolutely the one and only thing in the cussed world I would open that door for,' Kemp complained. I'd really ought to examine em, too.' He took a pry bar off a wall hook and tapped the nearest coffin indecisively with it.

'I'll help you do it if it's got to be done,' Conductor Purdy said, He looked queasy, his nostrils quivering. The stouter of the two women blew her nose violently. The other stared accusingly at the railroad men, her eyes glittering wetly through the veil. She lifted her chin at Kemp, waited.

'Madame,' he said in exasperation. 'Don't you think you might have done better to —'

'To plant them like dogs on that godforsaken mountain?' she flared.

Kemp knew he was being made to look bad now in front of the ladies and he didn't like it. He put the steel of the pry bar next to his pursed lips and deliberated. At that moment, the engineer blew two short blasts on his whistle, indicating that he was ready to go.

Kemp slapped the pry bar back onto its hook. 'Just don't never ask me to open my car up again,' he snapped, and slid the door back across the opening. The ladies boarded the car at the rear steps and entered the coach section followed by Dolan. The conductor lifted his arm and gave the high-ball, caught the grab-iron and swung up onto the platform as she began to roll.

The San Mig's stack gushed cindery clouds of smoke. The fireman's shovel clanged as he deftly sprayed coal onto his fire. He earned his pay on the mountain run.

From Aguila to the gorge by way of the old wagon road that passed near the Sheba was scarcely fifteen miles, but measured on the railroad iron, those fifteen miles stretched nearer thirty as the tracks snaked and wound back and forth into side canyons, straining for altitude before hitting the stretch of track on the narrow shelf cut into the wall of the gorge.

Laboring now at a man's walking pace as she neared the gorge, the San Mig sucked water from her tank in vast gulps to make steam. It was mandatory to take on water again, to top off her tank for the last long grade to the summit.

The coffins were made of pine siding from the Sheba's mill. The old wood was well weathered, though freshly planed, and was dotted with nail holes. Cushioned inside on a horsehair pallet from a cot in the Sheba's bunkhouse, Clay Russell wanted desperately to bend his knees. His body quivered to the limber springing and bucking of the car's floor. The deep rumble of steel on steel sawed noisily in his ears, the clicks of wheels on rail joints amplified to hammer blows that echoed the thudding of his heart. Light piercing the nail holes in the side of the coffin spattered his right cheek. There was only darkness on his left, so Zack's coffin had to be there.

Clay strained his head toward the cluster of nail holes – most of them drilled there by Blue – so that by moving his eye a little from hole to hole, he could see the entire end of the baggage room. There was blurred movement across the lamplight. A small man wearing an eyeshade got up from his saloon chair and scooped a little coal into the potbellied stove set in the corner near the foot end of Clay's coffin. The man closed the stove, tapped the vent with the scoop and returned to his chair, passing the bolted door to the passenger compartment and stepping over the outstretched legs of another man who sat with his back to the door. The small man with the eyeshade bent over the table. 'Fifteen two fifteen four and a pair is six,' he said.

'Damn,' the other man said. His shotgun was leaning against the wall behind his left elbow and he had now tipped his chair back so that the front feet were off the floor, with his heels hooked over a rung. Clay felt the car lurch into a curve. Wheel flanges binding against the rails squalled. In the coffin, the noise was like a shriek. Clay wished he had remembered to take a pee before they started.

Don't do nothing blind was what Blue had said. *One of you will be able to see and he is the one who makes the play.* Clay felt for the two latches near his elbows and slipped them back. 'Fifteen two, fifteen four . . .' the little man was saying. The other man was holding his cards with both hands. Clay lifted the coffin lid slightly, felt it come loose at the foot. In one smooth move he slid it to his left onto the other coffin and sat up with his heavy New Service Colt thrust out like a lance and his teeth bared in a wild grin. 'Fifteen six and eight is the game. *Don't move!*'

He swung a leg over the edge of the coffin and was on his feet, as the shotgun guard's chair came snapping down and the man swung awkwardly to get at the gun. Clay slapped his kneecap with the barrel of the Colt and the man doubled over. The little man crouched next to the window, his eyeshade somehow twisted over an ear. Behind Clay, both lids skidded off the other coffin and thudded against the timbered crib holding the Invincible. Murdock sat up squinting, his eyes slitted against the light. He swung his gun on Clay, then caught himself and scrambled out, still blinking. The guard, Malone, sat up gasping, holding his knee with both hands. Murdock thrust the pistol barrel under his chin. 'One squeak and we're finished, and by god so are you!'

Malone shook his head. Zack Murdock swung him around, whipped a coil of wire from his pocket and fastened his wrists, then slapped a big patch of sticking plaster over his mouth.

'You next, Pop,' he growled to the agent.

Clay took a saw from each coffin and set them aside. Then he and Zack Murdock lifted the agent and guard, one at a time, slung them each into a coffin. 'You stay quiet as corpses,' he said, 'and you'll live to climb out of there.' He clapped the lids back onto the boxes and they stacked one on the other. Saw in hand, Clay climbed up onto the top of the safe and crouched there, peering around at the little vent windows in the narrow clerestory space of the car's raised roof.

'We take out the roof over the second and third windows,' he said. He turned the teeth of the saw upward in the window frame and began to cut. Murdock climbed onto the stacked coffins and began his own cut on a line exactly four feet two inches away, parallel to Clay's cut. When they were finished, a short section of the roof would lift off like the lid of a box.

'A man who can't saw six feet in thirty minutes,' Clay said, 'don't know nothing about honest work.'

On the rocky bench above the gorge, Bassett stood at the head of one of the teams of horses hitched to the winch boom. The horses tossed their heads and snorted clouds of frost. Bassett swung his arms and stamped his feet. Here it was June and they had to crack ice in the water bucket to get coffee started in the morning. Looking along the winch boom to the far end where the other team was hitched, he saw frost on Naylor's wispy mustache.

The steel cable ran out some forty yards from the winch to the brink of the cliff, where it passed through a big pulley which was suspended from an A-framed pair of timbers, or shear legs. Then the cable dropped down the face of the cliff.

Packy Disbrow stood by the winch's brake handle, which was set just outside the horses' walking circle. He felt a yank on the string looped around his hand – the other end of the string was somewhere down the cliff face with the end of the cable and its burden. He eased off the brake, watching cable run off the drum – he was looking for windings of colored thread on the cable that marked off precisely measured points on its runout.

Owl Carver crouched shivering at the winch itself, where he would be able to control the tilt of the A-framed timbers with a second line, a length of heavy rope, also precisely marked with wrappings of colored thread.

Whatever happened now, Packy was glad to see the end coming, and at the same time, he was proud of the way Blue was making this bunch of gun sharks jump. Feeling a twinge of guilt, Packy cringed inwardly. He should have told the kid what he had learned about Israel, but just then he had blown his stake and – hell, greed did funny things to a man, or maybe not greed, but fear of finding himself old and sick and having to panhandle handouts at kitchen doors again. But one thing was certain, say they got out of this thing – the Pinks would be after him, now, like maggots after a corpse. He would really have to skin out, down to Old Mexico. For keeps. The cable ran on. On and on.

Packy heard the Owlhead and Naylor mumbling to one another at the winch, then a laugh. Damned trashy scum, he thought, without taking his gaze from the cable.

'You would do well to put a cork in it,' Bassett told them.

'We don't need to hear nothing from you about it,' Carver snarled.

'You won't hear the goddam train if you don't shut up,' Naylor said, suddenly nervous. Bassett grinned.

Packy suddenly knew who Preacher Bucklin put him in mind of – Birdsong. Leo Birdsong. The same loose and easy way, but always thinking. A man to tie to. The kid gave promise of being like that, except he had to clamp onto this damned train thing. Then Packy shivered – come right down to it, it was Birdsong who had gotten him blown up.

And Bassett, standing ready with his team, was like a man caught in a log jam. He could try to stop this now, sure, but he would set off a mess of shooting if he did – all of the wrong people getting killed, including himself, the way those things happened. No, better now to wait, because the slick way the kid had it laid out, there would be no shooting at all – no shooting, no noise, no tracks. Bassett knew he was going to have to pull the string on Blue, but he had the damnedest crazy desire to see the kid pull it all off. Which side am I on? he thought. The time will come, hours or even minutes away, and I'll have to step on him. But not yet.

CHAPTER XXIX

Blue Russell rode the steel cable down the face of the red wall. Sitting in loops of heavy chain slung from the steel hook, he held himself off the rock with his feet as the cable was paid out. Looking up he could see the cable disappearing through clumped branches of scrub oak. He could not see the A-framed timbers rigged and guyed to slant out off the brink of the cliff over him, nor the heavy pulley wheel suspended beneath them.

Looking down made him giddy. The tracks, still two hundred feet below him, were like two gleaming wires strung over matchsticks. And far below the tracks, in the blue shadows of the gorge, the river glinted like a ropy twist of raw silk.

The cable slipped, caught. Blue was jolted. For a crazed instant, he could not believe he was finally there. He put out his hand, touched the red rock. It was pocked and scarred. He saw powdery flakes of snow caught in the pockets, swirling now as the breeze touched them, sparking bright in the sun. Then the face of the cliff appeared to thrust out on both sides of him as he dropped, and he was into the declivity – a broad, deep chimney with one open side, choked with clumps of scrub oak that had taken root in pockets of soil.

A moment later his feet were on solid rock in the bottom of the chimney, some 25 feet above the tracks. He gave the string two sharp tugs, felt Packy's answering tug. The cable stopped. As Blue squirmed out of the sling, he heard the distant wail of the train's steam whistle, rolling, echoing in the canyon, then dying away to a growling moan. He waited.

Crouched in his brush-shrouded hole in the cliff face, Blue smelled the train before he saw it – the breeze was sucking smoke through the gorge faster than the train's creeping pace. He heard the labored *chuff-chuff-chuff*, then the steely grumble, and suddenly the train was there below him, the great stack gushing smoke and cinders up into his face. Then it was trundling past and through teary eyes he saw the fireman's face, his cheek bulging with a chew. A second later came the coal-heaped tender. The round cover on its water tank was the key to where he sat now – that water tank nozzle was exactly 103 feet away, around the curve of track on the cliff face. Allowing for couplings, two 45-foot cars and the position of the safe over the forward trucks of the third car, the safe would stop exactly 103 feet back from the water nozzle.

Tarred car tops rolled past, slower, slower. The third car crept into sight. Stopped. Blue could see the saw cuts across the narrow clerestory section of the roof, directly below him. He waited – in the weeks of waiting and preparing, he had watched the Shotgun Train three times as it stopped here for water. The guard from the locomotive always walked the top of the train. But where was he now? Steam was purged from the locomotive's cylinders with a whooshing roar. Blue heard voices, a laugh. Leaning out, peering though the oak leaves, he saw the stocky guard, shotgun cradled, walking carefully on spread legs, jumping now onto the roof of the third car – resolutely not looking down. The roof sagged a little under his weight, near the saw cuts. He bent down, grinning. 'Boys, who's ahead down there?' he called out and a muffled voice called back, 'Hell, not me.'

That had to be Clay, Blue thought. The guard laughed and

walked on.

And below, in the coach section of the combine car as the train rolled to a stop, Dolan put his head out the window and looked straight down into the gorge – seven or eight hundred feet, he thought, maybe more. There was not room next to the train for a man to stand. Dolan grinned at the other deputies. 'We ought to be out there walkin the train – we aint earning out pay.' Two of the deputies grinned back.

Nordstrom blinked pale lashes at him, grunted sourly. 'How the hell we going to do that here?' Nordstrom never joked.

'First you grow wings.' Dolan picked up his shotgun. 'Dillard's up there – reckon I'll walk it with him.'

Nordstrom frowned at the red wall of stone less than a foot from his window. 'That's one walk you can take alone,' he said. 'Caves, snakes nor ghosts, they don't bother me none, but by god, I hate high places.'

Dolan shrugged, turning toward the rear door of the car. 'Just never look down,' he said. The two widows were sitting together in the outside rear seat. As he approached, the smaller of the two, who was on the aisle, moaned softly and toppled onto the floor at his feet. At that moment, he heard footsteps on the roof of the car and a man called down, 'Boys, who's ahead down there?' That would be George Dillard, taking the walk on top.

'Please help me with the pore thing,' wept the stouter of the two women. Dolan set his shotgun aside and knelt over the slender woman. Dillard was up on top, and anyway, in the whole run, this was the one place Dolan always figured nothing could happen.

Dillard jumped onto the next car, walked on and in seconds he was out of sight around the curve. Blue gave the string three quick tugs. Three more. *Go. Go.* High above, Carver cast off his rope and let the A-framed shear legs on the brink of the cliff sag outward. They caught and held. The pulley was now precisely over the center line of the car. Blue was swung from the brushy declivity out over the car.

He dropped lightly onto the tarred roof, bent and rapped

with his knuckles. Instantly a section of roof was lifted from below by two pairs of hands. Blue saw Murdock's strained face, the teeth bared like a dog's, and Clay behind him, his wild grin flashing. They slid the section of roof forward, out of the way. Clay and Murdock were crouched on top of the Kruger Invincible. A chain harness was rigged around the safe, and Clay was holding a heavy steel ring that held the ends of chain together. Blue signaled. The hook lowered. The ring was clapped over it. He tugged again and the hook moved upward, the steel cable thrumming taut, and then the two-ton safe came free of its timbered crib and moved silently upward, carrying the two men.

It moved up exactly twelve feet, then stopped with its wheels just over the roof line of the car. Clay slipped down and he and Blue lifted the piece of roof back into place. They scuffed down shreds of tarred roof. Blue nodded. They scrambled back up onto the safe and Blue twitched the cord.

High above, Bassett and Naylor caught Packy's hand signal and each urged his team of horses ahead. The horses leaned into their collars. The winch boom creaked and quivered, turned slowly, and the drum wound in the cable. Owlhead Carver crouched at the winch next to the smaller take-off drum that protruded from the winch – an extension of the big drum's axis. Packy signaled. Carver whipped four or five quick turns of rope around the drum, drew them tight and the winch now drew back the top of the shear legs holding the pulley at the same time it was lifting the safe. And as the shear legs pulled back, the great safe swung massively sideways, crunching through scrub oak into its open-sided chimney in the cliff.

The shotgun guard George Dillard stood on the rearmost corner of the rearmost car of the train, carefully not looking down, but still admiring the long sweep of canyon and the snow-patched peaks. Then he rebuttoned his trousers and turned, starting back along the car tops. Seeing Conductor Purdy between the last two cars below him, he paused.

'Mr Purdy, I believe I have just peed farther than anybody in the whole world today.' Purdy laughed and waved. Dillard walked on and seventy seconds later was back on his seat in the locomotive.

The engineer gave two blasts on the whistle to indicate that he was ready to roll. He looked at his air gauge, the instrument indicating pressure in the brake lines. The needle dipped twice, his signal to go – since the conductor at the rear of the train was around a bend and out of sight of the engineer, he was responding to the whistle blast by cracking a valve. Olmstead eased in the throttle and the train began to roll.

The chuffing of the San Mig echoed briefly, then slowly died away as she wound out of sight along the flank of the red-walled gorge, climbing for the summit.

Clay Russell whooped suddenly, clapped his arms around Blue's shoulders and hugged. 'By god, little brother, we done it!'

Blue fingered the heavy steel ring that held the Invincible's chain sling – the ring was distorted, pulled down by the safe's great weight. He shivered. 'Not yet, we haven't.' He took a couple of turns of chain through the ring and the hook, then tugged on his signal cord. The safe lurched and began to rise, the three men on it ducking and hunching their shoulders against clawing branches of scrub oak in the chimney. The safe spun slowly, grating once against the face of red rock as it rose.

Above, on the open slope of the mountain, Bucklin and Naylor urged the two teams of horses on their circular path around the winch. The animals dug in, leaning into their collars and snorting clouds of steam. Around they walked, the drum winding in two-and-half turns for every circle walked by the horses – their speed, straining against the trace chains, was less than two miles an hour.

On the safe, Blue heard a high, keening note from the cable, the sound rising in pitch as they climbed. Once a hawk swooped close, inclining its head to look at them, its yellow eyes glittering coldly, and Blue heard Clay's reckless laugh.

It took fourteen minutes to crank the 4,000-pound load to the top of the cliff. As the safe rose past the brink Owl Carver quickly threw several turns of rope around the secondary drum and pulled them tight. Fighting the added strain, the lathered horses were suddenly halted. Heads down, shuddering, they held, and then Bassett shouted, lashed out with a length of halter rope and the horses lunged, moved again. The top of the hoist frame drew slowly back and up until the legs were vertical, straddling the safe. Bassett and Naylor halted the horses, Packy eased off on the brake and the great safe thudded down into a shoveled-out depression with walls diked up of earth and canvas.

Carver threw his hat on the ground and whinnied like a horse. Naylor collapsed laughing over his end of the winch beam. Murdock, jumping off the safe, slipped to his hands and knees. Furious, he snarled at them. 'Spose they find it's gone? They could be back here any time. You bastards get on up to the siding and keep an eye on the track.' Then he saw Bassett. 'No, not you, Preacher – you stay right here with us.'

Bassett grinned coldly, unhitched his horses and tethered them to a tree a few feet away. Blue saw Packy at the toolbox and sprang down just as Packy turned to him holding up the flannel-wrapped jar of nitroglycerin. He looked sick. 'Blue, we left the stuff out last night. It . . . it's froze almost solid.'

'Won't it explode?' Clay said.

'I spose it will go off all right,' Packy said, 'but it's got to be thin as water to run into the cracks.' He shuddered.

'We could get a fire going,' Blue said. 'Will it thaw?'

Packy drew a deep, shaky breath and shook his head. 'Maybe. I – I think it will. You get started drilling.' Holding the jar like a live rattlesnake, he limped away up the slope toward the little stream. Clay Russell flinched and backed away hastily, giving him room as he passed. Bassett followed and began collecting sticks to build the fire.

Blue turned to the toolbox and took out a hand-crank grindstone that was clamped onto a stout wooden bar. He anchored one end of the lever to the edge of the safe with a loop of rope, twisted it tight, and then Clay swung the free end to make the stone bear against the safe at a spot near the dial. Blue turned the crank. A shower of sparks flew from the steel as the stone whirred. 'The steel is only surface-hardened on this outer door,' he said, 'like a ball bearing. Once we grind through that, we can drill.'

'You mean you can't blow it?' Clay was suddenly worried.

Blue grinned at him. 'You'll see.' Breathing hard, he stopped grinding, felt the slight depression in the steel. He peeled off his coat and took a two-handed breast drill out of the toolbox, along with a box of drills and an oilcan. 'Keep the oil coming,' he told Clay when the drill was in place. He set his chest against the tool to let his weight bear on it, grasped the two handles and began to crank.

Up on the mountain slope, Bassett built a small fire against an outcrop of rock. Packy filled a bucket at the stream and set it on stones over the fire. 'You don't have to help with this,' he said to Bassett.

'It don't bother me none,' Bassett said, without truth.

'Wait till you see it go off once,' Packy said. He put a flat stone in the bottom of the bucket, then carefully set the jar on it, in the water. 'Swedish blasting oil, they used to call it. I remember in stir, there was an old-timer, a safe-breaker, too, did his first stretch in the quarries when he was a kid – it was before the war and there was no such thing as dynamite yet. He told me he started doing his time in December, and they gave him the job every morning of thawing oil in a skillet over a cookstove. Like lard, he said. And he couldn't understand why everyone cleared out of the shack – that being the only place a man could get warm – but he didn't connect the stuff with blasting.' Packy barked his sharp laugh. 'Then he saw a man throw an empty can of it into a trash pile. Empty, mind you. Blew the man's head off, just the little bit that was sticking to the can, see?' Packy turned the jar in the water, gingerly touching the greasy-looking mass in it with a forefinger. 'Before that happened, he said he had made up his mind to do his time like a little angel and go straight when he got out.'

'Didn't he?'

Packy laughed again. 'He was too scared to stay – he went over the wall. He got to be a nitro-man, too, the best in the game.' Packy dipped a finger in the water. A thin wisp of steam curled up from it. The he held up his hand. It was shaking. 'Me, I hate the stuff. It ain't my style.'

'Well then, why are you using it?'

'No way out, is why. Not if we mean to crack the box in the time we've got. But believe me, my friend, I still wouldn't touch it, except for the kid.' Packy suddenly sat back on his heels, his mouth twisting in disgust. 'What the hell – why should I blame it on the kid? I'm in it because it's my last chance to get a stake.'

Bassett was startled. 'I thought you and the kid were cleaning up.'

Packy laughed. 'We were, but I couldn't hang on to it, I was on the bum, see, too crippled up to work alone. I needed him. He was a natural, too – best I ever saw – except for one thing.'

'What's that?' Bassett fed small sticks to the fire.

Again the mocking laugh. 'I never could break the kid from thinking like an honest man.'

'He's traveling in rough company for an honest man,' Bassett said.

'Well, he thinks he's wanted on a murder charge,' Packy said.

'Thinks? Don't he know?'

Packy shrugged. 'I don't know why I'm telling you this, but it can't change anything now, anyway. I found out by accident that there wasn't no killing. He thinks he's got no selection, like he was doomed, bad blood and all, but he's been running from something that never happened. I didn't tell him because without him I would have starved to death.' He bent and looked closely at the liquid, then lifted his knife blade carefully – the fluid ran in a thin stream, like hot syrup. He grunted, then lifted the jar out of the hot water and stood up. 'And don't you go telling him, understand? Soon as we're clear of this, I'll tell him myself.'

Blue saw Packy and the Preacher coming back down the slope. He kept on drilling. His shirt clung to his back and sweat ran into his eyes. He thought of the slapping leather drive belts in Israel's shop, all powered by the huge Monarch motor, and he pictured one of the belts running down, connecting to his shoulders, driving his arms like pistons. So long as he thought about the job, buried his mind in it, he could keep himself from confronting the nightmare that was growing there. The nightmare was still shapeless, but in its fragments were glimpses of himself in the time after the robbery, not free but in a panic of sweaty fear, hiding, running. If I do this thing, he thought, I'm no better than Zack Murdock. To drive it from his mind, he made himself pump faster. He changed bits, pumped again and coiled slivers of steel unwound around the smoking bit. The drill broke through. With the pilot hole drilled, a larger-sized drill ran through quickly.

Packy fitted the headband of a medical doctor's mirror to his head, swung the circular mirror down over his good eye and peered into the hole. 'One little hole,' he whispered, 'but if you don't know where to put it, you could as well shovel sand with a stick.' He inserted a bent knitting needle, probed, feeling for the rim notches on the wheels. Turning the dial, he felt them turn, gear-driven by the dial. The needle dropped, caught. He noted the number on the dial and went on probing, dialing. In six minutes, the five wheels were aligned. He turned the dial gently, felt the fence drop with a solid *thunk*. Grinning, Packy looked at his watch. 'Ninety-two minutes for the first set of doors,' he said, and turning the handle, he swung them open.

The second set of doors was revealed, hinges buried in terraced edges of steel. Blue pried open a can of putty. Rolling a thick wad of it into a long snake, he thought suddenly of Anse and his band of yeggs, back in the County Treasurer's office in Cape Girardeau. And Hub lying dead. And saw himself, Blue Russell, lying dead, a corpse surrounded by law officers, a litter-load of jiggling meat.

'Snap out of it, Blue,' Packy said. Blue slapped the putty fiercely against the door seam.

CHAPTER XXX

Ninety minutes after taking on water in the gorge, the San Mig was making her last straight run up the narrowing valley into Telluride. The engineer played his steam whistle off the towering walls of the canyon.

Dolan left his seat in the combine and rapped on the solid, barred door to the baggage room. 'Let's move the goods, Kemp!' he shouted. There was no answer, but none was really needed – or expected, knowing Kemp's surly disposition. For two minutes Dolan thought nothing about it. He walked past the two widows and went out onto the open platform of the car where he leaned against the iron rail, squinting against the cinders to look ahead at the two waterfalls that hung in fantastically long, wispy twists from the cliffs.

Abruptly, he went back in and pounded on the doors again, then listened, frowning. He thought he heard a muffled thump, but there was no answer. 'What the hell,' he said to Nordstrom, 'get the fire ax off the wall.' The train was slowing now. The deputy began to swing the ax. Dolan suddenly thought of the two widows and looked back as the train halted. The women were gone. He ran to the platform. Scores of people milled around the train and the station area, including many women. He looked down. On the tracks between the cars he saw a length of tacky black lace netting.

Dolan kicked at the iron step and swore. He didn't even know what the women looked like. Nordstrom shouted inside the car. Dolan ran back in just as they kicked and battered an opening in the lower half of the door, below the bar. He crawled through the opening and stood up.

The safe was gone. The two men were gone. Dolan felt sick. He kicked off the lid of the first coffin. Kemp, bound and gagged, glared up furiously at him.

Dolan caught Nordstrom by the shoulder. 'Tell the engineer to cut this rig loose and get the engine headed out again, then get some men and horses in a couple of boxcars, ready to tie on behind it.'

The nitro welled up in the putty trough plastered along the upper seam of the safe doors as Blue poured, then slowly drained away. Blue stepped back, waiting for it to seep completely around the door. Murdock, pacing restlessly, whirled on him.

'There's a trainload of law on the way by now! What the

hell is holding you up?'

Blue held out the heavy sledge hammer. 'Maybe you want to touch it off?'

Murdock blinked, startled. 'I don't know nothing about the stuff.'

Blue grinned at him. 'You just give it a good full swing, right here.' He tapped a spot on the front of the safe.

Murdock stared back, then shook his head. 'No, you do it, only hurry.'

Blue settled himself to one side, then swung. The jolt of the hammer and the heavy *whump* came together and a thunderous shock traveled up his arms and flung him half around. He found himself on one knee, his ears ringing and fumes sharp in his nostrils. The doors, flung outward, toppled skidding with a screech of metal on stone. Pieces of paper slipped from mahogany pigeonholes and drifted down. But still intact across the lower half of the safe was the last of the doors.

Bassett quickly hitched his team of horses to the winch boom again. Blue looped chain around the top of the safe and hooked the cable to it so that the pull would be across the top and directly to the rear. He waved and Bassett urged his horses into their collars. The drum turned, cable drew taut, thrummed. The safe rocked back, toppled onto its back in the depression they had dug. Now the earthen and canvas walls of the dike rose around it.

Clay Russell and Zack Murdock wrestled a heavy board across the little stream that slanted across the slope. Stakes were waiting to receive it – the board was a floodgate. They dropped it into place. Water backed up behind the board, then flowed into a shallow ditch leading down to the dike that embraced the toppled safe.

Staggering a little from the explosion, Blue threw back the tarp covering the rest of their equipment – a steam-powered brass air compressor, a carbide generator tank, hoses, valves, pressure gauges. Then he stripped the canvas covering off the strange four-foot long assemblage of copper pipes that he had labored over long nights at the Sheba. He threaded hose fittings to the butt of the strange instrument.

Packy lighted the burner under the steam engine's boiler.

When he had pressure, he opened the throttle and engaged the compressor – the piston-driven arm began to move, pumping air, *choo-choo, choo-choo,* like a little locomotive. He worked with a twisted half-smile on his lips, as if he alone understood some secret joke.

Blue opened the valves, struck his torch alight – a languid yellow flame at first, sighing cobwebby strings of black soot – then he opened the line from the compressor. The sudden flow of air stiffened the flame into a roaring blade of fire. He pulled smoked goggles over his eyes and directed the flame to the steel door. Murdock stopped his pacing and watched with uneasy wonder. Under the flame, the metal glowed red, then orange. A ragged bead formed, blew away under the blast. A channel opened in the steel. Blue gouged it deeper with the flame. Water was rising now up over the front edges of the safe, pouring into the pigeonholes, filling them, then flowing over the face of the door under Blue's torch. Water spat and sizzled, grew deeper. The blade of flame knifed through the water, bit at the steel. Clouds of steam whipped away on the breeze.

Packy laughed and nudged Bassett. 'It would all burn up inside if the kid didn't do it under water. It's leaking through, too, so by the time he cuts through, the money will be soaking in water, protected from the flame. An artist, what did I tell you – the kid will set banking back a thousand years.'

'You mean this is the first time it's ever been done?' Bassett said. Packy nodded and laughed again. Fascinated, Bassett watched the bright tongue of flame burn through the water and into the steel. When I tell them Blue Russell burned through their precious tempered steel door with a crazy new kind of carbide blowpipe, *under water*, Bassett thought, they will throw me in with the lunatics.

Time fled in the roar of the flame and the *chuff-chuff* of the steam compressor. The cutting took an hour and forty-eight minutes – a few minutes less than four hours had elapsed since the safe was lifted out through the top of the railroad car. Blue levered up the cutaway section of door. It was more than half a foot thick, and heavy. Bassett and Clay Russell heaved it off.

It skidded off a hanging door and splashed into the water. Blue pushed up his goggles and stared down past severed hinges and boltwork, seeing through the water cylinders of wrapped gold coin and bundles of currency. For a long moment no one moved, and then Packy shut down the compressor. Blue turned off the blowpipe and silence washed over them.

The quiet was split suddenly by the wail of a train whistle. Clay pointed north, toward the summit. Against the distant green-black of pine forest, Blue saw a drifting streamer of smoke. He dipped into the water-filled safe, began lifting out bundles of money, which Murdock and Clay Russell stuffed into saddlebags, dividing the sixty-eight-pound weight of gold evenly among the pockets. There were four sets of saddlebags. Bassett unharnessed the horses and turned them loose with a slap and shout.

Blue disconnected the hoses from his blowpipe, carried it to the cliff's edge and flung it far out over the canyon. Down past the track it fell, turning over and over. He watched it until it was out of sight.

'We can leave everything else just as it sits,' he said. 'It will take them a while to figure out what happened, and from here on, there will be no tracks to tell them where we've gone.'

Carrying the four sets of saddlebags, they ran along the edge of the cliff to the cleft cut down through the red wall by the little stream that fed the water tank below. Water streamed down from ledge to ledge in a series of falls. They entered the cleft and climbed down by way of the ledges, passing back and forth through the splashing falls of icy water. Near the bottom, they climbed from the rock ledges onto the timbered framework of the tank's supporting tower, and jumped from there to the crushed stone roadbed next to the tracks.

Waiting for them on the tracks was an ore car from the Sheba's old siding above the gorge, its brake wheels, front and rear, manned by Naylor and Carver, who now loosened the brakes and let it roll downgrade toward them. Beyond the ore car, clouds of smoke from the approaching yet still-hidden locomotive drifted out across the gorge. The *chuff* of its engine was clearly heard over the rumble of the ore car. Each man caught hold and swung aboard as the ore car trundled past the tower on the downgrade. Naylor and Carver levered the spokes of the braking wheels with wooden clubs, and the car very slowly gathered speed.

For a sickening instant, Blue was certain the locomotive would steam into sight around the curve of cliff and run them down. Zack Murdock and Clay Russell drew guns and crouched low behind the timbered rear wall of the ore car. Bassett drew his own heavy Colt – instinctively he was thinking like a hunted man, a target for a shotgun blast from the train, yet his Colt swung toward Murdock's back.

Blue saw just the front of the locomotive appear – its cow-catcher, headlamp and stack – as it slowed. It was stopping at the water tank. White steam blasted from the cylinder cocks; then the curve of red rock blotted it from sight as the ore car pulled away. Blue's knees wobbled under him and he sagged against the side of the car. Packy looked at him, white-faced.

On the rolling ore car, with the quickening wind of the downhill run whipping at his clothes, Blue looked back through the purpling canyon. High above, the last of the sun's light licked at mountaintops with a fiery yellow tongue.

The shaken men were silent as they rolled, hearing now the steely clicking of trucks, the groan of wheel flanges on curving rails, with the wind stinging their eyes. The track bed dropped quickly to the level of the riverbank. Blue could see the bridge ahead, and beyond it on the other side of the river, the long siding above the Arapaho Girl mine, with its string of ore cars. Four miles from the gorge to the bridge. Another mile to the siding. He turned and looked back upstream, watching for smoke from the locomotive. There was none. Yet.

They reached the bridge and white water flashed below through open ties as the car slanted across, rumbling onto the west bank. From here, the mine buildings were masked by the curve of canyonside, but the siding and its string of ore cars swung into sight as they rolled down upon it.

Blue jumped down, ran ahead and threw the switch that would send the ore car onto the siding. He let it run through, swung the switch handle back to its normal position and trotted after the ore car. It nudged gently against the rear of the string and stopped. The men sprang down and followed

Murdock and Clay Russell in single file, staying close to the string of ore cars. From beyond clumped trees and the projecting shoulder of rock, they could hear the sound of stamp-milling machinery, like distant thunder.

Rounding the humped rock, they suddenly saw the great timber-framed sheds of the mill at the base of the mountain. Here was the lower tram terminal, where cable-hung buckets dumped their cargoes before starting their three-mile run back up the mountain to the upper mill. He could see buckets moving now, going and coming.

Russell and Murdock broke away from the tracks then, led them slanting up along the flank of the mountain, through brushy scrub and crags. Electric lights were flickering on at the mill. Blue ran easily, the weight of a pair of saddlebags slapping his chest and back. Just ahead of him, Packy, running with his peculiar hitching gait, broke stride, then stumbled as the slope steepened. Overtaking him, Blue heard the shuddering rasp of wind in Packy's throat. Packy tried to speak, but could not shape the words. Blue gave his saddlebags to Preacher Bucklin, got one shoulder under Packy's arm and ran on, awkwardly now, the others pulling ahead.

They climbed steadily, working to get above the Arapaho Girl sheds to where tram buckets swept close to jutting crags. With the sheds below them at last, they could hear the squeal of tram pulleys through the thunder of the stamp mortars crushing ore below.

Clay, crouching low to stay out of sight of the terminal shed, ran out onto a craggy shelf jutting close to the path of the tram buckets. Below him now, the terminal shed squatted sixty yards away, its open end darkly staring as it gulped a loaded, down-running tram bucket. Seconds later an empty bucket swept up and away from the platform, starting its run up the mountain, its path to the top marked by a file of tall, timber-framed towers. The bathtub-shaped bucket was suspended from a wheeled carriage that rolled on a heavy steel cable, pulled along by a lighter traveling rope at a walking pace.

Clay looked back. Murdock waved him on. The bucket stopped, jouncing – high above, at the upper terminal, a brakeman had stopped a bucket under the loading chute. Seconds passed. With a jerk, the bucket swept on. As it climbed past, Clay sprang out, caught the steel yoke and swung his legs in. The bucket bounced and swept on. Sitting on the rim, Clay grinned and waved, then slipped down inside.

Owl Carver and Naylor followed Murdock onto the shelf. The next bucket was just leaving the platform below, trundling back up toward them. I could pull out here, Bassett thought – let the others go on ahead. He was already carrying one pair of saddlebags, a fourth of the stolen money, and there was not likely to be a better chance to break away. The bucket was nearing the shelf. Bassett turned and helped Blue with Packy, hauling him up the last few feet, letting him sink down to catch his breath.

Murdock saw the two of them half-carrying Packy. Then he saw the saddlebags over Bassett's shoulders. Frowning, he stepped back from the edge of the rock and turned to Naylor. 'You and the Owlhead grab this one – I mean to stick close to Bucklin.'

Naylor hastily changed places with him. The bucket swung close, swaying. Owl Carver, his gun belt buckled across his shoulder and chest to hold the saddlebags in place, jumped first, into the bucket's lower end, catching the suspension yoke as he landed. Naylor jumped a moment later. Rock cracked away under his foot. With a startled grunt, he clutched at the passing bucket and caught it by the rim with one hand, his body twisting from that one hand as the bucket rose slanting away from the crag, the mountainside already sloping off scores of feet below it.

Carver snatched at Naylor's flailing free hand and caught the wrist, but at that moment the bucket stopped – braked by that unseen hand three miles up the mountain – and Naylor's grip on the rim was twisted off. Kicking, clawing, he hung from Carver's hand. His kicking wrenched him half around, swung Carver into a tortured backbend. With a jerk the bucket started up again, wheels squalling on cable. The jerk snapped Naylor's grip loose and he dropped, still kicking and twisting, his mouth open as he fell, the cry lost in the thunder of the pounding mortars.

The others stared after him in helpless shock. After a long

moment, Bassett said, 'They'll see him, you know.'

Murdock shook his head. 'It's near dark. They won't see him until the morning shift rides the buckets up to work on top. You go with me on the next one, Preacher.'

'You go on ahead, I'll help the kid with Packy.'

Murdock shook his head. 'No, by god – I want to see that money on its way.'

Bassett shrugged off the saddlebags, held them out. 'Pack the stuff yourself, if you want.'

'Too heavy for one man – catch the damned bucket, Preacher. I'll be right there with you.'

Bassett hesitated, then behind him, Blue said, 'Go on. We'll make the next one.'

Bassett nodded – the moment was gone, and with it any chance he might have had to get away. He could try to take Murdock now, but Murdock was watching him, that deadly rage of his barely contained. Packy struggled to his feet.

'That broken-down bastard is going to get you caught and strung up!' Murdock said to Blue. 'It should have been him down there instead of Naylor.'

'You didn't say nothing about that when he was helping to crack the safe,' Blue shot back.

'I'm saying it now.'

'He's just winded from trying to run. We won't be afoot again.'

'An hour in the saddle will be just as bad. He aint going to make it, and I'm damned if I'll let him hold us back.'

'He won't – leave him to me.'

The next bucket approached, swaying. Murdock made room for Bassett on the ledge. A moment later they made the jump and were gone, the bucket pulling away on the long curve of cable.

'I heard what Murdock said,' Packy gasped. His face was pale, his breathing ragged.

'He was just making noise – on account of Naylor falling.'

'Watch him close, Blue. He is like the hammer man in a slaughterhouse. Killing is what he does best and it don't mean a thing to him.'

'Clay will look after our end.'

'Don't be fooled, Blue – Clay is just like him. They're both shooters. All rip and tear, see?'

Then the bucket was there. Blue took a firm grip on Packy's left arm and shouted 'Now!' lifting as Packy jumped and jumping himself, all in one motion. They were in and clinging to the iron frame, climbing toward the long line of towers, the bucket springing and bobbing above the sheer-flanked ravine. Blue looked down. A hundred feet below him, Naylor's body was sprawled on tumbled stone, face up, arms outflung, as if calling out to him.

Crouched down in the other end of the bucket, Packy held his ribs, his mouth open. 'Trying to breathe —' he gasped. 'It aint a payin proposition. A crippled . . . old dog like Disbrow . . . don't belong in the mountains.'

'Once we got beyond the ridge, it slopes off quick,' Blue said. Wind swung the bucket, sighing through the cables. The mill sheds and the railroad were already far down the mountainside, toylike. The pounding of the mortars faded into muted, distant thunder. The loudest noise in the bucket was the oily grumble of iron wheels on the steel cable and the breathy moan of the wind.

A vast long line of snow-covered peaks rolled slowly into view to the east and north as the bucket climbed, and beyond, those in distant ranks unfolded still more. The red gorge of the Dolores lay below the snow line, a bloody ax-wound on the mountainside. And as Blue watched, a stubby three-car train – loaded with deputies, he thought – crept down out of the gorge toward the Arapaho Girl, spitting tiny puffs of smoke.

Seeing the toylike train from that great height, like a hawk in flight, filled Blue with a strange and reckless joy. He laughed aloud.

The bucket carrying Murdock and Bassett swept high over another great ridge of rock ribbing the mountain. For a moment, the upper terminal and mill came into Bassett's view, a mile distant and another 1,000 feet higher, and then it was lost again behind dark-bristling pine on the swell of the mountain-side.

Murdock sat facing Bassett with his back to the mountain,

his left boot on the rim of the bucket next to Bassett's thigh. His hands were knotted into fists and his lips were tight against his teeth. He was ignoring Bassett, yet *watching*, his aimless fury barely subdued – like a damned calf-killing old bear, Bassett thought, jaws dripping blood and looking for bellies to rip. The bucket stopped, springing, then moved on.

And Bassett was thinking too, how Owl Carver and Clay Russell were waiting up there now with the horses. Once they were all off the tram, together, they were again too many for him to handle. But now – he had Zack Murdock and half the stolen money right there in the bucket with him. *Take Murdock now,* he thought – ride the tram right on past where Russell and the Owlhead waited, ride it on up to the mine at the end of the tramline. There, with Murdock in custody, he could be put in touch with the law by telephone – the trainful of deputies moving toward the Arapaho Girl could be flagged and pursuit organized.

Yet Murdock, glancing back from time to time to see how far they had gone, still watched him like a hawk. Bassett saw above him now the hogback where the cables slanted close – the jump-off, where Russell and the Owlhead would be waiting. The bucket swung closer, then stopped again, jouncing and swinging, just as Bassett saw Clay Russell standing there on the ridge, partly hidden by scrub oak. And behind him the horses were strung out on a picket rope.

Bassett's heart suddenly pounded. *Five* horses! There were supposed to be seven. With Naylor dead, they were still one short. Somebody draws his time right here, Bassett thought furiously. With a jerk, the tram started again. The ridge was just ahead. Murdock glanced away for an instant and Bassett's fingers curled on his gun butt – but Murdock, turning back in that moment, saw Bassett's move and kicked. His booted foot jammed Bassett's hand against the steel rim of the bucket and the revolver spun away as Murdock drew his own gun and struck at Bassett's head with the barrel. Bassett could not get his hand up to block it. The side of his head seemed to explode. He sagged into the bucket, his face skidding on the steel.

The ridge rose to meet the moving bucket. Murdock caught Bassett by the ankles, swung his limp body and the saddlebags with it up and out of the bucket as it crossed the ridge, then leaped out after him.

Sixty seconds later, Blue said suddenly, 'I see Clay – end of the line, Packy.' He swung Packy down and jumped, landed rolling, laughing as he scrambled up to face his brother. And froze, seeing Bassett sprawled on the ground, wagging his head feebly.

'Zack says the Preacher tried to jump him, Blue,' Clay said. Murdock unbuckled the cartridge belt that held the saddlebags across Bucklin's shoulder and pulled them free.

'Why would he do that?' Blue demanded. 'We're all partners in this.'

'Not now, by god,' Murdock said. 'This is where the Preacher gets his ticket punched – shake the bastard down, Owlhead. See if he's clean.'

Owl Carver put his foot between Bassett's shoulders and pushed him down, then bent over him and went through the pockets of his coat. Finding nothing, he ran his hands over Bassett's body. With a startled grunt, he lifted Bassett by one shoulder of his coat, tore open the front of his shirt and pulled out a flat, black pistol. He stared at it curiously, frowning, then held it up. 'Hell, Zack it don't even have a hammer. How do you make it shoot?' Fumbling, he pressed a latch in the butt and a narrow object slipped out and fell to the ground, cartridges glinting in a shell of steel. He leaned down and picked it up. 'Hell of a way to load a gun,' he mumbled.

Blue stared at the flat black pistol. A Browning. The skin across the back of his neck suddenly prickled. 'Let me see that thing,' he said softly. Grinning, Carver tossed the magazine down the mountainside, then handed Blue the pistol. Bassett stirred, got his elbows under him, lifted his head and shoulders. Blood trickled along his jaw from a cut over his ear and dripped onto his hands. Blue turned the pistol over in his hand. It was a Browning. He looked back at Bassett, shaking his head, remembering nothing. Then Bassett blinked, looked at him beneath drooping eyelids and Blue saw in the sunburned, gaunt lines of Preacher Bucklin's face another man's face – pale, bearded, yes, under a greasy derby hat. And he remembered the smell of rancid lard. *Wagenbach!*

'You're —' he blurted, and broke off, the name all but spoken, dying on his tongue. But where was the connection? 'You set us up!' he accused Bassett.

'Did I?' Bassett mumbled. 'You got away with it – but ask him who stays behind now. Ask him, Blue. There aint but five horses —'

'That's right,' Murdock said. He threw a pair of saddlebags behind the cantle of a saddle and fastened them there. 'We aimed to thin out the litter right here.'

'Hell, you can't shoot him on account of the noise,' Clay Russell said. 'Leave him for the law – they'll string the bastard up.'

'You don't understand,' Blue said. 'He —' but he broke off, knowing suddenly that Murdock would kill the Preacher – or whoever he was – that instant if Blue told what he knew about the Browning.

'Five horses,' Packy said. 'One was meant for Naylor. Who else did you mean to leave behind?'

Murdock laughed. 'You.'

'You can't mean that!' Blue said.

'Hell I can't – Owlhead, bring up the rest of the horses.'

'Clay —' Blue said.

'No use talkin, Blue.' Clay grinned easily. 'We never meant to take him along. It don't make good sense. You climb on that horse and come with us, hear? You'll have a bigger cut —'

'Cut? You mean dump my partner? Without us, you wouldn't have *no* shares – I only come in on this because of you.'

Murdock was already mounted. Clay swung into the saddle. Between them, they had three pairs of the saddlebags. Carver had the fourth.

'Let's go, Russ!' Murdock snapped and reined his horse around. He galloped around the jutting rock and was gone.

'Blue!' Clay said, wheeling after Murdock. 'Brothers belong together – I'm doin you a favor, don't you see that?' He reined his plunging horse. The animal reared. *'Russ!'* Murdock's voice drifted back. 'Hear me, Blue?' Clay shouted, 'Git on that horse and come with me!' He gave the horse its head and the animal plunged away after Murdock.

Owl Carver, mounted on one horse and leading one, left the picket line to follow Murdock and Clay Russell. But Packy suddenly lunged forward between Carver and the led horse. He waved his hat in the second horse's face, shouted *'Ha-a-!'* The horse reared and the reins were torn from Carver's hand. Packy caught at the saddlebags behind Carver and hung on. Carver wheeled the horse in a tight, rearing turn and clubbed at Packy's hands with his gun barrel. Blue sprang toward them.

Packy was caught in the tight arc of the horse's turn. He tripped on his crippled leg and went down under flailing hoofs. At the same moment, Blue took two bounding steps from the ground up onto a knob of rock outcrop, and from there sprang headlong onto Carver's back – his driving weight toppled the already leaning, off-balance horse. The animal screamed and crashed heavily onto its side.

Blue was flung clear. Rolling, he came to his knees. Owl Carver, on one knee, swung up his pistol and fired. Blue's face was powder-stung and the explosion deafened him as the bullet plucked at the shoulder of his coat. He saw Carver knocked down hard, a startled, wide-eyed stare freezing on his face. Dazed, Blue turned and saw Preacher Bucklin holding the Browing leveled at Carver. Blue had not heard the shot and did not remember dropping the Browning. The Preacher must have snatched it up and fired in an instant. A tremor shivered through Carver's legs.

'I kept a slug in the chamber,' Bassett said, crawling to where Carver lay, taking the heavy Colt from his fingers. 'He thought it was unloaded when the clip slipped out.'

Carver's fallen horse scrambled up and limped back to join the other two horses. Packy lay still, face down. Blue crawled over to him. Very gently, he turned him over. Blood bubbled lightly on his lips and the side of his face was covered with dirt and bloody mud. Blue wiped it away. Packy's eye opened. The eye, blue and bright with the last light of the sky, roved. Seeking. Blue thought it found him for a moment. 'Packy,' he breathed. Then the eye moved on past him. Stopped. Blue sat holding him, awash in sad and helpless fury.

Bassett, with Owl Carver's .44 Colt in his hand, ran along

the trail taken by Murdock and Clay Russell, passing under the tramway cables and around a buttress of rock. From there he could see most of the mountainside up to the ridge. They must have heard the shots, he thought – but they would have figured it had to be Carver doing the shooting. They will be expecting him to catch up along the way, maybe Blue with him. A puff of red dust stained the sky, far up along the slope. Murdock and Clay Russell, riding hard. He turned back, staggering a little.

Blue was still sitting, holding Packy. Bassett touched his shoulder. 'He's gone, Blue. His chest . . .'

Blue blinked and tears scattered on his cheek. 'He wasn't nothing but a damned old pickpocket —' His throat tightened, choked off the words.

Bassett let him sit a moment longer. He bent, and from a pocket sewn in his boot top he took a loaded clip of cartridges. He put Carver's .44 into his own holster, then loaded the Browning and slipped it back into the shoulder rig under his shirt. The kid is my prisoner now, he thought, as much a criminal as any of them. But stopping now, turning back to put him in the hands of the law – and all the explaining that would take – would let Murdock and Russell get away for certain. Bucklin would have trusted the kid with his life, but Bucklin was gone. He touched Blue's shoulder again. 'Kid,' he said carefully, 'you've got a full share of the money there, whatever it adds up to, and a horse. What do you want to do?'

'Money . . . I don't care nothing about the money. I'm going after Clay and Zack.' Blue turned and looked squarely at him. 'You were Wagenbach. Now you're Preacher Bucklin. If you weren't fixing to set us up, what were you doing?'

'I was only Wagenbach for the few minutes I spoke to you. I was after Murdock and your brother Clay and the rest of them, all right. I'm a Pinkerton dick, see? As Bucklin, I had to come with something to prove myself to them —'

'You conned me and Packy into the game to get them?'

'That's right. We were following everything you and Packy were doing anyway. It was a natural to try to bring you in on it. Then once we were into the train job, there was no way I could put a stop to it, short of spooking you all and maybe touching off a gun battle and getting half of us killed. I didn't want them to pull out and run. I wanted to see their hides hanging on the fence, see?'

'Mine and Packy's too . . .'

Bassett shrugged. If the cards fell that way. Hell, you're wanted men. But look here, Zack and Clay are getting away clean. It's time we started, Blue.'

'You're not going to try to turn me in?'

'Your brother and Zack Murdock are headed for Mexico – are you going to sit there and let them go?'

Blue stirred, gently moved Packy and stood up. 'I won't let the law get him.' He nodded down at the still form.

'What the hell does that mean?'

'Give me time to bury him where he won't be found – it won't matter to you, or to them.' Blue stood back and looked along the mountainside, then nodded. 'Up there . . .' He bent and picked up Packy's body. Carrying it easily in his arms, he set out along the rugged slope. Bassett untied a slicker from behind one of the saddles and followed.

The mountain was scarred with old slides where snow had carried down rock, earth and trees. They found an overhanging ledge of rock at the foot of a slide where the rockfall was held back by a pine trunk fallen aslant against the ledge. They wrapped Packy's body in the slicker and then Blue cleared a place under the ledge. Together they lifted the body and settled it into the hollow. Blue took up a stout branch, worked one end of it under the jammed tree and heaved his weight against it. The tree trunk groaned, then suddenly swung down and a torrent of earth and rock poured around the ledge. Blue and Bassett jumped aside. In a moment, the hollowed place was covered and the ledge was merely a tip of rock sticking up through the rubble.

CHAPTER XXXI

They crossed over the ridge in the lingering twilight, the third horse following on a lead rope. Blue looked back once. Snow-crowned peaks beyond the Sheba stood cold blue against the darkening sky.

Ahead, the mountain sloped off rapidly toward hazy, distant low country that lay like a molten red sea in the last glow of the fallen sun. The old rustler's stock trail they followed was a broad, irregular trace, splitting here and there around an outcrop of rock or clump of pine or aspen, flowing together again, winding gradually down the flank of the mountain. Zack and Clay would be on it, heading for the Dandy Crossing and the badlands beyond.

The horses settled into a racking downhill lope, time lost in the hot-slick slap of saddle leather and the chill rush of wind as darkness fell. Riding, Blue's mind seethed – he saw Packy's face smeared with bloody mud, saw the restless eye fixed, staring. Blue clamped his teeth together and tried to drive it from his mind.

The trail dropped into another steep canyon. There was a stream, water rushing white across a rocky ford. They stopped to let their blowing horses drink. They rode on, following the stream down. Abruptly the canyon wall receded and the ground spilled out onto a brushy flat. Blue smelled sage. And after a time, wood smoke. A dimly lighted window glowed yellow through the brush. Two dogs ran barking out of the darkness. Their horses were too blown now to shy. The pulled up in front of a squat adobe, near a small corral of twisted poles. A door opened and a woman's voice spoke sharply to the dogs in Spanish, then said, '*Quién es?*'

'*Amigos de Chavez,*' Bassett said.

'*Bueno,*' she said and pointed toward the corral. Horses stomped there. Blue slid off his horse at the corral, let down rails and walked among the horses, slowly and quietly, running his hand over their hides. There were four of them, two with lather dried hard and spiky in the hair, and two fresh. He told Bassett. While they were saddling the fresh horses, the door of the adobe squealed open again. The woman walked through the yellow stream of lamplight toward them. Blue smelled cooked beans and his knees went suddenly watery. She gave each an earthenware plate of hot beans, corn tortillas and a cup of goat's milk, and then she slipped quietly back to the house and closed the door. A bar thudded down.

They sat on let-down corral rails and ate. Suddenly Blue said, 'Clay must have figured that I would be coming along with the Owlhead only four or five minutes behind him and Zack. But we lost a half hour or more back there, taking care of Packy.'

'Well?'

'They must have waited here a little while – a few minutes anyway. Clay would have done that. And they left us two fresh horses. But I'm saying there won't be horses for us at the next relay stop. Zack will see to that – he is too suspicious.'

'What are you getting at?'

'We've got to take our relay with us, change horses now and then. If we don't wear down the horses pushing too hard—'

'We'll still catch the bastards,' Bassett said.

They set out leading the two horses left behind by Zack and Clay. After a few miles they changed and rode on. A lopsided moon skidded up behind them, flaring through fast scudding clouds, flooding the brushy hills with silver. In the moonlight, Blue saw the last of the pine and aspen give way to sage and juniper. They forded a river, the horses belly deep in fast water – the Dolores again, Bassett said, running north now after its long loop out of the mountains.

Near midnight, Blue smelled sharp juniper smoke. The horses found the place – it was almost invisible from a few yards away. An old Ute lived in a brush wikiup that was patched with pieces of tin and scraps of canvas. He ducked out through the low doorway and faced them, aged and bent, his seamed face dark as coffee in the moonlight. Only two horses were in the brush corral, the lather on them barely dry.

The old man pulled his blanket closer around himself. 'Hombres tek all him horse. No more – you.' He ducked back inside.

'You were right,' Bassett said. 'The next stop now is Chavez' place. Four hours or more. Their horses have had a little rest. We'll take them all – run them ahead of us. They know the way to Chavez' place.'

Time wore away under the climbing moon. They rode slower, saving the horses, changing often. Then the moon slid down the sky ahead of them. It was still hanging above the horizon as daylight broke. Blue saw that they had ridden into another country. Another world. It was open, undulating, matted with sage and dark-plumed juniper, the ghostly bones of dead junipers gleaming in the gray light. The red earth was cut by winding, sheer-walled draws, deceptive and deadly as pitfalls, but the old stock trail wandered through them and up and down broken banks with the certain logic of a natural force. The hazy purple mountains were far behind them, capped with snow and anvil-topped thunderheads, the sunrise striking fire through them as the sun rose. Flat-topped red buttes propped the sky ahead. The air, crackling dry, was like the hot wind of Blue's old forge. A few scrawny cattle moved through the brush, here and there.

Two buzzards circled ahead, spiraling down, then a third, seemingly out of nowhere. The faint scent of smoke drifted on the air. The two sets of horse tracks angled sharply away. They followed. Under a shallow cutbank they found the butchered carcass of a yearling steer. There was a bullet hole in the center of its forehead and a sizable cut of the loin was gone. Close by were a few burned sticks with dirt kicked over them.

Bassett laughed and dismounted. He looked closely at the exposed meat, then felt the ashes of the fire. 'An hour, maybe a little more.' He took a stock knife from his pocket and began cutting another piece of meat from the carcass.

'We're losing time,' Blue said.

'Not much. The horses need a blow and we don't want to go to hell hungry, do we?'

Blue got the fire going and in a few minutes they were tearing at broiled strips of beef. Bassett bit into a piece. Sitting back on his heels, he said, 'Have you thought what you're going to do when we catch up with them.'

'How the hell do I know!' Blue snapped. 'You know I don't have a gun. I'll talk em to death, or maybe throw rocks.' He subsided, then shook his head. 'I don't know what I'll do.'

Bassett grinned. When he finished eating, he stripped off his coat and shirt, unfastened the straps of the shoulder rig holding the Browing and handed it to Blue. He watched Blue strap it on against his ribs on his left side. Blue sat for a moment with his hand on the butt of the Browning.

'He's my brother,' he said. 'I aint going to promise nothing.'

Bassett looked at him but did not answer. They changed horses again and rode on, following the two sets of tracks, crisp-cut in the red earth.

The sun climbed. Blue's face burned in the hot wind. His eyes were scorched and grainy. Hours of riding left him muscle-racked, raw with saddle gall. But he found grim pleasure in it, wanting to fill himself with hurt, wanting the taste and feel of pain to go on – rather than come to whatever it was that was going to happen.

Two of the horses were stumbling wrecks. They left them behind, heads down and trembling, in a draw. For a time they followed a long sweep of cliff and yellow birds flickered through the brush before them, chittering. The two sets of tracks dipped into a narrow canyon. Blue's horse snorted and stomped.

'He smells water,' Bassett said. 'Chavez' place is just yonder. Let's move in slow on it.'

They rode on around the bend of the canyon and saw the corral and the squat stone hovel built in against the canyon wall. Wind drove sand along the floor of the canyon in a gritty shower. Two lather-streaked horses with saddle slicks on their backs tottered, legs quivering, along the red mud bank of a water hole that was fed by a thin trickle of water in the draw. The corral poles were down. A piece of tattered blanket flapped in the doorway of the house. There were plenty of tracks and droppings, but except for the two exhausted horses, the place was empty of life, desolate and sandswept.

'Gone, sure enough,' Bassett said. 'They have no way of knowing if anybody is following, and Chavez wouldn't want to stay around to find out.'

They filled their canteens and watered the horses, then reined away again, following the two sets of tracks west and a little south, moving at a shambling lope. Red buttes loomed close, then fell behind as they pressed on.

'Nothing has changed,' Bassett said. 'We came this way before – they're still headed for the Dandy Crossing.'

'And after that?' Blue said.

'If they get there before we do, it won't matter – by then we'll be crawling on our hands and knees.'

The sun burned down from a brassy sky. The red buttes shimmered in heat waves like coals in a forge. The horizon was lost in haze. A hot wind blew drifting streamers of dust and piled red sand in ribbed dunes against the bleached skeletons of junipers.

Humps of red rock shoaled out of the earth, the rock pitted, potholded, with muddy red water standing in the pockets. Blue nudged his horse close to one, scooped up water in his hand and tasted it. It was gritty, bitter. He blew it out of his mouth, his teeth on edge. 'Sooner drink lye.'

'Tolerable after a rain,' was all Bassett said.

The tracks they were following turned into a draw, winding down between shoals of red rock. Then the earth opened before them. The canyon was a red-tawny, sheer-walled, winding cut in the earth 300 feet deep. The flesh-smooth walls were streaked with random strokes of umber stain, and were darkened with blue shadow where they were undercut by great arching conchoidal fractures. A shallow stream of reddish water wandered along the pale sandy floor. Blue saw the tracks again, far below, etched in the sand closed to the stream.

'The way the canyon twists and turns,' Blue said, 'it will eat up their time.'

'But they've got the water down there,' Bassett said, 'the only water now, except for the pockets in the rock. And down in that canyon, they'll be out of sight all the way to the Dandy Crossing.'

'What do we —'

'Stay up on top, water or no water,' Bassett said. 'Up here we can ride straight as the crow flies, maybe kill our horses doing it.'

'They're near dead now,' Blue said.

'Saddle the best, turn the others loose.' Bassett was dismounting. Blue threw his saddle on a big chestnut with clots of white lather dripping through the red dust on its hide. And mounting, he felt the tremor in the animal's hind quarters. Bassett was on a tough, ugly roan. They left two behind. Now there would be no more.

The canyon snaked in endless loops, cutting deeper and deeper as it bore south and west toward the Colorado. Where a loop cut close to their path, they drew cautiously close to the rim, to look down onto the sandy floor. The falling sun marked away the searing hours – the tracks were always there in the sand.

With the sun blazing full in his face, Blue's lips felt like tree bark to the touch of his dry tongue. They cracked, bled, cracked again. Bassett was a lean, red-masked ghost in a shroud of red dust, eyes glittering in the shadow of his hat brim. They doled out their water slowly, a sip for themselves, a bandanna soaked full for the horses, squeezed onto slobbering lips and tongues. Until it was gone.

A draw opened before them, slanting down toward the canyon. Bassett rode into it and Blue followed. Without warning, his horse shuddered, stopped, head hanging. Wind wheezed from it in a long sigh and it crumpled under him. Blue scrambled free on hands and knees. The horse lifted its head, then fell back. Blue pulled off the bridle and loosened the cinch, so that the horse, if it rose again, would be free of the saddle. Then he walked after Bassett, who stopped a few yards down the draw and slid off the staggering roan.

Below him, the draw opened into a fissure, a ragged rip, cutting down through the layered red rock toward the blue depths of the canyon.

'It's a way down.' Bassett's voice was nothing but a raw croak now. 'There's nothing left.' He pulled the saddle off the horse and dropped it, then unfastened the coiled rawhide rope and handed it to Blue. Shouldering the saddlebags, he led the way down into the storm-cut fissure.

Jumping from ledge to ledge, they dropped rapidly, red dirt and loose rock showering around them. Then the dry watercourse spilled out onto a broad, sloping ledge on the curving wall, still 50 or 60 feet above the sandy bottom. They were at a bend in the canyon. Directly before them, upstream, they had a clear view of a straight stretch of canyon floor running toward them, a quarter-mile or more; then it bent in a sharp S-turn to their left, curving on around, lost to sight behind the wall on which they stood.

'The sand,' Blue whispered, 'it's clean. No tracks.'

'And no way down from here, either,' Bassett said. They crept to the edge and looked over. The stream on the shadowed floor mirrored the sky and pooled against the cliff wall below them, and the wall, facing that curving sweep of water in countless floods, was deeply undercut, forming a great open-faced cavern. Huge waterworn slabs of red rock were tumbled in the pool and through the bend of the canyon.

'We're sitting ducks on this open ledge,' Bassett said. 'You go on downstream, around the bend to the left – see if there's some way down. I'll try the other way—'

A single hollow chock of hoof on stone echoed in the canyon upstream. A moment later, two horsemen rounded the bend, moving toward them at a fast trot. Seconds passed as they rode. Suddenly they halted, looking up.

'Blue-e-e?' Clay's voice, in drawn-out, splintered echoes.

Then Murdock's. *'That's the Preacher with him!'*

Murdock drew his gun, kicked his horse into a run. Clay hesitated, then followed, the horses running heavily, sand and water spraying beneath their hoofs, saddlebags bouncing behind the riders.

'If they get past us now, we'll never catch them,' Bassett said. 'Go on – try to get down someplace near the bend before they get there.'

Below, Murdock and Clay Russell were closing the distance. Murdock raised his pistol, fired. The shot struck behind Blue and whined away. Blue ducked back on the ledge and ran crouching toward the downstream bend as Bassett leveled his Colt and fired back. The shot was wild. Bassett swore and crouched down, waiting directly at the foot of the bend they would have to pass.

'Blue! You stay clear of this!' Clay shouted. Both he and Murdock were firing as they swept into the turn, the shots reverberating in thunderous echoes. Blue ducked behind a great red sculptured rock that squatted froglike on the ledge, near the bend. From there he could see back under the curve of the overhanging wall, see the cavernous undercut and rock-strewn pool, and Bassett crouching on the lip above, firing down as their bullets spattered close.

In the turn, Clay galloped broadside to Bassett now. Bassett braced himself and fired again. Clay's horse clattered onto a water-slick slab of red rock and fell in a great sheet of white spray. The horse struggled to rise, sagged back. Clay was pinned. 'Zack!' He thrashed the water, trying to pull loose.

Murdock, ahead now and almost beneath Blue, reined in, skidding, spraying sand and water as he wheeled and galloped back. He swung out of the saddle as Bassett fired again, and hung low on the horse's far side, then pulled up and dropped rolling, close to Clay. Murdock came to one knee, aimed carefully and fired. Blue heard the slap of the bullet and Bassett's startled grunt, saw him thrown back against the slope – then, horrified, he watched him skid down, clawing for a handhold, and fall over the edge, turning once in the air as he fell, the pair of saddlebags spinning free of him on the way down. Water gushed up beyond tall rocks.

Murdock ran toward Clay. Blue drew the Browning, leveled it at Murdock's back. He saw Clay, trying to grin, stretch an arm up. 'Pull me loose, Zack – he's busted my leg.' His voice sounded hollow, floating up to Blue.

Murdock bent down. The Browning wavered in Blue's hand. He couldn't shoot. *Not while he's helping Clay*. He lowered the gun, left the shelter of the rock and ran on along the broad shelf looking for a way down. Just ahead of him the canyon twisted sharply back to his left and the ledge thrust out into the hairpin bend like the prow of a ship.

'Zack!' Clay's startled cry stopped him short. He whirled, saw Murdock evading Clay's outstretched arm, saw him catch the saddlebags behind Clay's saddle – two pair of them – and tear them loose. Clay gripped one pair, twisting his body, trying to reach Murdock's hands. 'Dammit, Zack ... you caint ... leave me ...'

Murdock pulled the saddlebags free, backed away. Clay swung his body furiously, heaving at the weight of the horse. 'We *soldiered* together, Zack!'

Clay lifted his heavy New Service Colt up out of the water. Murdock fired. Clay fell back, thrashed feebly, his face half under water. Stunned, Blue saw the swirl of red under him. Murdock threw the saddlebags behind his saddle and tied them there, an ungainly bulk, then mounted again. The horse turned under him and he had trouble getting his leg over the mounded saddlebags.

Blue shook with rage. He ran on across the projecting prow of stone. To get his hands on Zack, he had to get down. He was into the next bend now, the walls closing in, narrowing darkly over him, blotting out the red sky. The ledge under his feet broke into spurs of rock. He shook out a loop in the rawhide reata, threw it over the rocky knob, then swung off the ledge into the shadowed, narrow canyon. He let himself down, hand over hand, kicking off and dropping as his feet struck the wall. Twenty, then thirty feet.

Hoofs clattered on stone, hollow, echoing. Blue reached the end of the rope and hung there as Murdock rounded the turn, thirty yards away, the horse trotting heavily in water and sand. Murdock peered up along the canyon wall, the heavy Colt poised in his hand. He saw Blue and fired. The bullet stung Blue's face with chips of rock from the wall. Blue let go of the rope and plummeted down. He hit the water and sprawled, floundered to his knees tearing at the Browning. Murdock kicked the horse into a plunging gallop, water spraying up before him as he fired again.

'By god, Blue – you've drawed your time!' His shouts and the gunfire echoed, deafening.

Blue held the flat, back pistol straight out before him, felt it buck and kick in his hand. There was a great tearing burst of sound. Murdock, still firing, threw up his arms and rolled out of the saddle. Water sprayed, fell back. The riderless horse stopped among the huge rocks in the narrow embrace of the canyon and stood quivering and blowing, white eyeballs gleaming in the shadows.

Blue looked down at the Browning in his hand and saw that he had emptied it, the whole clip, in that one burst. He stood there a moment longer, then waded toward the horse. It shied back. Blue caught the reins, turned it and led it back the way it had come. Passing Murdock's sprawled body, the horse shied again and tried to break away. Hanging on, Blue looked down. Murdock's eyes stared up toward the narrow patch of flaring red sky. Water ran in and out of his mouth.

CHAPTER XXXII

Bassett lay face down on the sandy beach, his legs still in the water, the sand furrowed along the bottom behind him where he had dragged himself. His shirt was split down the back from the collar to his belt from the impact when he struck the water. He heard the shots down the canyon, the deep booming Colt, the long burst from the Browning, and waited then, groggy and apprehensive, but utterly unable to move. He heard footsteps, the sandy shuffle and click of hoofs. With an enormous effort, he lifted his head. He saw a blur against the canyon wall. The blur shimmered, became the kid. Blue.

Blue dropped the reins, tottered to the water's edge and dropped to his knees in the sand, his face masked in caked red dust. He scooped up water in his hands and sloshed it on his face, then sat back on his heels, the water streaming in mud-red streaks down his chest as he regarded Bassett, seeing the eyes blinking at him now, the lids fluttering. He shook his head slowly. 'Was . . . sure he . . . finished you.'

Bassett grunted. At length Blue crawled to him, pulled him up farther out of the water and propped him against a slab of stone. Blood stained his wet shirt bright red along his left side. He inhaled painfully, caught his breath. Blue pulled the shirt aside and looked at the wound. 'The bullet skidded along your ribs – could have busted a couple.'

Bassett grunted again. Blue staggered into the water and fished around in it, ducked clear under for a moment and came up with Bassett's gun and the heavy saddlebags, then waded out again. He dropped the saddlebags next to Bassett, who fingered a bullet tear in one of the pockets. Gold coins spilled out into the sand. Bassett laughed weakly. When he opened his eyes, he saw Blue spinning the cylinder of the Colt, punching out empties, all six of them, with the ejector rod. Instead of handing the gun to him, Blue rolled it in the sand, left it sticking there, muzzle down, half buried, well out of Bassett's reach.

'What the hell are you doing?' Bassett said.

'You can clean it up after I'm gone.'

'Gone? Without me?'

'I'll leave you a horse,' Blue said. He tugged at the cuff of Bassett's trousers, exposed the boot top and pulled the last clip for the Browning out of the narrow pocket. He shoved the clip into the butt of the gun and holstered it.

'Where do you think you'll go when you get out of the canyon?' Bassett said. 'You won't last two days.'

'I'll last. Just don't try to follow me.'

'No? Kid, you'd better understand – I'll follow you to hell, if I have to. I know the way, there and back.'

Blue shook his head. 'It won't do you no good. I've made up my mind – you'll never put me in the pen.' He turned slowly, as if forcing himself, to look along the sandy bank to where his brother lay, only a hand visible above the slabbed stone where his horse had fallen with him. The horse had gotten to its feet and hobbled a few yards, and now placidly browsed in a sparse patch of grass. Blood streamed down from a wound high on its neck. 'I won't go! I'll never go,' Blue said. 'Look at my brother. Look at Packy —'

'What happened to them was their own doing.'

'It won't happen to me, not that or any part of it. I was quitting the game anyway. The money is all right there. This is the last you will ever hear of Blue Russell.' He stood to go.

'Hold on, Blue.' Bassett squirmed painfully, pulled a sodden bandanna from his pocket. He shook it out and held it against his ribs. His breath hissed through his teeth, then went out in a slow sigh. 'Listen to me, Blue – something has been eating at me ever since we left Packy. This could turn it all around.'

'Turn what around? Packy's gone. Clay's gone —'

'Blue, who is to know that Clay Russell and Zack Murdock didn't get away to Mexico? Supposing —'

A knot lodged in Blue's throat. Sickness washed through

him. 'You too? You're no better than they are.'

Bassett raised a hand, grinned wryly. 'Damn it, Blue, don't get so feisty with me. Let us suppose now that a couple of fine-lookin gents – well-dressed and well-heeled, you understand – turn up in, say, San Francisco —'

Frowning, puzzled, Blue listened.

'— and let us suppose that these two dudes throw one dandy spree, hitting all the underworld hangouts, see, and spending plenty of money. Of course, by then, or anytime from now on, what happened to the Telluride train and the Invincible safe will be famous, notorious. All right? Then supposing the word gets around that these free-spending gents happen to be Blue Russell and Packy Disbrow?'

'What are you getting at? Packy is —'

'Just this – the sports will be flocking around, and among them no doubt will be some of the boys who have been blowing themselves to tatters trying to crack those same three-door safes, or others like them, here and there. If all this is so, then Blue Russell and Packy Disbrow will be in the way of a business proposition in no time. It's bound to happen.'

'But Packy is dead!' Blue flared.

'Is he?' Bassett said softly. He wrapped the bandanna around his head and tied it, letting a corner flap hang down over his right eye, then he pulled gloves from his belt and slipped one onto his right hand. He pulled himself stiffly, painfully, to his feet and leaned against the rock for a moment. Then, with his gloved fingers curled awkwardly, the arm bent and the shoulder slightly hunched, he turned his back on Blue and hobbled away a few steps through the sand, with a peculiar, hauntingly familiar hitching gait. He stopped, still with his back to Blue, and barked a sharp laugh, swaying a little as he stood with his weight resting on one leg, a posture at once jaunty and frail.

Blue felt his heart pound – there in the dim light under the great vaulted overhang, the illusion was chilling.

'You are not thinking, are you,' the voice said, echoing, ringing off the walls of the overhang, 'that a game old sport like Disbrow aint a match for these cheap stickups?'

He turned and hobbled back, the illusion slowly melting as

he drew close and sat down again. Blue sat utterly still, staring at the footprints, hearing the voice over and over in his mind.

'It was only after we buried Packy that I began to put it together,' Bassett said. 'When you said you wouldn't let the law have him. Secrets have a way of getting out, but this way, if I step into Packy Disbrow's shoes, you and I will be the only ones who will know that Disbrow is working with the law. And Blue Russell with him.'

Blue nodded. 'What about this?' He touched the saddle-bags.

'A few days will bring us to the Santa Fe line, south of here, and to a telegraph office. I'll arrange with my people to turn it back, but it will be done undercover and kept that way. I won't come in from the field, you see, and it won't do to tell them your part in it for a while, either.'

'Why not?'

'Hell, they wouldn't go for it – a man with your record, you can see that. You'll have to prove yourself.'

'I don't know nothing about you,' Blue said. 'You could as well get me strung out on this, then throw me in the bucket when it suits you. And I'm wanted for murder – it would mean the rope for me, if the law pulled me in.'

'I know,' Bassett said. 'Packy told me back there on the mountain when we were thawing the nitro. He also told me he had found out that your Uncle Israel was still alive – he got a hell of a lick, but he didn't die. Blue, you never were really wanted for murder.'

Blue was stunned. 'Packy knew that and didn't tell me?'

'He meant to, Blue. He wanted to, but he had to wait until the job was over. He was afraid you'd walk out on him. I knew myself, right from the beginning – I was in Cape Girardeau, investigating the burgled safe in the County Treasurer's office, and I got a line on you there. Just your name – Blue. When I got back to St Louis, I went around to Israel's shop to see if it could have been you, and I found out what had happened between you two. But Israel was still alive. Until Packy told me, though, I didn't know you thought you were wanted for murder.'

Blue laughed bitterly. 'All I ever wanted was to stay free of what the law would do to me. Now you're telling me I never was wanted! That's rich – I'm wanted *now*, sure enough.'

Bassett shrugged. 'That's right. But you throw in with me on this thing, Blue – it will look a whole lot different to the law when it's over. It won't be up to me, but I've known pardons to be given for less.'

Blue laughed again. 'You sound just like Packy, talking me into cracking the safe in Cape Girardeau.'

Bassett's face was set and flinty. 'There's a difference. The pay don't amount to much. Sand in your beans is more like it. And you could get a bullet, easy enough – but you'll never get the rope, Blue. Now I'm through talking. Are you with me?'

Blue was silent for a time. He stood and looked up at the sky. Clouds were smoky now, like coals in a forge, and edged with a dying red glow. The light was going fast. His face looked older, Bassett thought. Harder.

'I want to look after my brother,' Blue said. 'Maybe sit with him a few minutes.' He started to walk away, then he reached into his pockets and pulled out an odd assortment of pieces – brass, wood and bone – and put them into Bassett's hand. Bassett saw four silver dollars among them. There were holes drilled in the center of each dollar and each of the rims was notched.

'You could as well look these over,' Blue said. 'There's a lot I'm going to have to teach you.'

'There's one thing I have to know,' Bassett said. 'What really happened that night in Cape Girardeau?'

Blue grinned slowly, then turned and walked through the wet sand to his brother.

War

NO PEACE ON EARTH	Jean Larteguy	50p	☐
'H.M.S. MARLBOROUGH WILL ENTER HARBOUR'	Nicholas Monsarrat	60p	☐
THREE CORVETTES	Nicholas Monsarrat	40p	☐
MOSCOW	Theodor Plievier	60p	☐
STALINGRAD	Theodor Plievier	60p	☐
BERLIN	Theodor Plievier	75p	☐
ALL QUIET ON THE WESTERN FRONT	Erich Maria Remarque	50p	☐
WINGED VICTORY	V. M. Yeates	75p	☐

Western

KIOWA	Matt Chisholm	40p	☐
McALLISTER JUSTICE	Matt Chisholm	40p	☐
McALLISTER: THE HANGMAN RIDES TALL	Matt Chisholm	40p	☐
McALLISTER: DEATH AT NOON	Matt Chisholm	40p	☐
RAGE OF McALLISTER	Matt Chisholm	40p	☐
THE VENGEANCE OF McALLISTER	Matt Chisholm	30p	☐
JUBAL CADE: VENGEANCE HUNT	Charles R. Pike	40p	☐
JUBAL CADE: THE KILLING TRAIL			

All these books are available at your local bookshop or newsagent, or can be ordered direct from the publisher. Just tick the titles you want and fill in the form below.

Name ....

Address ....

....

Write to Mayflower Cash Sales, PO Box 11, Falmouth, Cornwall TR10 9EN.

Please enclose remittance to the value of the cover price plus:

UK: 22p for the first book plus 10p per copy for each additional book ordered to a maximum charge of 82p.

BFPO and EIRE: 22p for the first book plus 10p per copy for the next 6 books, thereafter 3p per book.

OVERSEAS: 30p for the first book and 10p for each additional book.

Granada Publishing reserve the right to show new retail prices on covers, which may differ from those previously advertised in the text or elsewhere.